All or Nothing

Claire Cross

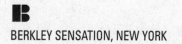

BERKLEY SENSATION, NEW YORK

THE BERKLEY PUBLISHING GROUP
Published by the Penguin Group
Penguin Group (USA) Inc.
375 Hudson Street, New York, New York 10014, USA
Penguin Group (Canada), 90 Eglinton Avenue East, Suite 700, Toronto, Ontario M4P 2Y3, Canada
(a division of Pearson Penguin Canada Inc.)
Penguin Books Ltd., 80 Strand, London WC2R 0RL, England
Penguin Group Ireland, 25 St. Stephen's Green, Dublin 2, Ireland (a division of Penguin Books Ltd.)
Penguin Group (Australia), 250 Camberwell Road, Camberwell, Victoria 3124, Australia
(a division of Pearson Australia Group Pty. Ltd.)
Penguin Books India Pvt. Ltd., 11 Community Centre, Panchsheel Park, New Delhi—110 017, India
Penguin Group (NZ), 67 Apollo Drive, Mairangi, Auckland 1311, New Zealand
(a division of Pearson New Zealand Ltd.)
Penguin Books (South Africa) (Pty.) Ltd., 24 Sturdee Avenue, Rosebank, Johannesburg 2196,
South Africa

Penguin Books Ltd., Registered Offices: 80 Strand, London WC2R 0RL, England

This book is an original publication of The Berkley Publishing Group.

First edition: April 2007

Library of Congress Cataloging-in-Publication Data

Cross, Claire.
    All or nothing / Claire Cross. — 1st ed.
       p.   cm.
    ISBN-13: 978-0-425-21499-2
  1. Waitresses—Fiction. 2. Thanksgiving Day—Fiction. 3. Mate selection—Fiction. 4. Mothers and daughters—Fiction. 5. Chick lit. 6. Domestic fiction. I. Title.
    PR9199.4.D45A79   2007
    813'.54—dc22

                                     2006100264

PRINTED IN THE UNITED STATES OF AMERICA

10 9 8 7 6 5 4 3 2

Chapter 1

"Are you gay?"

Jen glanced up from her toast. It was just before noon on a Friday morning and she'd thought herself alone in her mother's vivid yellow and cherry-red kitchen. She had been considering the problem of how to knit the skin of an avocado so that it looked real, but any internal debate about the pebbly merit of moss stitch would have to wait.

Her mom, as bright-eyed and bushy-tailed as Jen was not, was leaning in the doorway to the hall. Natalie had "that look," the one that meant trouble.

A casual observer wouldn't have guessed that Natalie and Jen were related, much less that they were mother and daughter. While Jen was tall and slender with cropped dark hair, her mother was petite, curvy, and possessed of what seemed to be several acres of corkscrew-curled auburn hair.

Jen's mother had found her niche in the 1970s and had decided to remain there for good. Natalie wore little round glasses, her jeans were worn, her sweater was hand knit (by Gran) and old enough to be embellished with many fuzz balls. She wore Birkenstock sandals all year around, baked the best whole-grain bread, and persisted in starting earnest conversations with her children at unpredictable moments.

Jen had forgotten the earnest-conversation bit when she'd accepted the chance to move back home two years before. She'd worked a double shift the night before at Mulligan's, was due in for the lunch shift today, and her feet were still begging for mercy. She wasn't really up for having her soul searched, her chakras aligned, or the fiber content of her diet analyzed.

Again.

Jen tried not to show any of her frustration. She changed the subject instead of answering, a ploy that sometimes worked. "Hi, Mom. The bread is really good this time."

"Don't you do that to me," Natalie said as she advanced into the kitchen. "I know you well enough to see you putting your shields up. I want you to be honest with me, Jen."

"I'm not putting—"

"You *are*. I can see you closing off the world. You've always done it, but now you're better at it."

Jen didn't know what to say to that so she ate her toast. She toyed with her knitting while she did so. It flopped on the table, not looking like much of anything since it wasn't yet stuffed. The pit of the avocado was done, because her plan was that the end result would look like an avocado cut in half. The round pit had been the easiest place to start. So, she had a purple golf ball with floppy frills around it and a lot of doubt.

Shouldn't the flesh be more yellow around the stone? Should she use more than one color of yarn? She could ask Teresa how to change from one color to the next gradually.

Jen's mom shook her head, which made her ringlets dance, then pulled out the chair opposite Jen with such purpose that she couldn't be ignored.

"Well, if you are gay, then you should know that I'm okay with it," her mother said with the compassion that characterized these discussions. "I'd just like to know—assuming, of course, that you don't think that's too much of a personal thing to ask."

So much for the diversion plan. Jen wondered at the timing of the question. "Why do you want to know? Shouldn't we have had this chat when I was sixteen?"

"I know, I know, and now your life is your own business, blah blah blah." Her mother sighed and grimaced, then leaned closer. "But you might as well know, it's because I need to decide what to tell your grandmother about Thanksgiving. You know, she's always after me about whether you're bringing a date or not."

"Just tell her no. It's worked before."

"Not this year. Gran saw some documentary on television and now she has this idea that maybe you're gay and we're hiding it from her." Jen's mother took a swig of her herbal tea. "She'll love it if you are, I've got to say. She's always insisted that I didn't know anything about raising children, and you know that she won't understand that being gay isn't a lifestyle choice. It's wired right in, we know that, but she's going to think that you've gone and chosen to do this to annoy her or me, and that you can be persuaded to change your mind and be 'normal' again, whatever the hell that is. I don't even want to imagine that campaign."

Neither did Jen. She ate her toast as quickly as she could, hoping her mother got lost on a tangent long enough that she could escape without answering the question.

The chances were slim, but it was worth a try.

"How many times have I told you not to wolf down your food?" Her mother fixed her with a stern glance, exactly the opposite of what Jen had hoped for. "I'm all for people expressing their own rhythms, but eating quickly only inhibits digestion. You, of all people, should be respecting your body's natural needs."

"Mom, I'm not sick anymore."

Her mother sat back, smiling slightly as if Jen had said exactly what Natalie had wanted her to say. "Really? How would I be able to tell?"

"Check out my new hair."

"Hair is only part of it. You mope around here like a ghost, or like a person with death sentence."

"I was a person with a death sentence."

"*Was* being the operative word. Past tense, Jen. You're better now, all better from what the oncologists say. Last I heard, your prognosis was excellent. You're one year clear."

"That's what I heard, too."

"So, when are you going to do something about it? When are you going to act as if you're alive, Jen, instead of marking time until you die?" Her mother leaned her elbows on the table and regarded Jen earnestly. "When exactly do we get the old Jen back?"

Jen swallowed the last bite of her toast and picked up her plate. "I don't know what you mean," she said with a shrug. "I've got a job and I go to work almost every day . . ."

"And what about going back to college?"

"I'm not sure what I want to do yet."

"What about traveling again?"

"I've already waitressed in sixteen countries. I'm good with that as a lifetime total." That wasn't it and Jen knew it, but she wasn't sure enough of herself to confess more to her mother.

Even if the woman had X-ray vision. She felt Natalie's gaze following her and knew she wasn't out of the kitchen yet.

"You used to have a lot of dreams and plans."

Jen said nothing. Not knowing how long you were going to live had a way of short-circuiting long-term dreams and plans.

Her mother tried another tack. "And what about your friends? What about Teresa?"

"I stay in touch with Teresa . . ."

"But you don't get together anymore. You don't go downtown and hang out with her as much as you used to."

"Teresa's really busy with her job. She's CFO now, you know."

Jen chose not to try to explain that she felt so out of step with her old friends. It was like Death was sitting on her shoulder, making her unwelcome company among people busy being vibrantly alive. "And after all, I don't care about power shopping or speed dating."

"Why not? That's what women your age should care about: clothes and music and parties." Her mother took a deep, fortifying breath. "And men, Jen. You should be crazy for men. But you've shown no interest in men lately. Which leads me back to the question: are you gay?"

It took Jen only a heartbeat to see where this was going and how a little white lie could be useful. "Maybe I'm not sure."

Her mother exhaled with impatience. "Then you aren't. There's no middle ground with sexual orientation. And for what it's worth, I don't think you are, anyway."

It seemed that Jen's inability to bend the truth was one constant in her universe. In a way, she was glad. "How would you know?"

"Hello. Don't you remember who caught you kissing Mark Desilvo behind the garage on your thirteenth birthday party?

"Maybe I was curious." Jen glanced up. "Maybe he wasn't very persuasive."

"That would explain why you cried your heart out every night for three entire weeks when Drew MacPherson broke up with you to date Annemarie Schultz instead?"

"That was pride," Jen insisted. She rinsed her dishes in the sink. "Drew didn't break my heart."

"Maybe it was Joel, then?" Her mother asked lightly, continuing before Jen could answer. "Or was it Steve?"

Jen caught her breath and was glad that she had her back to her mother. "You remember everything."

"I'm your mother. It's my job."

Jen pivoted to face her mother, feeling annoyed and defensive. "Is there a point to this? I need to get to work."

Her mother shrugged. "I just asked you a question. Are you gay or not?"

"It seems as if you've worked that out for yourself already." Jen dropped her mug and plate into the dishwasher, then let the door slam a bit more assertively than she'd meant to do. She felt like a cornered teenager, although that scenario was years behind her.

Maybe moving back home had stirred up a lot of old behavior patterns, like her mother meddling in her life and Jen resenting it. Unfortunately, waiting tables wasn't going to be the key to her financial freedom anytime soon.

Not with those medical bills still unpaid. One of her chemo buddies—they'd had a similar schedule and had quickly realized they were both uninsured—had joked that if the cancer didn't finish you off, the debt would. Now that she was healthy, Jen found the dark joke less funny.

Her mother, meanwhile, persisted in the day's theme of choice. "If you're not gay, when are you going to start dating again?"

"Maybe never." Jen strode to the door, wanting this conversation over ASAP. She picked up her avocado and her needles and decided that she could stop into that yarn shop on her way to work.

Her mother smiled the sweet smile that made people—other people—underestimate her. Jen folded her arms across her chest in anticipation of a direct hit to the heart.

It was too late to run for cover.

"Steve wasn't worth the trouble . . ."

"Forget Steve."

"Maybe you should forget Steve, Jen."

Jen knew that there was truth in that, but she wasn't going to admit it at this particular moment. "Do you want me to move out? Is that what this is about? Because I don't have to get married to move out of here."

"No, you don't." Natalie was annoyingly serene. "That was what I had to do, but you have a thousand choices. If you want to move and you want my help in any way, you're welcome to it. But that's not what this is about."

"You aren't going to tell me that I can't be happy without a man in my life, not you."

Natalie put her mug down on the table. "No, that's not what I'm going to tell you. We both know that I'm not a really great source of advice when it comes to men, at least when it comes to marrying them. I like men a lot and do think that they do add something to your life, but that's not what this is about, either."

Jen held her ground. Running away probably wouldn't work. Her mother would follow until she'd had her say.

"What then?" Jen asked, hearing surly sixteen in her voice again. "What's it about?" She fully expected a lecture on being purposeful or finding herself or getting in balance again, so her mother surprised her.

"It's about being alone. I don't care who you're with, or for how long, I just hate to see you alone. Maybe lonely." Her mother smiled softly. "You're too wonderful a person, Jen, for me to keep you all to myself."

Jen said nothing. She stood there and kept her arms wrapped tightly around herself. She felt her tears rise and wondered how the hell her mother could always see right through her.

Maybe that was her job, too.

Natalie got up and came to stand beside her. She raised one hand to Jen's face and caressed her skin, her words as soft as her fingertips. "Look at your hair. It's come in all curly."

"I know. Might not last." Jen's voice was thicker than she'd expected.

"I thought for a long time that I'd never see you like this again."

"Yeah. Me, too." Jen met her mother's gaze and the compassion she found there eliminated her frustration.

Just like that. It was a trick of her mother's. Natalie knew how to give Jen's sucker heart a squeeze and she did it now.

Natalie sighed. "And I don't know what to say to you. I don't know what to advise you to do, or even if I should butt my nose into your business, but it seems to me that you're just counting off the days, Jen. You seem to have insulated yourself from the world in a way I don't understand." Jen dropped her gaze. "It seems to me that—I don't know—maybe you don't believe that you've got this second chance. Or that maybe you're afraid everything will be snatched away again."

Jen swallowed, painfully aware of what cancer had stolen from her. It hadn't been just her breast. It had been her optimism and her sense of the future and her confidence; all of those had been sacrificed to the knife.

Every night, she looked in the mirror and saw the scar that would never stop reminding her of everything that was gone.

Every day, she walked among people who had no idea what it was like to have the foundation of your world ripped away.

Much less to fear that it could happen again.

Her mother touched her chin, compelling Jen to meet her gaze again. "But you've got this chance, Jen!" she said urgently. "It's all yours. I don't want you to miss out because you're afraid to live."

Jen took a shaking breath and tried to make a joke. "So, I should find a man and get married and have babies? You sound like Gran."

"No, no, that's not what I'm saying. I think you should get a date and have sex, lots of sex, because that will remind you that you're alive and well." Her mother grinned, looking young and mischievous. "I doubt your grandmother ever recommended that to you."

"No, I think I'd remember if she had."

"Sex is good therapy, Jen. I can recommend it on the basis of experience. An orgasm always makes me feel better about life, the universe, and everything. And the ones you give yourself don't have that same element of surprise." Her mom smiled and returned to her mug, filling it from the teapot.

Jen had always suspected that other people didn't talk so frankly to their mothers, and even after all these years of open discussion, her mother could still astound her. "So, Natalie's tip of the day is that sex is better than masturbation?"

"Provided you orgasm, yes." Her mother winked. "Get a date; you'll see. Just let me know if you plan to bring someone home and I'll make myself scarce."

Bring someone home. Jen's mind stalled on that concept. The thing was that she and her mother didn't work with the same set of assumptions. "Mom, I'm not going to have casual sex in your house."

"Then have formal sex. I don't really need to know the details."

"I mean, I'm not going to have sex with someone unless I'm in a serious relationship."

Her mother sighed and frowned, then shook her head. "I should never have let your grandmother read you all those fairy tales," she muttered, then looked up, her face pale and delicate within that halo of reddish curls. There had been a time when Jen had thought her mother must be an angel.

A thrice-married and thrice-divorced angel, with a child from each marriage and one son from before any of those marriages; an angel who was honest, creative, clever, and worked to her own unique moral code.

Maybe a naughty angel.

"Jen, this whole soul mate–Mr. Right thing is a notion created by and encouraged by men to ensure that women remain virginal until they're married, then chaste except when their husbands want something from them. It's a notion that serves men, not women, and one that is—or should be—deader than a doornail. You can have sex with someone without an ironclad guarantee that you'll be spending the rest of your life with him. Trust me. I know. Try it at least before you decide it doesn't work for you."

"Just because I can doesn't mean I want to. I mean, what about sexually transmitted diseases?"

"You can spell condom: I know because I taught you."

"When I was twelve."

"It's always better to be prepared." Her mother rubbed the bridge of her nose. "Jen, I just want you to have some fun."

"I am having fun."

Her mother gave her a cutting look. "Do not lie to me."

"Okay, maybe I'm not having that much fun. I just like to

believe that I'm having fun. And I'm knitting up a storm. The avocado is my biggest project yet."

Her mother heaved a sigh. "Lying to yourself isn't any better
than lying to me."

"But it's not that simple, Mom," Jen said, feeling dragged into
a conversation she wasn't sure she wanted to have. "It's hard to
meet people, to meet men."

"No, it's easy to meet men. Your problem is that you're trying
to meet your so-called one and only, and you want to recognize
him on sight." Her mother came to her side again and put a hand
on her shoulder. "You can't always tell a book by its cover, Jen,
that's all I'm saying. Just to mix our metaphors here, you need to
get into the pool, if you're going to prove that you can swim."

"What if I don't feel like doing any laps right now?"

"Then when will you?"

"Someday."

"Prove it," her mother said, challenge bright in her eyes. "Bring
a date to Thanksgiving dinner."

"Mom! I can't just order up a date, like you order a salad."

"You don't have to marry him, Jen. Just bring a date, a man
who is reasonably presentable, to Thanksgiving dinner at your
grandmother's. That's all."

"No, that's not all. I know you better than that."

Her mother contrived to look innocent and failed. "What's that
supposed to mean?"

"Bring a date or else what?"

Natalie grinned. "Or else I'll start fixing you up myself." Jen
knew her horror at that prospect showed because her mother
tapped the side of her mug with a fingertip. "There's a very nice, if
somewhat hirsute, young man working at the Birkenstock store,
for example. I understand he writes poetry . . ."

"Noooooooooooo!" Jen shouted and flung herself out of the
kitchen, only half joking. She heard her mother laughing, but knew
that this was a threat her mother would act upon. Jen made an es-

cape to work as soon as was humanly possible, though her mother still got in one last shot.

"Remember that boy at the natural-food store? He's always asking after you . . ."

Oh no. Not the bass-player-whole-grain-aficionado who never cleaned his fingernails and wanted to walk to around the world to protest the living conditions . . . somewhere. No, no, no. Anyone had to be better than that. Anyone had to think more clearly than that.

Jen had to be able to find a date somewhere. She'd ask her older sister for help, just like she always did.

Cin would know what to do.

Jen had one smidgen of time to call Cin before things got crazy. She'd taken a bit too long at the yarn store, seduced by a nubby dark green wool-and-silk blend that would make perfect avocado skin but was shockingly expensive. After much deliberation, she bought it—she only needed one ball, after all.

So she scrambled at work to get her tables set. Mulligan's was still empty and her section was ready by five to twelve. Jen knew that the place would be packed by quarter past.

She asked the older waitress Lucy to cover for her and called, praying that Cin would answer quickly.

"Nature Sprouts. How can I help you?"

"Cin, I need your help big-time. Mom wants me to bring a guy for Thanksgiving dinner at Gran's or she'll start fixing me up."

"Oh no!" Cin laughed and it wasn't a sympathetic sound. "Not the guy with the greasy little soul patch at the natural-food store? Hasn't he left to walk to Chile yet?"

"I don't know. I don't want to know. Cin, you've got to help me." Jen tapped her toe and watched the door swing open. Two guys came in and headed for the bar.

Not her section. She was free for another minute or two.

"Cin? I don't have a lot of time."

"No, you don't. It's next Thursday." Her sister was gleeful, instead of taking this seriously as Jen thought she should.

"Cin, this isn't a joke."

"You sure sound worried about it."

"I don't want to be fixed up. With anybody."

"You'd rather knit."

"What's wrong with that?"

"Okay, okay, no spinster-watching-the-world-go-by jokes from me. Hey, I have an idea. Remember how Mom hated Steve?"

"I am not calling Steve," Jen said firmly. Why did she have to hear that jerk's name so many times in one day? "I am not going to grovel for anything from that . . ."

"No, no, no. What I'm thinking is that you need to find a guy like Steve."

"I don't *think* so."

"You don't have to marry him, Jen. You just need to bring him to dinner once. Three hours, tops."

"Just enough time for Mom to hate him. What's your point?"

"That would be the point. Then you can lie—oh wait, I'm talking to Miss Truth. You'll have to learn to lie, but it's for a good cause."

"You can't lie to Mom . . ." Not for the first time, Jen was acutely aware of the differences between herself and her sister.

"Trust me, it can be done, but it's a learned skill. And it's worth it: if Mom hates who you're dating, she won't want to see him again. You can just pretend you're happily dating the invisible man and threaten to bring him to family functions every once in a while."

It made a dangerous kind of sense. "That sounds like something you would do."

"Well, you did ask me for an idea. For what it's worth, I think it's brilliant."

"But, Cin, how can I be sure that Mom will hate a guy I bring home? You know how unpredictable she is."

"As unpredictable as a trout rising to a fly," Cin said wryly. "All you need to find is an uptight, handsome, conservative guy. Someone who comes from money and is hot to make a bunch of it for himself, no matter what he has to do to earn it. Mr. Success at Any Cost. Boston is full of them. It should be easy."

Jen leaned against the wall of the waitress station, considering this. "You mean the kind of guy any other mother would adore."

"The very same. You know those ambitious types make her crazy, and corporate America is one of her hot buttons. Maybe you could find a lawyer—that would really send her to the moon."

"I don't know . . ."

"You did it once, little sister. You can do it again."

Jen winced. "But wouldn't I be using him?"

Cin laughed. "And this kind of a guy wouldn't be using you? It's pretty easily resolved, Jen: just don't put out and in three dates— max—he'll be forgetting to call you."

"But I don't know any guys like that."

And Jen didn't want to.

On the other hand, there was the prospect of a date with the guy at the natural-food store.

Maybe she just needed the right motivation.

"Come on, Jen, you must have guys ask you out all the time: I mean, you work in a bar and you're cute. Look at it this way: there's no chance of you getting hurt, is there? I mean, you're not going to make an emotional investment with a guy like that, are you?"

"No. Still it seems kind of mean."

"You got a better idea?" Cin lowered her voice. "You should know that there's a new guy working at the Greenpeace office. I'll bet Mom knows him and, you know, he's got to be just about your age."

"And?" Jen clutched the phone.

"Be afraid, Jen. Be very afraid." Another phone rang and Cin cursed under her breath. "Gotta go, sis. Just think about it."

Jen hung up the phone, seeing the potential of Cin's idea but filled with doubts all the same. After all, she'd missed out on the devil-may-care gene that both her mother and sister seemed to possess.

What was she going to do? Proposition some guy in this place? She'd probably lose her job.

Behind her, Lucy sighed. "No rest for the wicked, that's for sure. Look, of course, they're going to sit in my section."

Jen glanced up and saw the four guys heading for a front table. They were carousing together, laughing and joking, and three of them were in suits. They were all tall and buff, handsome and privileged, roughly Jen's contemporaries.

"This town is full of them," Lucy muttered as she grabbed cutlery out of the bin. "God's own gifts certain the rest of us were born to serve them. As if I didn't have eight tables of them last night, demanding this and that pronto." She sighed again and gave Jen a look. "Just another day in paradise. You gotta be glad that you always get the back section: these flashy boys prefer it up by the window so they can check out the women."

Which was really all Jen needed to know. "I'll trade sections with you, if you like," she suggested, as if she didn't really care where she worked. "I'd kind of like a change of scene."

Actually, she felt like she was channeling her sister. Cin's scheme wasn't the kind of thing that Jen typically did but here she was, doing it.

"They're cheap bastards, all of them," Lucy confided. The four guys were already looking over and one was snapping his fingers. "No tips to speak of. You sure?"

"Yeah, I'll give it a try." Jen took the menus from Lucy as the pushy one hooted for attention.

"Hey, how about we pool tips today and split them?" Lucy asked kindly. "I don't want you to get ripped off for giving me a break."

"Thanks. That'd be great." Jen turned and marched for the table, hoping that just putting things in motion would be enough.

One of the suits winked at her. Maybe Cin's plan would work out, after all.

The big problem, Jen realized en route to her new section, was that Jen didn't possess her sister's easy charm. Cin's plan seemed to suddenly have serious flaws.

Well, one flaw, really.

It had to be executed by Jen.

One thing Zach Coxwell could count on was his buddies. They showed up for lunch, dead on time.

There had been a time when the four of them had cut class to sit here, drink beer, and watch women. It hadn't been that long ago, at least not to Zach's thinking, but his buddies had been transformed. Instead of students in jeans with haircuts made to last a few weeks too long, they wore Italian suits and shoes with leather soles. Their ties were silk and perfectly knotted: Trevor even wore a white shirt with French cuffs.

Zach, in his old uniform of polo shirt and jeans, felt under-dressed. He slung his battered leather jacket over the back of a chair and knew he looked like an unemployed bum in comparison to his pals.

Which in a way, he supposed he was. And his pals were lawyers, because they hadn't dropped out of law school, and they dressed for success.

But what did clothes matter? The fact that they had showed up in their old haunt reassured him.

He needed evidence that some things didn't change. Zach had been killing himself for much of the last year, doing drudge work for no thanks and little benefit. Lunch with his old buddies had seemed like the perfect tonic. It might even motivate him to go back to law school, when he saw how much they enjoyed practicing.

Lunch had taken longer to set up than he'd expected, but hey, they all had day jobs now. As Scott had noted on the phone, needing to be somewhere sixty or eighty hours a week cuts into a guy's leisure time.

The four shook hands after they scored a table by the windows. Zach noted with satisfaction that it was their regular one, the one with the great view of the intersection on Massachusetts with the stiff crosswind. Skirts got flipped skyward there all the time. Zach settled in with anticipation.

"Scoring the best view?" Scott teased.

"Might as well." Zach grinned. "It's up to Jason and me now that you and Trevor are married."

"A guy can still look," Scott protested.

Jason nudged him aside. "Gimme the view, man. I know Anna's work number if you get out of line."

"Hey!" Trevor shouted in the general direction of the waitresses before he'd even sat down. He snapped his fingers imperiously. "Let's get some service here."

Scott tapped his watch, a fancy steel piece of work that must have set him back a paycheck or two. "Good point. One hour for lunch and I've blown fifteen just finding a parking spot."

"You could have walked," Zach suggested, then was surprised when the other three laughed in unison. He was used to people laughing at his jokes, but that hadn't been one. "It's not that far," he began but got no further before they laughed again.

"As if." Trevor rolled his eyes and spoke as if explaining something simple to a slow child. "The whole point of driving a flash car, Zach, is to be seen in it."

"Maybe it's different if you don't have to make the payments," Scott said and the three grinned again.

Zach didn't.

A tall waitress showed up beside the table then, with a fistful of menus. She was dark-haired and cute, if a bit serious. "Hi, welcome to Mulligan's," she said. "I'm—"

"You're gorgeous," Jason said, winking at her so boldly that Zach was embarrassed. The waitress looked at Jason as if he were a primitive life-form come to torment her.

Jason grinned at her, apparently oblivious to her response.

"Look, we're in a hurry," Trevor said crisply. "I'll have a San Pellegrino with a slice of lime. Do you have fifteen-minutes-or-free lunch specials?"

"Yes, they're right here on the back of the menu . . ."

"Is one a sandwich?"

"Yes, there's a chicken club sandwich . . ."

"Great, fine, I'll have that but leave off the bacon and mayonnaise and put it on whole-grain bread. Salad instead of fries, vinaigrette dressing on the side." Trevor checked his watch. "Twelve-sixteen. I'm counting."

"Same for me," Scott said, shoving the menu back across the table.

"Hey, we can spare a minute to hear her name," Jason said smoothly.

"Missed your chance," the waitress said, unimpressed by Jason's suave charm. Zach stifled a smile. "What will you have? Time's a-wasting, or so I've been told."

Zach laughed, although this time he laughed alone. The waitress met his gaze, a wary twinkle in the depths of her dark eyes.

Jason sensed competition and moved closer to the waitress. "Hey, don't cut him any slack. He's been in jail this year."

"Great. A felon in my section," she said, then pointed her pen at Zach. "You pay cash."

The other three thought this was funny. Zach didn't smile and neither did the waitress, though she was watching him.

"I'll have the club, too," Jason said, trying again to draw her eye. "But I'll have the bacon on mine."

The waitress scribbled then glanced up at Zach.

"What beers do you have on tap?"

She listed about fifteen while Trevor drummed his fingers on the tabletop. Zach picked one from a local microbrewery, flipped over the menu, and chose the burger with a salad.

"Thanks a lot, Zach," Trevor said. "Twelve-nineteen and the order hasn't gone anywhere."

The waitress gave him a look that spoke volumes.

"I'm not in a rush," Zach said to her. "So, don't worry about bringing everything at the same time if it will hold them up." She nodded. He smiled but she was already hurrying away.

"A pint of beer at lunch on a weekday!" Scott nudged Zach. "How long has it been, guys?"

"And in no rush." Trevor whistled through his teeth. "There's the life of leisure for you."

"Why couldn't my daddy have left me a trust fund?" Jason asked the universe in general and the three laughed together.

Zach straightened, not finding the reference very funny. It hadn't quite been a year since his father had committed suicide and it would be a long time, he suspected, before he could take a reference to that man in stride. "Actually, I don't have a trust fund—"

"Do the details really matter, Zach?" Scott interrupted him. "You were born on easy street and we have to bust our asses to get there. It's that simple."

Zach didn't know what to say, which was something for the guy known in his own family to have an answer for everything. He felt a definite thread of hostility where there had never been one before and began to wonder whether he really could count on his buddies forever.

Or for much of anything.

"I'd forgotten how slow this place was," Jason groused. He grinned and shook his head. "Though it's not like we had anywhere to go when we hung out here."

"What a grubby joint," Trevor agreed, brushing some crumbs from his seat. "I'd forgotten."

"Me, too," Scott agreed. "Who picked this place anyhow?"

"Me," Zach admitted. "I though it'd be like old times."

Scott laughed. "It is that. Gives us a chance to see how far we've come, if nothing else." He perched on the edge of his seat in his navy pinstripe suit and kept glancing down at the upholstery. "Anna will kill me if I send another suit to the dry cleaners this month."

"Spending more than your wife on dry cleaning?" Jason teased. "That's a feat."

"I don't like how she irons my shirts, so I'm already going there to take my shirts in." Scott was a bit defensive and Jason went for blood.

"What, you got married and didn't get a domestic slave out of the bargain?"

"Don't let Anna hear you say that!" Scott said, then shrugged. "Besides, she says 100 percent cotton is too much trouble and I don't like to wear synthetics."

Trevor laughed. "Maxine won't even try to iron mine. She showed me the ironing board when I asked her about it, and they've been going to the cleaners ever since."

Jason eyed the pair of them. "Where do you take yours? I've yet to find a cleaner who gets it right. It's the attention to detail that really makes it work . . ."

"So, wait, who does yours?" Scott asked. "Your mommy?" Trevor started to laugh.

"No." Jason stared between them both, as if daring them to mock him. "I do my own."

"Let me see the cuffs," Trevor demanded. Jason slipped one arm out of his suit jacket and let the other two check out his workmanship.

Zach sat back and stared. The guys he'd hung out with would never have been so interested in white dress shirts, let alone how well they were pressed. Obviously, they'd been surreptitiously replaced by aliens and all he had to do to save his buddies was find the pods.

He glanced under the table. No luck.

Trevor whistled in admiration as he examined Jason's cuffs. "So, what do you charge? I'll send you mine."

"Dream on," Jason said. "You can't afford me."

"What do you mean?" Trevor asked.

"You can dress up corporate practice at a bank, but you can't take it to dinner." Jason punctuated his comment with a sneer at Trevor's cuff links. They were costume jewelry, Zach had noticed that right away, but funky enough to be forgiven.

Trevor straightened his jacket cuffs so that his cuff links were partly hidden, defensive in his turn. "We can't all defend criminals with deep pockets."

Jason wagged a finger at his friend. "Innocent until proven guilty. Let's all remember the basics."

"Where is that waitress?" Scott said, looking across the restaurant. "I don't have all day to hang around this hole."

The waitress brought the drinks then and Zach was glad to have a beer. If he drank it fast enough it might dull his sense of alienation. What ever happened to job satisfaction? His buddies seemed to be worried about stuff that didn't matter.

"So, trust-fund boy, got a wild adventure to share with us this month?" Trevor asked. The waitress glanced up from putting a dish of lime slices on the table.

"Yeah, something involving gorgeous models, naked except for their designer logos," Scott teased.

"Fast cars," Trevor added.

"Private jets!" Jason contributed.

"Bathtubs filled with caviar and champagne on the side," Scott said wistfully, then shook his head. "Shit, I wanna be Zach Coxwell when I grow up."

They laughed again and toasted him with their sparkling water.

The truth was somewhat more mundane: Zach had spent the past eight months executing his father's estate, which had involved enduring a lot of appointments with dry-as-dust officials, copying documents, tallying inventories, and visiting notaries. His father's assets had been distributed in a thousand little stashes and it had seemed that every time he expected to be done soon, he'd found another. His mother had been little help, determined as she was to put her married past behind her, and his brothers had pretty much been ignoring him since his adventure in that New Orleans jail the previous winter.

Which he might have been willing to admit had been a major case of bad judgment, but no one in his family was giving him a chance to admit to anything.

Being the black sheep was proving to be lonely business.

"Maybe you could introduce me to your sister," Trevor suggested. "Get me on the gravy train, too."

"Afford some real cuff links," Scott muttered, but Trevor ignored him.

"You're married!" Jason protested to Trevor.

"So's my sister," said Zach and the guys laughed. He wasn't used to people laughing at things he said, not when he wasn't trying to be funny. He inhaled some beer, hoping it would make him feel better.

The waitress shook her head minutely and left.

"Twelve-twenty-four," Trevor called after her.

"And you still haven't given me your number," Jason added.

Zach began to wish he was sitting at another table. This plan to cheer himself up and find a plan for the rest of his life really wasn't going well.

Chapter 2

Jen had never been so glad to be getting rid of anyone as the guys at table twelve. What a bunch of jerks. At least she'd avoided the temptation to dump that side of vinaigrette down the front of the first loser's fancy suit. Her first impression had been the right one: she couldn't have asked one of them out, much less put up with one of them at Thanksgiving dinner for three or four hours.

She'd have to find another solution.

Maybe she'd knit herself a date. He'd be quiet, that's for sure.

They could be a close-knit couple, ha ha.

The casually dressed hunk seemed to be the most normal of them all, but the fact that he even hung out with them told her that they were four of a kind.

After all, they called him "trust-fund boy," which meant that he had money, lots of it. He'd eaten a burger and wore a leather jacket, which put him in the carnivore, planet-trasher, methane-dispenser category of men, no endorsement in Jen's view.

His pals said he'd been in jail, but she gave that less credit. Handsome rich guys never got busted, at least not for long. It had probably been a joke these three had played on him that had gotten him arrested.

With friends like that, a person didn't need enemies.

But then, they probably deserved each other.

Maybe she'd leave the country for Thanksgiving. Maybe she should date the earnest guy at the natural-food store, strap on her Birkies, and walk to Chile. She'd never waited tables in South America, after all.

Jen brought separate checks to the table without even asking, because she guessed they'd be expensing lunch individually: splitting the tab from the outset on the computer would save her grief later. Also, Lucy had called it right, these types were always cheap: splitting the check meant that she might actually get some tip out of it.

As opposed to none.

Or as opposed to the very worst case, that of the cash left on the table being short of the total bill. That would mean that she'd get to pay up for them after they were gone. She watched the change and bills hit the table as the three suits bailed and tried to not conclude that their departure was too quick to be a good thing. She waited until they were away from the table, though, sick of the fair-haired guy without a wedding ring hitting on her.

She'd cover the difference to not have to take more of that.

The fourth guy, the comparatively normal one, was left alone to finish his beer. Jen moved quickly to count the cash left on the table while there was a chance of someone ponying up any outstanding difference.

"Catch you later, Zach!" shouted the one who had harassed her about the time.

"Twelve-fifty-one," Jen muttered as that jerk ducked out the door. With luck, he was gone for good.

Zach laughed. "That's funny."

Jen looked at him with surprise. "I didn't think you'd hear me."

"It's okay, I won't tell." His eyes danced with mischief but Jen wasn't interested in making friends.

Maybe she did need a date but for a different reason than satisfying her mother: just being in the presence of a good-looking guy was making her heart beat faster. She could feel it thumping under her knitted prosthesis. It was the peach angora one with the Chinese good-luck charm embedded in the stuffing, the first one she had knit.

Maybe this would be her lucky day.

Maybe she should count the money. To her relief, there was enough cash to cover and a 10 percent tip. Not a fortune, but she'd take it. She glanced up to find the last guy watching her. She knew that look. Her mother would have said that the universe was setting her up to make her move.

He was a carnivore. He came from money. He had the same smooth charm as Steve and the same expectation that the world was his oyster. He was a perfect candidate for the Plan.

Too bad her tongue had rolled itself into a knot.

He smiled ruefully. "Guess I was underdressed for the occasion."

"It was lunch in a pub." Jen glanced over him. He was tall and sufficiently handsome that she didn't think it would much matter what he wore. Anywhere. He'd always look good. Maybe her age, maybe a couple of years older, he still looked like a university student. Maybe he still was, if his daddy was paying. Jen felt a tiny pang of jealousy, knowing she could have happily been an eternal student if the tuition bills hadn't gotten so scary. "I think you look okay."

He grinned at that and leaned closer, the sudden intensity of his attention making Jen want to bolt and run. "Thanks. We met in law school and haven't seen each other in a while."

Jen's ears perked up. A lawyer. Plus her mother hated anyone with a trust fund, as she believed such individuals to be incapable of work and unable to understand the realities of life.

Come to think of it, Jen had some issues with that—and the conspicuous consumption it implied—herself.

Never mind the Plan. She heard the ding of the bell in the kitchen, knew the meals for table eight were ready, and chickened out. She pointed to the last bill on the table. "If you give me a credit card, I'll put that through."

"I thought I was supposed to pay cash."

"That was a joke."

"Then why didn't you smile?"

"Not my style."

"So I see." He pushed the bill back across the table toward her. "I'm not leaving yet. I'd like another beer, please."

Jen glanced toward the door where there was a small line of people waiting for tables. "Well, then, could you move to the bar, please? I'll transfer your balance."

His smile faded. "Do you serve at the bar?"

"No. Murray, the bartender, serves all patrons at the bar."

He lounged back in his chair and gave her a wicked smile. "Then I'll stay here."

Jen's heart skipped a beat. "Why?"

"I like you." He squinted at the bill, where she'd written her usual thanks with her name. "Jen."

Jen glanced to the line again and back to him. He followed her gaze, but didn't budge. "Maybe you've noticed that there's a line of people who'd like to have lunch," she said, as politely as she could.

"So I see. I think I'll have a pint of the same, please."

Jen straightened. "But this is a table for four."

"So it is. And I'm sitting at it for the moment."

If he thought his confidence would persuade her to his view, he was wrong. Jen had been raised on a steady diet of Natalie's insistence upon social justice and his sense of entitlement annoyed her as nothing else could have done.

Who did this guy think he was?

Maybe she'd inherited her mother's perspective on rich jerks. Either way, she'd had enough of the guys at table twelve.

Jen braced her hands on the table. "Maybe you misunderstood me. This is a table for four people. *Four*. No matter how you count it, you are one person. It is just before one o'clock on a Thursday, a very busy period for us that will last through two."

"So? I'll pay for the beer."

"Your friends said you have a trust fund, so let me explain a little bit of waitressing reality to you . . ."

"Hey, you were listening!"

"This is how I make my living and incidentally it's not a really great way to make a living. Because every buck counts, I need a full section for every meal. I need to turn tables as quickly as possible and fill them as full as possible or answer to Murray."

Zach followed her gaze to the bar. "He looks like a barrel of laughs."

"Here's your chance to find out. You want to hang out alone and drink, I'd prefer you did it at the bar. Please."

He gave her a charming smile that did nothing to aid his cause. "The tip will make it worth your while."

Jen bristled. She knew better than to believe anything a guy like this said. "As if," she retorted. "'*Don't bet on the Bruins*.' I get that one all the time. Or pennies in the bottom of the water glass. Ha ha. You guys are all such jokers. I'll move your tab and Murray will pull your beer at the bar." She pivoted and waved to Lucy, who was seating new arrivals. "I've got a table for four here, Lucy."

"Hey, but Jen . . ." He stood up, displeased with the situation, and made a last appeal.

Jen had to look up, way up, but she wasn't intimidated. She was mad and the fact that he expected to charm her into giving him what he wanted only made her madder. "Move it. Now. The bar or the door. Your choice."

She supposed she shouldn't have been so surprised that he did move. Her mom always said she could be fierce.

She *was* surprised that he went to the bar, because she'd been sure he'd walk right out the door with her $14.45 plus tip.

But that couldn't mean he was any different than his pals.

Just more stubborn.

It was too bad that she could relate to that.

• • •

Okay, Zach's plan was showing serious weaknesses. He'd never had the sense before that he'd been left behind after the train had left the station, but that feeling had been unavoidable today.

His buddies had careers, wives, mortgages, car payments—or some combination thereof—and wore suits. He'd known all of that, but this lunch had really made the differences clear. They had purpose—or at least obligations—and clearly weren't enjoying it. He hated how they'd been bickering about nothing and had no ambition to become like them. Why was it suddenly a bad thing to have come from money? Wealth sure hadn't made his life any easier, as far as he could see.

Zach had even—apparently—lost his ability to charm women somewhere along the line. Any idea of saving the day by chatting up the waitress was bombing out. He settled in at the bar with no clear plan, other than not doing what Jen expected him to do.

On principle. She thought he'd leave and he was going to prove her wrong. It was a start.

"You the guy with the pint?" the burly bartender—Murray—asked. He was in the middle of pulling a beer that looked less good to Zach than it might have.

"Yeah, that's me. I haven't paid for my lunch yet, either."

"Right. Want it all together?"

"Sure."

An older waitress came to the bar and plunked down her tray, sparing Zach the barest glance. "Two pints of Stonecroft and another gin and tonic."

"You could crack a smile, Lucy," Murray said. "Wouldn't kill you and you might get better tips."

Lucy snorted. "You could do us both a favor and put more beer in those glasses than foam. And do more than introduce the gin to the tonic this time—put some of it in there. The guy at twenty-two complained that the first one was too weak."

Murray snorted this time, but he put a good hit of gin in the glass. "Undo a button, Lucy, and you won't have to complain about your tips."

"Huh. I didn't think this was *that* kind of a bar." Lucy swung her tray to her shoulder, winked at Zach, and sailed off to her section.

Jen came to the bar then and ignored Zach thoroughly. She was still annoyed with him, he could see that, and although he knew better than to push his luck, he'd do it anyway.

It wasn't as if he had much to lose.

"So, Jen, do you know why California has the most lawyers while New Jersey has the most toxic waste dumps?"

She spared him a glance and he sipped his beer. She sighed with forbearance as she waited for her drinks. "No, why?"

"Because New Jersey got to choose."

Murray snickered. "Hey, that's not bad."

Jen, though, gave Zach a hard look. "Maybe one of you could explain to me why poisoning the planet is funny."

Both men sobered. Zach sipped his beer. Murray put a martini and a 7-Up on the counter, which Jen claimed, then she sailed away.

"I'd count that as a strike," Murray muttered. "Unless you're trying to score points with me."

"Sorry. You're not my type."

"Fair enough. You're not mine." Murray grinned. "So, know any other jokes?"

"All lawyer jokes. I kind of collect them."

"Suits me. Lemme have 'em."

"What's black and brown and looks good on a lawyer?"

Murray scoffed. "A doberman. Everybody knows that one."

"Okay." Zach settled his elbows on the bar, rising to the challenge. "What's the difference between a vulture and a lawyer?"

Murray shrugged.

"The vulture doesn't get frequent flyer miles." Murray laughed, as if surprised, and Zach slipped into his usual rhythm. "What do you call two dozen skydiving lawyers?"

"I dunno."

"Skeet."

Murray snorted as he laughed, then wagged a finger at Zach. "I gotta remember that one. Come on, gimme another, kid."

At least *someone* thought Zach was funny. "What's the difference between a female lawyer and a pit bull?"

Murray pulled a beer for Lucy as he shook his head. "Dunno."

"Lipstick." The pair laughed, but Zach was on a roll. "Did you hear the one about the terrorist who hijacked a 747 full of lawyers?"

"No," Lucy and Murray replied in unison.

"He threatened to release one every hour until his demands were met."

Lucy and Murray laughed.

"He's not bad," Lucy said, then nodded at Murray. "Funnier than you."

"Thanks a lot. Faster than you, too," Murray retorted and Lucy hurried away. "Know any more?"

"What's the difference between an accident and a calamity?"

"I dunno." Murray braced a hand on the bar, his eyes sparkling as he waited for the punch line. Lucy glanced over her shoulder as she headed back to her tables.

"It's an accident when a bus full of lawyers goes off the road into a lake. It's a calamity if they can swim."

"Isn't that the truth?" Jen muttered, making an abrupt appearance in Zach's peripheral vision. "Murray, where're my margaritas?"

"Coming, coming."

"No crushed ice," Jen added.

"Have you got something against lawyers?" Zach asked.

Jen shrugged. "No more than most people."

"Phew!" Zach made a show of wiping his brow. "But then maybe I've got a loophole."

"A loophole for what?" Jen faced him, a hand on her hip.

"For asking you out. You might go to a movie with me."

"Why would I do that?"

"Because I'm asking. And we'd have fun."

She hesitated for a heartbeat, a hesitation that encouraged Zach, before she rolled her eyes. "Come on, Murray," she said then. "Ticktock."

Murray had a heavy hand on top of the blender, which was whipping the drinks. "The two women at nine again? What's this, their third?"

"Yowzer," Zach said. "You put real tequila in those or just introduce the bottle to the glasses?"

"Very funny," Murray grumbled good-naturedly. "Don't push your luck, kid."

"Those two are on a lunch of no return, that's for sure," Jen said.

Zach grinned. "I like that. A lunch of no return."

She gave him another of those hard looks. "A luxury for those with money and time to burn." The tray with the margaritas was hefted to her shoulder and she was gone.

Murray and Zach watched her go, then the older man leaned closer. "Has it occurred to you, kid, that you're not doing real well here?"

"Yeah. I noticed. You seem to be enjoying it."

"Both the jokes and their reception."

"Shouldn't you be on my side? You know, support your own gender and all that?"

Murray snorted. "I'm on Jen's side and don't you forget it."

Zach chose not to take offense at that. "So, you know the difference between a lawyer and a bulldog?"

"Nope."

"A bulldog generally has the sense to let go." Zach realized a bit too late that that analogy could have been applied to him in this particular situation, but he charged on. "How do you prevent a lawyer from drowning?"

"Tell me," Murray said with a smile. "In this biz, I might need to know."

"Shoot him before he hits the water." Zach paused only a beat for the bartender's laughter. "What do you call ten thousand lawyers at the bottom of the ocean?"

"A good start," Jen interjected.

Zach jumped. He hadn't seen her coming. "Hey, the punch lines are mine."

"Then you need better jokes," she retorted. "What do you call an honest lawyer?"

Zach searched his memory but didn't know that one. "I don't know."

"Me, neither," Murray admitted.

"An impossibility."

Murray laughed. "I like that."

Jen leaned a hand on the bar while she waited for her drinks. "So, the devil visits a lawyer and offers him a deal. He says he can make the lawyer rich enough to afford everything he could ever want, give him three months of vacation every year, ensure he lives to be a hundred. In return, the devil wants the immortal souls of the lawyer's wife, his children, and any grandchildren, to burn in hell for eternity. So, the lawyer thinks about this for a minute, then asks, 'What's the catch?'"

Murray laughed so hard that he had to wipe away a tear. Even Zach found himself chuckling, but Jen, he noticed, never cracked a smile. She rapped a nail on the counter. "Murray, get it together and pull me those two beers, please."

"Yeah, yeah, coming, Jen, coming."

Zach sipped his own beer, then leaned forward himself. "So, a guy goes into a brain store—"

"A brain store?" Jen interrupted, her manner skeptical.

"Yes. A brain store."

"And where would be the closest brain store?"

"Just go with it," Zach said with some irritation.

"A brain store," Jen muttered and shook her head.

"This guy goes into this brain store to get some brain . . ."

"Of course," Jen said deadpan. "It's on my to-do list all the time."

Murray snickered. "Let him tell it."

Zach raised his voice slightly. "This guy goes into a brain store to get some brain and is confused by the prices, which are listed by occupation. 'How much is engineer brain?' he asks."

"These are human brains?" Jen demanded. "This would be a *human* brain store that he's shopping at?"

"Just go with it," Zach repeated.

"What's he going to do with what he buys?"

"I don't know. It's just a joke!"

Jen snapped her fingers. "You know, come to think of it, there's one of those places opening down the street from my mom's house. It's part of a national chain, a franchise of *human brain* stores."

Murray, apparently, couldn't stop laughing.

Zach didn't appreciate how Jen was mucking up his joke. Or stealing his thunder. He was the one who was supposed to make people laugh.

She wasn't even smiling.

He decided to ignore her. "'How much is engineer brain?' the guy asks and the guy in the store says it's three bucks an ounce. 'How much is mathematician brain?' he asks and the guy says it's four bucks an ounce. 'How much is lawyer brain?' he asks and the guy says it's a thousand bucks an ounce."

Murray whistled under his breath.

"Obviously a rare commodity," Jen murmured.

Zach gave her his best death glare for wrecking the punch line. "The guy in the store says it's a thousand bucks an ounce for lawyer brain. And the guy who came into the store is surprised. 'But why does it cost so much?' he asks and the guy in the store . . ."

"This would be the *human brain* store."

". . . says, 'Do you know how many lawyers we had to kill to get an ounce of brain?'"

Murray nearly fell down laughing.

Jen gave Zach a pitying look. "Maybe there *should* be a national franchise of human brain stores." She hefted her tray and was gone again.

"Ouch," Murray said as he wiped away a tear.

Zach took another sip of beer and watched Jen serve her tables. She was polite, even charming, but she didn't smile. Which was weird, when he thought about it. Waitresses always smiled. As Murray had said, it made for better tips. He was pretty sure Jen would have an attractive smile—she was pretty enough even when she didn't smile. "Does she ever smile?"

"Not since . . ." Murray fumbled with his glassware. "Well, not anymore."

"Not since what?"

"Hey, the story's not mine to tell." Murray held up his hands. "I just pour the beer and sign the checks around here."

"That'll be the day," Lucy said, slapping her tray on the bar again. She thunked a glass of water on the counter, shoving it toward Murray. There were pennies in the bottom of the glass. "Drain that and fish out my tip, will you? These kids are all sooooo funny."

Having left a tip the same way once upon a time himself—and having thought it was hilarious—Zach busied himself with the rest of his beer. Come to think of it, it had been the beer that had made it seem funny.

"Three Diet Cokes. I punched it in a thousand years ago."

"Coming, coming, coming."

Zach pretended to watch the soccer game on the television over the bar while Murray and Lucy bickered amiably. He was surreptitiously watching Jen, intrigued and mystified by her.

He liked that she was quick with a comeback. It was more than her being cute: she was smart. (And okay, the brain store joke *was* based on a lame premise.) She had a bit of attitude, especially toward guys—no, especially toward guys with money. Trevor's crack about Zach's trust fund had really gotten her attention.

Maybe that was why she was needling him.

Even given her attitude, Zach was pretty sure he could make her smile. He'd cracked up Murray, hadn't he?

Zach was looking for a challenge, and Jen the waitress might just be that.

Lawyer jokes. Honest to God, how long had it been since she'd heard someone tell so many lawyer jokes? Jen rolled her eyes as she turned back to the bar and saw Trust-Fund Boy still parked there, working on that pint. He was watching her and pretending not to, something that made her pulse leap a little bit.

But she knew better.

It ought to be illegal for a guy to be so handsome, that was for sure. And rich, too. Jen reminded herself that it was unlikely his daddy had made his fortune by saving rain forest.

The thing was that her mother would hate him. It was a gimme.

The problem was that Jen might not. She'd learned plenty from Steve about men who were used to getting what they wanted, even more about them knowing how to turn on the charm to, well, get what they wanted. She'd also learned from Steve how little emotional investment these kinds of men made, even when they insisted otherwise.

How else would it have been so easy for Steve to toss her back once he'd discovered that she was defective merchandise? He'd obviously never given a damn about her personally, roses and pretty pledges to the contrary. She'd been a prize, though she wasn't sure why. She just knew that her status had been rescinded once she'd been diagnosed with cancer.

She hadn't seen him since. Just the realization reminded her how much that had hurt, how being abandoned in her time of need had made her treatment and recovery so much more challenging.

The big problem was that Jen didn't trust herself not to make the same mistake all over again. She had this idea that it would be better to learn from her mistakes, rather than make them over and over again.

Even if it meant being lonely.

This guy, for example, was trouble with a capital T. She was aware of him in that dangerous way, especially since he'd started trying to charm her, and she felt that little warning surge of adrenaline when she made him smile.

Once you want to make someone laugh, in Jen's opinion, you're half gone. She wasn't going any further. She marched back to the bar with purpose, wishing he'd finish his beer and vamoose before she had to pick up another round of drinks. She doubted she'd be that lucky. The kitchen bell rang with the salads for the margarita girls, who'd have to be poured out the door at some point this afternoon.

"A glass of red and a glass of white, Murray," she said, ignoring the hunk watching her so avidly.

"Isn't that a Billy Joel song?" Trust-Fund Boy asked.

"Nah," Murray said. "That's a *bottle* of red and a bottle of white."

"Sad song," Jen contributed, unable to keep herself from saying something.

"Why do you say that?" the hunk asked.

She gave him her most withering look. "It's about divorce."

"It's about reconciliation, in a way, or making peace with change." He shrugged and Jen found herself fascinated by a glimpse of emotion she hadn't expected. She lingered, knowing she shouldn't. "Divorce isn't always bad."

"You divorced?" Murray asked the question Jen wanted to ask.

Trust-Fund Boy shook his head. "No. My parents. It was a good change for my mom."

Murray snorted. "And your dad?"

To Jen's surprise, the hunk paled a bit. "Less good for him," he said grimly, then drained his glass.

Something changed in him, some spark was extinguished. Jen

saw the change and couldn't explain it, not any more than she could explain her urge to reach out to him.

Danger, danger. She picked up her tray and should have bolted, but instead she found herself trying to make him smile one more time. "So, what do you call a lawyer with an IQ of seventy-five?"

Murray looked up with relief. "Hey, I don't know that one. What?"

"Your honor."

"Ouch!"

The hunk gave Jen a dark look, then pushed to his feet. "I'll square up with you now," he said, pulling out his wallet. "I've got to go."

So much for making him smile.

"Hey, thanks for the jokes," Murray said, jovial as ever. Maybe he was a bit more jovial because of the change in the hunk's mood. Or because he was leaving.

"Like I said, I collect them. What do I owe you?"

Jen hesitated, not knowing what she'd said. It was clear to her that she was responsible for the change in his attitude, clear that she'd somehow pretty much pushed him out the door. She wasn't sure how or why, and she instinctively wanted to make amends.

It didn't count that she'd wanted him to leave as little as five minutes before.

It was, however, a bad sign.

Learn from your mistakes. Jen stifled the impulse to make nice, picked up her tray, and went back to her tables. This time, she didn't feel his gaze following her, and despite herself (and everything she knew), she was intrigued.

"Miss? Miss? Can we order, please?"

Jen hurried to table seven, apologizing for the delay. She glanced over her shoulder, her pen hovering over her order pad. She completely missed the fact that the woman wanted salad instead of fries with her chicken sandwich.

Until the woman repeated her demand in a shrill voice.

See, Jen told herself. *You don't even know his name and he's messing up your game. Don't even go there. He's leaving and you'll never see him again.*

And that's a good thing.

Really.

Zach suddenly felt as if he couldn't breathe. Two references to his father in rapid succession, however unwitting, were two reminders he didn't need. He was still struggling to come to terms with the fact that his father—Judge Robert Coxwell—had blown his own brains out in his study, immediately after Zach had called for assistance from a jail cell in New Orleans.

He'd spent his whole life trying to get his father's attention, and it wasn't much consolation that completely getting that man's attention had led to the result it had.

The beer seemed to curdle in his gut, which beer technically couldn't do, but Zach felt like he was going to hurl after all. He had to get out of there, get some fresh air, walk it off.

Out of the corner of his eye, Zach saw Murray settle a heavy elbow on the table. "So, it's none of my business," that man said, "but if you're thinking of hitting on Jen, you think about this. You mess up that girl and you have to answer to me."

"Mess her up?"

"Break her heart, leave her pregnant, stand her up, crack her fingernail. Doesn't matter if the crime is big or small. I'll collect the due. Got it?"

"You're protective of her."

"I like 'em smart."

"Why? Is she your daughter?"

Murray snorted. "So, a man is only allowed to be protective of his own blood? Where are you from, kid? She's a fighter and she deserves a break, not some hotshot stomping all over her heart."

"You don't even know me . . ."

"I don't have to. I know your kind with your confident walk and big talk. Your kind come in here every day, thinking you own the world. And maybe you will. Maybe you do. Maybe you *are* entitled to everything you think you want." He wagged a finger. "But not Jen. Understand?"

"Yeah, I think I do." Zach held the older man's gaze for a charged moment.

He was suddenly tired of people and their assumptions. What difference did it really make whether he made a waitress smile or not?

Lucy dropped her tray on the bar and exhaled in disgust. "My dogs are killing me. Where're my two 7-Ups?"

"Coming up, sweetheart," Murray said.

Lucy raised a brow at Zach. "Now, I'm in trouble. When he starts calling me sweetheart, I know something's gonna hit the fan."

Zach smiled because she seemed to expect it. He sure didn't feel like smiling. "Maybe you could give me my bill when you have a chance."

Murray glanced pointedly at Jen. "I thought you were here for the duration."

"No, I gotta go. The world is kind of high maintenance these days."

That won him a grudging smile from the bartender. His bill appeared immediately and Zach pulled a fifty out of his wallet.

He handed it back to Murray. "Give the change to Jen."

Lucy whistled.

Murray looked skeptical. "What? It's got your number on it?"

"No. My friends are cheap tippers and she worked hard. Tell her to keep it."

Murray regarded him with doubt. "That's it?"

"That's it. Ciao."

Zach scooped his leather jacket off the back of the stool and headed for the door. He didn't even look for Jen, didn't think beyond getting out of this place. He needed a better plan than winning a waitress's smile, or finding reassurance from a past that was long gone.

It was starting to snow, the first flakes swirling out of a gray sky. Zach wasn't the kind of person who got the blues but he felt a major funk coming on.

He could walk, walk and think, and see what came of it.

Jen was shocked by the sight of the crisp fifty-dollar bill. "But his tab was less than twenty bucks," she protested. "Even with a good tip."

"Half is mine," Lucy said. "We're pooling, remember?"

"Don't look a gift horse in the mouth," Murray advised.

Jen shook her head. "I can't accept this, not in good conscience."

"A conscience is what gets people into trouble," Murray said, but Jen didn't hear him.

She strode across the pub and leaned out the door, certain that Trust-Fund Boy couldn't have gotten far. He was tall enough that she'd be able to see him.

And she did: he was already half a block away, moving quickly with his head down and the collar up on his leather jacket. It was snowing, big pretty flakes that looked playful but might add up to something serious.

"Hey! Wait! You forgot your change!" Jen shouted, but the hunk kept walking. He was moving fast and not listening to her. She glanced back to her section, then took another step out the door. "Wait! You, who left the fifty!"

He glanced back then, briefly, just long enough to wave her off before he turned and strode away. Jen swore, looked back one last time, then ran after him.

She would not take pity money.

At least not from him.

It was colder than she'd thought and her shoes slipped on the snow underfoot. Her white shirt was too thin for the weather and the change in her apron jingled as she ran.

"Stop!" she shouted. "Wait!"

People in the streets paused, then stepped aside to watch. They probably thought she was after a thief. They probably expected cheap entertainment.

At least they moved out of the way.

Jen knew she looked like a lunatic running down the street waving a fifty, but she couldn't let him leave so much. "Stop! Wait! It's too much."

He turned a corner, apparently oblivious to her shouts. Jen ran faster, certain she'd lose him. She raced around the corner, slipped on the sidewalk and collided with something that nearly knocked her off her feet.

That something was Trust-Fund Boy. He caught her by the upper arms and steadied her so she didn't fall. His hands were warm and his grip was strong and she told herself that it was only sensible that she liked that he didn't let go. After all, she was just hanging on to him because he wasn't slipping and she was.

That didn't even sound plausible to her.

"Easy! Where's the fire?"

She looked up to find his eyes twinkling. "Don't laugh at me."

"I'm not." He frowned deeply, pretending to be serious. "I'm a profoundly solemn individual. Ask anyone."

"I don't think so." Jen wagged the fifty at him. "Look, you can't leave this much."

"Why not? It's my money and I can do what I want with it."

"But it's too much."

He shrugged. "It's a tip, Jen. Just keep it."

"No. It's too much."

"I don't think so. Trevor was a jerk."

"Not that much of a jerk." She pushed the money toward him. "Really. You must have a twenty instead."

"Nope. No luck. Hey, you're going to get cold." He gave her upper arms a quick rub, spun her around, then lifted his hands away. "Get back there before Murray comes after me."

Jen turned back to face him and blinked. "What?"

What had Murray said to this guy about her?

"Don't worry about it." He shoved his hands into the pockets of his jacket. "I gotta go. Take care." He turned and started to walk away, leaving a cold Jen with a fifty in her hand.

She had a definite feeling that she wouldn't see him again.

He was hurting, she didn't know why, but she knew it was somehow partly her own fault. It just wasn't in Jen to let him walk away, not like this.

Even if it was a mistake. She took a deep breath and said the words on impulse. "Hey, do you want to come to my Gran's for Thanksgiving dinner?"

It sounded weird, just blurted out like that, but once it was said, it was said. Jen wasn't usually impetuous and she regretted the words almost as soon as she'd said them.

He stopped, then pivoted slowly. His expression was—big surprise!—confused. "Excuse me?"

Jen straightened with a confidence she didn't quite feel. She bolstered herself with the memory of the guy at the natural-food store, with the sad puppy eyes. "I just invited you to Thanksgiving dinner at my grandmother's. Next Thursday. Four o'clock. No jeans, but no tie."

He looked away, looked back at her, then walked back to face her. It could have been said that he approached her with some caution.

As one approaches a wild animal.

Or an insane person. Jen wondered which he considered her to be. In a strange way, it was reassuring that he found this invitation as odd as she did.

Not that they could have anything in common.

He stopped in front of her, his gaze searching her expression. "You don't have me confused with someone else, do you?"

"No, I'm not that particular flavor of nitwit."

He grinned. "What flavor of nitwit are you, then?"

She was relieved when he smiled, as if she'd made something better. "You'll have to figure that out yourself."

"At Thanksgiving?" He sounded as skeptical as she had about the brain store. "Surrounded by your family?"

"Pretty much, yes."

"Between the candied yams and the mashed potatoes?"

Jen considered telling him that their Thanksgiving dinner was mostly vegetarian but—given that he'd had a burger for lunch—concluded that the tofu probably wouldn't be a temptation. He might actually like candied yams, while refined sugar was an illegal commodity in her mother's household.

Might as well keep it simple.

Jen met his gaze steadily. "Exactly."

He watched her for a long moment. He had green eyes. They seemed lighter when the wind played with his hair, making it look more blond. He cleared his throat. "You don't think that maybe we should get to know each other a little bit first?" He half smiled and Jen's mouth went dry. "Like maybe you should know my name?"

"Good idea. It would make introductions easier." Jen kept her expression deadpan. She was good at that. "What's your name?"

"Zach Coxwell."

"Good. Great. Zach. Hi, Zach." Jen forced herself to say his name, which was a bit tougher than it would have been if she hadn't been hyperventilating.

"And do you have a surname, Jen?"

"Maitland. Jen Maitland."

"Nice to meet you, Jen." Zach smiled a crooked little smile that made her sucker heart clench and shook her hand. His skin was warm, his grip was firm, and the glint in his eyes was definitely trouble with a capital T.

"Ditto, I'm sure," she said, taking an icy breath of air. Zach didn't let go of her hand right away and Jen didn't pull it away. She was sinking fast, a very bad sign.

It was time to plan an act of extreme vengeance upon her sister.

Unless, of course, this worked.

Chapter 3

"So, Thursday then?" Jen asked brightly.

Zach looked at her for a long moment, then straightened. "You don't think that maybe we should have just one date before I meet your family? Even coffee?"

Jen took a deep breath and made something up. She hoped it sounded plausible to Zach, even if it sounded nuts to her. In fact, she had a voice of dissent right between her ears. "I understand why you're surprised."

Hoo boy, did she ever.

"My family is a bit different, you see."

There was an understatement, maybe the understatement of the century.

Zach watched and waited, clearly unpersuaded so far.

"It's a family tradition." *Liar!* "My grandmother insists upon meeting any guy herself before any of us are allowed to go out for a date."

"Us?"

"My sister and I. My brothers are somehow exempt from the rule." She wrinkled her nose and shrugged. "We're kind of protective of each other that way."

"There's a lot of that going around," he muttered.

"I beg your pardon?"

Zach looked into her eyes so directly that Jen jumped. "So, what you're really doing here is asking me out, providing your grandmother approves?"

Jen found herself blushing. That he was smiling at her like that didn't help much. "Well, yes. Um. Pretty much."

Liar, liar, pants on fire . . .

"I don't believe you." He took the fifty, folded it, and put it into her apron. "But you should still keep the change."

"That's not why . . ."

"Of course not. Just so you know, though"—he leaned closer to whisper and she shivered when she felt his breath against her temple—"I can't go out with you."

"Even Thanksgiving?"

"Especially Thanksgiving. Murray promised to thump me if I made a move on you."

Jen put a hand on her hip and scoffed, because it seemed the safest option. "Wait a minute. I just asked out a guy who's afraid of Murray? He punches like a girl."

Zach laughed. "Okay, then, you're on. Thursday. Four o'clock. See you there." Jen's relief was short-lived, because he turned to walk away.

"But you don't know where!" He hadn't changed his mind: he was teasing her, that much was clear. He wasn't really accepting—how could he be when he didn't even ask where her Gran lived?

Zach, however, was the image of confidence. "I'll find out."

"But . . ."

"Ticktock, Jen. As I understand it, you've only got until two to make your tips and your section *was* full."

"Oh God, my section . . ." Jen paused to look back at him. "You actually listened to what I said."

Now he looked embarrassed. "Well, duh. Hey, you'd better hurry. And I've got to go anyway. Roxanne's waiting on me." With one more flash of that cocksure grin, he pivoted and strode away.

Roxanne.

Roxanne!

Jen had just asked a guy to Thanksgiving dinner who had a girlfriend. How smooth was that? She fingered the fifty, stared after him, and felt stupid. She should have asked if he was seeing someone. There was her inexperience screaming loud and clear.

No, the real problem was that she shouldn't have believed Cin's plan could work for her. And, she shouldn't have been so easily charmed by this guy. Her heart shouldn't be leaping and she shouldn't be watching him walk away, much less checking out his butt (it was a good one). She shouldn't have been having fun matching wits with him.

Nope. None of the above.

Zach Coxwell was totally not her type. That was, after all, the point to Cin's plan. So, it was a good thing that Zach had been just putting her on, that he wouldn't be coming to dinner, that she wouldn't see him again, even that Roxanne—who must be gorgeous and rich and endowed with two perfect breasts—was tapping her toe, waiting impatiently for him. Right?

Wrong. There was no arguing with the fact that Jen was disappointed.

Obviously, she was losing her mind as fast as she was losing her tips.

Women were a mystery. Zach could think of no other explanation for what had just happened. Here he'd been sure that he was striking out, that Jen wouldn't have given him the time of the day, and she'd been interested in him all along.

Who would have guessed? No matter how old he got and how many women he talked to, Zach knew that he'd never be able to read their responses with 100 percent certainty.

Maybe that was a good thing.

Maybe mystery—or inscrutability—added a little chemistry. There certainly was chemistry with Jen. He hadn't wanted to let go of her hand. He certainly hadn't wanted to walk away, at least not just yet.

He'd been thinking about scoring a kiss.

No doubt about it, the day was looking up. Zach was interested in Jen, in how quick she was, and curious about how serious she was, and the idea of spending a bit of time with her suited him just fine.

Even if she had some weird ideas. He could live with a bit of quirkiness. It kept things interesting.

In fact, he felt a lot more purposeful now than he had just a few minutes before.

He'd go back tomorrow and get the details straight. Right now, Roxie needed him. It had been four hours and he knew his dog well enough to know her maximum bladder capacity. He headed for his small condo in Cambridge and a large Bernese mountain dog with all four paws crossed.

His mistake, he decided later, was using that alley shortcut to get home sooner.

Zach was only a dozen steps down its trash-strewn length when he heard a familiar voice behind him.

"Hey, Zach, man, long time no see."

Zach looked up to find Snake-Eyes beside him, as twitchy as ever. The guy made as much noise as a shadow and always had given Zach the creeps. Tall, thin, and wasted—in both the colloquial and literal sense of the word—Snake-Eyes wasn't the kind of guy anyone wanted to spend a lot of time with. He'd been a customer of Zach's for years, one who Zach had insisted pay cash. Snake-Eyes had always looked as if he wouldn't last much longer.

Zach hadn't seen Snake-Eyes in a while, and the other man was looking a bit the worse for wear. That was saying something. He appeared to be more edgy than usual, and not in a good way. His gaze darted from one side to the other and his hands were shaking. Zach speculated that his indulgences had graduated to harder substances—he'd seen that happen a thousand times, always to the detriment of the user.

Which was why Zach had always kept his own indulgences modest: a beer once in a while and the occasional cigarette were his current sins. He'd always limited himself to a single joint, at most, and hadn't had one since that fateful night in New Orleans. He doubted he'd ever have another.

That chapter of his life was done.

"Hey, Snake-Eyes, what's going on?" Zach asked the question rhetorically, in a friendly tone even though he wasn't particularly interested in the answer. Nothing was ever going on with Snake-Eyes: he was either high or working on getting high.

Zach supposed that kept life simple.

"Not much, not much. Hey, Zach, you got any stuff?"

Zach glanced at his companion. "Stuff?"

"Yeah, you know. Some weed. You always have weed, man, and I could use some."

Zach shook his head. "I don't do that anymore, Snake-Eyes." He expected Snake-Eyes to leave it be, because it was pretty easy to lay hands on weed in a university town, but he'd called it wrong.

"I don't care whether you *do* it anymore, man." Snake-Eyes's voice rose slightly, one of the first times Zach had ever heard him irritated. "I asked whether you had any."

Zach shook his head again. "No. I don't do it and I don't sell it, either. That's over."

"Liar."

"No, really. I've quit." Once again, Zach made to walk away.

Snake-Eyes grabbed him by the shoulder, his fingers digging in like claws.

"Hey, cut that out." Zach did his best Bugs Bunny imitation, brushing off his shirt with exaggerated gestures. "You'll wrinkle the material."

Snake-Eyes didn't back off. "You mean you're not selling any to me, that's what you mean. What's the matter? My money's not green enough for you?"

Zach spoke firmly, intending to be understood. "No, that's *not* what I mean, Snake-Eyes. I don't sell anymore. It's been almost a year. I don't have any weed. I'm done with it. Ask anybody."

"I'm not asking anybody. I'm asking *you*." Snake-Eyes punctuated the last word by jabbing his finger into Zach's chest.

"Hey! I'm being straight with you."

Snake-Eyes laughed. "You've never been straight with nobody." He leaned closer, his eyes gleaming. "I want some stuff and I want some of yours. You can sell it to me or I can take it."

Zach took a step backward, not liking the tone of this conversation. The alley was empty, just his luck. "Snake-Eyes, you know that if I had any, I'd sell it to you."

Hell, if he'd had any weed right now, he would have *given* it to Snake-Eyes.

"I *don't* know that," Snake-Eyes argued. "In fact, I'm thinking that you're holding out on me. I'm thinking that you're saving your stash for a better customer . . ."

"You were always a good customer, Snake-Eyes, one of my best, but . . ."

"So, how come you're holding out on me?"

"I'm not!"

"Bullshit!"

Zach had no chance to argue because Snake-Eyes decked him. His punch caught Zach right in the eye and was harder than Zach could have expected.

The world spun and Zach lost his footing.

"Hey!" He staggered backward. When he raised his hand to his eye, it came away with blood. "What the hell did you do that for?"

Snake-Eyes put out his hand. "Gimme some stuff, man."

"I don't have any. I swear it to you."

Zach's pledge didn't persuade Snake-Eyes.

Instead of answering, the other guy punched Zach in the gut and while Zach was doubled over—giving serious consideration to the possibility of ralphing that burger on the pavement—Snake-Eyes went through his pockets.

Then Snake-Eyes stepped away with disgust. "You don't have any stuff! What's up with that?"

Zach coughed and spit on the pavement. He straightened with an effort and regarded the other man warily. "Just like I told you. I don't do that anymore. You've got to work on your trust, Snake-Eyes."

The other man just swore and shook his head. He glared at Zach. "You've changed, man. I thought I could count on you."

"Yeah, well, ditto." Zach raised a hand to his eye and winced that it was swelling fast. He never would have imagined that Snake-Eyes could have even thrown a punch. The guy's usual tactic was begging. Maybe he'd gotten lucky. Or Zach had gotten unlucky. "I guess times have changed, Snake-Eyes."

Snake-Eyes smiled, suddenly contrite and about as trustworthy as a rattler. "I guess so, man. Hey, sorry about the eye." He offered his hand as if shaking would make Zach's injuries evaporate.

This time it was Zach who stepped back. He saw his former customer more clearly now, saw how years of substance abuse had eroded Snake-Eyes to sinew, saw the future he'd evaded by leaving that life behind. Weed was the least of Snake-Eyes's problems.

He glanced at Snake-Eyes's outstretched hand for only a moment, then decided to take a pass on touching the other man.

"Yeah. So am I." Zach turned and walked away, grimacing at the ache in his gut. He hoped he hadn't broken a rib.

"Hey, see you around, man," Snake-Eyes called after him.

"Not if I see you first," Zach muttered. The way his eye was puffing up, he wasn't going to be seeing much from that side for the foreseeable—ha ha—future.

He was going to need some ice.

Actually, he might need more than that. His eye was closing so rapidly that he was frightened. Should he go to the ER? He needed advice from someone who knew about such things.

He and Roxie would have to inflict themselves on someone.

Unfortunately, the one person Zach knew who was most likely to know what to do about his eye was married to the one person who disapproved most heartily of him. There was some kind of cosmic rule wrapped up in that, but Zach wasn't in any shape to figure it out. His sister-in-law Maralys was street-savvy and would take the injury in stride, as well as know whether or not he should seek medical assistance. The price of her consultation would be not only her cutting commentary, but possibly a lecture from Zach's oldest brother, James.

Fun wow. It said something that even knowing that, he'd go to their place ASAP.

Not thirty minutes later, Maralys opened the door and smiled at Zach. He blinked, because she was a redhead today and had been a brunette when last he'd seen her, but it was still his sister-in-law.

The wicked smile gave her away.

"Nice, fresh shiner," she said.

Roxie, recognizing the house, darted past them both and headed for the kitchen with her tail wagging in anticipation. She'd be busy doing the perimeter sniff for a good twenty minutes.

"Glad you're amused," he said.

"Should I ask about the other guy?"

"His knuckles might be bruised."

"Were you being gallant, or were you completely trounced?"

"Hey, no need to build up my ego here."

"You're a Coxwell." Maralys stood back to let him come in. "There's no need to build up the egos of any of you."

"I heard that," James called from further in the house.

Zach stifled a groan. He'd hoped to talk to Maralys without seeing his oldest brother, but James was sauntering into the foyer. There was, he thought, no point in disguising his feelings. "Great. You would be home when I come begging for mercy."

"Nobody said you had good luck." James snagged his suit jacket from the chair in the hall. He was obviously heading back to work. "Just home for lunch. Hey, nice eye. Was she worth it?"

"Very funny. You should be congratulating me."

"On getting thumped? That'll be the day." James paused to give Maralys a kiss so thorough that Zach felt he should leave.

Something had changed in his brother since he'd been with Maralys—although she was prickly and opinionated, she seemed to have softened James's edges. His brother was more at ease in his own skin. Happier maybe.

Not to mention that the two could generate heat like no couple Zach had ever known. He looked everywhere but at them directly. This was his oldest brother, after all. The man was in his forties and had three kids. The evidence that James knew about sex was there for the looking.

Come to think of it—which Zach would have preferred not to have done—James had probably come home at lunch for a quickie.

Zach was thinking that the plate glass in the windows was going to liquify, just from being in the vicinity of this kiss, and couldn't stand it anymore. "Hey, keep it legal, you two."

To his relief, they parted, but neither looked particularly embarrassed.

James grinned and shrugged into his suit jacket. "Behind closed doors and all that."

Zach gestured to the front door. "It's open."

"That's your fault," Maralys said. "Come in already."

James paused on the threshold to look at Zach's eye. "That looks new. What happened?"

"Doesn't matter."

James arched a brow. "It does if you're going to be making another one of those calls for help from the big house."

Zach felt his mood sour even more. "I came for medical advice, not career counseling."

"Good." James held his gaze steadily. "Because you know that you can't call me anymore."

Zach straightened. "Or Matt. You two have made it pretty clear that I'm on my own. I'm not so stupid that I didn't get that." Zach turned to his sister-in-law, who was watching this exchange with interest. "So, Maralys, I was just wondering whether I needed to go to the hospital, or whether you think it's normal for it to swell this much this fast."

She folded her arms across her chest and leaned against the door frame to the living room. "Because I know so much about black eyes, street fighting, and otherwise troublemaking dudes?"

Great. She was insulted. "No. Well, yes." Zach fumbled with the words. "Because you know stuff, all kinds of useful stuff."

Maralys smiled, proof that he'd found the right words.

"Let me see." Zach jumped when James touched his eye. James put on his glasses and frowned slightly as he checked it out. "Easy. Just let me look at it." James lifted the lid gently as Zach stood motionless, then touched the swelling with his fingertips.

James's manner was patient and paternal, which surprised Zach. He hadn't been used to a lot of consideration from his brothers, especially in recent years. But then, James did have two teenage sons of his own. He'd probably checked out a lot of minor injuries in his time.

This certainly had never been their own father's attitude—Robert had shouted a lot and been preoccupied more. Zach couldn't remember his father ever showing interest in an injury. Getting into trouble had gotten him yelled at, but at least it was an acknowledgment of his presence.

James stepped back and peeled off his glasses. "There's no cut, no glass in it. I'll guess you just got popped a good one."

Zach felt an uncharacteristic need to be straight. He figured that's what kindness did to him—it threw his game. "You don't need to guess. That's what happened."

"Scary when it swells up so fast, isn't it?" James asked with a sympathetic smile.

Zach felt better. The accord between them wasn't familiar and probably couldn't be relied upon to last, but it felt good to not be completely at odds. "I feel like I'm going blind."

"Just for a day or two. It'll be better if you get some ice on it."

"Come on," Maralys said. "I'll make you an ice pack." She gave him a teasing smile. "But you've got to promise to show me the fab display when the bruise comes."

"You're only helping me for the entertainment value," Zach complained, although he was relieved.

"Well, you haven't offered much entertainment lately," Maralys replied. "We've got to make do with what's available."

Zach made to follow his sister-in-law but was stopped by his brother's softly asked question.

"What really happened, Zach?"

Zach paused, then was surprised to find himself answering. "One of my old customers didn't believe I wasn't selling anymore. He thought I was holding out on him."

"And were you?"

"No."

James and Maralys exchanged a look.

Zach heaved a sigh. "Is it that hard to believe that I'm on the straight and narrow?"

"Yes," they said in unison.

"Especially as this is the first we've heard of it," Maralys said.

So much for honesty. "Well, then I came to the wrong place." Zach whistled for his dog, who did not come running, but James put a hand on his shoulder.

"Sorry, Zach. You just surprised me. If you've really given it up, that's a good thing."

"You can't blame anyone for not expecting you to change," Maralys said softly. "It's been a long time, Zach."

"Well, I have given it up. You can believe it or not, whatever you like." Zach couldn't dismiss the sense that James was taking a wait-and-see attitude, but then, his brother had bailed him out of trouble enough to have earned the right to be dubious.

"Don't tell me the justice system finally reformed you."

To Zach's surprise, James's tone was light. He wasn't used to seeing his brother anything but serious and judgmental.

Pretty much an echo of their father's manner.

Maybe he'd come to the wrong house.

Maybe he'd stepped into a parallel universe.

"No, it wasn't that," he said cautiously. "I just got done with it."

"Since when?"

"Since New Orleans." Zach stifled the urge to squirm because James was watching him very closely, probably seeing a bit too much.

To his surprise, James teased him. "If I'd known it would be that easy for Matt to change your thinking, I would have inflicted you on him years ago."

Zach couldn't resist the chance to needle his big brother in return. "So, maybe he's just more persuasive."

"Right." James smiled. "He just declined to help you out."

"The power of the word 'no'," Maralys said with satisfaction.

James was watching Zach so carefully that Zach almost fidgeted. "That was a neat scheme for Mom you came up with this year," James said softly.

Zach shrugged. "Father's expectation that everything pass immediately to the four of us seemed unfair, especially as a big chunk of the family money came from Mom's side. She could have challenged the will."

"But you negotiated a neat compromise instead," James said.

"You should have come by yourself to pick it up: I would have liked to have told you what a nice piece of business that contract was."

Maralys folded her arms across her chest and leaned in the doorway, watching as well.

"It was a sound plan to have the four of us agree to wait until Mom's passing to split the estate," James continued. "And a logical argument that Father must have assumed he would outlive her."

"If not one that would have been in character," Maralys muttered but both men ignored her.

Zach shrugged, uncomfortable with his brother's approval. "I didn't want Mom to worry about money. She's never worked, after all. I just did my best."

"Beverly knows everything about etiquette," Maralys said. "She could set up one hell of a consulting business."

"But the choice should be hers," Zach said, speaking emphatically. "I didn't think it would matter that much to any of us and I wanted her to be without worries."

"It didn't matter to me," James acknowledged. "Or to Philippa. And Matt is okay with the payout scheme you devised for him buying our shares of Gray Gables. But are you okay with it, Zach?"

"Who cares?" Zach tried to shrug off the question with a grin. "I land on my feet."

"*I* care," James said with force. "If you need cash, you come to me first."

It was an unexpected offer and it surprised Zach. "I don't need much," he said but got no further.

"I know you're frugal," James said, interrupting him. "But I don't want you to feel that you have to go back to selling to make ends meet."

"I'm done with that."

"Good. But if you need a loan, this branch of the Bank of Coxwell is open. I'm your big brother and I'm running late on taking up that responsibility."

"Well, I don't know. You've already saved my butt a bunch of times. Thanks for that."

"New start?" James asked, offering his hand.

Zach smiled, genuinely pleased. "Okay. Thanks. New start." The two brothers shook hands, sealing this unexpected accord.

For the first time in his life, Zach felt attacked by warm fuzzies in the presence of his family.

Maybe he should have gotten decked sooner.

Then Maralys shooed James out the door. "You're late, Mr. Coxwell. I promise to tell you all the juicy details tonight, if there are any. Let's have a quick review before you go."

James paused on the walk and started to tick items off with his fingers. "Okay, official synchronization: Zoë and I are on the road tonight. Soccer for Jimmy at six-thirty; swimming for Johnny at seven; pick them up at eight and eight-fifteen respectively; pick up your father from euchre at the community center at eight-thirty; everyone back here for the bath and tooth-brushing routine, then I'll see you at Casa Pickle at nine-thirty."

"I didn't know you were domesticated," Zach teased, getting his own back.

James grinned. "You bet."

"It can be done," Maralys intoned. "We have the technology to harness the wild Coxwell male . . ."

The two exchanged another one of those hot looks and Zach cleared his throat lest they go at it on the porch. "What's Casa Pickle?"

"Maralys's studio and office," James said. "It used to be a pickle factory."

"No kidding?"

"No kidding. When the humidity is right, you can smell the vinegar." Maralys grimaced. "But the space is phenomenal."

"Even with Antonia making art all around you," James joked.

"I'm getting used to it." Maralys smiled, then shooed him away. "Synchronization right the first time, counselor. You're clear for takeoff." Maralys waved at James, then nudged Zach. "There's that incisive Coxwell legal mind at work again."

James turned and shook a finger at her. "You'd better be ready to leave by nine-thirty, Maralys. Tonight I'll need a glass of wine, with you and no computer code."

"Ten."

"Nine-thirty."

"Definitely by nine-forty-five."

James heaved a sigh of forbearance. "Well, I'll just have to change your mind." He winked when she laughed, then strode toward the T.

"Doesn't that sound promising," Maralys said, her eyes dancing with anticipation. "Funny how you don't find your brother persuasive. I find him irresistible."

"That's probably a good thing," Zach said. "I can guess how he persuades you and I'm really not interested."

"At all, or just with your brother?"

"You figure it out." He gestured to his departing brother. "Since when has he had a sense of humor?"

Maralys laughed and slipped her hand through Zach's elbow. She ignored his question. "Come on in. I've missed you, Zach. You always liven things up. Let's get some ice on that before you're legally blind."

"There's a good plan."

"Where do you think Roxanne's gone?"

"Where's Zoë? Where there's a toddler, there's spilled food . . ."

Maralys laughed. "And that's where you find a smart dog like Roxanne. Don't you feed that beast?"

"Right. Take a look at her and tell me that she's just wasting away."

"Hardly. She's bigger every time I see her."

"You haven't seen her since I dropped off that contract. She was only a puppy then."

"Note that I wasn't the one to say how infrequently you come by."

Zach chose to ignore that. "It's the fur. I'm sure that if I had her trimmed, there'd be a third as much dog left."

"Ah, but then everything you owned wouldn't be garnished with four-inch dog hairs."

"That would be a loss," Zach agreed solemnly.

They got to the kitchen and discovered that they had called it right. Zoë was sitting on the kitchen floor, feeding cheddar Gold-fish crackers to Roxie, one at a time.

With great concentration, Zoë pinched each cracker between her index finger and thumb. It was apparently of critical impor-tance to present the cracker face-first to the dog and to hold the fish tail. Her hands were were a bit gummy, probably from dog spit, which might have added to the challenge. Roxie sat obediently and calmly in front of the little girl. Even though the dog was half the age of the toddler, she had to outweigh Zoë four pounds to one.

"Scene of the crime," Maralys said.

"But Zoë is in total control." Zach refused to be insulted that his dog did what a toddler told her to do and not always what he told her to do.

"Of course, she is. She got that from me." Maralys cast him a devilish grin, then stepped toward the freezer.

Zach sat down, as he was told, and held the pack of ice over his eye, as he was told, and tried not to speculate as to why the kitchen table looked like it had been cleaned off in a hurry. He also tried to not feel that he had woken up on an alien planet, one that looked a lot like the one he knew but was populated by clones of people he knew who acted unpredictably.

James had been concerned about him. It boggled Zach's mind.

It was kind of a nice feeling. That boggled him even more.

He was distracted by Zoë, who came to stand right in front of him. "Zach fish," she said, offering him a sticky cracker for his very own.

Roxie stood immediately behind the little girl, avidly watching the cracker in transition. The dog salivated.

Zach accepted the present, to his niece's delight, then surreptitiously passed it to the dog after Zoë turned away. "I haven't been gone that long," he told Maralys. "Zoë remembers me."

"She's naturally brilliant," Maralys said. "Not that I have a biased opinion or anything."

"She's more cute than should be legal."

"And has charm to spare." Maralys sighed benignly as she watched her daughter. "She's going to give me a serious crop of gray hair in ten or twelve years."

"Only if I teach her everything I know," Zach threatened and Maralys laughed.

"What's it going to cost me to get you to keep that information to yourself?"

"I'm an artist. I can't be bought."

"A hazard of dealing with a family who has more money than God." Maralys shook her head. "So, what? You want a date for Thanksgiving? Or do you want me to be nice to whoever you bring? *That* will cost you big, avoiding the Coxwell initiation process."

Zach blinked. He hadn't attended a family Thanksgiving dinner for a couple of years, and was skeptical that the day would be celebrated in his family at all. "Mom isn't cooking Thanksgiving dinner, is she?"

"Be serious. With those two poodles underfoot and her life in transition? I think not."

"I thought she had moved everything back to Gray Gables already."

"She did, but it's not easy for her."

Zach could relate to that. Visiting the family residence in Rosemount was something he would avoid as long as possible.

Forever would be workable, in his opinion.

"She's still grieving for your father, Zach."

"But Mom and Father were getting divorced."

"Even so. That's the house where they spent most of their married life together. It has emotional power for her." Maralys sipped a cup of tea and looked wise.

Zach decided he was better off leaving that topic alone for the moment. "Well, what then? If Matt and Leslie are cooking turkey at Gray Gables, it's pretty safe to assume that I'm not invited. Especially as I haven't been and the big day is next week." And that was good, because he wouldn't have to decline and/or make up an excuse to not be there.

"Nope, you got it wrong again."

"Philippa's too busy to cook . . ."

"True. A new baby, a landscaping business to run, a toddler older and thus even busier than Zoë, Nick's imperious grandmother making demands . . . phew! I'd say your sister is busy right now, even with Nick helping out."

"And Nick wouldn't let me into their house anyway."

"You are a popular date, aren't you?" Maralys pulled out the opposite chair and sat down to consider him. "The truth is that no one Coxwell wants to host the feast, but I suspect everyone has a mild desire to get together."

"A *mild* desire." Zach fought a smile at her choice of words.

"Nobody will move mountains, that's for sure, but no one is running screaming into the woods at the idea either. And I'm thinking we should make more of an effort to do family stuff, to get together and all that."

"You're losing your edge, Maralys."

"You sound like James!" she said with a laugh, then sobered. "No, really, I'm serious. It's easier to not get along when you never see each other. We've been having dinner with Matt and Leslie and they're okay. Their Annette and our Jimmy haven't killed each other yet, which is a good sign."

"You've got to take them where you find them."

"My thinking exactly. We could all benefit from a bit more time together." She watched him closely, obviously waiting for his reaction to whatever she intended to say. "And I shouldn't say so, but it's a whole lot easier with your father gone. It might even be easier to be the prodigal son, without anyone calling you on it every five minutes."

Zach fought to hide his response. Maralys was too damn perceptive, though, and he was pretty sure she'd seen him wince. "The ice is really cold," he said by way of excuse.

"Uh-huh. So, tell you what, I'm going to have Thanksgiving dinner here."

"As of when?"

"As of right now."

"Does James know about this?"

"Obviously not."

"Shouldn't you talk to him about it?"

Maralys's smile was mischievous. "I'll *persuade* him to my point of view." She tapped a finger on the tabletop and Zach thought again about lunch breaks. "Next Thursday, three o'clock. Bring a bottle of wine. If everyone gets a bit buzzed, it will be even easier."

Fat chance of that happening. The last time he'd seen his brother-in-law Nick, the guy had nearly decked him. The last time Zach had seen his brother Matt, the guy had chewed him out and abandoned him to the Louisiana justice system. Even given the unexpectedness of James's attitude today, he knew that a Thanksgiving dinner with his family would be a special kind of hell.

Not for the first time in his life, Zach saw the universe turn in his favor. There was, apparently, a cosmic reason for Jen asking him to dinner—and his impulse to accept had been dead on the money. It wasn't the first time that he'd acted on instinct and it had saved his bacon, but this was definitely a big save.

"Sorry. I have a date," he said.

"Oh yeah?" Maralys was unpersuaded. "Funny. I didn't know you were seeing anyone."

"Well, I am."

"What's her name?"

It was easier to go with a version of the truth than to completely fabricate something. There was less chance of messing up later. Zach had learned as much years before. He'd just embellish his virtually nonexistent relationship with Jen a bit to satisfy Maralys. They'd never meet: Maralys would never know. "Jen."

Maralys arched a brow. "No surname?"

"No need to supply you with references, is there?"

She leaned back to watch him. "I don't believe you. You're making this up. Not that that's ever happened before."

Zach found himself getting defensive. It was usually the best offense anyway. "Her name is Jen Maitland. I met her at the bar where she waits tables. She's tall and dark-haired and funny in a wry kind of way and very sexy."

"And Roxanne approves? Hey, Roxie, tell me about this girl."

The dog wagged her tail, more interested in scoring another cracker than supplying references. Zach was glad she couldn't talk.

"She hasn't met Roxie yet." At Maralys's skeptical look, Zach improvised. "She has allergies, so we're working up to that intro."

Maralys rubbed Roxanne's ears. "I'll bet. You're not going to ditch the dog for her, are you?"

"We'll solve it. If it's meant to be, we'll all get along fine."

"Maybe with a cleaning service and crates of antihistamines."

"Maybe."

Maralys seemed to think for a moment, then turned a bright glance on Zach. "Still doing photography?"

Zach was surprised by the change of topic. "Well, sort of. Why?"

Maralys came in for the kill. "Because if you're going to skip out on my family reunion Thanksgiving party—planned, let's add, specifically for your benefit—I want *pictures*. I want photographic evidence of you having Thanksgiving dinner, next Thursday with this dark-haired, tall, sexy Jen and her family."

"Or?" Zach had to ask.

Maralys smiled. "Or you'll live to regret it. I'm trying to be nice to you, Zach. It's not my best trick, so if you're evading this bit of goodwill, I'll make you regret it forever." She shrugged and flicked her red hair. "Not that I'm vengeful. Not me. Just ask James."

And she smiled a smile that made Zach wonder where, exactly, he'd stashed his favorite camera.

The phone was ringing when Jen unlocked the back door that night. It was after nine and she was bagged. The phone kept ringing, a good sign that her mom wasn't around.

She dumped her bag, lunged across the kitchen counter, and snagged the receiver on the fifth ring. "Hello?"

"So?" Cin asked. "How'd it go? Snag a date yet?"

"Hang on a second." Jen went back to shut the door, took off her shoes, and hung up her coat. She put the kettle on and found some dried green stuff in the mug she usually used. Propped beside it was a note in her mom's handwriting: *Drink this. Trust me.*

Alice in Wonderland stuff. Would it make her taller or shorter?

Jen shook her head and picked up the phone again. "Sorry. I was just getting in."

"What's so funny?"

"I'm not laughing."

"No, but you never are. Your voice sounds lighter, that's all."

"There's a note from Mom with some dried stuff in my mug."

"Ah, better living through chemicals, the Gaia way. Well, it can't hurt."

"How do you know?"

"What do you mean?"

Jen leaned against the counter, fed up with this insistence upon the positive. "Well, if it can help, then by the same logic, it could hurt. I mean, expecting it to heal means acknowledging that it has some power."

"You're too skeptical. That's your problem."

"If so, it's the least of them." Jen stretched her left arm and wiggled her fingers. While she was on the phone, she did some of the exercises to keep circulation in that arm. She was careful at work to lift on the right, but lymphedema was always an unwelcome possibility.

"Soooooooooo?" Cin prompted when Jen didn't say anything. "How's the dating game going?"

"Mixed results."

"Sounds juicy. What happened?"

"Are you at work?"

"Yup, night shift on the order desk. I had the afternoon off and am back in the salt mines, so to speak, until ten."

"Those would be naturally dehydrated sea salts, I assume, not anything from a mine."

"Technically, yes. Baltic or Indian Ocean?"

Jen leaned against the counter. "Don't you have an obligation to do something for your employer while you're being paid to do something for them?"

"Break time. I get to play for fifteen minutes. I'm not letting you off this phone until I know, because one thing I do know is when you're holding out on me. Like now. Cough up the story, sis. I can smell that it's a good one."

"It's not. I asked a guy to Thanksgiving dinner. He said yes, didn't get the address where, then left because someone named Roxanne was waiting on him."

"Ouch. So who's Roxanne?"

"Duh! His girlfriend, obviously."

"And he's so committed to her that he was chatting you up."

"You don't know that . . ."

"I know you and you have zero balls."

"Thank God for that. Life would be even more complicated then."

Cin laughed. "Jen, I'm not joking. You would only have asked him out if he'd given you some encouragement. There must have been some chemistry, which implies that he's not very committed to this Roxanne."

"Or he's a rat."

"Or that." Cin accepted this possibility more easily than Jen could. "But then, isn't that the point? Was he perfect for the dastardly deed or what?"

"I thought so. Ate a burger. Wears a leather jacket. Went to law school. Comes from money and has expectations."

"That's good enough for me."

"Yes, but I think he must have been putting me on. Why else wouldn't he have gotten the address? Or even my number? He just bailed."

"Maybe he plans to come back before the big day."

Jen chewed her lip and considered that. It was possible. He had wanted to get to know each other better. "I have a bad feeling about this."

"You and your bad feelings. Did you get his name?"

"Zach Coxwell." Jen regretted the confession as soon as it was made, because she heard Cin typing. "Hey! Do *not* Google him."

It was too late, of course.

"Honestly, Jen, you've got to get with the times," Cin chided. "*Of course*, I'm Googling him. Do you want to be stalking a serial killer?"

"I wasn't planning to stalk anyone."

"Your mistake."

It was too late, both to stop her sister and to argue with her assumptions. Jen made her tea and waited for the bad news. Whatever the dried leaves were, they smelled awful once the water was poured over them. The scent was both minty and astringent, with a bit of mold on the side. The resulting "tea" was a yellowish green, not the most tempting beverage Jen had ever confronted. She closed her eyes and took a cautious sip.

"Bingo!" Cin shouted into the phone.

Jen jumped and spilled her tea down the front of her white

shirt. Oh well, it was destined for the laundry anyway and it was just a work shirt.

She'd have been a lot less philosophical about staining one of her vintage gems. This was a plain white cotton man's shirt from the thrift store and she already knew that the fabric was tough.

"Yowser, but you have snagged a good one, Jen. Good eye!"

"What are you talking about?" Jen asked, not at all sure that she wanted to know. After all, she couldn't really define "good one" in Cin's perspective with any certainty.

And that wasn't a good omen.

Chapter 4

Cin's cheerfulness only increased Jen's sense of impending doom. "There's only one Zach Coxwell in Boston, son of that judge who blew his brains out last year, younger brother of those two lawyer brothers who fought opposite sides of the Laforini case. Remember that?"

Jen did remember that, vaguely.

She remembered more clearly that Zach had left the bar in a hurry when she had made a judge joke. She guessed that she had hit a nerve and felt badly all over again.

She also was pleased that she'd read his response correctly. How much of a selfish jerk could a guy be who mourned his father's death?

Less than she'd expected, that was for sure.

But then, according to the Plan, that wasn't a good thing. Jen frowned and rubbed her forehead. This wasn't going to be as easy as Cin had made it sound.

Meanwhile, Cin was still chattering in her ear. "It was on the front page of the paper. His big bro is a hotshot lawyer in the district attorney's office. Whoa, Nelly, but these people have money and to spare. And he's in the phone book, with a condo in that flash building that overlooks the river. You know that one, the one we look at all the time?"

"Not that building? Condos in there cost a fortune."

"*That* building," Cin said with satisfaction. "Want his number?"

"No, thanks." Jen poured the rest of the "tea" down the sink. "If he comes back, we'll go with it. Otherwise, I'm done with your plan."

"You big chicken."

"I'm not a chicken . . ." Jen protested, but Cin was clucking into the phone. "Okay, maybe I *am* a chicken. Maybe I'm just not good at making a fool of myself."

"Even for a good cause?"

"Even for that."

"Even for eternal freedom from Mom's matchmaking schemes?"

"It won't last *that* long."

"Look," Cin said sternly. "Roxanne might be his goldfish or his pet name for his car—which, hey, is probably a Ferrari. You could get over that, couldn't you?"

"I don't care about cars and neither do you. We were trained from the cradle to carry transit passes or walk."

Cin continued as if Jen hadn't said anything. "You don't know who Roxanne is, and I think you should find out."

"How?"

"Phone Zach."

Jen's heart skipped, but she shook her head. She would not beg. "I don't think so."

"You always sit around and wait for the good stuff to happen all by itself. Sometimes, Jen, you've got to ask for what you want."

"Oh, I've done plenty of that," Jen said wryly. "It doesn't always work. After all, it's not always good stuff that happens all by itself." She only had to look at her shirt—at the prosthesis in her bra and at the stain on the surface—to see proof of that.

"That's just more reason to go and get what you want, because you don't know how long you've got to wait."

"Thank you for that reminder."

Cin's voice softened. "Jen, I mean all of us: 'you' in the general sense, not the specific sense. None of us get guarantees."

Jen frowned. "I know. I know."

"I just want you to reach out of yourself, that's all."

"Seems everyone has that on their Christmas list this year."

"Well, people like you. Go figure. Oooo, lookie, there are *pictures*."

"No!"

"Yes!" Cin was giddy, never a good sign. "Funeral pictures from the paper, all nicely hot-linked for you and me. It probably comes up because the caption lists the family members. Here they all are, carrying the coffin." She whistled through her teeth. "What a bunch of hunks. It'd almost be worth being dead to be able to look up at this bunch. These people aren't just loaded, they've snagged the best DNA."

Jen wished she hadn't answered the phone. "Why don't I ever learn that trusting you is a big mistake?"

Cin ignored her question. "Which one is Zach? Oh, here he is, the youngest and the yummiest by far. Oh, Jen, sorry, but I have to phone him myself."

"What? Why?" Jen didn't want her sister to plea on her behalf. Anything but that.

Well, maybe not quite anything.

"I'm going to have to have his child," Cin said and Jen felt her mouth drop open. "For the benefit of humanity. You know, to improve the view. I'm such a sucker for that dark blond ski-bum look. Maybe he'll grow a couple of days of beard stubble just for me. You know I like 'em disreputable, handsome, and rich. We would have the cutest child in the universe."

"You wouldn't . . ." But Jen wasn't sure.

"Oh yes, I would. No jars and turkey basters for me, though. Nuh-uh. We'd have to get right down to it. At least a dozen times. It would be one heck of a weekend. You know, Roxanne could watch. I wouldn't much care."

"It's all true then," Jen said with a sigh. "I *was* raised by wolves. Or aliens. We can't possibly be related."

Cin laughed, right from her gut. "Oh, Jen, I remember when you found out that there *hadn't* been a mix-up at the hospital. You were so convinced that you didn't belong with us."

"Imagine that."

"And were upset to find out that you did. You were so cute."

"If emotionally devastated."

"Well, there was that. Hey, tell you what, I'll name the baby after you. How about that? Kind of a consolation prize."

"You're not serious about this."

"Aren't I?"

"But you're married. Or almost married."

"Nope, I'm in a common-law relationship. *Was* in one. It could end as of now. Much easier to wiggle free of the informal stuff, you know."

"But you wouldn't . . ."

"Sure, I would. I'm a serial monogamist, you know that. Maybe it's time for an upgrade."

The problem with her older sister was that Jen couldn't predict with 100 percent accuracy when Cin was putting her on. This was mostly because Cin might change her mind, based on Jen's response. "What about Ian?

"What *about* Ian? He's a big boy and can take care of himself. I think his number's up, and it starts with a seven."

"No!" Even while she protested, Jen heard a dial tone. "You will not call . . ."

"Dial nine for an outside line," Cin said as pertly as a telemarketer. "Then let's see, seven . . ."

"*No!*"

The sound of her sister punching in numbers didn't stop.

"There we go," Cin said as a phone somewhere began to ring. Jen wished she had the moral fiber to hang up the phone, but she was curious.

The line clicked and her heart nearly stopped. Then the answering machine started.

And it was Zach's confident voice that came down the line. So much for getting the wrong number.

"Hi. You've found me, but I'm either ducking your call or I'm not home. So, talk to the machine, if you want, and if I want, I'll call you back. Ciao."

The beep sounded. Jen was suddenly terrified of Cin leaving some outrageous message.

It was something her sister would do.

Jen managed to make a choking sound of protest before the line clicked again and Cin hung up the phone. Then Jen sagged against the counter in relief.

Great. Now Zach would come home to the sound of strangulation on his machine. At least if he pulled up the last number that had called him, it would be that of Nature Sprouts, alfalfa and mung bean sprout suppliers to the eastern seaboard.

"Gotcha," Cin said with satisfaction.

"Isn't it illegal to give people heart failure?"

"Yummy voice, too," Cin continued. "Feel better just hearing him?"

Jen did, but she figured she had already admitted too much to Cin. Information was being used against her. "Doesn't matter to me. After all, I was just trying to use him, on your advice."

Cin laughed. "And if I believe that, you're going to try to sell me a bridge. Look, Jen, it's your choice. Because one of us is going to call this guy again before Thanksgiving. And just so we understand each other, I'm not going to be doing any intervention here on your behalf. If I call, it's for me and the future of the species. And you know that I won't take no for an answer."

"Yes, I know." Jen shook her head, admiring in a way the

formidable force that was her older sister. "He'll never know what hit him, but he'll feel like he's been run over by a Mack truck."

"Some of them like it that way. Come on, Jen, you or me?"

"You're merciless."

"It gets results. Next Wednesday night, I'll call." Cin cleared her throat. "Unless, of course, you tell me that you've talked to him and straightened out all the pesky details."

"I could lie to you."

Her sister laughed. "But you're such a lousy liar that I'd know. Hey, here's his number."

Jen wrote down Zach's telephone number on the pad beside the phone, uncertain that she'd call despite her sister's threat.

"Just let your fingers do the walking," Cin advised. "And do it soon. You know how I hate doing things at the last minute."

"You love doing things at the last minute."

"True. You're the power planner. Hey, so if you don't call over the weekend, then I'll know that you aren't going to, given that you always have to arrange things well ahead of time . . ."

Jen glanced up at the wall clock and knew she was saved from answering that. "Hey, your fifteen minutes are up, Cincinnati Mc-Kee. You'd better get off the phone and go make a living."

"Such as it is." Cin laughed her throaty laugh, the one that came from her heart, the one that always made Jen feel better. "Good work out there, today, kiddo. I never thought you'd snag a winner so fast—and I'm proud that you asked him out. You're making progress, Jen. Keep me updated."

And with that, Cin hung up the phone.

Jen chose not to think about her sister's threat for the moment. She turned on the kettle again, rinsed out her mug, and got a tea bag out of the box of green tea.

The telephone number niggled at her, drawing her eye to the notepad from across the room. Should she? Shouldn't she? Could she? Who was Roxanne? If she just phoned Zach out of the blue; the guy would think he had a stalker.

The thought of any man having a stalker who wanted him to come to Thanksgiving dinner at her grandmother's house was so ridiculous that Jen was tempted to call and say exactly that.

It would probably make him laugh. The door banged and she glanced over her shoulder to find her mom arriving with groceries.

"Hey, is that a smile?" Natalie demanded with obvious pleasure. "You've got to tell me what—or who—is responsible for that. And, more important, is he coming for Thanksgiving dinner?"

Oops. Think fast.

"Just glad to be home, Mom," Jen said brightly.

"Uh-huh." Natalie clearly wasn't convinced but to Jen's relief, she let it go. She looked pointedly at Jen's mug. "So, how'd you like the tea?"

By Thursday morning, Zach had only one eye in working order thanks to the skepticism of Snake-Eyes. His left eye had swelled shut and was already turning an impressive shade of purple. One look in the mirror and any scheme to drop by Mulligan's to see Jen was nixed.

He had to look better than this the next time he met up with her. He wanted to make her laugh but at his jokes, not at his appearance. His scheme to return to the pub for details about turkey day would have to wait a few days.

Meanwhile, job one was to find his favorite camera. He was amazed that it could be so hard to find something in what was essentially an empty apartment.

In fact, Zach's condo showed little evidence that he had owned it for six years. It was a one-bedroom unit, although the bedroom was small. The balcony faced the river and its view—from the sixth floor—was pretty good. Its other big selling point had been that the sun came through the two pairs of French doors that opened to the balcony, a feature that appealed mightily to Roxie.

One could have been forgiven for taking a glance at Zach's unit, though, and assuming that no one had ever moved into it. Or for assuming that it had been used to kennel the pets for other condo residents while they vacationed. Other than a liberal embellishment of dog hair, it was pretty much empty.

The walls were still painted in the standard contractor beige, albeit with a few scuffs here and there. The hardwood floors were as bare as they had been on the day Zach had gotten the keys. He never gotten around to finding rugs or paintings or drapes, or for that matter, furniture. There had always been better things to do than nest, better places to go than home decor stores. He'd never dated a woman long enough that she'd managed to change his mind.

Much less his environment. Letting a woman decorate his place would have been a step away from booking the wedding, to Zach's thinking, and he wasn't ever going there.

Zach did have a futon, which had seen better days. His current choice of bedding was an old sleeping bag, which suited Roxie just fine. He usually came home to find her sprawled on the futon in a stray sunbeam, queen of all she shed upon. (And that was a much larger territory than the casual observer might assume.)

The kitchen appliances were standard issue and white—no upgrades for Zach—and were holding up well, despite the lack of maintenance. That could have been because Zach only used the fridge—for beer—and the microwave—for leftover take-out food and the occasional frozen burrito.

Even the cabinetry was pristine. Zach possessed one kitchen knife and one big spoon, and, since Roxie's arrival, generally had a roll of paper towels around. The cupboards held three dinner plates, a collection of cheap glasses of various sizes and shapes—embellished with various logos, evidence of their "borrowed" origins—a pot big enough for making two boxes of macaroni and cheese at once, and a handful of stainless steel cutlery that had somehow become stained. None of this cluttered the space—he fit it all in one drawer and one cupboard.

The bathroom was white—standard fixtures, again—and, like the kitchen, fastidiously clean. Zach wasn't without his good habits and the insistence upon a clean bathroom was one of them. In fact, the bathroom had been one of the reasons Zach had bought this unit: it didn't have a window and it had a long vanity counter. It was the location of his only upgrade: the bathroom had a pair of stainless steel kitchen sinks mounted in that vanity.

The bathroom was also the site of the sole modification done with Zach's own hands: the door frame had black foam all around it and the door itself had a wedge of foam attached to the bottom. The combination made the room devoid of light when the door was closed. The sconces had red lightbulbs in them, so Zach could use the bathroom as his darkroom.

He hadn't done that in a while, though.

And that must have been why he couldn't find his favorite camera. Zach couldn't even remember when he'd seen it last.

If Maralys wanted pictures, well, he'd get her some. But he needed his camera to do that, and he wanted his favorite 35 mm with the sweet zoom. It wasn't in any of the boxes in the bedroom closet, although he had found a bunch of contact sheets and the film he'd shot in Venice. There was a bit from New Orleans, too, and some killer shots from Savannah. He'd taken some great stuff in Paris, as well.

He'd lost the night before to a one-eyed review of his own work. He'd actually been good at photography. It was a welcome revelation that he'd been good at something other than ticking off his father.

And he missed taking pictures, another surprise. Zach remembered an art teacher—Mr. Nicholson—telling Zach years ago that if he ever decided to give a crap about anything, he'd make something of himself, but that otherwise Zach would just be another aimless rich boy, taking up space and wasting oxygen.

For a long time, he had despised Mr. Nicholson.

Now he wondered what had ever happened to Mr. Nicholson.

Morning had brought a new sense of purpose—and a new range of color in the bruise surrounding his eye. Zach was determined to find that camera. It wasn't in any of the kitchen cupboards, or the front hall closet. He was running out of options. Had this place come with a storage locker? Zach couldn't remember. And if it did, where had he put the key?

He pulled open the louvered doors of the utility closet with some impatience. The stackable washer and dryer had never been used— Zach still frequented the same coin Laundromat he had used as a student. His rationale was that a guy could never meet women doing laundry in his own utility room, although lately the women at the laundromat had seemed too young and too giggly to be interesting.

(Where did Jen do her laundry? He would have paid good money to know, so he could "accidentally" run into her and have her trapped for an hour as the laundry whirled in the dryer, compelled to talk to him. He was sure that he could make her laugh in an hour of solo time. Guaranteed.)

There was an enlarger parked on top of the washing machine, the dust on it offering evidence of how long it had been since Zach had used it, and how often he had to move it to open the lid of the washer. In fact, the manuals were still inside the respective machines, and as he stood there, he considered the merit of using them.

"I could become one of those eccentric hermits," he suggested to Roxie, who was sniffing inside the unfamiliar territory of the closet. "Never leave the unit, have my groceries delivered. I could just sit back and watch my toenails grow longer. You and me, Roxie, we could just have each other."

The dog snorted a dust bunny, sneezed, and gave him a look.

"Right. That wouldn't work too well for you, would it?" Zach found a dirty T-shirt and cleaned the dog snot off the appliances while it was still fresh. He had learned that it was much harder to remove later. "I tell you, the prime achievement of my life was training you with six stories between us and the grass."

Roxie stepped back and sat down, the expression on her face hinting that, given the chance, she'd contest whose achievement it had been. She trotted to the front door and returned to look at him expectantly.

"There would be the power of suggestion. Just give me a minute, Roxie. There's a box on the top shelf." Zach didn't have a chair or a step stool—which left the mystery of how the box had gotten there in the first place—so he climbed the appliances.

He could have waited, but that wasn't his style.

He opened the dryer door and put one foot on the opening, managed to get his toes beneath the lip of the dryer and the washer above, then pulled himself up by the door frame. He nudged the box open Roxie-style (with his nose), peered into the box, and shouted in triumph.

"Ha! There it is. Bonus!"

The trick was that he had to let go of the frame to reach into the box. There were, after all, limitations to how many tricks he could do with his nose. Chances were good that he'd fall.

But he wanted the camera. Now.

The sensible thing would have been to get down, to go find a chair or a step stool, but Zach had never been one for sensible responses. He liked the immediacy of surrendering to impulse.

It had led to some of his most memorable experiences. It probably was responsible for the majority of disasters he'd experienced in his life as well. On the whole, he thought the balance came out in favor of impulse.

"I don't suppose you'd spot me, Roxie?"

The dog sat below him, watching, and thumped her tail against the floor.

"No. I didn't think so. Well, here goes."

Zach moved fast. He barely had time to reach into the box, snag the camera and clutch it to his chest before he lost his balance. He fell backward, just as he had anticipated, except that his fall was louder.

And it hurt a lot more.

"Ow!" he yelled when his butt hit the floor. His ankle banged off the dryer, his elbow hit the louvered door and sent it slamming against the wall. His shoulders hit the floor hard and he thunked his head, making the standard white ceiling with its standard cheap light fixture spin.

Roxie barked at the noise and ran around him.

"You're a big help," he told her and she licked his face. "You're probably just relieved that I'm not dead. That way there's hope of my opening the kibble bag tonight."

The dog barked again, then ran to the front door. She returned, proudly bearing her leash and dropped it onto Zach's chest. The metal clip missed the camera lens, which was a major stroke of luck.

"If you had opposable thumbs, Roxie, you wouldn't have any need for me at all."

She licked his face again, indicating that she had other reasons for putting up with him. She made him smile, she always did, but a dog's affection didn't quite seem like enough anymore.

He laid there for a minute and considered the plain box of his apartment—albeit an inverted, spinning version—and knew it wasn't like the homes of any of his buddies. They had moved on from under grad minimalism. Most of them had houses, with furniture and rugs and paintings and actual food in the fridge.

They had committed to staying, to putting down roots. But if he wasn't committing himself to this place and this life, then where was he going?

Or was it just that he didn't want to be tied down, in case he decided to go somewhere or do something?

That sounded pretty lame, even to a guy who had hit his head, never mind one lying on the floor and talking to his dog. Zach got up and put the camera on the kitchen counter. He got the box from the bedroom full of prints and film and contact sheets, and rummaged in it for a minute. The dog tap-danced in the foyer.

"Give me a minute, Roxie," he said just as he found the print he wanted. Just the sight of it made his pulse leap. It was a color shot he'd taken in the rain of the Bridge of Sighs in Venice, but the image was virtually black and white. It was awash in tones of grey with a whisper of blue and green. It was moody and evocative and perfectly echoed his sense of Venice in the winter.

This was one time that he'd nailed an image perfectly and he stared at it, surprised that it was as good as he'd remembered, Zach knew that this was the only time that he'd felt any satisfaction in any of his achievements. He'd had it blown up, once upon a time, in honor of that, but had never managed to mount and hang it.

That would have put his pride in his accomplishment in full view, and would have provided the opportunity for his family to mock what was important to him.

Zach decided that it was past time he stopped worrying about family response to his actions. He slid the print into an envelope with a piece of cardboard to keep it from bending, tucked the envelope under his arm and took Roxie for a walk.

He'd stop at the framing store around the corner when he was out, get an acid-free mat and a frame. Then he'd have art on his wall, not some homogenized image out of the Ethan Allen catalog. Ha. And he'd pick up some film, too.

He would take more pictures, and not just of Jen. He'd rediscover the world around him, through the lens of his camera. He didn't have to travel far to look at the world his own way.

"We'll do a couple of road trips, Roxie," he told the dog, who was more interested in a more immediate exploration of the outdoor world. "We'll go up the coast, Nantucket, Cape Cod, Provincetown, even back to Rosemount, and blow off a bunch of film. You can check out the beaches or roll in dead fish if you'd rather. It'll be fun."

Just talking about it put a bounce in Zach's step. He'd felt this way when he'd gone off to Europe in pursuit of beauty, but not since. That was such a good thing that he wasn't going to think about it any further. He'd just enjoy it.

He'd just go with it.

Although it would be more fun to do those road trips with someone who would keep up their side of the conversation. As a bonus, next Thursday he'd be seeing Jen again. Maybe in a week, he'd think of a way to make her smile.

Lawyer jokes, after all, just weren't going to cut it.

By the following Wednesday, Jen had run the entire gamut of possible responses and tactics. She'd quickly resolved not to ask anyone else out—because her luck was such that as soon as she did, Zach would show up, asking directions. She'd end up with two dates for Thanksgiving dinner, which wouldn't please anyone.

She'd worked up the nerve to call Zach twice, but had gotten his answering machine both times. (She hadn't worked up the nerve to leave a message.) She'd just happened to walk in the vicinity of his condo building, purportedly on other missions, but hadn't caught a glimpse of him. She'd lingered at Mulligan's before and after her shift, as well as working extra hours, hoping he'd turn up.

No luck.

And now it was Wednesday, the day before the big day, and she had no answers. The only thing Jen knew was that Cin would call Zach tonight.

Unless she called him first. That afternoon, on her way to work, she'd decided to give him one last chance to show up—and if he didn't come in for dinner, she'd call him after the dinner rush. Cin was working until nine, so Jen figured she had a small window of opportunity left.

Maybe.

It was enough of a concern to distract her from the prospect of finishing the knitted avocado at work tonight. She wanted to finish it before Thanksgiving, so she could show it to her Gran, but it had given her nothing but trouble. For all she knew, she'd be up half the night, trying to get the silly thing done.

It was snowing like crazy when Jen headed to work, and had been snowing all day. Cars were mired in the unplowed snow at the curb and the world was painted with swirling white. Jen walked from the T, her shoulders hunched against the cold, and was surprised to find her mood lightening. The snow was so pretty, and all of the people out shoveling their walks and driveways greeted her—as they never would when it wasn't snowing. Bad weather seemed to bring out the best in people.

Although that almost certainly wouldn't be true at the airport, where thousands of anxious travelers were trying to get to Thanksgiving dinner on time. She was glad her family was pretty close together. They could all take public transit the next day.

Jen was startled from her thoughts by the new sign on the cleared sidewalk in front of Mulligan's.

KARAOKE! EVERY WEDNESDAY NIGHT AT SEVEN.

"Karaoke? Be serious," Jen said to no one in particular when she stepped inside. Lucy grinned and Kathy, another waitress, shook her head. No one apparently had any doubt what Jen was talking about.

But they left it to the boss man to explain.

Once upon a time, Murray had bought a karaoke machine at a sale of another bar's chattels. He was convinced it was a prize, but it had proven to be so well used that it was uncooperative about ever working again.

Experts—mostly regular patrons falsely convinced they could fix anything, either independent of the influence of alcohol or because of it—had fiddled with the machine without result. Lucy and Jen had joked that if Murray ever got it working, it would be a miracle. Ultimately, the machine had been retired to a corner to collect dust.

Until now.

Murray was whistling as he polished the karaoke machine, which had been set up at the end of the bar since Jen's last shift. It was as large and ugly as only old technology can be. "I *am* serious.

This thing is going to be a gold mine for us." The small stage that never hosted bar bands anymore had been cleared and one of the bar televisions had been pressed into service on the wall behind it.

Lucy rolled her eyes as she marched from the kitchen to her section. "A gold mine. Like the glitter disco ball. That brought them in, didn't it?"

"Until the Smithsonian came and commandeered it for their collection," Jen said, shedding her coat.

"I've still got bruises from that twentieth-century curator," Kathy interjected, looking up from setting her tables.

"She was one mean piece of business," Lucy agreed.

"And she took my mood ring, too," Jen complained.

Lucy and Kathy laughed together, but Murray wasn't amused. "You three can yuck it up, but you'll see. I'm on to something here. Retro is in right now. Everyone's reliving the past. This is going to be a huge hit. You'll see. Tonight we won't be able to keep up with the crowd."

"If that Smithsonian chick comes back, don't seat her in my section," Jen warned.

"Ha!" Kathy agreed. "I'll pop her one before she gets the jump on me again."

"No abuse of the customers!" Murray called after her. "It's bad for the insurance rates."

Lucy came to look at the machine and gave it a little poke. Something rattled deep in its belly, behind the smoked plastic cover. "Is the music on eight-tracks?"

"LPs?" Kathy suggested.

"It's been updated to CDs," Murray informed them huffily.

Lucy peered at it. "What music is on there? Handel's *Water Music*?"

"Worse," Kathy said. "Duran Duran."

"Men Without Hats," Jen said. "The Police. Devo."

Lucy brightened. "Hey, maybe the Eurythmics."

Murray shook his head and patted his new baby. "It's loaded up with classics, so everyone will know the words."

Murray peered at the console. "See? Motown. Elvis Presley. The Beatles. All the good stuff." He buffed the plastic with pride, removing Lucy's fingerprints from the dark Plexiglas cover.

Jen was intrigued despite herself. "Wait a minute. You've got Motown on there? Like what songs?"

"You don't know that stuff," Lucy scoffed. "You're too young."

"I love that stuff. My mom plays it all the time."

Murray grinned with triumph, glad to show off his baby's charms. "See, it works like this." He handed Lucy the microphone—which was still wired into the console—then turned the beast on.

The words of the first verse came up on the television screen as the background music began. A little red ball bounced on the left, apparently awaiting its cue to skip over the words to be sung.

"You be Diana Ross," Lucy said and handed Jen the microphone. "I don't sing outside of the shower: it's a public health hazard."

Jen didn't need much encouragement. "You're on." Murray had chosen "Stop! In the Name of Love," one of Jen's favorites. She told herself that this was the only reason she was even contemplating doing this, but knew it wasn't true.

Besides, there were no witnesses. Her coworkers didn't count. That wasn't the reason, either.

She just loved to sing, even though she hadn't for a long time.

"Do it, Murray," Jen said. "Let's try this baby out."

"If it's going to choke, it might as well do it now," Lucy agreed.

"Still time to take down the sign," Kathy agreed.

"Skeptics, every one of you," Murray retorted and punched the button.

Jen took to the stage, clutching the mike. The cord was barely long enough. "So, do I get backup here, or what?" she asked, feigning indignation when Lucy and Kathy didn't follow her.

"Excuse me." Lucy straightened her apron. "The diva has spoken.

I've heard about these singing babes and how much trouble they are."

"I want a sequined miniskirt," Kathy complained.

"A beehive hairdo," Lucy agreed.

The two stepped behind Jen as she sang the first verse. She didn't even have to watch the bouncing ball: she knew all of the words. After a wobble or two, all three found their pitch and their rhythm. Jen started a bossa nova step, and Lucy and Kathy followed her lead. Murray tapped his fingertips on the bar and nodded approval. When they sang the word "stop" in the next chorus, all three of them held up a hand in unison.

"Hey, this is good," Murray said.

"It'll cost you big," Lucy warned, before returning to her back-up warbles. Jen closed her eyes and let her voice go for the solo. This was the music she'd been raised on, the music that made her joyous no matter what was going on in her life. How had she lost track of it the last two years, just when—ironically—she'd needed it the most?

There hadn't been much to sing about, that was for sure. But her mom was right—she was alive.

And maybe, just maybe, she was ready to sing again.

The last chorus was triumphant, their three voices finding a good fit together. None of them heard the door open and close. Jen had her eyes shut. Their voices came together for the last chorus, held the note, then let it fade to nothing along with the music. Jen even took a bow to the applause of her coworkers.

"Good job," Murray said, clapping. They were all laughing and proud of themselves, and Jen flushed a little at the enthusiasm of the others.

"I didn't know you could sing," Zach said and the bottom fell out of Jen's universe.

Jen pivoted to discover that Murray, Kathy, and Lucy weren't the only ones clapping. Her heart did an awkward bossa nova step that took it all around her chest and she had a hard time catching her breath.

Zach had snow in his hair and a sparkle in his eye. He looked even better than she remembered, and this despite the battered leather jacket that showed his wanton disregard for our fellow creatures on the planet. Jen's fingertips brushed the telephone number stuffed into her pocket and she was glad that she wouldn't have to use it.

Unless, of course, he'd stopped by to cancel.

Chapter 5

Zach grinned. It was one surefire sign that a woman was interested when she blushed as red as a beet and Jen was redder than red. She also couldn't look straight at him, which was a shame because he wasn't sure whether her eyes were hazel or brown. He wanted to know.

Especially since he hadn't lost his touch, after all.

"There are lots of things you don't know about me," she said.

"I can think of lots of ways to fix that." Zach settled into a seat at the bar with satisfaction.

Jen propped a hand on her hip and he couldn't read her expression. "So, let me guess. You're here because my sister phoned you, wanting to have your love child, and you dropped by to find out whether insanity runs in my family or not."

The other waitresses laughed. Zach blinked, feeling again that Jen had shifted the field of play on him. Didn't she understand that he was supposed to be the one who made people laugh? "No. I came to have some dinner and get directions."

That sounded boring, even to him, and Zach Coxwell wasn't used to sounding boring. He frowned. "How are you doing?" he said to Murray, his mood having changed from triumphant to something more disgruntled in two bats of a pretty waitress's eye.

"Hey," Murray said, his reply concise. "You want a pint? Same as last time?"

Zach nodded. He didn't really want the beer, but he supposed he should order something. He put his fave camera down on the bar with care. At least it didn't steal his punch lines. He felt Jen move away and was a bit surprised that he was as aware of her presence as that.

It must just be the challenge she presented.

"So, now he's a regular," Lucy said with a roll of her eyes. "You're getting desperate for business when coming here once makes someone a regular."

"So, how's the other guy look?" Murray said, ignoring Lucy.

"It was a pity shot," Zach confided. "I let him take it."

"Uh-huh." Murray glanced toward the waitresses. "So, now I'm paying you to stand around."

"You started it," Lucy retorted. "You turned on the machine."

"And you can really sing, girl!" The third waitress patted Jen on the back.

"Thanks." Jen seemed embarrassed. Zach took the opportunity to look. She was every bit as attractive as he remembered. Not flashy, but he didn't like women who showed their assets to everyone in the neighborhood, as the other unfamiliar waitress was doing. It looked as if Jen was wearing a man's white shirt with the sleeves rolled up. This and the fact that she wore no makeup or jewelry, ironically, made her look more feminine. Zach couldn't figure it out, so he looked more carefully.

She flicked him a glance, catching him in the act. Zach smiled, but Jen turned away.

With pink cheeks.

Ha.

"So, I've got an idea," Murray said and the three waitresses groaned as one. "You three can start off the karaoke tonight, get things going."

"As if I'd do this in public," Lucy retorted. "You won't find me scaring small children."

"There won't be any kids in here tonight," Murray said. "And besides, I'm making it part of your job."

"Then you can pay me more." Lucy propped her hands on her hips, which made her look formidable. Zach thought this was a more effective way of scaring small children, but he wasn't foolish enough say so. "Add to the job description and you can add to the check. It's that simple, Murray."

"We need sequined miniskirts," the blonde waitress insisted. "In coordinated colors."

"Maybe not the beehive hair," Jen said dryly and the blonde laughed. Zach noticed again that Jen didn't crack a smile.

"The shoes though," the other waitress insisted. "We need the shoes, dyed to match the miniskirts. Sweet little pointed toes, sling backs with kitten heels."

"Vintage," Jen said with surprising resolve. "One pair lime, one pair pale yellow, and one pair shell pink."

Interesting that she was so definite about color. Zach felt a kinship with her. "You'll all look like you're the reincarnations of Jackie O," he said.

The blonde propped her hands on her hips, then looked him up and down. Her smile turned appreciative. "And what's not to love about that?"

Zach turned back to his beer, uncertain whether she meant the look or him, well aware of Jen's watchful eye.

There was another clue that he wasn't spitting into the wind here—if Jen wasn't interested, she wouldn't be worried about him going for the other waitress. Zach decided to take encouragement where he found it.

"One song," Murray said. "One song, that's all, just to get things started. Jen can pick which one."

"Now, come on," Lucy began to complain. "As if a busy section isn't enough, now I've got to embarrass myself . . ."

"I think it might be fun." Jen straightened when Zach looked her way and avoided his gaze.

"You'll knock 'em dead. You're really good," Zach said and she glanced his way. "Maybe we should call Berry Gordy and see how his talent lineup is looking these days."

Her eyes twinkled a bit, as if she was glad to have his support.

"I'm not singing. Forget it," Lucy said.

The fair waitress nodded agreement and made to turn away. Jen's disappointment was visible, which was a big clue as to how badly she wanted to do this.

Her next words were an even bigger one.

"If you two don't want to, I'll do it alone," Jen said, her tone defensive as she addressed the other waitresses.

"Go ahead," Lucy said. The blonde shook her head and kept walking.

Jen wilted.

Zach had a rare heroic impulse. He wanted Jen to have what she wanted, if only to see her smile, and so he leapt in where angels might have feared to tread. "It might be good for tips," he said and the other two waitresses stopped cold.

"Ah," Lucy said as she paused to glance back.

"Cash is good," the blonde noted, then nibbled on her bottom lip.

Jen's eyes were bright with her excitement, which was all the reward Zach needed.

Strangely enough.

Murray grinned. "Found the nerve, kid. Okay, no pooling tips tonight unless you all sing. It wouldn't be fair to Jen."

"There's a guilt trip," Lucy said. "We can stand aside and let her face the lions alone."

"Not a chance," the blonde said. "I'm in. Bring on the cash."

"Okay, me, too," Lucy agreed and the pair high-fived it with Jen, who looked a lot happier than the other two women. Zach saluted her with his beer. He was hoping she'd say something to him, but Murray punched him lightly in the shoulder.

"Good job, kid. That beer's on the house."

"Oh. Thanks."

By the time Zach acknowledged Murray's comment, Jen had already turned away to wipe down the tables in her section. Maybe she'd sing a song just for Zach.

Maybe he had nowhere to go for the moment.

"So, here's the playlist, Jen." Murray poked at the machine so that the list came up on the display. "Pick a song."

Jen didn't come any closer to Zach, to his disappointment, and he was right beside the machine. "Does it have 'You Can't Hurry Love?' she called.

"Um, yeah, it does."

"Then that's it. That's the one we'll start with." She spoke with such resolve and with such a quick glance at Zach that he knew the choice was deliberate.

You can't hurry love? Well, who was trying to? Love was not an agenda item for Zach. He liked his relationships uncomplicated. He shrugged when Jen glanced his way, signaling his agreement with the concept. Jen studied him for a long moment.

"But . . ." Murray protested.

"I've got to set my tables," Jen said quickly. "Look, first dinner patrons through the door." She gestured to the door and sure enough, a trio of women stood there, shaking snow out of their coats.

"'You Can't Hurry Love' is a good choice: I even know our words," the blonde said, giving Lucy a nudge. "I think they're 'doo wop.'"

"Don't be silly," Lucy said. "They're 'mmm mmm mmm.'"

"Wrong, wrong," Jen called from across the restaurant. She wasn't laughing but her voice was lighter. It was a good start, in Zach's opinion. "It's 'bop bop' and then 'oooo oooo.'"

Zach smiled as the two waitresses grinned. "We can do that," Lucy said. She marched past Zach to tend to the new arrivals, muttering at him in passing. "You would have to bring up the better tips question. Kathy is always hot for more cash."

"Not you?"

"If it doesn't work out, sport, I'm going to hunt you down and hurt you."

"Fair enough. But I've got some good hiding spots."

"I should hope you both know the words." Murray spoke gruffly, even though he was obviously pleased. "Just don't spill any drinks while you sing. Patrons get cranky about that."

"Picky, picky, picky," Lucy said.

"It's always something," Kathy agreed, but she winked at Zach. "You're right; this might be fun. You gonna stay to watch?"

"Probably," he conceded. "I deserve fair warning if Lucy is coming after me."

Murray snorted and Kathy laughed, but Jen didn't seem to have heard anything Zach had said. The woman's smile was going to be elusive, that was for sure.

Zach settled in to strategize.

"So, you gonna duck him all night?" Lucy prodded Jen with her elbow, which was surprisingly sharp given that every other bit of Lucy was well insulated. "You hiding from the stud or what? I think he likes you."

It was the doldrums between the dinner crowd and the evening crowd, and Jen's section was empty. It would be a good time to find out what Zach wanted. The only problem was that Jen had been trying to think of something clever to say ever since he'd come in and had failed completely.

She didn't want to sound desperate, after all.

Or pushy.

"What's going on?" Kathy asked. She followed Jen's glance and smiled. "So, you know the hunk at the bar?"

"Not in the biblical sense." Jen said.

Lucy clicked her tongue. "I should hope not."

"Is there any other sense that counts?" Kathy demanded. "'Cause if you're not calling dibs, then I am. We've got half an hour before things start to hop again and I'm ready to put that time to good use."

"He came to see Jen," Lucy said, affronted on Jen's behalf.

"You don't know that," Kathy argued. "He hasn't talked to her yet . . ."

"She's been working!" Lucy argued.

"Where there's a will, there's a way," Kathy insisted. "I think he's just hanging out, and that puts him in the clear."

"You can't do that to Jen . . ."

"Do you know my sister?" Jen asked, then waved off Kathy's confusion. "Don't answer that. Just give me five minutes." Jen marched across the floor with purpose. She reached the bar just as Murray put a second pint of lager in front of Zach. The head was perfect, a trick Murray only performed for his favorites.

"That's some kind of antique you're toting around," Murray said, gesturing to the camera.

"I guess it is." Zach seemed to be unaware of Jen standing just behind him and to one side, and Murray didn't give her away. "Just because it's old, though, doesn't mean it isn't any good."

"Why don't you get one of those digital ones?"

"I don't want one."

Jen stopped to listen. She'd assumed that someone like Zach would want all of the newest expensive toys as soon as possible. She expected him to be the kind of person who spent a lot of money on consumer goods and found little satisfaction in any of them—which would just drive him to spend more.

She expected him to be shallow.

That he might not be was news.

"Why not?" Murray asked. "It's easy. Point and shoot. And you can see what you've got right away." He gestured to the 35 mm. "Those babies are way too much hassle."

"Depends what you want," Zach said. "If you want mostly okay pictures that are mostly in focus, then digital is the way to go."

"You make that sound like a bad thing."

Zach shrugged. "Maybe I think the lowest common denominator isn't that appealing of an objective. In photography or anything else."

Jen listened avidly, shocked to hear her own perspectives echoed by Trust-Fund Boy.

Murray braced a hand on the bar. "What do you want then?"

"Control." Zach picked up the camera, cradling it in his hands. "With this, I can control what is recorded on film with the aperture setting and the exposure."

"Say what?"

"I can manipulate what is in front of me to make it look the way I want it to look." Zach glanced over his shoulder and gave Jen a smile, his surety of her presence surprising her. He spun the lens and the shutter clicked, his shot taken so quickly that she couldn't respond.

"Hey!" Jen protested. "I don't like having my picture taken."

"Then, get over it," he retorted. "Beauty should be captured on film whenever possible."

Jen blinked at the unexpected compliment, but Zach had already turned back to Murray.

He was indicating the settings on the camera, which was again resting on the bar. "See? I set the aperture wide because it's comparatively dark in here and I didn't want to use a flash."

Jen found herself drawn closer, interested by what he was saying.

"I like the way the light softens appearances," Zach continued. "Kind of like chiaroscuro in the paintings of Da Vinci."

"Chiaro? Wasn't she a singer? That blonde with the guitar, you know?"

Zach gave Murray the kind of hard look that his joke deserved. Jen bit back a smile. "Chiaroscuro's a technique of using shadow and in this kind of light, you can get a similar effect with film. Also

having the aperture wide shortens the depth of field. Jen's face will
be in focus and what's behind her will be blurred, like a painting.
And having the aperture as wide as possible makes the exposure
time as short as possible—still a fifteenth of a second, but not half
a second which would show blurring. I'll show you the results
when I develop the film."

"Nobody processes that stuff anymore," Murray complained.

"That's why I do it myself."

"You develop your film yourself?" Jen asked, intrigued that he
might do anything of the kind. She was standing beside him without any recollection of having moved there. It was as if a magnetic
force had pulled her closer without her being aware of it. She decided not to think about that.

"Well, yes."

Jen nodded in understanding. "Because you want to control the
result."

"Exactly." He smiled at her and her heart went thump.

At close range, she saw the vestige of purple and yellow bruis-
ing around his eye. "What happened to you?"

He shook his head and smiled. "My past jumped me from behind when I left here last week. Happens sometimes."

"Hazard of having a past," Murray opined.

Both Zach and Jen ignored him.

"I thought maybe Murray had improved his right hook," Jen
said. Zach laughed and Murray glowered, getting busy with his
glasses behind the bar.

"Nope, Murray can't take credit for this one." Zach shrugged.
"Maybe he still punches like a girl. Do I really have to find out?"

"Hey!" Murray protested to general disinterest.

"Presumably you're fast enough to duck." Jen considered Zach's
eye. "But then, maybe that's an unfair assumption."

"Surprise, he got me by surprise," Zach insisted. "If I'd guessed
he was going to get violent, he wouldn't have touched me."

"That's what they all say," Jen teased, enjoying herself more
than she knew she should. "Believe what you need to."

"You need me to pop this guy, Jen?" Murray asked. "Maybe I need to defend my honor, if he's going to be saying such things about me."

"Except she said it first," Zach said and Jen strove to look innocent. Zach chuckled and she liked having made him laugh.

Murray scoffed. "My girl Jen? I don't think so. You know, it's not very chivalrous to blame a lady for your own shortcomings."

"Chivalry, is it then," Lucy said as she put her tray on the counter. "Aren't we going upmarket? You should have warned me, Murray. I'd have painted my nails, brought a thesaurus."

The pair commenced their usual bickering, and Zach turned a shoulder to them. He winked at Jen and she reminded herself to not be charmed. "I didn't want to frighten you. It was pretty spectacular."

"I'll bet." Jen wiped the bar counter a bit, feeling immeasurably better. He'd stayed away for a reason. Or at least he cared enough about what she thought to make up a reason. Either way, Jen was reassured. "So, how was the steak special?"

Zach blinked. "I didn't have it."

"What did you have, then?"

His expression was skeptical. "You're that interested in what I ate?"

"Diet says a lot about a person." Jen shrugged, well aware that he must be thinking she was nuts.

Or maybe that insanity did run in her family.

"I had the pasta, the one with the chicken in pesto cream sauce. It was pretty good."

"Oh." Jen wasn't sure whether she was pleased that he was eating chicken—and thus a perfect candidate for the Plan—or disappointed.

Murray was watching the exchange, his gaze dancing between the two of them, even as he talked to Lucy. It was kind of cute that he'd threatened Zach on her behalf.

But if he was worrying about people using other people, maybe he should have warned Zach against her.

Zach cleared his throat. "So, do you think I'll pass inspection tomorrow, or will your grandmother think you're bringing home a troublemaker?"

Jen stared at him, not understanding. Her grandmother had no issues with people eating meat. "Because you ate chicken?"

"Because of the shiner."

"Excuse me?"

"I wouldn't want your grandmother to disapprove of me, or think I was a certain kind of person because of this." He grimaced. "It might nix the whole dating prospects thing."

This time Jen blinked. Zach actually was afraid that her family would think poorly of him because he had a black eye.

He had a lot to learn about Jen's family.

She wondered briefly about his own family. Did they judge by appearances alone?

But what difference did it make? She had no business thinking about it. She'd never meet them and shouldn't speculate on the kind of people they were. Curiosity was just another step closer to being involved.

And she wasn't going there.

So, Jen shrugged as if indifferent. "So long as you lay off the lawyer jokes, you should be fine."

Zach laughed, his eyes dancing, and her pride in having made him laugh triggered a warning alarm deep inside Jen.

It was one day.

One meal.

In front of witnesses.

She could do this.

"You're going to have to give me the address, then."

"Right." Under Murray's watchful and disapproving eye, Jen gave him her grandmother's address. She couldn't help feeling a bit of anticipation when their fingers brushed over the scrap of paper. "Oh, and if you get a call from a crazy woman tonight—"

Zach arched a brow. "Offering to have my love child?"

Jen nodded, liking how his eyes sparkled. "That would be my sister. She's mostly harmless." When he grinned, Jen pivoted to return to her section, thinking the matter resolved.

But Zach surprised her one more time. "So, should I tell her we've got that all worked out already?"

Jen glanced over her shoulder and his mischievous expression made her want to laugh as much as the idea of putting one over on Cin. "Tell her I'm pregnant already," she said impulsively. "That'll give her something to choke on."

"Will do," Zach said, toasting her with his beer.

He'd make it sound plausible, too.

It was almost worth "forgetting" to call Cin to tell her that all was arranged, but Jen couldn't do that. She returned to her section, feeling as if she'd conquered the world.

If she'd thought about it, she'd have realized that it had more to do with making Zach Coxwell grin than with the probability of Cin's plan being a success.

Zach wished he had brought a flash, because he was fascinated by Jen when she sang. On the other hand, the flash might have disconcerted her. A tripod maybe. He should bring a tripod one Wednesday so he could use a long enough exposure.

She sang like a siren, all sensuality and invitation, her range of emotional display in complete contrast to her usual deadpan manner. Her voice was lush, richer than he'd expected. The way she could hold a note gave him goose pimples. Again, the contrast with her appearance, with that tailored shirt and cropped hair, was fascinating.

How could she look so biteably sexy?

How much more sexy would she look in a sequined dress with red lipstick, turned out in full-throttle femininity?

Or would she look less sexy that way?

It was a mystery worth pondering. Zach considered the question

each time she took the stage and couldn't come up with a persuasive answer. He listened to Jen sing and watched her work and
itched to take more pictures of her.

Here was a woman who would never be predictable. And Zach
liked that. He liked it a lot.

At nine-thirty, he realized Roxie would be waiting for him and
settled his tab with Murray. He was trying to figure out how to
have a quick word with Jen before he left without disturbing her
rhythm of serving her section when he saw that she was taking a
break. She came out of the kitchen with a single plate, spoke
quickly to Lucy, then headed for a back room.

Zach followed, glad they'd have a chance to talk in comparative privacy.

Jen took three bites of her salad, then dug out her knitting.
She had fifteen minutes to make a difference in the progress of the
avocado. The pit, where she'd begun, was a perfect little golf ball,
already stuffed. She'd picked up stitches all around the pit and
shaded the "flesh" of the fruit itself, knitting an oval shape. Then
she'd changed to the dark green, and done the skin in moss stitch,
picking up stitches on the other side and working from the bottom
up. There probably was a better way to have done it, but it didn't
look half bad. She'd started to stuff it, and planned to make a seam
between the flesh and the skin along one edge.

"What's that?" Zach spoke from behind her and Jen nearly
jumped out of her own skin—which was not knitted in dark green
in moss stitch.

"What's what?" she said, making an unsuccessful attempt to
stuff the knitted avocado back into her bag.

Zach leaned in the doorway of the break room, so avidly interested that Jen knew his attention couldn't be easily diverted. "That
thing in the top of your bag. The green thing."

Jen immediately pushed it farther into the bag. "Nothing."

"It's not nothing. It's something green, like a ball. Do you carry tennis balls around with you?"

"No. It's not a tennis ball."

"Then what is it?"

Jen gave him a look that should have told him to disappear, but he held his ground.

"Come on, I'm curious." He smiled a little, making her heart go thump. The break room was a very small space and seemed suddenly very full of a handsome, confident hunk. "Is it a secret?" he teased.

Jen doubted that showing him the avocado would persuade him that insanity didn't run in her family. On the other hand, it might be interesting to see what he thought of it.

She didn't expect much. She reached into her bag and put the avocado, still with three needles sticking out of it, on the table. Then she took a bite of salad, as if she carried such things around all the time.

Because she pretty much did.

Zach frowned at it. "It looks like a voodoo ball. Sort of."

"You might as well know that it's a knitted avocado," Jen said with some pride.

Zach blinked. "A knitted avocado?"

Jen nodded.

Zach stepped closer, which brought him close enough to touch. He bent and peered at the avocado, apparently uncertain whether he should touch it. "So it is," he acknowledged, flicking an amused glance her way. "With a knitted pit. What exactly do you have against avocados?"

"What do you mean?"

"It looks like a voodoo doll, like a way of remotely inflicting pain on, um, an avocado."

"But it's not. It's just a knitted avocado."

"Ah." Zach seemed to be trying to look as if this made sense and failed.

"I knitted it as if it's cut in half," Jen agreed. "I like how knitting the skin in moss stitch made it look pebbly." She picked up the avocado, unable to resist touching it. She turned it in her hand and frowned, considering her own workmanship. "I'm glad I did it that way, although it was a bit of a pain."

Zach braced his hands on the table. "Wait—*you* knitted this avocado?"

Jen sat a bit straighter, prepared for him to question her sanity. She met his gaze squarely and found only curiosity in his eyes. "Yes."

Zach seemed to be at a loss for words. He frowned, as if contemplating the mysteries of the universe. Jen fought a smile, impressed that he recovered so quickly. "And why, exactly, would someone knit an avocado?"

"Just because."

"And here I thought you were a pragmatic person."

"You said there was a lot you didn't know about me."

"And I should say it again. A knitted avocado."

"Be prepared, that's my motto," Jen said, hearing her tone lighten. "I mean, if you needed a knitted avocado, wouldn't you want to have one already?"

"Good point." Zach nodded solemnly. "But why would one need a knitted avocado?"

"You never know."

"But you're ready. For anything."

"Exactly."

He pulled out the other chair and sat down, his knee bumping against hers in the small space. Goose pimples paraded over Jen's skin, at just that casual contact. She could smell that he wore some kind of aftershave—it was light and sexy—and also that he didn't smoke. Worked for her.

In fact, it worked a little too well for her.

He smiled at her. "So, what does one do with a knitted avocado?"

"Nothing. Admire it." Jen made a show of admiring her handiwork.

Zach chuckled. "Nice shading around the pit," he said, touching the avocado with one fingertip. "Very realistic."

"Thank you. I did that six times to get it right."

"Six times!"

Jen nodded with pride.

Zach leaned closer. Jen was glad she'd stopped eating before he got here: her throat was so dry that she couldn't have swallowed anything.

Maybe her mother was right. Maybe she did need some wild sex.

She looked into Zach's dancing green eyes, thought about wild sex with him, and her circuits shorted.

It was awfully warm in the break room.

He braced an elbow on the table and came even closer. "So, is it possible to need a knitted avocado and be unaware of that fact?"

Jen considered this for a moment. She frowned a little bit when she answered him, her tone equally solemn. "I think it's likely that few people fully comprehend their need for knitted fruits and vegetables."

Zach laughed. It was an honest deep laugh, one that came right from his gut and pleased Jen enormously. "That was plural. Fruits and vegetables. You've made more?"

Jen sighed, knowing that the only way out was to confess the fullness of her addiction. Actually, she was surprised to realize that she was having fun. "It started with a knitted cherry."

"Just one?"

"Well, after making one, the sense of accomplishment is lost. I moved on to a strawberry." She cast him a conspiratorial glance. "The little seeds were a challenge, you know."

"I'll bet. How did you do them?"

Even though he was teasing her, she saw that he was intrigued. "With little beads."

"Brilliant."

"I thought so."

He plucked the avocado out of her hands, turning it to admire it. And he *was* admiring it, much to Jen's surprise. "Then?"

"Then an orange."

He gave her a mock frown. "That can't have been hard, not after the strawberry."

"No, it was more of a restorative break."

"Not a gimme?"

"No. I did it in half, as if it was cut crosswise."

"So you'd see the segments."

"Right. Then I felt I was ready for the bananas."

"More than one?"

She gave him a pitying look. "Did you ever buy just one banana?"

His lips quirked again. "No. Never. But then, I've never bought one cherry before, either."

"Picky, picky. It's a small bunch, just four, with shading. The ones on the left are more green and the ones on the right have a few brown spots."

"And the ones in the middle are yellow, in order to provide a restorative break," Zach guessed.

Jen watched him for a moment, then folded her arms across her chest. "Great. Now you think I'm a nut."

"No, no, not nutty." Zach paused for a beat. "Fruity, maybe."

Jen almost laughed at that.

Zach spun the avocado in his hand. "Or just possibly, you're bananas."

Jen groaned but Zach continued. "But not nutty. At least not so far, right?"

"That was so bad," Jen said.

"You set me up perfectly. You had to have seen it coming."

"I didn't."

"Then you're losing your touch." He winked at her and she caught her breath.

"So, why knit fruit?"

"Because it's manageable."

"What does that mean?"

Jen paused, unsure what to say. The truth was out of the question. "It's small; it's portable; you can see the end of the project right from the beginning," she said finally. "It's not a huge commitment in time and materials, but it's fun."

"But they're getting bigger," Zach observed and she was struck again that he paid attention to detail. "Are you knitting faster?"

"A little bit." Jen shrugged. She tried to take the avocado back, feeling suddenly protective of it. Zach held it firmly, forcing her to slip her fingers beneath his. He watched her, his eyes gleaming, and she liked the feel of his hand over hers. "And getting a bit more daring, too," she said quickly.

"An avocado is daring?"

Jen seized the avocado and jammed it into her bag, certain she'd confided in him enough for the moment. "You don't want to know what else I knit."

"When you look mysterious like that, I sure do."

"Your loss. I'm not telling."

He leaned back in his chair, considering her with a warmth that made Jen all tingly. "At least we're getting closer to establishing just what kind of nitwit you are—or is that knit wit with a k?"

"Oooo, that's bad."

"Let's see," he mused, undeterred. "Would the flavor of choice be Daring Cherry? Strawberry Shortcake? Agent Orange? Bananarama?"

"You forgot the avocado."

"It's a toughie. Give me a minute."

"You're out of time because so am I. I've got to get back to my section."

"You didn't eat your dinner yet."

"Oh well."

He looked concerned. "But I kept you from eating. I'm sorry. I just wanted to say good night to you before I left."

He was leaving already?

Jen fought against her disappointment, knowing it was stupid.

"Roxanne is waiting?" she asked archly.

"Actually, yes." He stood then. "Sorry about your dinner."

"It wasn't that good of a salad."

"You need to eat something."

Jen shook a finger at him as she stood up. "Do not start sounding like my mother."

"Fair enough." Zach grinned. He was standing in the doorway and when Jen picked up her bag, she found him standing right in front of her. They were close together, close enough to give a person in need of physical intimacy some interesting ideas.

Murray needed to make a bigger break room.

One with better ventilation.

"See you tomorrow, then?" His gaze dropped to her lips and lingered. Jen knew what he was thinking and was a bit disconcerted to find herself thinking much the same thing.

What did he taste like?

How would he kiss?

It was hard to believe that he'd be as hasty about it as Steve had been. No, Jen could imagine that Zach lingered over pleasure.

That was the beauty of having a trust fund and no financial worries, she reminded herself. A wealthy person could take his time savoring whatever he wanted to savor. He'd have no deadlines, no obligations, no responsibilities.

Except to Roxanne.

She reminded herself vehemently that she and Zach had nothing in common, and no future beyond dinner the next day. She shouldn't have needed reminding, but that was just lust working against her.

Because she'd have to be dead to not feel any yearning when a hunk like Zach leaned closer for a kiss.

And she wasn't dead. That, after all, was the point.

"Good night, Jen," he said softly and bent his head with purpose.

Jen took a step back, planting a finger in the middle of his chest. "Hey, don't get ahead of things here. You haven't been approved by my grandmother yet." She tried to make it sound like a joke, but it sounded desperate even to her own ears.

Zach caught her hand in his. "Right." He smiled at her as he put a kiss in her palm. She fought the urge to shiver and tried to give him a daunting glare. He didn't appear to be daunted. "The knitted avocado made me forget myself."

"My section . . ."

"Right. See you tomorrow." Zach stood back and Jen strode past him, forgetting her dinner plate in the break room for the first time ever. All she could think of was putting distance between an annoyingly attractive man and herself.

She told herself that she always walked that quickly.

It wasn't until the end of her shift that she realized that evening had lost its fizz when Zach left Mulligan's.

And incredibly, he hadn't thought her knitted avocado was a really dumb thing. Steve would have told her that she was wasting her time, but then, Steve had thought every waking moment should be spent pursuing money.

What did Zach pursue?

What did he want?

Jen had a moment's fear that he wasn't as predictable as she'd thought, that he wasn't the kind of guy she'd thought he was, but managed to dismiss it.

He was just being polite. That was it.

Besides, in twenty-four hours, she'd never see him again. She reminded herself that that was a good thing, then forced herself to think about something else.

Anything other than how much she liked talking to Zach Coxwell.

Jen was nervous. She didn't have Cin's breezy ease with deception and barely slept the night before Thanksgiving.

It had nothing to do with the fact that she'd thought Zach was going to kiss her in the break room, nothing to do with her own unexpected yearning that he do so, and absolutely nothing to do with her disappointment that he hadn't. It didn't have a damn thing to do with her curiosity about Roxanne.

She was using Zach, plain and simple.

She was not going to get emotionally involved.

She wasn't even attracted to him.

This didn't sound plausible in the middle of the night and only seemed less so in the morning. Once she met her mother in the kitchen and began gathering the appetizers, Jen faced the truth.

This could go quite badly. Her family, after all, would be in fine form.

And they were weird. One look at the contributions they had made and Jen knew that Zach might go into culture shock. Would there even be a turkey? She wasn't sure. Sometimes Gran cooked one just for spite.

Jen hoped this would be one of those years, but this year, that hope wasn't just because she loved turkey herself. Jen had been vegan for years—albeit with secret hankerings and the occasional indulgence in a hot turkey dinner when her mother couldn't witness the deed—but had begun to eat chicken and fish to combat the pernicious anemia she developed during her chemo treatment.

A hint of the adventures to come came in the car, when Jen shared a ride with her mother and Natalie's latest paramour, Gerry. She was wedged into the backseat of her mother's ancient Honda with their contributions to the meal, while Natalie drove.

This left Gerry free to pontificate. He was one of those people who couldn't talk without using his hands, so it was better for the life expectancy of all of them to not let him drive. Gerry was a difficult man for Jen to like, even though she knew his heart was good and that he treated her mother well.

He was just so intolerant of everyone who wasn't like him. Jen couldn't understand her mother's attraction to him—beyond the physical, and even that was questionable as Gerry was a tall, reedy man with thinning hair—as tolerance had been one of the anthems of their household for as long as she could remember.

"Look at this gasoline alley," Gerry began not five minutes after they got rolling. "It's got to be the ugliest street in Massachusetts, and what do they do, but add more to it . . ." He launched in a tirade about urban sprawl once they were all trapped in the car, a lecture that didn't bode well for the day ahead.

Jen tried to ignore him. She was kind of glad that there was another big box bookstore opening on this street—it was close enough that she'd be able to walk, and she did like having a coffee while she read a new knitting magazine, maybe cast on a new project.

"You're just warming up for the festivities," Natalie accused, her tone teasing.

The only sign of her concern was that she took a corner a bit too fast. Jen was glad she'd made the hummus extra thick: it didn't seem to have moved in the bowl, despite the g-force exerted on it. The tabouleh was holding its own; the baba ghanouj, however, had sloshed over the side of its container. Jen had packed the mini pita breads all around the perimeter to brace the bowls but it hadn't been enough.

She'd deal with the spill after they arrived.

"Warming up for what?" Gerry demanded.

Natalie sighed. "I know you don't approve of my mother's lifestyle choices, but maybe for the sake of harmony on a holiday, *we* should be a little more understanding today."

"But, Natalie, you know it's tolerance of the status quo that leads to indifference . . ."

"One day, Gerry. Just one day. She's my mother. Jen's bringing a date. Let's just all have a nice meal together, without any serious discussions about world peace or financial disparity between the first and third worlds."

"But . . ."

"Gerry, it's going to be hard enough for my mother that we won't eat her turkey. It's a festive day for her, as well."

"I'll eat her turkey," Jen volunteered. "I didn't know she was making one." The special plate at Mulligan's couldn't begin to compare to her grandmother's turkey dinner. Homemade stuffing

with sausage. Giblet gravy. These were delights long abolished
from Natalie's vegetarian kitchen, gastronomical pleasures that
had attained mythic status for mostly vegan Jen.

Natalie flashed Jen a smile in the rearview mirror. "Just for
you. She knows you love it and she's glad to have the excuse to
make one."

Gerry, predictably, turned in his seat to challenge Jen. "Do you
know how those birds are raised?"

"No," Jen said firmly. "And I don't want to know."

He shook a finger at her. "Avoidance of the truth doesn't
change anything . . ."

"Gerry," Natalie interrupted. "You're doing it again. Besides,
my mother bought an organically raised bird at my insistence."

"Yum. I bet it'll be good," Jen said.

"Yes, and we'll hear about the price of it at some point in the
day," Natalie said with a smile. She shook a finger at Gerry. "And
you will not talk about mass food production techniques that result in lower market prices but obscure the true environmental
costs. Promise?"

Gerry settled into his seat, the way he exhaled telling both
women that he was annoyed. "So, am I allowed to say *anything*?"

"You know that saying," Natalie said benignly. "If you can't
say anything nice . . ."

"Then don't say anything at all," all three of them said together.

Gerry sighed. "Fine. Tell us about your date, Jen. That's the real
reason your mother wants me to shut up."

Jen's heart stopped, then took off at a gallop. She tried to sound
casual. "It's just this guy I met at work."

"You must like him."

Jen met her mother's gaze in the rearview mirror and strove
to keep from fidgeting. She tried again to act like her sister and
was pretty sure she failed. "Oh, I do. I think he's just great." She
swallowed and fought to sound convincing. "He might even be
the One."

"Romantic nonsense," her mother sniffed.

Gerry chuckled. "Wouldn't life be boring, if we only got one chance at true love?" He slid a fingertip up Natalie's arm and Jen looked away.

Natalie laughed. "You can say that again."

Jen stared out the window and hoped they were wrong. Maybe she was ridiculously romantic, but she liked believing that there was one soul mate out there for each of us.

What if hers was Zach Coxwell?

Impossible. Zach was a means to an end, a way to gain herself time to find Mr. Right without her mother's interference. It would be better if she could remember that and not think about the way he smiled. She certainly shouldn't think about how much fun it was to match wits with him. She reminded herself that she wasn't doing anything he might not do to someone else, and still felt crummy about her decision to go with Cin's plan.

She wanted this day to be over. Right now.

Chapter 6

Jen's suspicion was confirmed when Cin answered the door to their grandmother's house. She was jubilant, pretty much bouncing in anticipation of a good show. Her eyes were sparkling and she could hardly stay still. She was five feet of pixie on a sugar buzz. Just watching her made Jen's head hurt.

"So, where's the hunk?" Cin demanded.

"He's coming."

"Didn't want to scare him off by making him ride in the Honda, balancing the guacamole, huh?"

"It seems a bit early in the relationship for that," Jen acknowledged.

"So, is this serious?" Jen's brother M.B. took the tahini from her hands and gave her a buss on the cheek. He'd surrendered to his hair loss since she'd seen him last and had shaved his head bald.

"I like it," Jen said, rubbing the top of his head for luck.

"No use fighting the inevitable," M.B. said in his usual somber tones. He was the reliable one, everyone's Rock of Gibraltar, and he had the deep, melodic voice to go with that role. She couldn't remember ever hearing him raise his voice or get excited—and in this family, that was a feat.

"Plus you look like the magic genie who lives in a bottle," Jen teased.

"There is that." M.B. gave her a steady look. "This guy is the One?"

Jen nodded, finding it harder to lie to M.B. than to her mother. "Maybe. I'm thinking so."

"You're probably hoping so," M.B. said. "Dating is such a pain—don't let your heart get ahead of you, Jen."

"You know he's the One," Cin said supportively. "He's such a hunk, after all."

"Beauty is more than skin deep," Natalie interjected.

"Not when you have to sleep with him," Cin said before she sailed off to the kitchen with the pita bread.

"I hear we're going to be planning a wedding," Jen's grandmother said, looking as perky as ever. She was tiny, evidence of where Cin had come by her petite stature, but full of fire. She gave Jen a tight hug and stretched up to ruffle her hair. "I like it curly like this," she said briskly, then changed subjects immediately. "Does he have a job?"

"Uh, no, actually. He has a trust fund."

Gran's eyes widened in approval while Jen was sure she heard her mother hiss behind her.

"It'd be nice to have someone in the family with spare change," Ian said, his voice lilting. Ever the pragmatic one and Cin's partner (and foil) for ten years, Ian was unloading the Honda with efficient gestures.

"I thought you'd wear a kilt today," Natalie teased.

"Can't have Cin jumping my bones when the family's around," Ian retorted, only the sparkle of his eyes revealing that he was joking. "Might frighten Jen's date away forever."

"Good point," Natalie said. "We should all try to behave ourselves, right, Gerry?"

Gerry glared at Natalie. "Point taken," he said coldly.

"Why? Have you finally decided that we're unconventional, Mom?" Pluto demanded. He was sauntering up the sidewalk from the bus stop, his fair ponytail bouncing in the wind. He'd brought nothing but himself, typically.

"What's your contribution?" Natalie asked him with mock severity.

"Unless that guitar case is full of chocolate, you're a dead man," Cin said.

Pluto pretended to be insulted. "I brought my guitar, of course. My gift is my song and all that. Music soothes the savage beast."

"We're not that bad," Natalie said.

"I'm counting on Jen's date wanting to make a run for it at least once during the course of the day. I can lull him back into complacency. Hypnotize him, if necessary."

"You?" Cin demanded. "You're more likely to play something from Aerosmith than a mellow ballad."

"You never know. It might be his thing."

"Great," Jen felt the need to interject. "I bring a guy home for once and you're all planning how to scare him away."

"On the contrary," Natalie said, "we're trying to ensure that we don't scare him away. We're making a plan."

"No wonder I'm afraid," Jen muttered. M.B. grinned and gave her a hug.

"Don't worry, Jen," her grandmother said, patting her on the shoulder. "I'll protect him, if necessary."

Oddly enough, these reassurances had precisely the opposite effect upon Jen. She was thinking she should phone Zach and cancel the whole thing.

After all, she still had his number.

It was too late for that, of course. No sooner were they inside and sorting things out in the kitchen than her grandmother's doorbell rang. Jen had all the jitters of a first date. Under Cin's bemused

eye, she ran to the front door, half afraid Zach wouldn't turn up after all.

But she opened the door to find him on the porch, carrying a
bunch of cut flowers. He was wearing khakis that looked new, a
crisp button-down shirt, suede desert boots and—best of all—a tweed
jacket. He looked reputable, conservative, and sufficiently uptight
to fit the bill.

Jen relaxed slightly. They should hate him on sight.

And she shouldn't feel guilty, like she was leading Zach to the
lions. Who knew—he might be entertained. Or oblivious. "Hi. You
didn't need to wear a jacket."

"Seemed better to err on the side of caution." Zach held out
one sleeve. "What do you think? I borrowed it from my brother."

Jen actually liked it, her taste being more traditional than that
of her family. It made Zach's shoulders look broad and the bit
of green in the tweed made his eyes look more vividly green. She reminded herself to not be charmed. "It looks good. Very Brooks
Brothers."

Zach grimaced. "Probably is, knowing James. The man spends
a fortune on clothes—or he used to."

"Got over it?"

"Got married—to the queen of vintage. Reduce, reuse, and recycle is Maralys's mantra. Maybe it's vintage Brooks Brothers."

Jen paused for a moment, surprised by this comment. Zach's
sister-in-law sounded like someone she would like. She wondered
where the sister-in-law shopped—the great indicator of personality,
in Jen's view—then caught herself. After all, Zach's manner indicated that this Maralys might not be universally accepted in his
family.

It didn't matter. This was the only time she'd ever see him. She
was *not* going to be curious about his family.

He gestured to her shirtdress and beaded short cardigan. "But
then it looks like you've got the vintage bug, too."

Jen blushed. "It's an addiction, that's for sure."

He smiled easily and her heart thumped. "It suits you. Very Coco Chanel. Or maybe a young Audrey Hepburn."

"Well. Thanks." Jen was disconcerted by his compliment, as it was dead on the look she was after. Coincidence, that was all. She and Zach didn't really think the same way, or have anything in common.

Jen gestured Zach into the foyer to meet the rapidly gathering cluster of curious relatives, ignoring her awareness of him. She introduced him at lightning speed—experience had taught her that it was the best way to get through the array of strange names without a lot of questions. Polite people always assumed that they had heard incorrectly if Jen said her siblings' names fast.

"Everyone, this is Zach Coxwell. Zach, this is my eldest brother, M.B. Sommerset."

Zach offered his hand. "M.B., like Milton Bradley, the game company."

"Not exactly." M.B. was as solemn as only he could be, openly assessing Zach. "I don't play games."

Jen moved right along. "This is my other brother, Pluto Nazinsky." She paused, then felt obliged to explain Pluto's appearance. "He's a composer and musician."

"Great stage name," Zach said with an easy smile.

Pluto's smile was thin. "Except it's not a stage name."

Zach faltered for a beat. Jen felt badly for him. "My sister, Cin McKee," she said. "And her partner Ian Gallagher." Zach shook hands all around, like the good little private-school boy he had been.

Perfect. It was just too perfect.

So, why was she feeling so awful?

"Pleasure," Ian said grimly as he shook Zach's hand.

"Hi, Zach, I've heard so much about you. I just couldn't wait to meet you." Cin gushed as only she could gush. "You know, I just have to tell you that I love a wedding, maybe a spring wedding . . . ?"

Zach glanced to Jen with some alarm and she shrugged, as if

she had no idea what her sister was talking about. He nodded then, apparently remembering her comments about her crazy sister.

He looked about to say something outrageous and Jen was so afraid he'd tell everyone she was pregnant that she said the first thing that came to mind.

"Then maybe *you* should get married this spring," Jen said to her sister. Cin flushed and Ian snorted. "Zach, this my mother, Natalie Sommerset, and her friend, Gerry Smith."

"Nice to meet you," Zach said, shaking the hands of both of them and apparently not noticing their disapproval.

"And my grandmother, Mabel Sommerset."

The older woman stepped forward with purpose and shook Zach's hand. "Welcome, Zach. I'm very pleased to meet you and hope you have a good time today."

"Thank you. I'm certain that I will. I didn't know what to bring, so I thought some flowers might be nice." Zach offered a large bouquet of red and white flowers to Jen's grandmother, who smiled with pleasure. Natalie and Cin dug their elbows into Pluto's ribs, one from each side, as if he should take a lesson. He grimaced but said nothing.

"Aren't they lovely?" Gran enthused. "How thoughtful of you, Zach."

Before the moment could pass, Gerry stepped forward to finger a petal. "Oh, look," he said. "Would these be asiatic lilies and roses?"

Zach glanced at the bouquet. "I guess. I don't know much about flowers . . ."

"Lilies and roses!" Gerry exclaimed. "In Massachusetts in November." He turned a narrowed gaze on Zach. "They must have come from a hothouse."

Zach smiled, still apparently at ease. "Actually, they came from the Dash-In market around the corner from my apartment."

Gran snickered and Jen saw her life passing before her eyes. Cin was grinning, however, triumphant that her scheme was proceeding as if she'd scripted it.

"Here we go," M.B. muttered and rolled his eyes.

Zach had time to look puzzled. Jen had time to want to intervene, then to remember that she shouldn't.

"Then they're from Ecuador!" Gerry cried.

"I guess." Zach was clearly confused, a normal reaction for a normal person confronted with Gerry on a rampage.

Jen might have intervened, but Cin gave her a covert thumbs-up, reminding her that this was all part of the plan.

"I thought you were going to be nice," Natalie muttered, but Gerry couldn't leave this one alone.

Gerry raised his hands, the usual precursor to a lecture. "Do you know that Ecuador exports over twenty-six thousand tons of fresh flowers every year?"

This was Gerry's sole talent as far as Jen could see—the man could remember copious quantities of trivia and could stop any conversation dead in its tracks by dissecting the GNP of a country no one else had ever heard of.

Although, of course, she'd heard of Ecuador. The guy at the health-food store was going to walk through there on his way to Chile.

"No, I, uh, didn't know that." Zach looked at Jen, who fought her urge to help him out. She returned his glance benignly.

"Twenty-six thousand tons," Gerry intoned, "of the biggest, most vivid flowers. How do you think they do that?"

"Airplanes, I'd guess," Zach said.

Pluto snickered. "Good one, man."

Gerry wasn't having any of it. "I mean, how do they make them so big and vivid?"

Zach shrugged. "TLC?" Pluto chuckled again.

"No! Pesticides," Gerry hissed. "Lots of them."

"And virtual slave labor, it must be said," Natalie contributed, being drawn into one of her favorite arguments against western capitalism and its effects on the third world, and this despite her admonition to Gerry in the car.

Did Jen's family have to be so weird so quickly?

She reminded herself that this wasn't a serious date.

Mercifully.

Natalie took a deep breath. "The wages for the workers are outrageously low and they work long hours to earn them. Never mind the exposure to fungicides after the flowers are picked . . ."

"Here we go," M.B. muttered. "And we're not even out of the foyer. Come on, people, can we at least shut the door?"

Gerry raised a finger, ignoring M.B.'s voice of reason. "Pesticides and slave labor, all to fill jets with roses and lilies, to export them to the western democracies to please housewives and lovers . . ."

M.B. intervened with resolve. ". . . thereby poisoning the planet and diminishing ozone and creating greenhouse gases for the sake of a wasteful, nonsustainable lifestyle, and when exactly are we going to eat?" He delivered this soliloquy with his usual deadpan manner, then reached past Zach and flicked the door closed with his fingertips.

Zach looked briefly as if he wished he'd made a run for it while he could. Jen sympathized completely, although it was a bit disconcerting to find that they had something else in common.

"We'll eat soon," Gran promised, carrying the bouquet toward the kitchen with a flourish. "And thank you. I think they're pretty. Always liked red. Good choice. There's something to be said for a man who thinks to bring flowers." She cast Jen a proud smile and gave Gerry a dirty look en route.

"I don't suppose we'll catch you making that kind of a careless blunder again," Gerry said, so superior in manner that Jen despised him all over again.

Zach was undaunted. In fact, he straightened and looked Gerry in the eye. "Well, I don't know. My mother always said to bring a gift that pleases the hostess. If I'm lucky enough to be invited back, I'd have to consider red flowers, whether they're from Ecuador or not."

Natalie looked upon Jen's date with narrowed eyes, then turned away, apparently biting her tongue. Jen felt admiration for Zach, for standing up for his beliefs regardless of the regional response to it.

Come to think of it, wasn't that the kind of strength of character her mother always said she admired?

Zach watched Natalie, then glanced at Jen. Was he aware of his faux pas? Or didn't he care? Or were his manners just so good that his thoughts couldn't be read? Jen couldn't tell. He certainly didn't appear to be ruffled by rudeness.

That might stand him in good stead on this day.

He trailed after Gran and the others, after offering Jen his hand. "That turkey smells really good, Mrs. Sommerset."

"Does it?" Natalie murmured.

Gran beamed, Natalie glowered from the threshold to the living room. "I bought an organically raised one this year, and although the price was outrageous, I must say that I was very pleased with the bird itself . . ."

Gerry whispered to Natalie. "I'm sure we could find some more statistics on the Internet about flower production . . ."

Cin winked at Jen. "Good job," she whispered.

Jen followed, very aware of Zach's gentle touch on her elbow, unable to quickly sort out her mixed feelings. His hand was strong, warm, and he was comparatively sane. She felt an overwhelming urge to apologize to Zach for her family's rudeness.

But that wasn't how Cin's plan was supposed to work, was it?

Something weird was going on.

Zach could smell it. Having been raised in a family with its own brand of weird, in which nothing was ever expressed verbally, Zach had learned young to sense emotional undertow—and avoid it for his own well-being.

There was lots of emotional undertow here. More even than he was used to. The difference from his own family was that a lot of opinions were being expressed, but they weren't the real ones, any more than the oppressive silences in his own family revealed the actual issues.

On the upside, Jen looked great and he was glad to see her. He'd never seen her wearing anything other than the standard waitress uniform, but today she was wearing a coral pink dress. It was tailored like a shirtdress, again showing that contrast between a comparatively austere design and a soft fabric. No frills and rosebuds for Jen, just crisp pintucks in a feminine color.

She wore shoes that were almost flat, shoes that let him admire the perfection of her long legs. The young and scrumptious Audrey Hepburn had invited him for dinner. The color of the dress was perfect for Jen, made her look soft, and showed that her eyes were golden brown. Her lashes looked thicker and darker, and she might have been wearing a bit of lipstick. Her lips certainly looked soft and inviting.

This should have been a good thing, meeting her family and getting to know Jen herself better, but it wasn't working out quite that way.

Jen's family hated him. Zach was sure of it. Even worse, he didn't know why. Zach hadn't even done anything that would get him in trouble in his own family. He'd been careful and it was backfiring completely. Zach couldn't figure it out. It was as if he was the enemy simply because he existed.

Maybe they were protective of Jen, like Murray was. But they didn't know him, and they didn't seem to want to know him.

Well, he had to amend that as he glanced around the dinner table and took a tally. Not all of them hated him outright.

Jen's mother and Gerry had decided against him, apparently on the basis of the flowers alone. Who could have guessed that would be a bad move? Not Zach, whose mother practically chucked guests out the door who didn't bring either wine or flowers. Wine had seemed like the riskier option to Zach, which was funny if he thought about it.

Or it would be funny later.

Pluto wasn't far behind the older couple, although he covertly laughed at Zach's jokes. His eyes were cold though, unwelcoming, and that wasn't just due to their pale blue color. M.B. and Ian were still deciding about his merit, or else were too hard to read easily. Zach wasn't sure. Cin was a flake who could be thinking anything, independent of what she said. Zach wouldn't have trusted her as far as he could throw her and had a new appreciation for Jen's earlier comment about her sister being nuts. Jen's grandmother was Zach's sole supporter.

And Jen, he was pretty sure, had expected nothing different. He wasn't even sure that she was in his corner, given how she sat back and let events unroll as if none of this had anything to do with her.

Yet she hadn't warned him. She wasn't protecting him or even setting him up. It was really odd. She almost ignored him in her grandmother's house, even though he was supposed to be her date.

It made no sense.

It was Ian who explained to him the various unfamiliar appetizers. Zach tried everything, as he'd been taught to do, and swallowed even the ones he didn't like, as he'd been taught to do. He complimented the various contributors, finding something to admire in each concoction, just as he'd been taught to do.

This didn't get him any points, either.

Zach was relieved when the turkey was presented, though surprised at its relatively small size given how many of them were in attendance. There were cabbage rolls and roasted vegetables and something tofu in a roll to be sliced and three kinds of pilaf. The turkey, to Zach's relief, had the familiar trimmings of gravy and stuffing and mashed potatoes. No candied yams, which was okay by him.

It was only after he had taken some turkey that he realized that he and Jen and her grandmother were the only ones partaking of the traditional feast.

Jen's grandmother beamed at him and urged him to take a little more. "If you like, you can take some leftovers home," she offered. "There's always a lot left and I don't eat that much these days."

"Thank you, that's very generous of you."

"Well, I know that single men living on their own don't always eat a good dinner."

Jen looked suddenly as if she'd swallowed a lemon. Why was she scowling at him? Zach was mystified.

He was also confused as to how could there could be much potential for leftovers. "Doesn't anyone else take leftovers home?"

"We don't eat meat," M.B. said flatly.

"But it's turkey."

"Just the same. It was alive. We don't eat things that bleed when they're killed," Pluto said.

Zach looked down at his plate, uncertain how to proceed. The turkey did smell good. He couldn't remember the last time he'd had a homemade turkey dinner.

He smiled at his only ally and told her so.

Jen's grandmother sat three inches taller. Jen's mother watched Zach with pinched lips. Ian took a sliver of turkey out of some kind of camaraderie. Jen just ate, as if all of this was perfectly normal.

Or as if she'd been turned into a robot.

And as soon as plates were filled, the interrogation began.

Zach had expected to be asked a few questions, of course, but the comments over the flowers were nothing compared to what happened over the dinner table.

"So, Jen says you have a trust fund," Pluto said as an opener. "What's it like, having all the money you could ever need without having had to work for it?"

"Soul destroying, I'm sure," Gerry said. Natalie nudged him but his attention was too fixed on Zach for him to notice.

It wasn't too hard to guess what these two thought of it. Maybe that was the issue.

"Actually, I don't have a trust fund." Zach watched Jen look up.

"Then you have a job?" Gran asked, pert with the prospect.

"No, I don't."

"Between jobs, then?" Ian suggested, cautious but helpful.

"No." Zach looked down at his plate, then decided to just go with the truth. The mood couldn't get much worse. And maybe he'd startle them enough to shake their game.

Playing along certainly wasn't getting him anywhere. "I've never actually had a job," he confessed easily.

Jen sat straighter and blinked. "I thought you met your friends at law school."

"I did. The difference was that they finished and I dropped out." Zach had a feeling that his wasn't the right answer.

"Just like Jen," M.B. teased. "Unable to decide what she really wants to do, so she waits tables everywhere."

Jen looked down at her plate and said nothing in her own defense. Even M.B. looked a bit surprised by this.

"Going to college, then," Gran suggested with approval. "You can't go wrong with a solid education. You must have changed majors."

Zach took his time with a bite of stuffing and gravy. "No. After I dropped out of law school, I never went back. It just wasn't for me."

Gran's lips thinned and she stabbed her fork into her turkey with unnecessary force. "That seems to be quite the fashion," she said, flicking a glance at Jen.

"I'm starting to see what you two have in common," M.B. teased and Jen blushed.

Had Jen dropped out of university? Zach was intrigued even though Jen didn't look ready to confide any more information than that.

"Dropped out? Man, I can relate to that," Pluto said with a smile. "You've got to step out of the system to find yourself."

Zach could see that this would be like negotiating a diplomatic treaty: winning one person's approval would mean losing that of another. The truth was the only way to go, in that case.

"What are you doing now?" Natalie asked.

"Well, I was doing some photography."

M.B. leaned closer. "Where? What kind of photography?"

"I went to Venice and then around Europe a bit. I came back to Savannah and New Orleans," Zach smiled at the memory. "Shot some great stuff."

M.B. and Ian laughed. "It's easy to see how you two found so much in common," Ian said to Jen. She flicked a lethal look at Zach, but still didn't say anything.

"Jen has waited tables in twenty-eight countries," M.B. supplied with some pride.

Zach tried to not look shocked. That Jen had a wanderlust to match his own seemed to be something he should have known already. "That many?" he asked her.

Jen met his gaze, her expression sober. "Only sixteen, really, but who's counting?" She shrugged. "I couldn't decide on a major, so I bought a plane ticket instead of paying my tuition."

Zach stared at her in awe, trying to hide his response. No wonder he felt such a strong connection with her.

"And traveled far and wide," Natalie said with satisfaction. "I've always believed that backpacking around the world was the best way to both learn about the planet and to find oneself."

"Absolutely," Zach agreed.

"I doubt you travel student class," Gerry said to Zach.

"Actually, I walk a lot," Zach admitted. "I'm more likely to snag a good shot that way."

"And here I'd thought you were a Club Med kind of guy," Jen said.

"But instead, he's environmentally responsible," M.B. said with a nod. "Bonus." Jen didn't look very pleased with this bonus. "You know, Zach, I'd love to see some of your work. I teach high school art, which doesn't mean I'm an expert by any means, but photography has always been something I admire."

"It would be great to have another opinion," Zach said, surprised by how easily the words came.

"New Orleans is some place," Pluto said with approval. The mood was changing around the table, Zach could sense it. They were starting to side with him, and he was determined to win them over even if he couldn't understand it. Quitting law school and going to Europe to take pictures had, after all, almost gotten him disinherited from his family.

Strangely enough, Jen had done something similar but her family approved. That was a bit weird, but he thought he could navigate this meal with the information at hand. He stuck with a safe and popular subject.

"New Orleans is a great place, unique in America," he said with enthusiasm. "All that wrought iron and old architecture, misty mornings, great coffee. The history is incredible . . ."

"There was money there before the Civil War," Gran said. "From the cotton trade. It was the biggest city in the colonies."

"Due to slavery and the exploitation of people who had no choice," Gerry interjected.

"True," Zach agreed. "It's not a part of our history to be proud of. New Orleans itself, though, has this artistic mood, this joie de vivre that's very seductive."

"We should go there," Cin said, giving Ian a nudge. "You could use some joie de vivre."

"Not in hurricane season," he said grimly. "I'm not much for snow, but you can shovel it out of your way and it doesn't destroy your house."

"See what I mean?" Cin said in an undertone.

"You should go for Mardi Gras," Zach said, always ready to convert another potential traveler. Jen, he noticed, was watching him warily. "That's what I did and I ended up staying afterward. I just couldn't get enough of it. You know, I'd probably still be there if I hadn't gotten busted . . ."

This wasn't strictly true. Zach had come home because his father had died and he'd been executor, but in his haste to keep that truth from ruining a social occasion, he made a blunder.

He knew as soon as he'd said the word.

"Busted?" Gran echoed sharply.

They all stared at him in silence.

"You mean, as in *arrested*?" Pluto asked.

"Well, yes," Zach admitted.

Jen chewed vigorously but her expression was benign. Or controlled. Zach met her gaze and her eyes widened slightly. It was as if she was daring him to dig his way out of this.

And there was a hard light in her eyes, as if she disapproved more than anyone else.

Zach was suddenly aware that he'd made a tactical error.

"You were arrested in New Orleans, man?" Pluto asked with a laugh. "Is there anything illegal in that place?"

"Busted in the Big Easy," Gerry said with relish. "Now, there's a story."

To Zach's surprise, they were interested, and not particularly condemning. He glanced to Jen who had developed a fascination with her stuffing and gravy. She looked grim and he understood that he was on his own. "Well, it was different from being arrested here, that's for sure . . ." he acknowledged.

"You've been arrested more than once?" Natalie demanded.

"Well, several times over the years . . ." he said but got no further before Jen put down her cutlery with purpose.

"Excuse us, please?" she said, interrupting Zach's story.

She didn't give anyone a chance to argue, just seized Zach by the elbow and hauled him from the table. She was stronger than she looked and her eyes were flashing with fury. Jen pulled him into the kitchen and slammed the swing door behind them.

One look at her face and Zach knew he'd made a mistake so big that there might not be a way to fix it.

"What are you doing?" Jen demanded. She gestured in the direction of the dining room. "What was that? How is it that you forgot to mention to me that you were in jail? More than once?"

Zach tried to talk his way out of a corner. "Well, it's not exactly something that comes up in everyday conversation, you know . . ."

"Bull! You knew I was asking you here to meet my family. It wouldn't have taken a rocket scientist to guess that jailtime served might be an important detail to share beforehand. You could have at least shut up about it at the dinner table."

"Sorry, it kind of slipped out."

"I guess that can happen, when you routinely spend time in the slammer. It just crops up, like all the other routine details of your life . . ."

Zach snapped his fingers. "Wait a minute. The guys were giving me a hard time about it at Mulligan's on the day we met. You must have heard them."

"I thought they were just teasing you." Jen's expression didn't soften. "I thought they'd played a joke on you. I didn't think that you were a career felon."

"I'm not."

"You just get busted all the time?" She folded her arms across her chest. "There's a credential."

"Look, I'm sorry. I just got talking and forgot myself." Zach was not going to tell her the real reason he messed up. He was not going to think about his father, not now. "It'll blow over. This kind of stuff does . . ."

"Not in my family."

"We'll go back in there and the conversation will have moved on . . ."

"I don't think so." Jen pinched the bridge of her nose, looking suddenly a lot more like her grandmother. "I can't believe this is happening."

"I think it will be okay," Zach said, trying to console her. "I think I can talk my way through it. They seem to be pretty understanding about it all."

She gave him a cold look. "That's exactly what I'm worried about." It wasn't the first thing someone had said since his arrival here today that Zach hadn't understood, so he let it go. Jen was leaving anyway, her hand already on the swing door.

"Wait a minute," he said. "Let me ask you a couple of things so I don't mess up again."

She paused, her expression wary. "Things like what?"

"Is Gerry your father?"

Something that might have been a smile touched Jen's lips then was banished forevermore. "If ever I needed proof that there is a God and She loves me, the fact that Gerry is not my father would be it."

"Then where is your father?"

"I forget. Baja California or Alaska. Maybe Bali."

Zach couldn't believe that she was as indifferent as she appeared. "Don't you see him?"

"No. The last time was in 1987, I think."

"But . . ."

"It doesn't matter, Zach. He might technically be my father, but he's never done much beyond that initial burst of enthusiasm."

Zach could see that it really didn't matter to her, even though he had a hard time understanding that. "Then he's not the father of all of you?"

"No. And"—she held up a finger—"I'll anticipate your next question here. Gerry is not the father of any of us. He's a recent addition. In fact, we all have different fathers."

Zach decided to guess. "None of whom are present and accounted for?"

"Exactly." Jen leaned in the door frame. "That's why we have different surnames."

"And your mother . . ."

"Decided to stick with her maiden name after her second divorce."

"That sounds as if she had more than two."

"A third, from my father." There was a definite twinkle in Jen's eyes. "She liked to be married when she was pregnant, although she calls it a concession to paternalism."

Zach tried to fold his mind around this family history without turning his brain into origami and failed. At least he managed to keep his expression neutral. "One last question. Did I hear your brother's name right? It's Pluto?"

"That's right."

"And that was his given name? *Pluto?*" Zach asked. The corner of Jen's lips was tugging upward, although she was fighting the impulse to smile. "I'll guess not Pluto after the Disney character."

"Nope." Jen looked at the ceiling and put one hand on her hip. She was losing the battle against that smile, although Zach was enjoying the show. "If I remember correctly, it was a reference to an orgasmic sensation, a kind of celestial journey." She looked at him, her eyes dancing.

"Astral travel during orgasm," Zach said.

Jen nodded as the smile curved her mouth. She looked like a spoonful of mischief. There was nothing Mona Lisa about this smile. It threatened to break free at any moment.

Zach leaned against the wall, entranced by the view. He was going to shake that smile loose before he went back into the dining room. He wished he had brought his camera into the kitchen. He was ready to do anything to keep Jen smiling.

And he was wondering—again—how she kissed.

After all, it seemed that he had passed muster with her grandmother, if not with anyone else.

He moved closer and Jen didn't run. "You know, the really scary thing is that that makes sense."

Jen laughed, surprise dragging the sound out of her, and Zach was charmed. She looked ten years younger and her eyes were filled with starlight when she laughed. He immediately wanted to make her laugh again.

"Here's another one for you," she said, her tone playful. "M.B. is short for Moonbeam."

Zach was skeptical. "Moonbeam is your brother's actual name?"

"He prefers M.B. It keeps the other teachers from razzing him."

"I'll bet. Never mind the students." Zach pretended to be serious. "I'll guess that Moonbeam refers to another such orgasmic journey. At a lower orbit."

"Ah, no, it's a reference to the sensation of riding a moonbeam."

"I've never done that."

"Neither have I."

Zach grinned. "Maybe we should try it."

Jen caught her breath then turned to the door. "Maybe we should go back and eat our mashed root vegetables before they get cold."

Zach put a fingertip on her arm. He felt her shiver. "Maybe you could tell me how you and your sister ended up with normal names like Cynthia and Jennifer."

Jen flashed a smile again. Zach was mesmerized by the change that happiness made in her features. "What makes you think those are our names?"

"Well, Cin. What else could that be?" Zach felt his eyes widen. "Unless it starts with an *s*, like *sin*?"

"Guess again."

Zach shook his head, watching the stars in her eyes. "I'm fresh out."

"Cincinnati."

Zach groaned. "Not because she was conceived there?"

"Bingo. She always counted herself lucky that her name hadn't been Ford Pinto instead."

This time Zach laughed. "And Jen . . . ?"

"I use Jennifer, but it's not my legal name."

"What is?"

"The old version." When he shook his head, she continued. "Guinevere."

Zach leaned against the wall to consider Jen. He still had a hand on her arm and he let his fingers slide over her skin. She smelled sweet and feminine, like a scented soap, not perfume. He watched the curve of her lips and had a hard time thinking about anything other than kissing her. "So you're named Guinevere because your father was Cin's father's best friend?"

"You're good at this." Jen tapped a fingertip on his chest and Zach caught her hand in his. To his surprise, she didn't immediately pull away. "It could have been worse: I could have been born a boy."

Zach let his admiration of her gender show. "That would have been worse."

Jen blushed. "I mean my name would have been worse."

"Lancelot?" Zach tried not to wince.

"No. Their child was Galahad."

At that, Zach did wince. Jen chuckled again. She stopped when he let his thumb slide across her palm and tried to pull away, but he held fast and she gave it up after a minute.

"And your mother has no idea that this is maybe a bit too much information?" He bent and put a kiss into the palm of her hand. Her eyes widened and she trembled a little bit. Her lips parted just a little, as if in invitation. Zach eased closer.

"There's no such thing as too much information in my mother's world," Jen said, her words breathless.

Zach couldn't resist. He bent and kissed her. Just a gentle kiss, but it was one that made his pulse go crazy all the same.

Jen froze for a moment, her lips firm beneath his. Then she relaxed, letting him ease into a primo kiss. Zach was ready to slide his arms around her waist and pull her closer, when she abruptly ducked away.

"What would Roxanne think of that?" she demanded and headed back into the dining room without waiting for an answer.

Zach was mystified as to why his dog's opinion would matter.

But then, Jen was a thousand mysteries rolled into one. And he was feeling very inclined to solve more than a few of them. She traveled. She defied expectation.

She'd smiled for him.

She'd laughed at his joke.

There was a bounce in her step.

He was winning, and that was enough to send him back into the fray.

Chapter 7

Jen was sizzling. She'd been out of the dating game too long, that was for sure, if one quick kiss that wasn't supposed to mean anything left her as hot and bothered as this. She knew she was blushing, knew her family were taking far too much notice of her response, and wished that this day would end immediately.

If not sooner.

Zach sauntered back into the room, the image of masculine confidence. Jen had the urge to chuck the gravy boat at him.

That only got worse when he smiled at her.

He smiled the way a wolf might smile at the chicken that it meant to eat for lunch. She licked her lips—big mistake—and tasted him. He watched her, his eyes bright and his expression knowing, and Jen knew she that her cheeks were scarlet.

So much for keeping her cool.

Roxanne, she reminded herself.

Natalie swatted Zach on the arm when he sat down. "No fair

ducking into the kitchen to neck, especially when your story is just getting good," she chided.

Zach looked startled by this accusation.

"We *weren't* necking," Jen argued but no one was persuaded.

"Right," Pluto said.

"I don't much care what you were doing." Natalie winked at Zach, who seemed surprised to be suddenly finding favor with Jen's mother. "All that's important to me is that you were doing something that made my daughter laugh for the first time in years. You keep doing that, whatever it is, but finish your story before you do it again. Why were you in jail in New Orleans?"

Zach tried not to fidget, even as all eyes turned upon him. "Oh, we don't need to talk about that today," he said, glancing in Jen's direction. She ignored him. He used an evasive device that she was coming to realize was his usual one. "Hey, you probably don't know that I collect lawyer jokes. Here's one: why don't sharks ever attack lawyers?"

"Professional courtesy," M.B. said dismissively. "Tell us about jail in New Orleans."

"Why don't hyenas eat lawyers?" Zach said, looking a little bit less confident of his joke's reception. Jen decided to let him deal with whatever her family dished out all by himself.

Even though she felt a teeny bit badly for him. After all, his kissing her and getting her all zingy hadn't been part of the plan.

"Even hyenas have their dignity," Gerry said. "You need newer jokes."

"A doctor told a patient that she had six months to live," Zach began, apparently not noticing the deadly calm that settled around the table. "'Isn't there anything I can do?' the patient asked. 'Marry a lawyer,' the doctor said. 'It'll be the longest six months of your life.'" Zach looked around, clearly expecting a chuckle, and found everyone serious. He glanced to Jen in confusion and she shook her head minutely, unable to stop herself.

He didn't seem to know what to do.

"I don't care about lawyer jokes," Gran said. "If you have a criminal past, I demand to know about it."

There was silence in the dining room. Zach was clearly considering about the best way to proceed. Jen reminded herself that in her scheme of things—in Cin's scheme of things—there really weren't any right answers.

Her family was supposed to hate him. That was the point.

Zach looked almost as uncomfortable as she felt. "Well, uh, it was a possession charge."

"Possession of what?" Gran demanded, jabbing her fingertip into the table to make her point. "Because it's the right of every citizen to bear arms and don't let them tell you any different . . ."

Jen almost groaned at the introduction of a familiar theme—and an equally familiar argument.

"Do not tell us that you're a member of the NRA . . ." Natalie began with outrage, mother and daughter squaring off as they had so many times before. M.B. raised his hands to referee, but against all expectations, there was one right answer and Zach found it.

"Actually, it was possession of marijuana," he admitted.

"Mary Jane!" Natalie and Gerry cried jubilantly together.

Jen groaned and rolled her eyes, simultaneous to her sister.

Zach felt the tide turn in his favor, but he couldn't explain it. His own family, after all, had been livid with him since that incident—and Jen's family took it as evidence that he was okay? He looked around the table, skeptical of his read of the situation.

"Marijuana is the most underrated palliative-care herb known to mankind," Natalie said, her manner triumphant. "You were fighting the good fight, fighting for legalization of a substance that has been demonized by the government . . ."

"Wait a minute," Zach said, incredulous. "You're happy that I was busted for possession of pot?"

Natalie nodded. Gerry leaned an elbow upon the table and

began to expound. "It's outrageous that the government has legalized both alcohol and tobacco, yet continues to enforce punitive fines for the much less hazardous substance known as marijuana. This is, of course, a result of the ridiculous profits they make on sin taxes . . ."

Zach blinked but they didn't stop. He'd been raised with a diametrically opposed philosophy, one that accounted marijuana to be the root of all evil in civilization. He looked around the room again, hoping to find some clue that the universe hadn't changed that much.

He found it in the censure in Jen's grandmother's expression. That was familiar. That was what he got at home.

"I hope you've left that nonsense behind you," she said, adjusting the master butter spreader on the butter dish for emphasis.

"Yes, Mrs. Sommerset, I have," Zach said, and it was true. "Since New Orleans, I've had nothing to do with it."

She glared at him. "And when was that?"

"A year ago."

"Really?"

"Really."

Jen's grandmother studied him for a moment. Zach knew she wouldn't find any evidence he was lying because he wasn't. He let her look until she settled back, satisfied. "Well, I suppose one must give people the chance to reform themselves. And there's no one more likely to keep you on the straight and narrow path than my Jen."

Zach inclined his head in agreement, noting how Jen evaded his glance.

"But we need to rise up and challenge the status quo," Gerry said. "It's people like you who fight the good fight by challenging the government, putting themselves at risk to ensure access for all to this wonderful helpmate of a plant. You have to head back into the battle . . ."

Zach had to interrupt him. "Actually, there was nothing heroic

about it. I had some stash. I was going to sell it and make a profit.
People were buying and I planned to make some money. It was capitalism, plain and simple."

"You're so modest!" Gerry said. As Gerry settled in to what
was clearly a familiar rant, Zach watched Jen and Cin exchange a
glance. The two sisters left the table, abandoning Zach to the battle lines being drawn between the tofu and the giblet gravy.

Pluto gave Zach a thumbs-up. "You are so in," he murmured,
only loud enough for Zach to hear. "Good on you, man."

But the look on Jen's face when she glanced back from the
threshold of the kitchen told Zach that being in with her mother
had come at the expense of being out with Jen.

This was the worst possible scenario, Jen was sure of it.

"It had to be pot, didn't it?" Cin demanded. She paced the
kitchen, ranting. "You had to find the one upper crust guy in
Greater Boston who's a convicted pothead."

"There's probably more than one," Jen felt obliged to note.

"The one who admits it, then! The one who brings it up in casual conversation." Cin flung out a hand. "I don't want to go back
in there. I don't want to see the lovefest while it goes down. You're
going to have to peel them off him to leave this place, you know,
and it's not going to be pretty. Even Gran is ready to forgive him.
And that's not the end of it. It's going to be 'When's Zach coming
over?' all the time. He's going to be moving into the spare room before you know it and there won't be a thing you can do to stop it.
Shit, you *will* be getting married in the spring, although I suppose
that will save you from dating the guy with the soul patch."

"Thanks for the vote of confidence."

"It's the truth. Mom loves him. And it's all your own fault."

The only thing Jen knew for sure was that she should never
have agreed to Cin's plan. Jen was a jumble of conflicting emo-
tions, just as she'd been from the beginning, but they kept getting

stronger. She could taste Zach's kiss still—and knew she'd liked it too much.

She was too lonely, that was it.

That made perfect sense except that his desperate look, the one he got when his considerable charm wasn't working, made her want to help him out. It would be like throwing a line to a drowning man . . .

But she wasn't supposed to like him. At all.

She was supposed to be glad to let him drown.

She wasn't supposed to be wondering what kind of photographs he took.

"Wait a minute! This isn't all my fault," she argued. "It was your idea. You got me into this . . ."

"No. No." Cin—characteristically—waved off her responsibility. "My idea was that you would find an outwardly charming but completely uptight rich guy for a fake date. Key to this strategy was that he would be like Steve, meaning that Mom would hate his guts. You didn't follow my plan. You made up some variation, and having strayed from the brilliance of the original scheme, you've created your own mess." Cin held up her hands. "Not my problem anymore." She pivoted, then paused to glance back. "But hey, if it doesn't work out, give him my number. I still think he's cute."

She shoved open the door to the dining room while Jen tapped her fingers on the counter. What a mess. What was she going to do? Moving to Zimbabwe sounded like a good choice. Even walking to Chile had its appeal. Jen heard a little squeak as Cin was surprised, then froze as she guessed what had surprised her sister.

"Thanks, but I don't need your number," Zach said smoothly. "I might be a crazy optimist, but I think things are going to work out just fine."

Jen heard her heart hit the basement floor far, far below her. Then she wondered just how much he'd overheard.

She looked and was afraid.

Zach was cocky. He braced a hand in the door frame and watched her, his stance confident, his smile brilliant. He was doing that radiant sunbeam thing again.

This was not going to be pretty.

He winked at Cin. "Even if Jen has strayed from the brilliance of the original scheme." Then he grinned, a smile that had trouble written all over it. "Or maybe because of it."

Oh no.

He strolled into the kitchen, letting the door swing closed behind him and came to stand beside her at the sink. Cin, predictably, abandoned Jen.

Jen was left alone with Zach and devoid of good answers.

The guy had been to jail and hadn't told her. He had been charged with possession of marijuana and hadn't told her. He had to hurry back to Roxanne all the damn time, which meant he was seeing more than one woman at once. Yet she felt guilty for using him, even though she'd done a crummy job of it.

She was some kind of wimp.

Jen couldn't even look at him. She was too busy praying that he hadn't heard everything.

"I only have one question," Zach said as he leaned against the counter beside her. "Who's Steve?"

Oh no.

Z**ach was ecstatic.**

Where confusion had reigned, now everything all made sense. He'd heard enough of the sisters' conversation to recognize a nefarious scheme, one he'd have been proud to have devised himself. Jen was embarrassed, as befit someone caught with her hand in the proverbial cookie jar.

Zach had always been one for following his instincts and it was now obvious to him why he'd been so attracted to Jen in the first place. They were two of a kind. Or at least they understood each other.

And that was a very good thing.

"I don't want to talk about Steve," she said, looking as uncomfortable as he'd ever seen her.

That was saying something.

"Okay, so let's talk about the Plan," he suggested. He wanted only to be encouraging, but Jen gave him a suspicious look. "What was the goal here, beyond having a date for turkey day?"

Her lips set. "It was Cin's idea."

"I picked that up already."

She watched him for a minute. "Aren't you insulted? Or hurt?"

Zach pretended to consider this, then shook his head. "No. We haven't known each other nearly long enough for me to be emotionally devastated by your decision to use me. That's why I was a perfect choice." He nodded approval. "Brilliant on your part to use a stranger."

"I wasn't using you, not exactly . . ."

"What then?"

She blushed. "Okay, maybe it was a bit manipulative."

"A bit? Take credit where it's due. This was a masterful piece of manipulation and, incidentally, typical of something I once would have done."

"Maybe you and Cin were twins tragically separated at birth."

"Ah no, I've gotten over that phase, but still I admire the impulse." He grimaced as she watched him. "Even if you lost a bit of power on the follow-through. We could work on that."

That suspicious glint got a bit brighter in her eye. "What are you saying?"

"That I can help you refine your game, if that's the way you want to go. A little finesse here and there, and you'll be giving Cin a run for her money in no time."

Jen folded her arms across her chest. She looked somewhat skeptical, it must be said, of the inviolable wisdom of Zach's conclusions. "You're going to criticize my technique?"

"Maybe just offer a few helpful pointers. Think of the things I could teach you."

"All things I don't want to know. I don't want to be better at be-ing manipulative . . ."

She was so indignant that Zach couldn't resist teasing her. "We could make a heck of a team, you know, with my experience and your smooth delivery."

Jen was unimpressed. "I can't believe you! You're not even in-sulted. You wish I'd done a better job of deceiving you and you're going to teach me how to do it! Doesn't it bother you, not even a little bit, that I tried to use you?"

"No." Zach shook his head. "Because I can understand why you did it." He leaned closer and liked how her eyes widened at his prox-imity. Maybe he should steal another kiss. "Because, let's face it, we both know that the very fact that you picked *me* isn't insignificant."

Jen turned away. "You don't know that. It was a random choice."

"You're a lousy liar," he said, his tone teasing. She looked dag-gers at him. "And I'm not going to teach you how to do better at that because I think it's cute."

"Cute!" Jen got three inches taller. "I am *not* cute! Cute is for puppies and kittens and small things that aren't threatening."

"You *are* cute." Zach closed the step between them and lifted her chin with his fingertip. "You're cute, you're funny, you're gor-geous when you smile, you have a stunner of a voice, and you kiss like a goddess."

"Liar," she had time to say before he kissed her again. This time, she didn't let the kiss get far enough to be interesting. She planted her hands on Zach's chest and pushed him away. "You have to stop doing that."

"Because it might upset my dog?" Zach was already learning that the best was to make Jen laugh was to surprise her.

"Roxanne is a dog?" Jen blinked, then smiled tentatively when he nodded. "Really?"

The smile didn't last long enough to suit Zach, but he knew now that it could be induced.

By him.

Repeatedly.

"Really." That was all the encouragement he needed. "A large dog, who is fond of me, but probably just because I feed her." He pretended to be pensive. "I don't think she's a possessive type, to be honest."

Jen watched him, her expression unreadable. There was a gleam of . . . something in her eye. "You couldn't be honest to save your life."

"I'm trying to save a date here. Isn't that a worthy cause?"

"It's not a date. Not a real date, anyway." Jen heaved a sigh. "I'm sorry. If you want to leave, I'll make up something."

Zach snorted. "As if anyone would believe you. I'm not leaving until the party's over."

She looked at him, her eyes bright.

"Just tell me what the Plan was," he invited. "Professional courtesy and all that."

Jen averted her gaze. "That they'd hate you, that's all."

"The way they hated Steve," Zach guessed.

Jen nodded. "So, my mother wouldn't start fixing me up."

Zach chuckled. "If Gerry's any indication, her taste in men is a bit frightening."

Jen began to smile, then stopped abruptly as if she would rather have not done so. "Got it in one."

"So what was Steve like?"

It took her a while to answer, one big clue that Steve had been important to her. Maybe he still was. Not that Zach cared about serious emotional commitment. Jen was welcome to pine after another guy while she had fun with Zach. "Successful, ambitious, conservative." She paused, then nodded as she added another attribute. "Carnivorous."

It sounded as if she should have picked Jason to have her plan come together with success, but Zach didn't tell her that. If nothing else, he was going to develop an affection for vegetables in the short term. "And once they hated me?"

"I could just threaten to bring you to family events. They'd insist I didn't."

"Ah, and meanwhile, we wouldn't even be seeing each other. You'd be dating the Fictional Man—"

"Not entirely fictional. They'd have met you."

"—and never have to deal with your mom's choices."

Jen wrinkled her nose. "Sorry."

"Don't apologize. I wish I'd thought of it myself."

"I didn't actually . . ."

"Lesson one, Jen: take credit where it's due."

"But . . ."

"Look, I can still get you off the dating hook. After all, I'm already here."

She regarded him with suspicion. "Why would you do that?"

"Why not?" Zach felt as if he was back in his rhythm again, following his impulse and seeing where it led. He could smell that this was going to be fun. He offered Jen his hand. "So, come on back in the dining room. I'll tell them jail stories and lawyer jokes and take some pictures and it won't be so bad. We'll get through it and ensure along the way that you don't have to be fixed up with anybody. You'll see."

Jen folded her arms across her chest and stood back from him. "Why are you making this easy for me?"

Zach grinned. "I told you already: you're cute and you're . . ."

Jen held up a hand, stopping him before he really got rolling. "No, no. I want to know the real reason. I want to know what's in it for you. I want to know what you want in exchange for giving me what I want."

Zach leaned close to whisper, watching her awareness of him. When he did score that kiss, it was going to be a good one. "Because if I play along, then you owe me," he whispered with satisfaction.

"Owe you what?"

"We'll have to negotiate that." He watched the fear light Jen's eyes, then headed back toward the dining room, certain she'd be right behind him.

He was right.

Jen felt as if she were six years old again, hoodwinked for the zillionth time by her older sister and unable to do anything to save herself. *It's not fair*, she wanted to shout, which was ridiculous. She'd gotten herself into this mess and she'd get herself out of it.

She had to have learned something from a lifetime of surviving Cin's tricks. Right. The most important thing to do was to take the initiative.

And ideally, to turn the tables.

She could do that.

She caught Zach's elbow in her hand and pulled him to a stop on the threshold of the dining room. He looked down at her and she wondered whether it was possible for any man to look as if he was having a better time than Zach did right now. His eyes sparkled and his lips curved, which also made her wonder if anyone could kiss better than Zach.

Maybe she'd just been out of the lap pool for too long.

Jen frowned and shook her head. There was nothing saying that she had to let Zach charm her into anything.

And there was nothing saying that she had to let him kiss her again.

Even if it didn't seem like that bad of an idea in this particular moment.

"There's no deal unless my mother hates you," she whispered, smiling sweetly up at him as if they were exchanging lover's secrets.

She saw his consternation and realized that Zach liked to be liked. "But . . ."

"Otherwise, I owe you nothing," she said. She stretched up to give him a chaste kiss, punctuating it with an endearment intended to make him wince. "Honey."

Zach flinched. Jen headed back to her place at the table, well aware of Cin's curiosity. Her sister looked between the two of them, obviously regretting her early departure from the kitchen.

She gave her sister her best "too bad" look.

Zach sat down, seemed to collect his thoughts, then had another serving of turkey. "You must use the liver in the gravy," he said to Jen's grandmother. "That's my favorite."

It was a brilliant comment. Gran beamed while Natalie glowered. Jen's siblings turned various hues of hostile and Gerry puffed up with indignation.

"It's in the stock," Gran confided. "I use all of the giblets to make the stock for the gravy, just the way my mother did, and you know, once the stock is done, I sauté the kidneys and liver in onions and butter. It makes a nice meal."

"I'll bet it's very tasty," Zach agreed.

"Must we review this senseless carnage at the table?" Gerry asked.

Gran smiled. "At my table, yes. And it's not senseless, Gerry, it's tradition. Natalie grew up tall enough and healthy enough, eating meat."

"My children grew up tall and healthy without it," Natalie countered.

"And Jen?" Zach asked, glancing to her.

"I eat chicken and fish," she admitted.

"She has an excuse," Natalie said with obvious regret and silence reigned again. To Jen's relief, nothing more was said about that.

Zach looked between the three of them, not as at ease with the conflict he'd awakened as Jen might have expected. "It's all delicious," he said, taking another cabbage roll as well.

He glanced Jen's way and she mouthed the word *chicken*. Zach glanced down at his plate, his eyes sparkling as he lifted the meat with his fork and shook his head minutely. *Turkey* he mouthed back at her and Jen nearly had an untimely attack of the giggles.

She shouldn't be finding him funny. Not at all. He was useful in only one way—and that wasn't supposed to be entertaining.

"No winning this one, man," Pluto said, settling back to chew and watch the show.

Jen wondered what Zach would want as recompense for playing along. Maybe he had the same kind of issues with his family and she could reciprocate. That would be the obvious quid pro quo. Even if, according to Cin's plan, Jen shouldn't want to know more about Zach.

But she did.

She wondered, actually, what kind of family he had. He'd mentioned brothers, as well as his dead father and his mom, who was presumably still alive. Did he have nieces and nephews? Did he make them laugh, too? She'd bet he was their favorite uncle, always ready for a game of whatever.

She wanted to know what kind of a dog Roxanne was, and if he treated her well, and if she really did adore him. She wanted to see the photographs he'd taken, because his whole face had lit up when he'd talked about them. She wanted to go to the places he'd been and see for herself why they were so fascinating. She wanted to take him to places she'd been and see whether he liked them as well as she did.

She wanted to make him stop telling lawyer jokes, but that seemed unlikely.

She wanted to make him laugh.

She wanted to surprise him, but he got to her first.

Zach glanced around the table brightly, which Jen would later realize was a clue that he meant to say something outrageous. "Maybe you're right, Cin, maybe a spring wedding would be just the thing." Jen choked on her mashed root vegetables and Zach winked at her. "What do you think, *honey*? Why should we wait?"

"Married? You've only just started dating," Natalie protested.

"Oh no," Zach said with such confidence that no one would doubt the truth of what he said. "We've been seeing each other for months now. Right, honey?"

Jen nodded, because she didn't trust herself to say anything.

Zach's eyes were dancing and she tried to match his enjoyment of the moment. Cin was astonished, which was kind of fun.

"I had no idea you were so serious." Natalie gave Jen a sharp glance.

Jen shrugged, doing her best to play along. "I wanted to be sure before you met. Not get your hopes up."

"Never hurts to take time to get to know each other," Gran said with approval. "Where's your ring?"

"We're still looking for the biggest diamond in Boston," Zach said, shaking his head with mock disappointment. "Because the size of the stone shows everybody the size of our love, don't you think?" Gerry nearly choked on his tofu at that. "The bigger the better is my thinking, given how I feel about Jen. But I think we might have to fly down to New York for lunch and shop at Tiffany. We're just not finding anything spectacular enough, here in town."

"Fly? For lunch?" Gerry sputtered, seeking the words to express his outrage over such wasteful consumption.

"Well, I'd rent a corporate jet. Just a little one."

Gerry was at a complete loss for words. Natalie fumed.

"How romantic!" Cin said.

"Don't be holding your breath," Ian muttered to her.

"After all, you've already got the green plastic Batman ring from the cereal box," Pluto teased Cin.

"That was a joke!" Ian protested, his neck coloring.

"You'll never live it down, my love," Cin said.

"Only because you had to tell them about it." Ian was disgruntled as he rarely was.

Cin ignored him, her gaze fixed upon Zach. Ian ate with stoic determination and couldn't possibly be tasting his food.

Looked like trouble in paradise. Jen wasn't going to get involved.

Meanwhile Jen's mother opined about marriage being an outdated institution and her grandmother argued forcibly in favor of tradition and dissent ruled the table again.

"Early spring or late?" Cin demanded, interrupting a familiar argument. "Lilacs or roses?"

"Depends when we can book the church," Jen said, raising the stakes a notch. "Have you phoned yet, honey?"

Zach snapped his fingers. "You're right, honey. I forgot again. When we go to church Sunday with my mom, we can maybe ask the minister. I'm sure he'll arrange it."

"Getting married in church?!" Natalie and Gran exclaimed simultaneously, although their reactions were opposite.

"You're going to church?" Natalie demanded. "I thought you were working Sunday brunches."

Jen nodded weakly, resolving that she'd reciprocate in kind at Zach's family dinner. They'd be living together like hippie flower children and *never* getting married, smoking dope every night and having love-ins on alternate Saturdays.

"I shall have to get a new hat," Gran said with satisfaction. "A church wedding. What a delight that will be! I never thought I'd see the day that one of my grandchildren would be married in a church."

"There's nothing wrong with city hall," Natalie said, her teeth gritted. "Marriage is a secular bond and religious institutions have no right to . . ."

"Oh, we have to get married in church," Zach said, picking up his cue with perfect ease. "Don't we, honey?"

Jen nodded. "His mother wouldn't hear of anything else."

"Maybe you know the big Episcopalian church in Rosemount?" Zach asked. "That's where it will be."

"Lovely!" Gran enthused.

"Wait a minute," M.B. interjected, his manner thoughtful. "Didn't Jen say your surname was Coxwell? Are you one of those Coxwells?"

"Which Coxwells?" Gran asked.

"That's us," Zach admitted, his manner less easy than it had been. "You must have read about my brothers in the paper last year."

"Yeah," M.B. said, leaning back in his chair. "I did. Your family is really old Massachusetts."

"I guess we are," Zach said. "Arrived on the *Mayflower* and all that, but you know, timing isn't everything." Jen watched him try to divert the conversation but she couldn't figure out why. "Anyone know the difference between a lawyer and a trampoline?"

"I didn't read about his family," Natalie said. "Or if I did, I don't remember."

M.B. wagged a finger at Zach. "Judge Robert Coxwell would have been related to you, then."

"He was my father," Zach said, with a dark glance at M.B. "Now, the difference between a lawyer and a trampoline . . . ?"

"Judge Robert Coxwell?" Natalie and Gerry straightened and inhaled in unison.

"He wanted to overturn Roe versus Wade," Natalie fumed.

Gerry nodded vigorously. "And his agenda for the Supreme Court would have set us back a hundred years . . ."

"He's dead," Zach interrupted more sharply than Jen had ever heard him say anything. He was serious, and she'd never seen him that way, either. He pushed aside his plate, then grimly delivered his punch line. "The difference is that you take off your shoes to jump on a trampoline."

No one laughed.

Jen didn't know what to say. Zach appeared to be quite upset. Or was he just putting it on?

"That's very sad that your father passed away, but still, his ideology . . ." Natalie began, but M.B. shook his head.

"Leave it, Mom."

"I don't think so, M.B. This is important. If Jen is going to marry into this family, we need to understand—"

"The judge committed suicide, Mom," M.B. interrupted flatly. "Maybe talking about that isn't very festive for Zach."

Natalie flushed and sat back in her chair.

"Thank you," Zach said quietly to M.B.

"No problem. It's a day for gratitude, not for mourning or grudges."

Zach nodded and toyed with his wineglass, apparently out of conversation for the moment. Jen met M.B.'s gaze and smiled at him. *Thanks*, she mouthed and he nodded once. M.B. was the one who made bridges in this family of divergent views and she was glad he had done it again.

She knew one way to make Zach smile again. "Maybe we shouldn't wait until the spring, honey," she said, her tone playful. "What about Valentine's Day?"

"A manufactured holiday," Gerry intoned. "Based upon nothing but generating the sales of greeting cards and imported flowers."

"You don't need time to arrange a simple wedding," Natalie chided. "And besides, there's no rush. Shouldn't you get to know each other better?"

"A simple wedding?" Jen asked, well aware of how Zach's eyes were widening. "Oh no, Zach's mother has already made it clear that we'll have to have at least five hundred guests. She was saying, actually, that she didn't know how she'd keep the list that small."

Gerry took a deep breath. "Big wedding ceremonies are a waste of money and prey upon the insecurities . . ."

"And they require flowers, Gerry, lots of beautiful flowers," Jen said. "You've given me an idea with this pretty bouquet, honey. I think we'll have asiatic lilies and roses. Do you think they'll be available in February?"

"I'm sure they can be flown in from somewhere," Zach assured her. "Cost is no object, if that's what you want, honey." Jen was ridiculously glad that he had rejoined the discussion.

Natalie hissed again.

"Red and white is lovely, especially for Valentine's Day," Gran enthused.

"And pink rose petals scattered down the aisle," Cin added with glee.

"Buckets and buckets of them," Jen agreed.

"Maybe we'll need our own jumbo jet to come from Ecuador," Zach said with a smile. Jen smiled back at him as controversy stormed over the table once again.

Zach had the definite feeling that the Sommerset clan liked to argue. Maybe it gave them something to talk about.

In a way, he enjoyed the repartee over the dining table himself, except for the bit about his father. Even with the dissent, this was far better than the brooding silences fraught with meaning and embellished with small talk that had characterized his own family functions.

He realized that he preferred having differences of opinion out in the open. They seemed less potent that way, than resentments left locked in the dark to breed. When no one talked about issues—as was the case in his family—the smallest things ended up casting long shadows.

If nothing else, it kept him on his toes. He tried to ensure that he picked up every hint from Natalie to put himself in her bad books, although it wasn't easy for him.

He became aware that his efforts were undermined every time Jen cracked a smile. Her mother obviously was pleased by this and was prepared to put her own opinions aside for the sake of her daughter's happiness. He tried harder, but Natalie proved more and more difficult to visibly displease as Jen looked more and more radiant.

In a way, Zach had to respect that. He could understand Natalie's desire to see Jen happy and smiling. It was noble. It was what parents were supposed to do.

In another way, he wanted to deliver his side of the bargain. He kept trying. By the end of the meal, he'd shot a roll of film, eaten too much dinner, come to like Jen's grandmother and to respect her older brother M.B., developed a new appreciation of cabbage rolls, and eaten tofu for the first time in his life.

Yet he still couldn't wrap his mind around the fact that the height of his maternal approval rating had been when he'd confessed to being arrested for marijuana possession.

Too bad he couldn't have introduced Natalie to his father. That would have made for some fireworks. The two would have disagreed on every single point of discussion. Interestingly, Zach knew that his father would have walked away from the discussion, as would have Gerry. Natalie, he suspected, would have tried to find some common ground.

The whole family worked together to clean up Gran's kitchen, the older lady looking a bit tired by the end of the meal. The brothers teased each other, snapping tea towels at each other like kids, as Cin started the washing and Ian loaded the dishwasher.

Gerry informed them of the evils of labor-saving devices and the impending doom of higher energy prices, but they all ignored him. Natalie sat with her mother, drinking a brandy as she watched Zach. It was convivial in a way that was unfamiliar to Zach, but he was glad to pitch in.

The Sommersets seemed to accept each other as they were, even if they made a lot of commentary about each other's choices. No one seemed intent on changing anyone else, which was a radical concept for Zach. Zach's father had always been hot to improve all of his children. Here there were lots of answers and they all got air time, but no one expected universal agreement—much less, adherence to an edict.

Even as Zach dried plates, he felt as if they'd known him for years. Or at least as if they'd let him wash dishes for years. Pluto snapped a wet towel at him. Cin bossed him around. M.B. talked to him about photography. Jen shook her head at her siblings and showed him where things went. Her grandmother smiled approval at him.

It was homey. And unfamiliar.

And *nice*. Zach struggled against an attack of the warm fuzzies. Usually he was immune, and in his family, there was little chance of having to defend himself against them. Pluto went to get his guitar, Jen went to the washroom, Cin and Ian headed into the living room to argue, followed by Natalie and Gerry.

Jen's grandmother came to Zach, took the wet tea towel from his hands and hung it up. She reached up, to Zach's astonishment, and kissed his cheek. "Thank you, dear. I shouldn't have let you help, but I do appreciate it."

"It's good to get the kitchen clean," Zach said, surprised by how touched he was by her gratitude. "They're just dishes."

"You like things clean, then?"

Zach nodded. "Kitchens and baths. I focus on key areas of biological invasion."

She chuckled, then dropped her voice. "My granddaughter is a very special girl," she said firmly, the glint in her eyes telling Zach that this wasn't the sum of what she wanted to say.

"She is," he agreed and he wasn't putting anything on.

"You be good to her and we'll have no quibbles, no matter what you've done in the past. Understand?"

"I understand."

"Then you can call me Gran, too."

Zach grinned, relieved that the approval of Jen's grandmother was his. "Fair enough."

Now he could ask Jen out for a date, and that wasn't all bad.

There sure was a lot of protectiveness going around. Zach didn't have a chance to say anything more before Jen returned. She came to his side and put her hand through his elbow as if they touched all the time.

Did she feel that little sizzle that he felt?

Was she thinking about that kiss, the one they'd had in this very kitchen only a few hours before, their first kiss? He sure was.

And he wanted another.

"We should go," she said brightly. "Don't we still need to drop in at your brother's place, honey?"

Zach was sure he hadn't told her about James and Maralys, much less Maralys's plans for Thanksgiving. On the other hand, she knew he had brothers plural and only one sister. Jen was guessing but she was good at it, and she left him room to correct her, if necessary.

Zach smiled, liking how smart she was. "Yes, Maralys wanted to meet you," he agreed. "She's going to love this dress. Although I should pick up Roxanne first."

"Roxanne?" Cin asked, her eyes wide. She was lurking in the doorway to the dining room, probably eavesdropping on everything.

"His dog," Jen supplied, as easily as if she'd known all along.

"Oh. Dogs are nice."

"This one is very nice," Jen said firmly, as if she knew anything about it, then led Zach to the door before anyone could ask any more questions. "Let's go, honey."

She really had to stop using that endearment.

And Zach had a couple of ideas of how to persuade her to his point of view.

Chapter 8

It was time to dump Zach.

The sooner, the better.

As far as Jen was concerned, Cin's scheme had come to its conclusion. Her mother had enough doubts about Zach that Jen could have considered the plan some kind of a success. The problem was that now there was supposed to be a wedding in February.

Enough was enough. The sooner she and Zach had a fatal fight, the better.

The sooner she and Zach resolved to never see each other again, the better the chances that Jen wouldn't do anything stupid.

Like kiss him again.

Or worse. She could start to like him, or like him more than she already did. It didn't help that she had fun with him. It really didn't help that he made her laugh. Was it her fault that he was funny? Was it wrong to be flattered by his attention?

No, but it would be stupid to think that there was more to this than that. Jen knew that she wouldn't be able to remember that for long. She was the kind of person who made emotional investments easily.

Even if Zach was confident in a way that was half forgotten to Jen, and she felt like she was standing in a sunbeam when she was close to him. He was optimistic and ready for anything, qualities that she could only envy.

And trading quips with him was too much fun.

No doubt about it: Zach had to go.

Maybe her mother would give her a year of slack to mend her supposedly broken heart. It was the best Jen could hope for at this point, and it was good enough. She refused to think about owing Zach anything, never mind how well he kissed, never mind that she might be tempted to make more of what was between them if she spent too much time with him.

Jen knew Zach's type. To prove it to herself, as they walked down the sidewalk together in silence, she made a mental bet with herself about his car.

Zach would have a new car. It would be flashy and expensive, since cost would be no object for a Trust-Fund Boy (or Inheritance Boy, whichever way it fell out). The car would have leather seats and flashy gadgets and in a year, he'd be driving something completely different. This was the kind of man who needed to turn heads and look good.

Jen decided Zach's car would have to be a silver sports car, European, like something James Bond would drive. A convertible, even though that would be impractical in New England. That impracticality, in fact, would be part of his style.

To Jen's astonishment, Zach stopped beside a red Neon that had seen better days and pulled out his keys.

"This is your car?" Jen asked, expecting him to say that it was a loaner because his sleek machine was in the shop.

He glanced up in confusion. "Yes. Why?"

"No reason."

Jen got into the car when he opened the passenger door for her.
Zach's Neon wasn't brand new, although she noted with approval
that it was clean and empty.

He took care of it, as if he wanted it to last.

"Sorry," he said as he got in and noticed her quick glance into
the backseat. "I didn't get the backseat vacuumed out since Roxie
was last riding along. Sometimes, it seems as if there isn't much
point in vacuuming—she's always shedding ahead of me."

Jen glanced back again and saw the layer of long black and
white hairs on the upholstery.

"She sheds a lot?"

"She's in the *Guinness World Records*. I think she sheds more
than she weighs." He started the car and eased out into traffic. Jen
said nothing. "That was a joke."

"I know."

"What's the matter?"

"Nothing. I'm still surprised. I thought you'd have a fancy car."

He gave her an incredulous look. "So you're going to dump me
as a fake date because of my car? I don't think even cellophane is
that shallow, Jen."

Jen straightened, knowing that this was the perfect opening.
"That's not why, but I am going to dump you. Mission accom-
plished and all that."

"What about the wedding?"

"Cancelled."

"The trip to Tiffany in New York to pick rings?"

"Cancelled."

"Rats. I was looking forward to that."

"Don't be ridiculous. You just made that up to drive my mother
crazy with the idea of ostentatious spending."

Zach smiled a little bit. "And it worked, right?"

Jen watched him, not trusting that smile. "Well, yes. That was
the point."

He cast her a bright glance. "You admit then that I kept to Cin's
plan and made it work?"

Jen didn't see any way around it. "Yes, but it's over now . . ."

Zach shook his head, effectively silencing her. "It's only just started."

"What do you mean?"

"I mean that you owe me. Like we agreed in your grand-mother's kitchen." He shook his head when Jen would have ar-gued. "I kept to the plan. I made your mother dislike me. Your grandmother, in fact, has approved of me, which was your original story. Now I get to name my terms and I get to ask you out, too."

"Wait a minute, this isn't fair." Jen wasn't afraid of what he'd say. He was enjoying this too much for it to be anything truly awful. Maybe meeting his family was a terrible prospect, to his thinking.

Mostly, she was curious. She argued because he expected her to.

"Of course, it's fair," he replied. "You got what you wanted and now I get what I want." He waggled his eyebrows at her, as if to remind her that he could have asked for a lot, and Jen fought a smile.

"Okay, then take me to meet your family now and I'll do the same thing."

Zach shook his head and Jen's heart sank. "Nope. That won't work, *honey*."

"Why not?"

He cast her a smile. "You could never make them hate you."

"What's that supposed to mean?"

"You're totally a straight arrow, Jen. They'll be crazy for you. They'll decide that you're good for me. In fact, they'll start inviting people to the wedding."

"No."

"Yes. They won't believe that I'm capable of doing anything so responsible as organizing a guest list, and they'll be worried that if you have too much to do yourself you might have second thoughts, so they'll take over." He sighed. "Somehow they'll work out that it was my fault that you left college, even though we didn't know each other yet. It will become clear that your impulses are superior to mine and so you should be encouraged to stick around and be a good influence on me."

"They don't really give you that little credit, do they?"

"Of course they do. I'm the official black sheep." He shrugged as if indifferent but Jen wasn't convinced. "I wonder sometimes what they'd talk about if I didn't show up or fail to show up or generally make trouble at reasonable intervals."

"That's nuts. We'll just talk to them about it and get everything sorted out . . ."

Zach laughed. "Oh, you really should meet my family. They're so different from yours."

"What do you mean?"

"No one talks about anything—well, not about anything important. Stuff is just resolved. Opinions are formed, then set in concrete. Sometimes they're dictated from above, like Moses getting the Ten Commandments, already carved in stone. There is no expression of alternate viewpoints because there are no alternate viewpoints that count. There is only one right answer chez Coxwell and so there's nothing to talk about."

Jen watched the road, unable to imagine a family dynamic like that. "How do you all get along?"

"Mostly, we don't. We're really good at avoiding each other."

Jen saw that Zach was trying to make light of the way his family worked, but she suspected it bothered him more than he would have liked her to believe. "So, you're alone. It's like you don't have family at all."

"Be serious: I have Roxie."

Jen looked out the window, feeling a bit sorry for Zach, feeling a little bit more appreciative of her own family than she had in a while. They might be a lot of trouble, and they might be weird, but there was a bedrock of love underneath it all.

Zach touched her arm with his fingertip, just a fleeting gesture that drew her back to the moment and made her keenly aware of his presence beside her. "How do you all get along? It seems that somebody has an opinion against everything."

"Well, they do. We used to joke that all perspectives were represented—"

"—and defended—"

"—in my mother's kitchen."

"So, doesn't that mean that all of you are wrong, all of the time, according to someone's point of view?"

"Probably," Jen admitted, then frowned as she tried to explain. "But it's not malicious. It's more a case of making information available." Because they cared about each other and wanted to help. It seemed rude to add that, when Zach's family didn't sound as if they cared much about each other at all. Jen's sucker heart twisted, even though she tried to stop it.

"Not of changing people?"

"No. My grandmother is never going to get rid of her dishwasher, for example, even though it's wasteful of energy. We all know that. My mother argued with her when she decided she wanted one, and she did pick a smaller and more fuel-efficient model than the one she'd looked at initially."

"So, you compromise or not, and then when the decision is made, you move on to the next issue?"

"Pretty much. It's done then."

"So, why did Gerry comment on the dishwasher?"

"He's new." Jen grimaced. "And hopefully he's temporary. I'm not sure anything makes him happy and it's hard to believe that he'll make my mother happy in the long term."

Zach laughed. "Maybe your mother has her own version of Cin's scheme."

Jen blinked. She hadn't thought of that.

"So, I'm thinking we should take this right to the wall," Zach continued, his manner cheerful. "Let's get the ring, book the church, ask the groomsmen and bridesmaids, order the flowers, buy the dress, then break it off right at the altar." He cast her a mischievous glance. "Give everyone some major entertainment, and lots to talk about."

Jen felt the color drain from her face. "You wouldn't!"

"Sure, I would. It would live up to everyone's expectations. My family would be convinced that you were too good for me, and that you were smart to dump me." He grimaced. "They'd probably invite you to their parties afterward instead of me."

Jen was horrified. "They wouldn't!"

"Don't bet on it," Zach said. "Your family would think that you'd made a narrow escape from conventionality. It would keep them off your back for years."

Jen noted that he didn't talk about the impact on his own life. Did he like living alone and unimpeded by family ties? She couldn't imagine anything more lonely, but then she couldn't imagine a family like the one he'd told her about. "I don't think so . . ."

Jen's doubts were perfectly countered by Zach's confidence. "Of course. It would work like a charm, Jen. Just think about it. How devastating would it be to be dumped at the altar? We could split up right in the church, right in front of everybody. You could throw your bouquet at me and storm out of there. Very theatrical. It would be quite the show."

"Make quite the picture."

"It would. You could blame me."

"You could blame me, then."

"Nope, wouldn't be what a gentleman would do. I'd just brood." He drew his brows together, presumably doing an impression of himself brooding, and Jen laughed despite herself.

"You can't brood."

"I could if you broke my heart," he said lightly, hurrying on before Jen could think much about that. "Think about it: both families would assume we were so emotionally scarred that we could both remain single forever."

"If we wanted," Jen felt obliged to add.

"If we wanted. If we changed our minds, they'd be ecstatic."

It made a scary kind of sense. Jen stared out the window, shocked and yet excited in a strange way. She could imagine her mother's face—and Cin's, too. It was so wrong, yet she was tempted.

"You're naughty," she accused.

Zach grinned. "It's a gift."

"It would cost a fortune," Jen said, ever practical.

"Lucky then that I have access to one, isn't it?" Zach said with a grin. "Even luckier that I don't particularly need to access it for anything else."

"That sounds like it isn't all yours."

"It's not," he said lightly. "My brothers and sister and I actually did agree on one thing, and it was even my idea. If you don't think there were long odds against that, think again."

"What kind of thing?"

Jen watched him as he drove, uncertain he'd answer her. "I was executor of my father's estate. He left everything to be divided between his four kids."

"That sounds fair."

"Except that my mother was the one who came from money."

"Didn't she have money of her own?"

"She'd given him a power of attorney years ago, and he used it."

Jen was so horrified that she couldn't say anything.

Zach frowned. "So, it seemed to me that my mother had good reason to contest the will and that a court would have good reason to agree with her and lawyers would get richer. So I suggested to my siblings that we jointly agree to cede our inherited stake until my mother passes away, whenever that might be." He spared her a smile. "I mean, after all, we're not exactly minors anymore."

"And they agreed."

He nodded.

She admired him for coming up with a solution more just than the one his father had put in his will. "So your mother has all the money."

"Pretty much. Other than allowances paid in the past and stuff like that. But she said that we could touch her for loans when necessary. So, it's accessible, like I said."

"You could spend it on better things."

"I'm thinking this is a pretty good cause. I would love to never be fixed up again. Wouldn't you say it was worth it?"

Jen watched him, knowing that he really would do this. "You're crazy." They stopped at a traffic light and he scooped up his camera.

"It's been said before, Jen. You need new material."

When she opened her mouth to protest, he snapped a shot. "Perfect," he said with satisfaction. "The moment of proposal, frozen on celluloid forever. The astonished bride-to-be. I'm going to start a scrapbook: the book of Jen."

"You wouldn't," Jen argued, suspecting that she was wrong.

"I would. I am." He put the car into gear as the light turned green. "So, what day's good for you for the trip to New York?"

"I'm not going to New York to pick out a ring."

"Okay, I'll pick one for you. Big rock, little one, colored or clear? Like any shape better than others, or should we just go with the big Tiffany solitaire? Name your preference and tell me your size."

"You can't do this . . ."

"I can do it and so can you. It'll be fun."

"I can't deceive people like this."

"Ah, Jen, I've got so much to teach you. It could take a lifetime. Maybe we really should get married."

Jen's heart made a weird leap in her chest then belly flopped. "You don't mean that."

Zach didn't answer. He drove and expounded and to Jen's surprise, he was both a good and a careful driver. Not reckless at all.

He confounded every expectation she had of him. She needed to stop having expectations of Zach, and just make observations.

"You see, the point is that you've already started to deceive them," he said. "If you give it up now, they'll figure it out. They'll know that today was just a scam. They might even figure out that Cin put you up to it. There's no victory there."

"I should be frightened by how reasonable you make it sound," Jen muttered.

Zach grinned. "It's an art. Or a gift. Doesn't much matter. What we need to do here is make the whole scheme more plausible. There's doubt because you never talked about me before, because they didn't know you were seeing someone and suddenly here I am and we're all serious. All we need to do now is go to the next step to bring this scheme to a finale."

"At the altar of the church."

"You've got to admit that it has a certain panache. I mean, why break up in the car, quietly and without witnesses? If this is a great passion we share, then we should end it with a flourish."

"But we don't share a great passion."

"Is that right?" Zach parallel-parked with astonishing speed, and put the car in neutral.

His hand was on her cheek, his fingers warm and strong, his lips on hers before Jen knew what he was doing. She gasped. At that, he angled his head and deepened his kiss, coaxing her to join him.

It was a sweet kiss, unexpectedly sweet, and his tenderness caught Jen off guard. Why didn't she expect him to be a gentleman? She found her eyes closing, found herself responding to his caress.

And why not?

Wasn't she supposed to live a little?

It was just a kiss.

If "just" could be said of a kiss from Zach. His tongue touched hers and she reciprocated, liking the feel of him, the smell of him, the weight of his hand on her shoulder. She put her hands on his shoulders, felt the strength of him, felt his fingers slide into her hair. She was dizzy with his kiss, lost in sensation.

It had been a long time since Jen had kissed a man.

Really kissed a man.

She hadn't kissed anyone since Steve.

And she had never kissed Steve like this. Everything was spinning, everything was boiling or churning or otherwise riled up. Yet Jen, queen of self-control, just wanted more.

This guy was bigger trouble than she'd feared.

She pushed Zach away at that realization, one hand in his chest. He didn't let her push him far, just pulled back a bit and let his gaze dance over her. His eyes were gleaming with satisfaction and he was smiling a smile that warmed her to her toes. He slid his fingertip up her cheek, then tucked her hair behind her ear.

She felt cornered, but not entirely in a bad way. She liked how he looked at her, the admiration in his gaze making her feel attractive for the first time in a long while. She liked the heat in her veins. She liked the way he kissed, and the way she felt warm and tingly afterward.

But this was just a joke.

And that look on his face wouldn't last if they did more than kiss. Jen knew better than to get involved.

Well, she knew better than to get *more* involved.

Zach cleared his throat. "What was that you said about there being no passion?" He winked at her, then glanced over his shoulder. "I think we fogged the windows, *honey*."

"Maybe they're just dirty," Jen said hastily. She reached for the door handle.

"Where are you going?"

"We've broken up," she said, feeling only a need to run. She didn't even know exactly where they were, but it didn't matter. She had her transit pass: she'd figure it out. "I told you—I'm dumping you."

"Not so fast. You owe me . . ."

"You just collected whatever I might have owed you, and you got a turkey dinner, too." Jen got out of the car and slammed the door before he could say something persuasive.

Zach rolled down the window. "But we have to make it look good, Jen."

"We did. It's over, Zach. Have a nice life."

"Hey!" Zach shouted after Jen as she strode away. She didn't look back. People turned to look. He sounded, to Jen's surprise, angry, but that must just have been because he wasn't getting his way. "What about Roxie? You haven't even met her yet."

"Give her a kiss for me," Jen said. When Zach swore, she was afraid he would get out of his car to follow her and darted down a side street. Her heart was pounding when she heard tires squeal.

Once around the corner, she ran, making sure she'd be out of sight by the time Zach got the car out of his parking spot. Three streets later, she ducked into a shop and hid in one front corner like the chicken that she was. She saw the Neon drive past and her breath caught, but Zach didn't see her and he didn't stop.

Jen waited but he didn't drive by again.

She knew she should have been relieved. But if she'd gotten what she wanted, why did she feel so disappointed?

Jen had disappeared, just like that. Zach drove up and down and all around for forty-five minutes but he didn't even catch a glimpse of her.

And he was mad, madder than he could remember being in a long time. Of course, they'd been close enough to the old North End that it would have been comparatively easy for her to give Zach the slip, but still. He liked his plan. He liked the elegance and showmanship of it. He wanted to follow it through. He wanted Jen to be awed by it and to agree to it.

She wasn't supposed to have run screaming into the afternoon at the prospect of taking her own scheme to the next level. (Okay, she hadn't screamed, but still.)

She wasn't supposed to be blind to the brilliance of his master planning.

She wasn't supposed to be immune to his kiss.

Maybe he really had lost his touch.

Maybe his timing was off.

Maybe he wasn't going to let this go easily. No, Zach was right and he liked Jen and she liked him—he could tell by the way she kissed. He wasn't a dope with women and had never had any romantic issues in the past—at least not beyond the usual one of girlfriends wanting to get married, which was really not a life goal of Zach's, and him not wanting to do so.

(He would not reflect upon the irony that he had been the one to suggest a fake wedding as a culmination to the fake date with Jen and that she had turned him down flat. And bolted. Better not to go there.)

Zach was certain that he couldn't be responsible for this particular romantic failure. After all, it had never happened before that he'd kissed a woman who had kissed him back and then she'd run.

No, he had been cheated of triumph by another variable.

He had been cheated by this Steve guy.

Whoever Steve was.

This Steve guy had messed up Jen and the shadow of those events, whatever they had been, was still spooking her. The obvious resolution was to (a) find out what Steve had done, and (b) do whatever was necessary to banish his memory.

It seemed pertinent—at least belatedly—to Zach that no one had ever really answered his question about Steve. Being a carnivore couldn't have been the worst of it, especially as Jen herself ate chicken and fish.

Come to think of it, it had almost been as if Jen had been avoiding his question. That was the kind of thing she would do, if she didn't want to talk about something, Zach was sure of it. Change the subject and evade the topic.

Fortunately, he had other sources of information. Cin's plan had been for Jen to find a man like Steve, because Jen's mom had hated Steve, which meant that the best place to obtain more information about Steve was from Jen's mom.

Zach was not going to be cheated of a great moment—and a bunch more great kisses—by some jerk in Jen's past. He thought of how Jen had smiled in her grandmother's kitchen and how laughter had transformed her.

This was his new mission. He chose to accept it. He would make Jen laugh, he would persuade her to follow his plan, and by the end of it, by the final scene at the church altar, she'd be happy and ready to go on with her life.

Job one was to find out more about Steve. Zach drove home to Roxie as he dialed Directory Assistance on his cell.

Lo and behold, Natalie Sommerset had a listed number.

The gods were with him.

Jen was certain she hadn't seen the last of Zach Coxwell. He wasn't the kind of guy who took no for an answer. He'd be back, to argue his case, to try to charm her into agreeing with him. He'd been quite excited about his revision of Cin's plan, after all. Jen couldn't imagine him letting it go.

It was only a matter of time.

Jen was determined to be ready for him. The ruse was over. They were done. She didn't want to see him again. (Well, not officially, anyway.) And she was ready to tell Zach so, bluntly if necessary.

But it seemed that she had called it wrong.

Even though she worked two doubles that weekend—Friday and Saturday—and served brunch on Sunday, even though she glanced up every time the pub door opened, she never caught a glimpse of Zach.

She was sure she'd find him leaning against the door when she emerged from the kitchen with a tray of turkey dinner specials.

She was positive he'd be sitting at the bar, sipping a beer with a perfect head of foam, every time she came into work.

She was certain she'd step off the T and find his little red car idling as he waited to give her a ride home (and a piece of his mind besides).

She sat facing the door of the break room, convinced that he'd appear in the doorway just as she was putting a forkful of turkey special into her mouth.

But Zach didn't show.

Jen couldn't make any sense of this. It was impossible that she'd read him wrong. He was stubborn. He was used to getting what he wanted. He wouldn't give it up that easily.

But then, she'd read him wrong before. He didn't have a flashy car, did he? He didn't just buy things for show, then forget them and buy something else, did he? And he hadn't wanted her to meet his family as his part of the deal.

Maybe she *didn't* know what kind of a guy Zach Coxwell was as well as she thought she did.

Maybe that was why she was curious about him.

No, that couldn't be it.

He must have had family commitments that kept him away for the weekend, although it seemed unlikely that he'd get caught up with family after what he'd said about them.

At that, she started to worry. Maybe Roxanne, his dog, was sick or injured. She halfway thought about calling Zach to find out.

Maybe Zach was sick or injured. Maybe his past had jumped him from behind again and he'd come out with more than a shiner.

She had to visit the yarn store to calm herself down at that thought. She strolled the aisles and fingered the wool and lost her heart to something that could be relied upon to not leave her weeping in a month.

There were a pair of socks in the window of the shop, a pair of socks obviously intended to be worn with Birkenstocks because they had a little cable on the heel that would only show with Birkies. Jen worked her way all around the perimeter of the shop before she could bring herself to really look at them. It was as if she was stalking socks.

Then they were there, right in front her, as soft as a cloud. She touched them and knew that she was a goner. The little cable was even more darling with closer scrutiny, the wool used in the sample showed more variations of greens than she'd thought possible. It was heathery but not fussy; earthy but not boring.

These socks were perfect for Natalie.

Jen hesitated. A pair of socks was a big time commitment: she would have to survive at least another week to finish them.

If she knit furiously.

But her mother would love them, and Christmas was coming, and Jen—filled with a newfound appreciation of her family and what they'd done for her—wanted very much to make a pair of socks like this for her mom. Her mom had stood by her and supported her, and taken her to chemo and had half carried her home afterward. Her mom had let her move back home and had loaned her money and never nagged about it.

Maybe Natalie was an angel after all.

When Jen learned that the scrumptious heathered yarn came in a blue, the battle was lost. Blue was Natalie's favorite color. Jen picked up the pattern and the wool and the needles she'd need and paid for it all before she could change her mind. Before her shift that Saturday afternoon, she'd cast on the first sock and had begun to knit like a crazy woman.

Maybe there was a different kind of insanity running in her family.

Jen vowed she would get the socks done before she died, even if she had to knit in the hospital, in the chemo waiting room, in the bathroom while she upchucked everything inside her, in the doctor's office, in palliative care.

Because that was the great terror of Jen's life: that the big C would come back and this time it wouldn't be vanquished and that all the things in her life that she had left undone would never be finished. She didn't want to leave that kind of legacy.

Which was why she knit small fruit.

It was why she had no wool stash, like other compulsive knitters. She'd given all of hers to Teresa when she'd been diagnosed and had never bought more than she needed since. It was too risky. It was an investment that might not pay off. It was betting on a future that might never come.

These socks were the biggest project she had undertaken in over two years. Jen knit at night, she knit in the morning, she knit before her shift and after it and during her break, and slowly, steadily, a sock developed beneath her busy fingers.

By the time she was heading home late Sunday afternoon, Jen had turned the heel of the sock. She was thinking she might finish the first one, but couldn't count on the second.

She was, however, ready to admit that she'd been wrong about Zach's determination to see her. The most probable explanation was that he'd bailed on her, that he'd found another woman who was easier to get along with, that he'd been distracted by a wink and a smile, that he'd thought she was too much trouble (or too slow to jump into bed).

Just like Steve.

Which should have meant that she was relieved to have seen the last of him. It would give her more time to knit.

Instead, Jen found it all a bit depressing. Had she ever met such an unpredictable man? It was kind of interesting to never know what would come next, if occasionally frustrating.

It would be kind of fun to be in love with Zach, even more fun to have Zach be in love with her.

She could admit that to herself, now that there was no chance of having anything come next from Zach. She supposed he would just bounce through life, savoring the moment and never worrying about the next one. Consequences would slide off him as if he were made of Teflon. Women would flock to him, like bees to you-know-what. (Maybe she'd touched on a deeper truth by calling him *honey*.) Money would appear and be spent, with him never sparing a care for the future.

It sounded like a good life, put like that.

It certainly would be good to have that kind of enthusiasm and energy again. Jen had forgotten what it was like to be so light on her feet. Maybe remembering that sense of opportunity, that conviction that fun was here for the taking, was good enough.

Maybe not.

It was probably only the ache in her shoulder that made her miss him, because she even missed his stupid lawyer jokes. She forced herself to remember that Zach had no plan. He was adrift.

She was tired, that was all. Her mood had nothing to do with the absence of Zach Coxwell in her life, nothing at all. She forced herself to consider the good fortune of having the next two days off. There was luck. There was a cause for joy.

There was a chance to sleep.

To take a load off her feet.

And to finish knitting those socks.

What an exciting life she led.

Jen opened the door to her mom's kitchen Sunday night to a chorus of greeting. Cin and Natalie were sitting at the kitchen table, drinking herbal tea and looking like the proverbial cats who had swallowed the flock of canaries.

Hmmm.

Jen took this as a bad sign. She almost looked for stray feathers, then decided not to give them the satisfaction.

"Hi," she said, closing the door, kicking off her shoes and dropping her bag. "Is there more of that tea?"

"It's rooibos," Natalie said. "Very good for the immune system." She poured a cup of the red herbal brew for Jen, who didn't much like it but took a sip anyway.

She couldn't help but grimace.

"You could put some honey in it," Cin suggested.

Jen tried not to flinch.

"Also good for the immune system," Natalie agreed. "Let me get it for you."

Jen regarded them both with some suspicion. "Why would I need extra immunity right now? What's going on?"

"Nothing!" Natalie said, her tone too cheerful to be trusted.

"Winter's coming," Cin said and giggled.

Jen sat down at the kitchen table and took a long sip of the hot tea. Her gaze flicked between the two apparently innocent parties, then she put the mug firmly on the table. "If you've fixed me up, you can forget it. Call and cancel. I'm going to bed for the next two days."

"Are you sick?" Natalie asked with concern.

"I'm tired."

"Not sick and tired?" Cin asked playfully.

"Not yet," Jen said. She sighed and rolled her shoulders, then began to do her arm exercises. "I have two days off and I mean to enjoy them."

"In bed!" Cin teased.

"Alone. Sleeping. It sounds like heaven."

"It could be more heavenly if you weren't alone," Cin replied but Jen ignored her.

"You shouldn't be lifting all those heavy trays," Natalie chided. "It's not good for your arm."

"Should you get one of those elastic sleeves?" Cin asked.

"I don't lift that many," Jen said. "I lift on the right and the guys in the kitchen are good about helping me out." She could feel the result in her left arm, though, and suspected that she had overdone it a bit. "There were just a lot of turkey dinner specials this weekend."

"I'll bet." Natalie came to stand behind Jen and started to massage her shoulders. Jen sighed and leaned back into her mother's magic caress. "You have to think about how long you can do this job, Jen."

"I can do it as long as I have to," she said, almost automatically. It wasn't worth calculating how long she would have to wait tables to pay back her mom. Jen had done that before and she was depressed enough right now.

No, not depressed. She was exhausted, which was different.

"You should think about doing something else," Natalie said.

"Something that puts your brain to work. You should find a job that uses your other talents."

"Such as they are. I hear there's a big market in knitted fruit. Oooo, that feels good."

"Zach said you were singing at the pub. You used to sing a lot." Natalie sighed, her fingers easing Jen's tired muscles. Jen closed her eyes, barely listening. "In fact, I don't know when I last heard you sing, even singing along with the radio."

"We'll book a concert," Jen said, then straightened in confusion. Her eyes opened wide to find Cin smirking. "Wait a minute. I don't remember Zach talking about my singing at Gran's. We didn't talk about the pub at all."

Cin smiled her Cheshire cat smile, the one that meant things were about to get interesting.

"Oh, it wasn't at Gran's," Natalie said. "It was here." Then she caught her breath as if she'd said something she wasn't supposed to have said.

It was too late. "Zach was here?" Jen turned to look at her mother. This was the woman from whom she'd inherited the inability to tell a lie.

Natalie shrugged as she smiled. "Just twice."

"Twice?" Jen no longer felt so tired. In fact, her heart was going skippity-bop. "When did this happen?"

"Friday, then again last night." Natalie smiled as she took the seat beside Jen. "You know, I was so wrong about him. I'm sorry, Jen, that I gave him a hard time at your grandmother's. False first impressions and all of that. He's so sincere and so concerned about you . . ."

"A regular prince among men," Cin agreed. "Snap him up or I will."

"But wait! What was he doing here? We broke up after Thanksgiving dinner."

Natalie regarded her with an understanding smile. "He said you would say that. He was quite upset about it, really."

Zach upset? Jen couldn't imagine him taking anything seriously enough to be upset about it. It was like trying to imagine Tigger the Tiger on antidepressants.

Zach was playing mind games with her mother, that was what he was doing.

Natalie sighed, obviously completely sold on Zach's performance. Jen felt a niggle of admiration. Her mother wasn't that easy to fool. "He thought things hadn't gone that well on Thursday and he was so sorry. He wanted to sort things out between us, so that there wouldn't be any obstacles. I understand now that his mother has a lot of social obligations that need to be answered with a big wedding. It's not his choice, either, but only one of his siblings had a big wedding and he wants to please his mother. It's quite reasonable, really, and Mom always said to consider how a man treats his mother when you want to know how he'll treat you. I suppose I will have to find an appropriate hat . . ."

"Stop!" Jen leapt to her feet. "Stop right there. You're telling me that Zach came here—"

"Twice," Cin interjected.

"—twice, and somehow, against all odds, persuaded you not only that a big church wedding would be a good thing but that you need a hat? Are you really my mother? This would be a church wedding with a minister and hymns and crucifixes? And you? With a hat?"

"No crucifixes in the Episcopalian church," Cin said. "Just crosses."

"Whatever," Jen said. "It's still church, you know, pawn of the patriarchy and all that."

Natalie smiled and shrugged. "There's nothing more persuasive than a man in love. And he's good for you, Jen. Anybody can see it." She wrinkled her nose at Cin. "I won't have to wear mauve, will I?"

"You get to pick before Zach's mom," Cin assured her. "That's how it works. I looked it up."

"Maybe blue would be better . . ."

Jen made an incoherent sound of exasperation. "He's not in love! At least not with me."

Natalie shook her head sadly. "Zach said you'd say that."

Jen was outraged that Zach had thought this far ahead.

On the other hand, it was kind of impressive.

Her mother waxed rhapsodic. "Zach really does understand you, Jen. I was so touched by his thoughtfulness. And the way he makes you laugh. Look at all the similar choices you've made in your lives. Well, anyone could see that you're perfect for each other."

Jen pulled out a chair and sat down beside her mother, determined to get to the bottom of this. "Mom, listen to me. Zach is not concerned. He's putting you on . . ."

"Jen! I don't know how you can say that!"

"He's putting you on, just the way that Cin does . . ."

"Me?" Cin protested. "I've never put anyone on in my life!"

Natalie ignored Cin as she patted Jen's hand. "Jen, give credit where it's due. He took the initiative to come here and talk to me about your past . . ."

A new terror ripped through Jen. "About *my* past? You talked to him about my past?"

"He wanted to know about Steve. It's only understandable. He thought that whatever happened between you and Steve was the reason you couldn't believe that he really loves you. And you know, I have to admire his insight. I've thought all along that the problem was your fear of trusting anyone again. There's an imbalance in your aura, my friend Karen said so, and only a very sensitive man would be aware of it."

Jen took a deep gulp of the hot tea. It didn't fortify her; in fact, it scalded her throat. But at least that proved that she was awake.

This was really happening.

"Mom, please tell me that you didn't tell Zach about Steve."

Her mother fidgeted. "I know it's private, Jen, and your personal business is your personal business."

"But?" Jen prompted.

Natalie averted her gaze. "I told him that you and Steve had been engaged and that Steve had broken it off suddenly, and that he had hurt you."

"That's all you told him?"

"Pretty much."

"What about the big C?"

Natalie met Jen's gaze squarely. "I didn't tell him about that."

Jen breathed a sigh of relief that one of her secrets was still her own. But this had gone far enough. She took a deep breath and prepared to confess her sins. "Mom, you need to know something about this."

"What's that?"

"Zach and I have never had a date. I brought him to Thanksgiving dinner so that you wouldn't fix me up with someone else. It was a trick and it wasn't a nice one, and I'm sorry, but we're not in a serious relationship."

If Jen had thought that confession would resolve things, she had called it wrong.

"I think you need to stop denying your feelings for Zach, Jen," Natalie said. "Nice men don't come along all the time."

"I'm not denying my feelings for him! I don't *have* any feelings for him. I barely know him."

"But you see, that's going to change," Natalie said calmly. She got up from the table and fetched a wad of papers from the desk. Jen felt her eyes round when she saw what they were: her mother was carrying astrological charts.

"You didn't," she breathed.

Natalie smiled. "Well, how else could I trust him so easily as that? And you know the strangest thing, Jen, is that there's a perfect conjunction between the vertices of your charts . . ."

"That means a fated relationship," Cin said with enthusiasm.

"I know what it's supposed to mean, but it's not rational . . ." Jen began to argue.

Natalie looked at her over the rims of her glasses. "Only those things that are rational are true then? What about love?"

"What about the fact that dozens of children are born in hospitals in the Greater Boston area every day and every night?" Jen demanded. "Does that mean that I could have a destined true love with every other guy who was born the same day as Zach Coxwell?"

Natalie removed her glasses. "Well, of course. That's why all this talk about a single soul mate is nonsensical. There are potentially dozens of soul mates for each of us, each one of whom could teach us something, any one of which could chart a path intersecting with our own at any point in time."

"Mom. Zach Coxwell is not one of my soul mates."

"That's not what it says here on your charts."

Jen knew she couldn't win that argument, so she appealed to Cin. "The whole fake date scheme was Cin's idea. Right, Cin?"

"I don't know what you're talking about," Cin said demurely and sipped her tea.

Jen regarded her sister with outrage. "What do you mean? You came up with the idea in the first place. Find a guy Mom will hate, you said, a guy just like Steve . . ."

"Zach isn't at all like Steve," Natalie said firmly. "And I like him. A lot."

"And he's cute," Cin said. "A Valentine's Day wedding is so romantic, Jen. I don't know why you're being so obstructionist about this."

"Because it's a lie!"

"Zach's right," Natalie said to Cin. "Steve really did leave an emotional scar. I had no idea it was so bad. Even with her aura."

"It's sad when someone like Jen can't trust anymore," Cin agreed.

"Don't you have to go?" Jen demanded of her sister. "Isn't Ian waiting on you?"

Cin smiled sweetly. "He's working late. I'm in no rush to leave."

"It's downright tragic when we hold ourselves back from love."

Natalie gave Jen a concerned look. "Do you want me to book a consultation with Karen? You know she's the best at balancing auras. She could massage your energy forces and fix you right up. I'm sure she could come by in the next two days."

"No, thank you, I'm fine." Jen got to her feet. Funny, but she didn't feel so tired anymore.

In fact, she felt murderous.

"But where are you going?" Natalie asked when Jen hauled on her coat and boots.

"Out."

"You just got home!"

"I have to go kill somebody." Jen grabbed her hat and gloves. "And it has to happen now."

"That's so bad for your karma!" Natalie cried.

"Oh no, Mom. This must be love," Cin said, assuming her "wise" expression. "Look at all the energy she has, now that she's going to see him. She won't kill him. She'll kiss him instead." She waved her fingertips. "See you tomorrow, sis. We won't wait up."

"I am not going to have sex with Zach Coxwell!" Jen shouted.

"Maybe you should," Natalie said worriedly. "You're very tense, Jen. That's not good for a bride-to-be."

"An orgasm might be just the thing," Cin agreed.

"I'm only energized because I'm ready to get the dirty work behind me." Jen glared at her mother and sister. "In fact, I should have killed Zach sooner. It would have made things much simpler."

Cin swallowed a smile. "You could just break up with him instead."

"I tried that already: it didn't work."

"Violence is never an answer," Natalie began, but Jen interrupted her.

"It is this time. Trust me."

"I think you're being too sensitive, Jen. Let me call Karen. Zach is such a caring individual and once your aura is balanced . . ."

"If you believe that, then he's got you fooled, Mom."

"But Jen, you can't lie," Cin said, laughter underlying her words. "You'll get caught in the act and go to jail forever."

"It'll be worth it." She spared her sister one last glance from the doorway. Natalie's back was turned, so Jen pointed at Cin and mouthed the words *you're next*.

The last thing she heard before she closed the door was her sister's laughter.

Chapter 9

Zach stood at the window of his condo, leaning against the trim as he watched the road below. He didn't think it would take long for Jen to show up and chew him out, and he smiled when he saw that he was right.

She came out of the T station like a whirlwind, then strode through the snow. Her jacket was open and blowing in the wind, she was only wearing one glove and had the other one clenched in her fist. Her every step was filled with fury as she made her way to his apartment. Her mom had said she was working until four: factor in transit time and Jen must have come straight here. It was only 5:10.

Perfect.

It was already getting dark out, the winter light turning that pearly dusk that was just right for romance. He lit the candles, reminded Roxie to behave herself, and turned on the music. He didn't have anything sufficiently saccharine for the wine and roses thing, so he played R.E.M.'s "Losing My Religion."

It applied to the situation quite well, given that the closest thing

Zach had to a religion was a determination to live without any ties. Proposing marriage, even a marriage that wasn't going to actually happen, was definitely a breach of faith.

But it would be worth it.

There was a buzz from the lobby and he dispensed with the formalities of chat. He let Jen in immediately. He checked the pair of champagne flutes and the temperature of the bottle in the fridge, ensured that Roxie hadn't scarfed the chocolate truffles, then someone rapped on the door.

It was a decisive knock.

An annoyed knock.

It was precisely the knock he'd been expecting. Zach was ready. He swept open the door, confident of his plan, to find Jen on the threshold, her eyes flashing.

"Ah, you're gorgeous when you're angry," he said with a grin.

"Another cliché and I reserve the right to blacken your other eye," she said, then stepped past him. "Mind if I come in? We need to talk. And then I'm going to kill you."

"You don't appear to have any weapons."

"My bare hands will do."

"Sounds kinky."

She gave him a dark look. "Don't push your luck. I don't punch like a girl."

"Wouldn't killing me be against the whole nonviolence thing?"

"I'm making an exception."

"You know, I've always thought I was exceptional."

She gave him a cutting glance. Zach moved out of the way, anticipating that her attitude would change when she saw the roses.

Jen, however, had no chance to see the roses because Roxie launched her considerable self at the new arrival.

"Down, Roxie!" Zach shouted, to no discernible effect.

The dog ignored him—as usual—barked with joy and planted two large paws on Jen's shoulders. Surprised, Jen fell back against the wall, then put one arm protectively over her chest. Roxie landed a big slobbering lick on Jen's cheek.

"I'm the one who's supposed to get to do that," Zach joked, embarrassed by his dog's enthusiasm. He snagged the dog's collar and pulled her down.

Jen seemed to be busy with something under her coat. When Zach glanced up, she blushed furiously, then gave Roxie her undivided attention. "Don't you get out much?" she asked and Roxie wagged her tail so hard that Zach thought it might fall off.

"Oh yeah, she's completely neglected."

"The glossy coat and cold nose are big clues," Jen said.

"What's that supposed to mean?"

"She's healthy. That means you take care of her." Jen straightened and gave him a look that seemed a bit less angry. "I guess it's all those kisses." Roxie nudged Jen's hand, demanding more attention, her tail thumping on the floor.

"Roxie, go and lie down." Zach's command made a big impression, as usual.

The dog began to lick Jen's fingers.

"She also seems to think that you're a pushover," Jen said with the barest smile. "Who's alpha in this place anyway?" She looked around then, her expression turning incredulous. "I thought this was where you lived."

"It is." Zach followed her gaze, unable to find anything wrong. How could she miss the red roses on the sill? They'd make a great backdrop to the shot, with the darkening sky behind them . . .

Jen gave him a hard look that stopped his planning cold. "How would I be able to tell?"

Zach resisted the urge to squirm. "Oh, you mean furniture."

"Most people have at least one item. A chair. Or a table."

"I have a very minimalist vision . . ." Zach began, suddenly aware that the yawning vacancy of his apartment might not be seen as an asset.

"You can't be minimalist with a dog like this. You just don't really live here."

Zach was insulted that she even implied that he was lying. "Of course I do. My name's on the door buzzer in the foyer."

"So you have another place."

"No, just this one."

"I don't believe you."

"Well, you should. It's true."

"It doesn't make sense. You're supposed to have big bucks. I thought your place would have been decorated by professionals and filled with fancy gadgets. Antiques. Persian carpets. Something like that."

Zach shook his head. "I don't need stuff to be happy."

"Just money?"

"It does take the edge off."

She looked again. "You must have a mingy trust fund."

This was not the direction Zach had anticipated the conversation would take. The change affected his sparkling good temper and his next words sounded irritable.

Maybe that was because he was irritated. "I don't have a trust fund. What I had was an allowance, one which my father didn't think was sufficient for anyone to actually live on."

Jen glanced at Zach and he knew he'd have to cough up more.

"That was his plan, you see. It was supposed to be motivational. Or keep us begging before his checkbook, or something."

Jen folded her arms across her chest. "Let me guess: it didn't work."

"Why do you guess that?"

"Because nothing works with you the way anyone would expect it to work."

Zach could have returned the dubious compliment, but he was pretty sure it wouldn't improve the tone of their conversation. He shrugged instead. "I enjoyed proving to him that someone could, in fact, live on that much money."

Jen's eyes were bright, her gaze too knowing. "I'll bet it ticked him off."

Zach smiled. "You'd win that one."

"But didn't you say he was dead?"

Zach nodded as he sobered. He would not think about his

father's death, or his own culpability. He tried to be offhand and change the subject a bit. "But, you know, old habits die hard. I'm kind of used to this lifestyle now."

"And you can touch your mother for access to the fortune now?"

"Roxie and I don't need much."

"Or you have less to prove now that your father's gone." Her words were uttered softly but they cut right to Zach's heart. "Is that why you don't seem to do anything? Because he isn't around anymore to give you something to defy?"

Zach stared at her, startled speechless by the truth in her guess.

She held his gaze for a long moment, then abruptly shook her head and looked away. "Sorry. It's not my business."

Zach tried for his usual sunny manner. "Well, why not? We're getting married, after all."

"Are we?" Jen shed her wet boots, then took a couple of steps into the apartment. Her gaze lingered on the four dozen blood red roses arranged in vases on the windowsill. She flicked a glance at him that he couldn't read and shook her head a bit, then moved on.

So much for the impact of that investment.

Jen spent more time looking at the framed print of Zach's that was now hanging on the wall. That made him nervous, especially as he couldn't read her expression. He held his breath, but she didn't say anything about it, something that disappointed him more than he thought it should have done.

She glanced into the bedroom, where the futon had been left in splendid disarray by Roxie, and peeked into the kitchen. There was an empty six-pack of beer on the floor and two empty boxes of macaroni and cheese peeking out of the trash. It did seem kind of barren, now that Zach thought about it, but it was clean.

Jen glanced back at Zach and her expression wasn't encouraging. "How old are you? Seventeen?"

He bristled, not liking the sense that he wasn't measuring up. He figured he should have been used to that by now, but with Jen, it was different. "What's that supposed to mean?"

"You live like a teenager. Or an undergrad. This place even echoes."

"It's easier to clean."

"Is that what the maid service tells you?"

Zach folded his arms across his chest. He was quite certain that romantic proposals didn't usually follow a script like this one. "No. I know it myself. I don't have a maid service. I don't want anyone poking through my things."

"And what things would those be?" Jen asked, with another survey of the empty living room.

"I like my privacy. I do it myself."

"I doubt that."

"What's that supposed to mean?"

She squinted at him, then shook her head. "It means that I can't see you with rubber gloves and a toilet brush."

Zach marched into the kitchen, annoyed beyond belief that his perfect scheme had been hijacked and left to die on a tarmac in deepest, darkest Africa.

He hauled open the doors of the cupboard below the sink, Roxie looking over his shoulder just in case the dog biscuits had been moved. He hauled out his heavy-duty yellow rubber gloves and wagged them at Jen. Roxie gave them a sniff of disdain and returned to Jen, as if she was the dog's only ally. "Extra large. Mine, thank you very much. I may be a lot of things, but I'm not a slob."

Jen glanced to the dog. "Is he putting me on, Roxie?" The dog leaned on her leg, obviously smitten with her, and drooled on her black pants. The spit shone on the cotton and Zach knew it would harden like shellac.

Which maybe was Roxie's point—to embellish everyone she liked with her bodily fluids—but didn't strike Zach as particularly elegant or appropriate.

Zach snagged the roll of paper towels, ripped off a few, and handed them to Jen. "Here, you've got to get that before it dries. Otherwise, it could be used to mortar bricks."

Jen took the paper towels, their fingertips brushing in the transaction. Her fingers were cold and Zach had an urge to grab her hand and warm them up.

Nothing doing in that department, though. She pulled back quickly. She bent to wipe up the mess, then glanced up at him through her bangs.

Suddenly she looked mischievous and playful and completely kissable. "Okay, you've convinced me," she said with a smile that made his heart twist. "A slob wouldn't know anything about the consistency of dried dog spit."

"Thank you for that. I think." The atmosphere in the kitchen warmed slightly and Zach felt that he was back on track. "Can I take your coat?"

"No, thanks, I'm not staying."

"Just stopped by to kill me," he felt compelled to remind her.

"Right." She snapped her fingers but looked a lot less angry than she had.

Zach made the most of his moment, such as it was. It probably wouldn't last. On the other hand, it kept him on his toes, matching wits with Jen.

He reached into the fridge and pulled out the bottle of champagne. "Care for a drink first?"

"No, thanks . . . that's real champagne!" Jen eyed him with suspicion. "I'm thinking I should wait and have it to celebrate your untimely demise."

Zach grinned as he peeled the foil from the cork. "You know what they say about going out with a bang." He popped the cork, right on cue. He eased it from the bottle the way he'd been taught, and though it made a pop rather than a bang, it didn't leave his hand.

Jen shook her head at his joke, then nodded to the cork as he put it on the counter. "Maybe you missed your calling as a sommelier. That was smooth."

"Thanks. My mother has issues with flying champagne corks. She says it's vulgar."

"As well as dangerous."

"Someone could get a black eye," Zach said.

"And you've already had one this month."

"It wouldn't be me: it would be you. And I don't think it would be a good look for you."

"Plus Murray would blame you."

Zach pretended to shudder. "Don't even talk about it."

Jen almost smiled.

He poured into the two champagne flutes and handed one to Jen. They were funky glasses, with red twisted stems, handblown by a local artist. Zach didn't own much, but what he owned, he really liked.

Jen looked at the glass in her hand with something that might have been appreciation, then looked up at Zach. "So, we're drinking to your death by unnatural causes?" she said and he was sure it was a joke.

Pretty sure, anyway.

"I thought we were celebrating our pending marriage."

"Oh, so we're drinking to your talent for meddling in my life."

"I knew you'd be angry that I talked to your mother, but it's okay, Jen. This is going to work like a charm." Zach moved into his full-press persuasive mode. "Is Tuesday good for you for the trip to New York? I'm guessing you don't work a lot of shifts at the beginning of the week."

Jen had been in the act of sipping champagne, but stopped without imbibing any. "I'm not going to New York."

"Sure you are. We've got to go to Tiffany and add to the photo montage. It'll be great for credibility . . ."

Jen blinked. "The photo montage?"

"Yeah. Of course. I showed the pictures from Thanksgiving to your mom already. She really liked a couple I took of you."

"You showed your pictures to my mom?"

"Jen, you've got to stop repeating everything I say to you. They're just little words and not that hard to understand." She swatted him in the shoulder and he laughed, relieved when she smiled.

Even if she had smiled after inflicting a blow on him.

"Of course, I showed her the pictures," Zach continued, intending to bowl her over with details. "I mean, it was part of the whole setup. She loved the Book of Jen. Now, we'll go to New York and I'll blow another roll or two. Maybe we'll go the Empire State Building, or take one of those carriage rides around Central Park."

"In November?"

"We're just two people crazy in love." He winked at her and she sipped her champagne, avoiding his gaze. "Maybe you could wear something that matches the little blue boxes. We could do a mock '50s thing . . ."

The base of Jen's glass hit the counter firmly. "I'm not going to New York, and you're not buying an engagement ring, because we're not getting married."

Zach waved off this protest. "I know we're not getting married and you know it, but nobody else needs to know. Yet."

"I dumped you . . ."

"That's why I went to see your mom. Breaking up was a brilliant touch, really, as I think they were a bit skeptical about how quickly things were moving. This gives the whole scheme a greater plausibility, some emotional nuance . . ."

"We are not doing this!"

"Of course we are. It's too good of a scheme to *not* do it . . ."

Zach had a heartbeat of warning as Jen's eyes flashed, then she stepped closer to tell him off. "How can you even think about doing this? What about people's feelings? What about their expectations? What about consequences?"

"There aren't going to be any consequences. People cancel weddings all the time . . ."

"No, no. My mother likes you. My mother thinks that you're perfect for me, although it's a challenge to figure out that one."

"She does?"

"Don't preen. You tricked her."

"Hey, that's a bit harsh . . ."

Jen didn't slow down, though. She was spitting sparks again. "You manipulated her and you got her hopes up and you don't care one bit that this will disappoint her in the end."

"Well . . ." Zach didn't have much of an answer for that, but it didn't matter. Jen was on a roll.

"What about my grandmother? She likes you, too, and she'll be mortified if a big wedding comes undone at the altar. What will her friends think? What will *your* mother's friends think? What will they say?"

"I don't really care what a bunch of gossips have to say about me . . ."

"Then what about your own mother? Won't she be embarrassed and disappointed? Won't she be sad that you tricked her?"

Zach suspected that his own mother would never think any woman was good enough for him—because she'd said as much in the past, after each of his relationships had ended—but he didn't think it a good time to express that idea. "No one will ever know . . ."

Jen shook a finger at him. "One thing I've learned watching Cin is that these schemes always come out. People always have a suspicion if they've been tricked and it erodes their trust in the people who tricked them. It would, in fact, be handy if this one came unraveled right now."

"But you started it."

"I was stupid." Jen picked up the glass of champagne and knocked back the rest of its contents in one gulp. "I listened to my sister and I should have known better. The truth is that I have nothing to fear from any guy my mother fixes me up with. I should have faced that in the first place." She spun on her heel, patted Roxie on the head, and made for the door.

"Why not?"

She paused, one hand on the knob. Her attitude was triumphant.

"Because if I'm not attracted to them, they can't hurt me. And I won't worry about hurting them. Simple."

It was simple all right.

And it was fascinating.

Zach sauntered after her and spoke just before she opened the door to leave. "Why does that sound like you have something to fear from me? Like maybe you're attracted to me? Like maybe you're running because I could hurt you?"

Jen's expression turned skeptical. "Be serious."

"I am serious. I like you. I think you're funny and smart. I like how you smile, although you don't do it often enough."

"Flattery isn't going to get you anywhere."

"It's not flattery; it's the truth. I have fun talking to you and that's not very common." He put down his champagne and pursued her. He noticed how her cheeks turned pink and didn't think it was the alcohol.

"Don't kiss me," Jen warned, her tone lethal.

"Why not? If you've got nothing to fear from me, then it's no big deal to kiss. It would be like, oh, I don't know, like kissing your brother." He watched her battle over that, watched her eyes glitter as she considered the consequences of either option.

"I don't feel anything when I kiss you," she said with such conviction that he didn't believe her. "It *is* like kissing my brother. It's just for show."

Zach felt compelled to point out the problem with that argument. "Except that most of the times we kissed, no one was watching."

Jen started at him and the room seemed to be steaming up. Her eyes were wider than usual, and darker, too. He liked that he could almost see her thinking.

And yet, he didn't really know what to expect.

The woman was a mystery wrapped in an enigma.

And he liked that, liked it a lot.

In the end, Jen surprised him completely. She closed the distance between them with a decisive step and reached up to frame his face in her hands. Her fingers were still cold but Zach barely jumped. "I'll prove it to you, brother Zach," she promised, then touched her lips to his.

Her mouth was cold, too, but firm and sweet. Her kiss went straight to his head—and to another part of him—a lot more quickly than champagne. Zach felt as if everything in him was suddenly pulled taut.

If this was how Jen planned to kill him, Zach wasn't going to fight her off.

Zach tasted too good.

Or he was too experienced of a kisser.

One or the other had to be why Jen couldn't stop kissing Zach. She certainly wasn't attracted to him, and she certainly wasn't enjoying this. She was proving a point.

That's all.

And really, it would take a little bit longer to ensure that her point was made. His hands were around her waist, holding her against him but not trapping her there. She was pressed against his chest and felt the evidence that he worked out. She had her hands on his shoulders and then around his neck and then wove her fingers into the thick waves of his hair. She liked the bit of stubble on his chin, the way his tongue teased hers, the way he used his teeth, just a little, to drive her crazy.

Roxie leaned against them and made a little whimper in a bid for attention, but Zach ignored the dog. If anything, he lifted Jen closer and deepened his kiss.

She liked that he gave their kiss—the kiss she had initiated—his undivided attention. She liked that she could feel his hardness against her belly, yet he didn't force or push her. The way he held her made her feel that she was in charge, that she could bring it all to an end or drag him off to be her love slave for the afternoon. She felt strong and sexy as she hadn't in a long time.

The choice was hers.

And it was too tempting.

He would only hurt her, she reminded herself, because she couldn't just savor the moment and walk away. It wasn't in her. She would make an emotional commitment, just as she had the last time with Steve, and it wouldn't be reciprocated. Zach was ready to have fun, and nothing more than that.

Jen couldn't do it.

The fact that he expected her to do so made her angry.

She planted one hand in his chest and pushed, backing away and breaking their kiss. "That's it," she said, her voice husky in an unfamiliar way. "That's enough to prove my point."

Zach grinned, unpersuaded. "And what would that point be?"

"That kissing you is like kissing my brother."

"Then your family really is odd." He tapped a fingertip on the end of her nose. "Give it up, Jen. You've lost this one. That is not how anybody kisses a sibling."

"What do you mean? I didn't feel anything special." Jen tried to lie and failed spectacularly, as usual.

Zach laughed. "Then you're dead and you don't look it. That was a killer kiss, one for the Hall of Fame, in my opinion, and nothing to be ashamed of."

"I'm not ashamed of it . . ."

"Then why are you trying to lie about your response?" He folded his arms across his chest, his eyes sparkling. His gaze swept over her and he smiled, proof positive that he had noted all the damning evidence.

Jen straightened. "I came here to kill you."

"What a way to go."

"Don't make fun of me. What you're trying to do here is wrong . . ."

"And if I get one last wish before I die, I want another one of those kisses."

"Do you take anything seriously?"

Zach cocked his head, as if considering this. "I try not to. As a matter of principle. I mean, stuff happens whether you worry about it or not, so why bother?"

"That's not what I mean. Don't you take your actions seriously? Don't you think about the impact of what you do?"

"No. Never." Zach shook his head, once and firmly, decisively changing the subject as Jen had seen him do once before. She'd hit a nerve, she was sure of it, and she was intrigued.

But then, maybe that was just part of his game.

"Look at this," he invited and curiosity drew Jen after him, despite her better judgment. Zach pulled out a pile of prints out of one of the kitchen drawers and offered them to her.

Jen hesitated in the doorway.

"I promise not to bite."

"I was looking for a sharp knife," Jen retorted but he laughed.

He held out the prints, unafraid. She sighed, then took them from him. They were his shots from Thanksgiving Day and they were good. She would have loved to have been able to just toss them aside, but they were too good. He seemed to have a knack for catching people in action, often in the midst of a characteristic gesture. This was her family, distilled and captured at their best.

Jen lingered on the ones of her grandmother, knowing she'd never seen any better shots of Gran. She couldn't think of a thing to say, especially when Zach hovered so close beside her. He obviously was anxious about her response and she knew from that alone that his photography was important to him.

"They're good," she said, not even wanting to lie. "You really caught their characters."

He grinned, looking ready to bounce again. "I'll give you some prints. Just pick the ones you want and I'll blow them up."

Jen shoved a hand through her hair with impatience. It was exasperating how he kept coming back to the same issue, how he insisted upon building bonds between them. "Look, Zach, we're not going to do this. You don't have to pretend to be in love with me.

We're not going to pretend to get married. We're not going to build fake links between our lives just for the fun of destroying them. There will be no performance, understand?"

He was insulted, she saw that immediately. "That's not what this is about. You like the shots. I'll give you some prints."

"Why would you do that? Why would you bother?"

Zach winked. "Because I'm head over heels in love with you, of course."

"That's it!" Jen dropped the prints on the counter and reached for his throat with both hands. "Liar! How could anybody trust anything that you say?"

Zach evaded her easily. Worse, he caught her hands in his and they ended up dancing—sort of—around his kitchen. He was enjoying her anger too much. "Okay, I won't give you prints if that makes you feel better." He nodded to one drawer. "The knife's in there, but you'll have to let go of me to go for it."

There was nothing more annoying than not being taken seriously.

Jen pulled her hands from his with impatience. "You don't understand. I don't want to do any of this," she said, her words low and hot. "I don't want to lie to my family. I don't want to pretend."

"But it'll be fun . . ."

"Only to you." Jen turned and stepped away from him. She had to get out of there before he persuaded her to do something she'd regret.

"Wait a minute. You were the one who was laughing about your family in your grandmother's kitchen."

"No!" Jen shook her head. "I was laughing at *you*."

Zach sobered instantly. "At *me*?"

"At your shock that anyone could be so weird. My family is unconventional in some ways, but we care about each other, and we don't deliberately hurt or embarrass each other." Jen felt herself lecturing but she didn't care. "If that's the difference between having money and not, I'll go with not having any, thanks just the same."

"So, it's about money. That's really why you're saying no."

"No. It's about principle," Jen said firmly. "It's about values. It's about trust."

"Why wouldn't you trust me?"

"Why *would* I trust you?"

Zach smiled. "Because I'm charming and funny and a better man than Steve."

"A different man than Steve, maybe," Jen insisted despite the untimely skip of her heart. "Whether you're better or not is anyone's guess."

Zach's eyes narrowed. "What's that supposed to mean?"

"Is it better to ditch someone a month before the wedding or at the altar?" Jen held up her hands. "Seems like hairsplitting to me."

"I didn't know he did that to you."

"You didn't ask."

"But it's not the same, Jen. You can ditch me, if you'd rather. I'm good with it."

"That's not all of it."

"Then tell me."

Jen hesitated. She glanced around his apartment and knew she could end this for once and for all. She could make a comment that would cut to his heart, but she didn't want to hurt his feelings.

But then, it was his feelings or hers.

"Go ahead," Zach urged. "Dish it out. I can take it. I had my Wheaties this morning."

"Why would any woman marry you?" Jen asked abruptly, putting one hand on her hip as she gestured to the apartment with the other one. She took a deep breath and plunged on, despite the shock in Zach's eyes. "You live like a kid. You eat like a kid. You think like a kid, focussed on fun and nothing else. You survive on your daddy's money and it seems that the only motivation you ever had was to tick him off. You have no plan, no job, no ambition, and no dream. You're neither old enough nor young enough to get away with that crap. No one with a speck of sense would even pretend to be marrying you."

There, it was said.

And she felt badly, but she would not take it back. Jen knew she should have marched out the door right then and there, but she couldn't do it. Not yet. She had to wait for his response.

Did she want him to be devastated?

Or to bounce back, unaffected?

She didn't have time to decide before Zach—as usual—found another option altogether and, one more time, surprised the heck out of her.

Zach hid his thoughts, making a point of patting the dog while he decided upon his comeback. Okay, it was an unexpected assault but not an unjustified one.

It was clear that Jen expected him to be shattered by her truth-telling, but the real truth was that he'd been thinking much the same thing, on some level, for a while. It was kind of reassuring to have it said out loud, maybe a bit less scary that way than when it had just been rattling around in his brain.

But this seriously struck him as a case of the pot calling the kettle black.

Zach considered her, trying to gauge her fragility. She stood with her hands on her hips, eyes flashing, as invincible as he'd ever seen her. She was the Amazon queen. Maybe that was why she was turning him down: she would prefer to choose her own love slave and drag him off by the hair, rather than just go with a volunteer.

Zach decided to say what he thought. "And I'm supposed to be wounded by this observation, coming as it is from a woman who lives with her mother and waits tables for a living." He spoke lightly but Jen caught her breath. "I don't see a lot of evidence of your plan, ambition, or dream, Jen, and even you admit that your job is a crummy one."

To his surprise, she didn't give back as good as she'd gotten. Not this time. He'd found the Achilles heel of his Amazon, if mythology could get that mixed.

Jen's eyes filled with tears, which she blinked away furiously. She didn't want him to see them, he could understand that, because she liked to be seen at her strongest. All the same, he knew he had hit a nerve.

He felt like apologizing, except she'd hit harder than he had.

"I'm sorry," he began but Jen interrupted him, one hand held up between them.

"Fair enough," she said, her voice husky and her pose defensive. "I guess now you can see why this just isn't going to work." She hauled open the door and headed for the elevator, without looking back.

Zach watched her, wishing he knew how to fix this. Roxie whimpered and Zach had to hold her collar to keep her from following Jen.

"I'll see you around, then," he called, his characteristic optimism taking a dive when he noted how savagely Jen pressed the elevator button.

Jen gave him a dark look, but he could see that she was going to cry. He might have gone after her, but he already knew that she'd prefer him to not see her tears.

"You'd better not," she said tightly. "Or I'll call the cops."

Zach didn't think of a brilliant comeback before the elevator came. For once, it arrived quickly. Jen didn't look at him when she got into it, just focused on the control panel as if it was the most fascinating thing she'd ever seen. The doors closed almost immediately, leaving him with the conviction that he'd never see her again.

It wasn't a good feeling.

Roxie whimpered again and nudged his hand.

"Yup," he told the dog. "She's gone. After a particularly smooth move on my part." Zach closed the door to his apartment. Roxie went to the window, apparently wanting to catch a glimpse of Jen as she departed. Zach knew the dog watched for him this way, because he'd seen her from the street below.

He stood at the door and looked around. His apartment felt

vast and empty. The sound of Roxie's nails echoed as he'd never noticed before.

"You were a big help," he said, his heart not really in his complaint. "Couldn't you have begged for a belly rub or done something cute? Women go for that kind of thing."

Roxie ignored him, her attention caught by something below. Zach found himself standing beside her, watching a dark-haired woman turn up her collar against the swirl of snow as she walked away from his building with long, decisive steps. This time her hands were bunched in her pockets, fists driven deep by anger.

Or sorrow.

It was as if she couldn't put distance between them quickly enough. She wiped at her face with one hand and Zach felt like a bigger loser than he ever had before.

Which was saying something.

When Jen disappeared into the T station—presumably to disappear forever—Zach returned to the kitchen, snagged the bottle of champagne, and settled in to finish it himself. It would only go flat, otherwise. He had to admit that his brilliant plan hadn't exactly come together.

There were quotes from famous people on the matter of champagne printed on the label. Zach paused after he filled his glass to read the one from Winston Churchill.

In victory I deserve it; in defeat I need it.

Zach could drink to that.

Jen was fuming.

A waitress who lives with her mother.

Zach's charge had power because it was true. What was her dream? What was she doing to accomplish it? And who was she to call him on his chips when her own life didn't look so hot?

She raged home from the bus stop, ignored her mother's query about Zach's health and took the stairs two at a time to her room.

She heard Cin make some comment about a lovers' spat and resisted the urge to kill her sister instead of Zach. She chucked her coat on the bed, fired up the computer, and clicked to the website of the college she had attended.

It took an hour of going back and forth through the calendar, of reading the rules for admission and readmission, and a ping to an admin that got a quick reply, to tell Jen what she needed to know.

She could reactivate her student number, by crossing the admissions department's palm with silver.

Big surprise. Money fixed everything.

The thing was that she could finish her degree by the end of summer term, if she went full-time in the winter and again in spring and summer term. She'd graduate with her bachelor's in business administration.

In less than a year, she could have her degree. She could have a real job and make real money to pay off her very real debt.

It was a big step from committing to the construction of a piece of knitted fruit or even a pair of socks. Eight months of intense study from here to graduation. The thought nearly stopped Jen's heart. The possibility of doing it part-time was unthinkable. Could she envision herself surviving even eight whole months?

Could she afford to do it?

Could she afford to *not* do it?

Jen pushed back from her desk and looked at the screen. All it took was money and time. She was suddenly very jealous of Zach Coxwell, but she wasn't going to think about that.

She was going to appreciate what she had. Or at least, she would begin to appreciate what she had more than she had been appreciating it for the last couple of years.

Natalie was right: Jen was alive and it was time to start living again. It was time to make a commitment to something bigger than another small knitting project and another shift waiting tables. She would have liked to have given her mother credit for the change, but Jen was honest enough with herself to admit that it had been a certain infuriatingly confident man who had finally pushed her to make something of herself.

Too bad Zach would never know.

Impulsively, she returned to the part of the website that would let her reactivate her student number and did so. Jen was going to do this and no one was going to change her mind. She paid the fee by credit card and waited for the confirmation with her heart pounding.

How would she pay for this? Jen stifled the voice of doubt that had gotten far too much airtime lately. Once upon a time, she had gotten on a plane to England with no firm plan other than to see the world. Once she had walked into a taverna in Italy and asked for a job in her mediocre Italian. Once she had taken chances, been bold, faced risk.

This was nothing. Jen registered for a full roster of classes for the winter without any further hesitation. The balance due posted to her account nearly made her lungs seize.

This was the right thing to do, she reminded herself. She logged out, then went downstairs to negotiate a loan from her mother.

She might be living here, paying it back in increments, for twenty years, but Jen didn't care. She had a purpose. She had a dream. And she was going after it.

It must just have been human nature that made her want to call Zach and tell him so.

Or maybe do something truly mature, like say "nyahhhhh" into the phone and hang up on him. That would impress him. Guys went for that behavior all the time.

When they were six.

Which, she reminded herself, didn't exactly put Zach out of the picture.

Did six-year-olds kiss like he did? Jen didn't want to know.

Chapter 10

Jen had hit a nerve. It wasn't strictly true that Zach didn't have a dream or a goal, but it was true that he hadn't visibly done much about pursuing his objective. He had never even named it, for fear of his father's decimation of it.

Zach wondered whether his father would rise from the grave to destroy the notion of his son becoming an "artsy-fartsy liberal." If sheer willpower was the only credential necessary to haunt someone from the great beyond, Zach figured he could count on his father showing anytime now.

There hadn't been room for Zach's dreams in his father's universe: Robert Coxwell's children were supposed to want what Robert Coxwell had decided would be best. The only possible choice was to become younger versions of Robert Coxwell: to get good enough grades to go to law school, to graduate with honors and ace the bar exam, to practice criminal law, and thus amass fame and fortune. Especially the fortune bit.

But Zach had never been that wild for money.

Even so, the fate of Zach and his two older brothers had been decided when they had made their first yells and the particular shape of their genital equipment had been noted.

Zach had hated law school. He had hated it so much that it had been impossible for him to put up and shut up, as he expected his brother Matt had done, to just get through it and do something else afterward.

He sat on the floor and liked that photo from Venice more with every passing minute. He could remember now how he'd spent hours as a kid with *National Geographic* magazines, not reading the articles but looking at the pictures. He'd "borrowed" money from his mother's purse to buy every issue.

Come to think of it, they must be stored at Gray Gables somewhere. It was such a big house that nothing ever got dumped or given away: it just got nudged aside. The attic was an amazing place and had been another haunt of his as a child.

Maybe he should get the magazines back. Matt, who had bought out his siblings' shares in the house after Robert's death and moved in with his family, wouldn't care. If anything, Matt would probably be glad to be rid of them. Zach could put them in a bookcase, right over there.

Of course, in order to do that, he'd have to go to Gray Gables to ask for them and to pick them up, and that wasn't going to happen anytime soon. Gray Gables was where his father had been when Zach had called from New Orleans. Gray Gables was where his father had died.

Zach decided not to think about that.

He certainly wasn't going to think about Jen's kiss melting his Jockeys and how things could have proceeded in a really interesting way from there.

If he had had a bed.

He thought about photography instead. He could remember now how he'd always been framing views in his mind's eye, always composing things for a better effect. It was intuitive and it was the only thing that made him feel connected to the world.

It made him feel alive. The impulse to quit school, become a photographer, and go to Europe to learn his craft had been a good one. Like most intuitive choices in Zach's life, he had found a truth about himself without really looking for it. Maybe that was the only way to find the great truths in life: to guess, to follow instinct, and see where it took you. Zach didn't know. He did know that he liked the sense of adventure.

The less happy truth was that he'd chickened out of his big adventure. His grand tour hadn't lasted nearly long enough, and he could attribute that to his own weakness. It's hard to be the life of the party when there's a language barrier. No one in Italy or France had gotten his jokes. That had given him more time to think than he'd been used to having.

In a strange way, he'd missed the relentless disapproval of his father. At least when Robert was chewing him out, Zach could be sure that the man knew Zach was alive. It had, in fact, been the only way he could get Robert's attention. James had excelled at following in Robert's footsteps, Matt had done so well in English classes—both lit and lang—that even though Robert hadn't valued the humanities much, he'd been compelled to express approval. With those two options spoken for, Zach had gone with making trouble as a way to get noticed.

It had worked like a charm. Jen had nailed it in one.

In fact, marijuana had been the best charm of all. Robert had been convinced that the downfall of American society could be traced to the growing prevalence of recreational use of marijuana in the 1960s, so Zach had figured that selling pot would be the best way to guarantee that his father's eye was on him. It had taken a surprisingly long interval for his father to associate the demon weed with his youngest son, and that blind eye had led Zach to be more daring all the time in his exploits.

He wouldn't think about the last one, not now.

He wouldn't think about finally pushing his father too far.

He wouldn't think about his stupid prank being the straw that had broken the camel's back.

Zach looked at the Bridge of Sighs, captured in all its moody splendor. He thought then about traveling with Jen, how it would be fun to discover a place with her and to talk about it. They would get each other's jokes. He would take pictures. They would, he was sure of it, be cheap about the same things and expansive about the same things.

Of course, that would only work if she started talking to him again, which didn't seem to be particularly probable at this point in time. He had a nasty feeling that there was only one way out of this mess, only one way back into Jen's universe.

He was going to have to tell her the truth.

All of it.

Zach hated when that happened.

His whole future hinged on the answer to one question: was it possible for a son of Robert Coxwell to do something other than what Robert Coxwell had determined was the ideal and thus sole possibility for that child's future?

The evidence was scant. Eldest son, James, was still a lawyer, albeit one practicing in the district attorney's office. But number two son, Matt, had cast all of that aside. He'd written a book, from what Zach had heard, not just the one on Boston's history that he'd been pecking at for years, but a novel.

If anything smacked of being artsy-fartsy, it would have to be writing fiction.

Of course, the last time Zach had seen his brother, Matt—other than at his father's funeral—had been when Matt had refused to help him get out of jail in New Orleans, if not for free than at least at a minimal charge. They'd come close to a fight then, for the first time ever, and Matt had given Zach a dose of hard truth.

Kind of like Jen. There seemed to be a lot of that going around.

He shied away from the prospect of confronting Matt, of facing whatever truth Matt would see fit to deal out this time.

Matt would be found at Grey Gables, and Zach wasn't going there anytime soon. At least not voluntarily.

Then he had a thought. His baby sister, Philippa, had never finished law school but had started a successful landscaping business instead. Maybe Robert Coxwell's rules had been different for girls.

Zach didn't think so, though. His father had really given Phil a hard time, especially about her choice of partner. Nick Sullivan had been condemned without a hearing by Zach's father. Maybe he and Nick, who were contemporaries but had never been friends, had more in common than Zach had realized. Maybe Philippa could give him some pointers about charting his own course.

Maybe it was time he found out.

Roxie sighed and stretched, putting her chin on Zach's knee. He rubbed the back of her neck, liking her warmth against him. "We never took Phil and Nick a gift for their new baby's arrival," he told the dog, who didn't appear to be inclined to discuss the matter.

In fact, her only reply was a long whisper of a dog fart.

Zach sipped his champagne, wishing Jen had stayed to drink some of it with him. It didn't taste that good to him in her absence. "Jen would have told me that I was wrong," he told Roxie. "Just the way Matt told me what was wrong and I told him he was wrong even though he was right. Jen would have told me to apologize, to straighten up and treat my family the way I'd like them to treat me."

He eyed the framed photo, then put his half-empty glass aside. He remembered Jen's defense of her family and their idiosyncrasies, on her insistence upon their mutual respect. Maybe his family wasn't close because none of them ever bothered to say they were sorry. Maybe they weren't close because they didn't treat each other with any tolerance and respect. Zach suspected that Jen would have said that apologizing, especially when he had to admit he'd been wrong, was something an adult would do.

Zach was ready to be an adult.

Let the rest of the champagne go flat.

"C'mon, Roxie, let's go for a ride in the car." The dog bounded to her feet, instantly awake at the prospect of one of her favorite activities. Zach was sure that she'd learned "ride in the car" immediately after "out" and "walk." He was still working on "no" and had a feeling he always would be.

He picked up her leash and his keys, a combination that never failed to delight her. "We're going to score a baby gift, then we're going to Rosemount. Not Gray Gables. The other side of town where the troublemakers are. Who knows? Maybe it's where I really belong."

Something was wrong with this picture.

Nick Sullivan opened the front door to find his brother-in-law standing on the porch with a gift and a large wagging dog.

Nick looked Zach up and down, in no mood to cut him any slack. "Got the wrong address?" he asked.

It sounded almost as irritated as he felt, having spent the night bouncing a screaming baby, trying to ensure that Phil got some sleep so that she could prep today for her big presentation tomorrow. This morning, his grandmother, Lucia, who actually owned the house, had insisted that it was time to repaint the kitchen, that it had to be done today, and that it had to be chartreuse, although she couldn't decide upon the precise shade of limey green. Michael, Nick's four-year-old son, had woken up with a messy cold that precluded his going to nursery school, and Phil had been on the phone all morning.

Nick was not in the mood to entertain his troublemaking brother-in-law and he was not in the mood to be hoodwinked, blackmailed, or otherwise bamboozled into anything he might regret. He stood on the threshold, barricading entry. The dog sat down, apparently understanding from Nick's attitude that it should stay put.

"I don't think so," Zach said with his usual easy charm. "Doesn't my sister live here?"

"She's out," Nick lied. He made to shut the door. "You'll have to come back another time."

"Then why is her truck here?" Zach asked. He gestured to the pickup in the driveway emblazoned with the logo of Phil's landscaping company. He grinned with familiar confidence. "Or are you just not that happy to see me, Nick?"

"How irrational that would be," Nick said wryly.

"Okay, so we didn't get along when we were teenagers . . ."

"There's the understatement of the century."

"But we're family now . . ."

"Don't remind me."

"And I'd like to patch it up." Zach jiggled the box as if it would tempt Nick. "I even brought a present."

Nick eyed the pink bow atop it. "Presumably not for me."

"I'm not sure the terry jumpsuit would fit," Zach said with some solemnity. "And you probably don't need the snaps in the crotch these days." He winced. "At least I'm hoping so."

"Thank you for that."

"But the sales clerk assured me that it was just the thing for a baby girl."

Beverly Lucia screamed right on cue, then began to wail. Nick passed a hand over his forehead in exhaustion as Michael began a hiccuping cry for attention.

"That's some duet you've got going," Zach said.

"I don't have time for your games today, whatever they are." Nick started to close the door, but Zach stopped him with one hand on the knob.

"I'm not bad with kids," Zach said, to Nick's astonishment. "Maralys even says so. You want a hand?"

It was tempting to shut the door in Zach's face, especially as this would traditionally have been a setup to a joke that led to further inconvenience and frustration. Nick hesitated. Maralys *had* been saying lately that Zach had a special touch with Zoë. "Why are you offering to do this?" he demanded, knowing his eyes were narrowed with suspicion. "We both know that playing nice isn't your game."

Zach looked away, then glanced back at Nick with a rueful smile. "But I'm trying to be an adult. I have to say that it's not as easy as it looks."

"Why now?"

Zach shrugged, so obviously and uncharacteristically awkward that Nick was intrigued. "It's kind of past due, wouldn't you say?"

"Why do you need to see Phil?"

Zach looked around himself, so uncomfortable that Nick expected either a bald lie or the truth. Zach met Nick's gaze abruptly and he put his dime on the second option. "I need to ask her how a Coxwell can *not* be a lawyer."

"With difficulty," Nick said quickly.

"That's what I'm afraid of."

"Maybe it's easier now that your father is gone."

Zach shoved a hand through his hair, looking and sounding considerably more human than Nick had ever remembered him being. "I'd like to think so, but Phil will know better."

Nick tried to fight his impulse to agree. "Why wouldn't you want to be a lawyer?" Nick leaned in the door. "You did a great job with that contract to take care of Beverly. Phil said it was a masterpiece and that you didn't even ask for help from any of them."

"As if I would!" Zach said with a shake of his head. "Wouldn't they have all loved it if I'd admitted failure?" He straightened before Nick could say anything. "No, I had to do it myself. I was glad everyone agreed that it was the right thing to do."

There was a glint in Zach's eye that was new, new to Nick anyway. That document rejigging the distribution of Robert's assets had been a surprise, not just because it was an admirable legal document but in the thoughtful impetus that had driven it. Was Zach changing? Finding his conscience? Thinking about other people for a change?

But Nick wouldn't be suckered, not by Zach anyway. "I shouldn't let you in here. You're a bad influence. My kids could learn things from you that I'd rather they didn't know."

Zach leaned closer, his manner confidential. "Then I'll make you a deal. Let me talk to Phil today and I promise that I won't teach Michael how to drive." Zach looked serious.

Nick considered this. "You're the one who taught Phil to drive," he remembered, speaking with some caution. He'd seen his life pass before his eyes far too many times when Phil was at the wheel. It was the only time she was aggressive and devil-may-care.

Not a big surprise, when you considered who had taught her how.

Zach nodded, mischief in his eyes. "We turned doughnuts on the ice on Mary Lake in the winter. She was my star pupil."

"And you taught her to pass."

"You bet." Zach nodded. "Gotta gear down for the acceleration and just go for it. You gotta know what your machine can do."

"And if you're wrong, you use up a life."

"You learn the limitations *before* you use up a life."

Nick thought for one heartbeat about Michael driving like Phil and his decision was made. "Deal," he said abruptly and flung open the door. "Come on in. Phil's in the conservatory with Annette."

Zach paused. "What's Matt's daughter doing here?"

"Homework. Studying the operation of a small business." Nick grimaced as he strode down the hall, leading the way. "She could babysit, or paint the kitchen, but no. She's doodling in the margins of Phil's landscaping plans instead, making more work for Phil, who is too nice to say anything."

"Bad day?" Zach asked lightly.

"It's in the running for worst day of the century."

"The century's young yet."

"I'll still put my money on this one." Nick heard Phil's voice more clearly as they approached the kitchen. She was on the phone again, probably trying to finalize details for her presentation the next day.

"Nick!" His grandmother called as they stepped into that room. "This green or the darker one? I think I prefer the lemon tones of this one. It's more scrumptious, in a way . . ."

"I'll be right with you, Lucia." Nick pointed Zach in the direction of his sister and niece as Michael's wail gained in volume. The dog bounded into the conservatory and Annette squealed with delight.

"This must be Roxanne!" she cried and immediately made a fuss over the dog.

Phil frowned and put a finger in her other ear as she leaned away from the noise to talk urgently into the phone. Nick shrugged an apology and she smiled a little.

He headed back for the stairs and a very unhappy toddler. "I knew that nap was too good to be true," he muttered.

"What a voice," Lucia said with approval as she listened to Michael wail. She nodded confidently to Zach. "He gets it from me, you know. It's in his blood." As she began to sing some part in Italian from an old opera, adding to the household concerto in her own way, Nick fought the urge to yell for silence.

Zach nudged him, bringing him back to sanity or its closest approximation. "Bring me a niece or nephew, your choice," he murmured conspiratorially, "and I'll do what I can."

"You might regret that offer."

Zach grinned. "I'll just add it to the list. After all, I'd rather regret what I have done than what I haven't."

The scary thing was that Zach was making sense. Nick wasn't going to give credence to his impression that his brother-in-law had changed just yet—his observations might be affected by his lack of sleep, after all—but he wasn't going to turn down an offer for help, either. "You're on," he said, resolving to entrust Zach with whichever kid was screaming the loudest.

It would serve him right for volunteering.

"The lighter green or the darker one?" Lucia demanded and Nick did not care. He opened his mouth to say so but Zach spoke first.

"The light one," Zach said decisively. "The yellower tone of that chartreuse brightens the room and picks up the greens from the leaves in the conservatory." He moved across the room and held up his hands, framing a view. "See? Look here and picture that lighter color on the walls. Then look at the darker one against the floor: it makes it look dingy and you probably don't want to lay a new floor."

"Not right now anyway," Nick muttered. As he headed down the hall, he glanced back.

Lucia looked around the kitchen, then smiled at Zach. "You know, you're right. I didn't know you had an eye for such things."

"Hey, I just do what I can."

That was a switch, but Nick wasn't going to argue.

Not on this day anyway.

It was dark by the time Zach drove away. He'd talked—apparently earnestly—to Phil for a while and stayed for dinner. He'd also painted one wall of the kitchen with the can of test color that Lucia had bought, promised to come back the next day to finish the kitchen. And he'd managed to lull Michael to sleep with some story about a stuffed toy that he'd seemed to make up as he went along. They'd barbequed some chicken breasts to make life simpler, and Nick was ready to crash out himself.

Phil was nursing the baby, still occasionally getting up to add to her sketch. Nick watched her, liking the way her hair was swept up into a ponytail, liking the way she shifted the baby's weight so easily. She had licked or eaten off all of her lipstick, and looked smooth and soft and natural.

The way she did first thing in the morning. She was filled with that nervous energy she always had before a meeting and he suddenly felt a bit less sleepy than he had.

He could think of one good way to expend that energy of Phil's.

He'd bribe her with chocolate, if he had to, and volunteer to help her work off the calories if she complained about them.

"I gotta go." Annette was packing up her notebooks.

"I'll walk you back to Gray Gables," Nick offered before Phil could give him a look.

"It's not that far," Annette protested, her tone revealing that she knew she'd lose.

"I could use a stretch."

Phil cast Nick an impish grin, the one that made his heart skip. "You could use some silence," she teased. "It's just an excuse to get out of this madhouse for a few minutes."

"He might go out for milk and never come back," Lucia teased. "He's done it before."

"Not this time," Phil said with confidence before Nick could protest his own innocence. She smiled warmly at him and he knew he'd be walking home double-quick. "He doesn't do that anymore."

"He grew up," Lucia said with approval. "Just like your brother is doing."

"Who was that, anyway?" Nick asked, gesturing toward the door as he got his jacket. "He looked like Zach and sounded like Zach but sure didn't act like Zach."

"He said he's trying to be an adult," Lucia offered.

"It's not new," Phil said with care. "Father's death had a big effect on him. Remember that contract?"

"I don't know." Nick laughed. "Being an adult will be a big change for him. You watch, he won't come back to paint tomorrow. That promise will be out of his head before he reaches the highway tonight."

But Phil shook her head. "I don't think so. He'll be here in the morning, you'll see, all bright-eyed and ready to go."

"This would be your brother Zach we're talking about?" Nick asked, not hiding his skepticism.

Phil laughed. "He doesn't make many promises but he's always kept the ones he does make. Trust me. He said he'd do it and he will."

"Why?"

Phil's lips quirked slightly, and Nick knew she was laughing at him. "Maybe it's pity."

Before Nick could argue with that, Annette spoke up.

"I think he's in love," she said with a teenager's resolve. The adults exchanged smiles.

"Do you, then?" Phil asked. "What would you know about that?"

"It makes perfect sense," Annette said, her manner haughty. "It happens in almost every show on TV and in every movie. The sexy heartbreaker hunk who sleeps with every woman but doesn't commit to any of them finally falls in love. And then he changes."

Lucia nodded. "The child is right. It's a classic theme in operas, as well."

"And when the woman is convinced of the change in him, they live happily ever after?" Nick said, unable to keep from teasing Annette.

"Be serious," Annette said.

"I think not," Lucia said at the same time.

Nick and Phil exchanged a glance. "What then?" Phil asked.

"Well, the woman dies, obviously," Annette said with the considerable scorn that can be mustered by a fourteen-year-old.

"It's the climax of every tragedy," Lucia agreed. "Thematically, the hero has learned his lesson about using other people for his own pleasure, and thus is robbed of his own pleasure for all time."

"Right. The cowboy is such a wreck that he can't ever love again," Annette concluded with a shrug. "Happens every time."

Nick saw that Phil's dismay at that prospect. "Hopefully not this time," she said.

"Maybe she'll just dump him instead," Nick suggested. Phil smiled, slightly reassured, but neither Annette nor Lucia were convinced.

Not that it mattered to Nick. If Zach really painted the kitchen the next day, Nick would have to give serious consideration to the prospect of forgiving and forgetting.

But he wasn't going to rush into anything.

• • •

For the first time in Jen's recollection, the prospect of Christmas lacked a certain zing. Even the invitation from Teresa to stay at her apartment in Boston for a few days for the solstice didn't put a bounce in Jen's step. She reminded herself of all the great vintage places in the vicinity, the holiday sales, and the adventure of a different, more urban locale, but couldn't manage to persuade herself.

Teresa would talk all night about her fab job. Her apartment would be perfect, her clothes would be chic, and she would drink a lot. The phone would ring incessantly, or maybe it would be her BlackBerry demanding her attention. Teresa's knitting wool stash would be impressive, both in quantity and in quality (and thus expense). She would have knit glittery things that Jen couldn't imagine wearing. Jen would have almost nothing to say to her former best friend, no experience or anecdote of any relevance to a high-powered female executive destined for corporate glory.

Jen would wear the black cashmere breast prosthesis and it wouldn't help. She certainly wouldn't make the mistake again of showing Teresa the very neat prosthesis, having already made the mistake of assuming that a fellow knitter would be intrigued by the clever decreases and vintage button used for the nipple. On that unforgettable occasion, Teresa had stared at Jen's empty bra cup instead, making her feel like a freak when she'd been trying to establish common ground.

Nope. She wouldn't do that again.

Maybe she'd "catch pneumonia," cancel, stay home, and knit.

She finished the socks for her mother and was enormously relieved. It seemed to energize her with possibilities. Jen then embarked on a pair of qiviut mittens for M.B. in a wonderful chocolate color. It wasn't so terrifying to embark on a bigger project the second time—although she still did knit like a fiend and didn't take a deep breath until they were done.

It was easy to commit to the intricate hat that would be perfect for Cin. It was a onesie, after all, not half of a pair. She felt triumph when it was done.

No goals? She had goals.

Jen embarked on a lacy shawl for her grandmother, knowing that it would take until the eve of Christmas itself to finish it, if she knit like crazy. She worried a bit about making the deadline, but for the first time in a long time, she forgot to worry about whether she'd be alive by then or not. She even went for her routine mammogram without spending the night before puking her guts out in terror.

If that wasn't progress, she didn't know what was.

Meanwhile, not very far away from Natalie's house, a skeptical Maralys was pushing prints back across her kitchen table toward Zach. "Fair enough," she said. "But it could have been staged."

Zach pretended to be outraged. "Don't you trust me?"

Maralys smiled. "No. Why should I?"

There was that. Zach gathered up his prints of dinner at Jen's grandmother's house and started to put them back into the envelope. Roxie was scoring oatmeal cookie crumbs from Zoë, who had parked herself on Zach's knee.

"Zach cookie," Zoë said, offering him the gummy remains of the cookie she was eating. She had sticky crumbs all over herself, and Roxie was salivating as she watched. Zach thought that maybe the dog should just lick the toddler all over, but wasn't sure Maralys would approve of that idea.

"You'd better finish that one yourself," Zach said with a smile. The little girl hesitated and he pretended to be horrified. "Isn't it any good?"

She giggled and held on to it with both hands. "Good cookie."

"Oh, then you eat it up."

Zoë leaned against his leg contentedly, took another bite of the cookie, then handed the rest to Roxie.

Roxie didn't give her a chance to reconsider her offer.

Maralys tapped a fingertip on the table. "Christmas," she said and Zach was startled by the firmness of her tone. "Bring Jen to Christmas dinner and then I'll believe you."

"But wait a minute . . ."

"I hosted Thanksgiving dinner, planned purely to reconcile you with your family, and you skipped out with an excuse. I don't have to let you off easy. Think about it: thirteen Coxwells trapped in this small house for seven hours together."

Zach shuddered. "It must have been slice of hell."

"Actually, it was kind of fun." Maralys shook a finger. "But you still owe me. Christmas dinner with Jen and we'll call it square."

Zach felt obliged to make an observation. "But we don't have a family Christmas dinner."

"Wrong! We worked it out at Thanksgiving. You would have known that if you'd bothered to show."

"Go ahead, rub it in."

"I will."

"But, uh, Jen and I broke up . . ."

"How convenient is that?" Maralys demanded, a gleam in her eye.

"Actually, she didn't want to get married," he said, going with a variation of the truth.

"You proposed to a woman and she turned you down?"

"Well, yes."

Maralys grinned. "Now I have to meet her."

"Impossible."

"Nothing's impossible, Zach."

"Well, this is."

"Are you telling me that your charm isn't enough to persuade her to make one guest appearance, for old times' sake?" Maralys tapped the side of her coffee cup. "Oh right. Jen's immune to your brand of charm. Otherwise, she'd be wearing your ring." She leaned an elbow on the tabletop, her eyes dancing. "So, what's it like, having finally met your nemesis?"

"She's not my nemesis . . ."

"You proposed for the first time in your life and Jen said no. Who knows? She might be perfect for you. Aren't you going to go back and ask again?"

Zach met the challenge in Maralys's eyes and knew he had to make this happen somehow. Rather conveniently, Jen still owed him—and it had been her own suggestion that the trade be attendance at their respective family dinners.

He'd been a dope to turn down her offer, but maybe that meant there was a chance of recovery.

"Deal," he said, picking up his envelope. "Are you going to tell me where dinner is and when, or is that a surprise?"

"It might be a surprise. Gray Gables, two o'clock on the big day."

Gray Gables.

Zach sat down again. He wasn't in a hurry to go back there and he suspected that Maralys knew it. "That's early. We can't all be getting along that well."

Maralys smiled. "Leaves time for presents. We did a lottery." She rummaged by the phone for a minute or two, then came up with a sheet of paper. "That's right, you drew Matt's name."

"I wasn't even there!"

"By proxy. See? You should have shown up. You might have picked someone easy all by yourself."

"Go ahead, rub it in."

"It's an innate talent," Maralys said with a smile that told Zach she was enjoying herself. "I can't wait to meet Jen," she called when he snapped his fingers for Roxie and headed for the front door. "She must be really something."

"She is," he muttered, wondering how he was going to make this happen. There was a way: he just had to think of it.

In the meantime, he had another appointment. Photography was what Zach wanted to do, and that meant that he was going to have to show his work to somebody. His old art teacher, Mr. Nicholson, had retired, but Zach had hunted him down and Mr. Nicholson had agreed to look at Zach's work. He'd even expressed some curiosity.

Zach had decided it was time to get another opinion and he trusted Mr. Nicholson to tell him the truth.

No matter how ugly it might be.

All dire predictions to the contrary, karaoke night at Mulligan's was a huge success. The pub was crowded every Wednesday night and the jar for pooled tips saw some serious action. They had to clear some of the tables away to make room for the crowds—and the dancing—each Wednesday after dinner. There was almost zero work for the kitchen after seven and most of the revenue was from the sale of alcoholic beverages.

Murray, not surprisingly, gloated. The margins on booze were enough to make him downright gleeful.

Jen was very glad she'd registered for winter classes and would be cutting back her hours. She hefted so many trays of beer on Wednesday nights that her mother was always ready and waiting to give her a massage when she got home. Jen now understood that she couldn't do this job forever, although it had taken karaoke night to bring the point home.

But that was okay. She had plans and dreams and goals to achieve.

On the Wednesday before Christmas, Mulligan's was hopping early. People came for dinner and stayed. It didn't hurt that classes were over for the term and that people would be heading home for the holidays—this might be a last chance for hanging out with friends.

Murray was merry, which made the waitresses exchange glances as they waited for their orders.

"You look the way my kids did when they'd done something bad and figured they couldn't get caught," Lucy observed as she loaded four pints of beer on to her tray.

"Holiday spirit," Murray said with a smile.

"So, he's been into the brandy," Jen said.

"That explains a lot," Kathy agreed.

"And tells us that profits are way up," Jen said.

Lucy laughed but Murray shook his head. "Not me. I learned early that the owner belongs behind the bar if the joint is going to make any money."

"Spoilsport," Kathy complained, probably because it was expected of someone. "I could use a shot of something right about now."

"Get over it," Murray retorted. "You've got another group seated in your section."

Kathy harumphed. "Well, if you'd make those margaritas for table five in this lifetime, I could get back over there."

"Cheeky, cheeky," Murray retorted. "If they were guys, you'd have been over there already, even without your margaritas."

"Now, don't go acting jealous, Murray," Kathy teased, blowing him a kiss as she hefted her tray of margaritas to her shoulder. "I still love you best of all."

Murray shook his head as he pulled the cork on a bottle of Merlot. "What's your choice for a starting song tonight, Jen?" he asked as he poured a glass of wine.

"'Come See About Me,'" she said impulsively, hoping no one realized she was thinking of Zach doing just that. She hadn't heard a word from him, which wasn't irrational given what she'd said to him before she walked out of his apartment.

But still.

Life had certainly been more lively with Zach around. She'd stopped looking up every time the door to Mulligan's opened although she hadn't quite stopped looking for large black-and-white dogs or red Neons that had seen better days.

The man might have fallen off the face of the earth.

Which, despite everything she'd said to him, was a pretty disappointing prospect.

"Good choice," Kathy said, waiting for a couple of Diet Cokes when Jen returned to the bar for another order. "Mind if I beckon to the cutie at twenty-seven?"

"That's my section," Lucy snapped.

"And do you want him?" Kathy propped a hand on her hip. "Should we give Joe his walking papers?"

Lucy shook a finger at the younger waitress. "You're going to get yourself a disease, girl." ·

"But I'll die with a smile on my face." Kathy shrugged and sailed back to her tables, unpersuaded.

"How about something a little more upbeat?" Murray suggested to Jen. "You could do a second song, something to get them dancing."

"A second song?" Lucy demanded. "Here we go, here's the escalation that we knew was inevitable." She nudged Jen, who didn't agree.

"We've done every song the machine has," Jen said, trying to remember the list without taking the time to look.

"Except Elvis," Murray observed.

Jen gave him a look. "I refuse to wear fake sideburns."

"How about the white jumpsuit?" Lucy teased.

"I could never hit the low notes anyway." Jen shook her head. "Maybe a Beatles tune." She was skeptical though, unable to think of one that would be what Murray wanted. "How about 'I Hear a Symphony'?"

"Works for me," Lucy said.

"I thought you were against doing a second one," Murray said.

Lucy tossed her hair. "It's not the same. I know the words to that one now."

"Dance music," Murray muttered. "I want them dancing, because that makes them thirsty."

"Then you should have loaded the machine with Donna Summer," Lucy replied. She patted Jen on the shoulder. "You sing what you want, Jen, and don't let him give you a hard time. This stupid karaoke machine is only a success because of you, and don't you let Murray try to make you forget it."

"Hey . . ." Murray started to protest.

Lucy silenced him with a glare. "Give her a hard time and none of us will sing."

Murray glowered and wiped the bar. "A little dancing never hurt anyone," he muttered, but no one was listening.

If Jen had thought about it, she would have realized that he gave it up more easily than was characteristic.

But she didn't.

Not until much, much later.

Eight o'clock came quickly that night, with no lull between dinner and the crowd for karaoke. Mulligan's was dark, crowded, and already getting warm. Jen propped open the door to the street to get a breeze.

At Murray's whistle, she scurried to join Kathy and Lucy, and when she took the stage, some of the regulars cheered.

"Demand a raise," Lucy advised.

But singing was reward enough. Jen took a bow, blushing, then they launched into "Come See About Me." Murray had preprogrammed the machine and it rolled directly into "I Hear a Symphony." The trio barely missed a beat. The bossa nova step had become second nature to the three of them, Lucy and Kathy finger snapped together, and it was as if they'd been singing together for years.

It was fun.

"C'mon, let's do another," Kathy said, waving to the guys in her section who were egging her on.

Lucy hesitated.

"C'mon," Kathy urged and Jen saw Lucy relent.

"Itching," Jen shouted to Murray and he punched up "Love Is Like an Itching in My Heart."

Being bitten by the love bug was about the size of it. Jen let her voice go. She was happy.

The crowd cheered and moved closer to the stage. Lots of fingers and toes were tapping, and Murray cranked up the volume. The six women from eighteen took to the dance floor together and were joined by two couples. Murray gave Jen a big thumbs-up.

The song was over all too soon. The trio were taking their bows when a motorcycle could be heard outside.

"The lazy bugger is driving it right up to the damn door," Lucy muttered in disapproval, then hurried back to her section.

Whoever was riding the bike did drive it up to the door: Jen could see his shadow through the etched glass in the pub windows as she went back to her section. The bike engine was given one last loud rev, as if the rider wanted to fill the pub with the smell of gas fumes. Or if he wanted to make sure everyone knew he had arrived.

That part worked.

Everyone glanced toward the door, although Jen's heart was probably the only one that stopped cold. A tall guy in black biking leathers paused on the threshold for effect.

She had a sneaking suspicion who the guy was, given his athletic build and apparent love of drama, and her heart began to gallop. She was pretty sure she remembered that battered leather jacket.

"Yum," Kathy whispered from the far side of the bar. "Be still my heart." Her voice carried in the comparative quiet and launched a ripple of female laughter. Or agreement. The guy pulled off his helmet and Jen's knees nearly gave out.

It *was* Zach.

With big, black fake sideburns and sunglasses.

He handed his helmet to a woman sitting at the table closest to the door with nonchalance. She smiled up at him in adoration.

"Thank you, thank you very much," he said in a passable imitation of Elvis. Jen bit back a giggle. The man was a lunatic.

And she was far too glad to see him again.

Zach swaggered down to the bar, winked at Murray, then took the stage. He held the microphone with casual ease.

Come to think of it, he was built a lot like the young Elvis. His dark blond hair was a bit incongruous with the dark sideburns, but he'd styled it with some kind of gel that made it look darker.

"It's mighty fine to be here tonight," he drawled. The women began to whisper and edge closer to the stage. Zach peeked over his sunglasses and winked at Jen. She smiled back at him, unable to help herself.

Then the karaoke machine began to play "Jailhouse Rock."

Jen choked back a laugh, then stared—just like every other female in the bar. Not only could Zach sing—and hit those low notes—but he could dance. He mimicked Elvis's hip moves so well that the temperature in the bar practically doubled. The women from table eighteen crowded the stage, clapping and hooting with appreciation.

The man knew how to make an entrance: she'd give him that.

But why had he bothered?

Chapter 11

Jen went back to the bar to get her drinks and found Murray tapping his fingers as he watched with approval. He was not surprised by Zach's sudden appearance.

"You knew," Jen accused.

Murray shrugged. "He phoned. He came in when you were off. He wanted to check what songs we had."

"You never told me."

"I wasn't supposed to. Come on, Jen, who am I to argue with *this*?" Murray shook his head in admiration, then Lucy demanded her four margaritas from the far side of the bar.

"Here I thought Elvis was in a doughnut shop in Kalamazoo," Jen said, unable to keep herself from turning to watch.

"Lucky for us," Kathy said.

Zach was gyrating low and the women were going wild. He was eating it up, obviously in his element. One of the women from eighteen was jitterbugging with him as the others bounced in excitement.

"I thought this wasn't that kind of a bar," Lucy said, though there was little censure in her tone. "What do we do when the women start throwing their underwear at him?"

"Kick the undies aside so they don't block the view," Kathy said.

"He's going to split those pants," Lucy observed.

"That's what we're all waiting for," Kathy said with a grin.

"Here I just thought you were appreciating his voice," Jen said. She wasn't sure what to think of this, besides enjoying the view. Why had Zach come here to do this?

Was he teasing her?

Or was he trying to show her her mistake in walking away from him? If he thought having teams of other women drooling over him was going to change Jen's mind, he could think again.

He was so unpredictable, though, that she couldn't be sure what his plan had been. He spun, dancing with the microphone again, then peeled off his black leather jacket and tossed it straight at Jen with a flourish.

She caught it instinctively, and the women from table eighteen glowered at her with dislike. The coat was warm and to Jen's surprise, even knowing that it was made from the hides of dead cows that probably would have preferred to keep their hides, she wasn't anxious to let go of it.

Zach was wearing a tight white T-shirt—very James Dean—which showed his muscular build. The women from eighteen were so busy swooning that they forgot to hate Jen.

Kathy rolled her eyes. "You'd have to be dead to not be thinking about what other good stuff he has."

Jen looked again, because she wasn't dead.

Not by a long shot. She fingered Zach's jacket and couldn't help hoping that this performance was for her benefit.

And she liked it a bit too much to be sure of what she'd do next. The bar, in fact, had become *really* warm. She passed Zach's jacket to Murray, giving it one last instinctive stroke. Then she hefted her tray, forced her way through the crowd, and tried not to think about how much fun it would be to jitterbug.

She had work to do.

Although that didn't preclude her sneaking the occasional peek at the eye candy Zach provided. On her way through the crowd, Jen noticed people pulling out their cell phones, more people than were usually using them in the bar, and wondered how they could hear anything.

The cell phones made sense when more people started pushing their way through the door. Suddenly, Mulligan's was crazy busy and it was all Jen could do to get drinks to her section.

"We're getting killed!" Murray shouted with glee, grinning from ear to ear and giggling to himself for the first time Jen could remember.

"All Shook Up" was next. Zach tossed the microphone from hand to hand as he danced and feigned the thump of his heart with one hand. At least the women in Jen's section didn't care how long it took for their drinks to come.

Jen caught Zach's eye, entirely by accident, and he lowered his sunglasses to give her another slow wink. The patrons in her vicinity turned to look at her, and although she tried to pretend she was indifferent, her blush gave her away.

At least the music was loud enough that no one could hear the thump of her own heart.

"Oh my God," Kathy breathed as the karaoke machine segued into "Twist and Shout." She was standing at the bar when Jen got back there, her hands over her mouth and her eyes wide as she stared.

Jen decided it would be safer not to look.

"Those women are salivating on the dance floor," Lucy commented as she banged her own tray on the bar. "Make sure you don't slip on your way to your section."

"Thanks for that safety tip," Kathy said. "Maybe I'll just stand here and enjoy the view instead. Yum!"

"Maybe you'll take care of your section or you'll be cut out of the tip pool," Murray said.

Kathy gave him a glance. "Might be worth it."

"Not tonight," Murray said with a shake of his head.

Meanwhile, Zach claimed a bar stool and perched upon it. He peeled off his sunglasses and chucked them into the crowd with a theatrical gesture. The women from eighteen squealed and there was screaming as one caught them.

"This one's for a special lady," he said in his Elvis voice, then started into "I Want You, I Need You, I Love You." He worked the low notes and Jen felt the back of her neck burning, but told herself not to look.

He could *not* be singing to her.

Not after what she'd said to him.

But the feeling that she was being watched only grew. Murray's grin and Lucy's nudge were also big clues. Jen was sure that her face was as red as a beet, she was so hot. She surrendered at the second verse and looked.

Zach was singing straight to her.

At her.

For her.

She would have to assume that he had forgiven and forgotten.

The details weren't important. The man looked good enough to eat with a spoon. Or without one. She remembered how he kissed and her mouth went dry.

Jen stood, a tray with three margaritas and two glasses of red wine on her shoulder, and could not for the life of her remember where she had been going. Or why.

"Give me that," Lucy said, spinning the tray out of Jen's hand. "You'll lose your tips."

"I can do it."

"Not when your feet are rooted to the floor."

It was true. "Table twenty-two," Jen whispered, unable to look away from the gleam of Zach's eyes. "I think."

"Yup, twenty-two," Murray confirmed.

Lucy paused to whisper in her ear. "Remember that it's not often a man will make an ass of himself for a woman."

"Even this one?"

Lucy glanced at Zach before she smiled at Jen again. "Especially this one," she whispered, then made off with Jen's tray.

But was that true? Most men would never have pretended to be Elvis, but with Zach, who knew? What was too much for a man who did everything to excess?

One who would do anything to provoke a reaction?

Zach drew out the last note and the women cheered. He did his "thank you very much" routine, then turned to address Jen. His eyes were sparkling and his lips were curved, as if he was on the verge of laughter, as if he was laughing at himself.

Those fake black sideburns were enough to make Jen smile back at him.

(Or maybe it was something else that made her smile.)

"And now a duet," Zach said over the clamor for more. "But for this song, I have to be a Temptation"—the women cheered, but Zach just offered his hand to Jen—"and I'll be needing a Supreme." He was pretty much daring her to join him onstage, and Jen didn't think twice before she took his challenge.

Maybe she was hoping to surprise him. She had a definite sense that he'd been thinking he'd have to persuade her. The crowd parted as she strode to the stage and she recognized the music as it started.

"I'm Gonna Make You Love Me."

It was a frightening possibility, but Zach didn't have to know that.

"You won't," she whispered, smiling despite herself.

"Never underestimate the power of persistence," he murmured with a wicked grin.

"You're like Tigger the Tiger," she complained and he laughed.

"Remember that the wonderful thing about Tiggers is that I'm the only one," he said, quoting the character's signature tune.

Jen didn't say anything, because she suspected it was true. There couldn't be another man like Zach anywhere.

And he was singing with her.

Meanwhile, Zach sang the first verse, pledging all the things he would do as he looked into Jen's eyes as if he meant it. She halfway thought she wouldn't be able to sing the chorus, her mouth was so dry.

But their voices fit together pretty well. Once she got going, she had a great time. Even her solo verses were easy, because Zach mugged for the crowd. It was as if they'd sung together a hundred times. Jen was half laughing, half singing, and it was a good thing she knew the words as well as she did.

She was alive and even better, she was enjoying it.

When the music faded and the crowd began to cheer, she had one warning glimpse of the mischief in Zach's eyes before he caught her around the waist, dipped her low, and winked. "Having fun?"

Jen had a heartbeat to realize that she was. She laughed, but before she could answer, Zach bent lower. He kissed her quickly and she pushed at his shoulder, embarrassed to be the center of attention. "Don't. Not here."

He arched a brow, his expression wicked. "Afraid you'll lose control in front of witnesses, because you missed me so much?"

"As if," Jen retorted. She curled a hand around the back of his neck and pulled him closer. "Brother Zach."

He laughed then, but Jen gave him a lasting kiss, tasting his surprise as she did so. When she might have broken the kiss, Zach deepened it, kissing her as if he'd never get enough of her.

Jen was dizzy.

And she didn't care. She just closed her eyes and hung on.

Zach's plan was going well so far.

Really well.

It was going better even than expected, which was saying something. He'd come with three objectives: to see Jen again, to make her laugh, and to persuade her to attend Christmas dinner. That

last one was going to be sticky—especially as he didn't particularly
want to attend himself—but he thought he was doing pretty well
so far.

The way she had stared at him without expression when he'd
arrived had spooked him a bit. Maybe she'd been incredulous.
Maybe she'd been skeptical. Maybe she'd really meant all that stuff
she'd said. None were particularly encouraging options. Her response had had a serious impact on his sense of triumph.

He'd thought then that his good news should wait.

It had been better when Jen started to sing. He loved how joyous she looked when she sang, loved how she sparkled like a diamond when she was happy.

The kiss was a total bonus.

He spun her triumphantly after breaking their kiss, liking the
color in her cheeks and the way her lips were swollen. Her hair was
disheveled and he had a definite sense that he'd jangled the order of
her universe a bit.

That had to be a good thing.

"We need to talk," he whispered to her.

"I don't think so," she said, but there wasn't a lot of conviction
in her tone. She looked too happy for him to be deterred. "I
thought you were gone for good."

"I was working."

"You expect me to believe that?"

"No rest for the wicked," he said with a grin. "Proof positive
I've been busy."

"Doing what?"

Zach decided to go with the truth. "I've been working on this
adult thing. I think I'm doing pretty well, for a novice."

"With no shortage of confidence," Jen said wryly.

Zach laughed. "Hey, we make our own reality. Believe you can
do it and you can, etcetera, etcetera."

"Now I am worried. You sound like my mother."

"No need to worry. We just need to talk."

Jen folded her arms across her chest. "Why?"

"You still owe me and I've come to negotiate."

Jen's protest came low and fast. "You had your turkey dinner . . ."

"See? I told you we needed to talk."

Jen gave him a quelling look. "We're *not* going on a date. We're not going to start seeing each other . . ."

"Then what's your suggestion? Aren't you curious? Don't you want to even hear my idea before you turn it down?"

Jen regarded him steadily for a moment, and there was a glitter of curiosity in her gaze. "Okay, I get off at one. You can come back here and meet me then."

That wasn't an ideal situation, to Zach's thinking. "It'll be late."

Jen scooped up her tray. "The talk will be short."

Zach knew when he'd hit a wall in a negotiation and he'd definitely reached one here. He'd just have to work with the opportunity presented. "You're right: I need my beauty sleep." He winked at her. "See you at one then."

"But what . . ."

He didn't linger for Jen's question, because he knew what it would be. Better to let her worry about it.

Instead, he took his bows, strode through the crowded bar, reclaimed his helmet and jacket, then got back on the motorcycle he'd borrowed from James. He revved the engine, then peeled off.

Jen hadn't forgotten him.

Yet.

She still kissed like a goddess.

And he'd be seeing her at one.

As missions went, this one had gone pretty well.

One of the women at eighteen was wearing Zach's silver sunglasses on her head. They treated Jen like a returning heroine when she brought their next round of margaritas.

"So, you know him?" the one with the sunglasses demanded.

The others giggled.

"What's his name?"

"Where does he live?"

"How do we find him?

"I've never seen him before in my life," Jen said, her expression deadpan.

"Then you can't introduce me?"

"Sorry, no."

"But he threw you his jacket!"

"I just was in the vicinity. I used to be a coat-check girl. Maybe a finely honed instinct just put me in the right place at the right time."

"But that kiss . . ."

"It wasn't bad, really. You know, though, I've had better." Jen hefted her tray, stifling a smile as she turned back to the bar. The women erupted into chatter behind her, one insisting that she shouldn't have given up waiting tables.

"What are you smiling about?" Lucy asked.

"As if you need a memo," Kathy said, slamming her tray on the bar. "Where are my tequila shooters, Murray?"

Lucy spared a glance to Kathy, then winked at Jen, apparently for reassurance.

The bar was jumping from that point on, too busy for chitchat. There was no shortage of men willing to sing for the women on the dance floor and no lack of women ready to sing themselves. They were serving drinks as fast as Murray could pour them. Jen thought she'd probably sleep for a week after she survived this shift.

At least, if her pulse ever slowed down enough for her to sleep.

What did Zach want? Even though she knew better than to be curious, Jen couldn't help wondering. Her shift seemed to last forever and she had plenty of time to think of possibilities.

By 12:45, she was dead on her feet. She was wiping tables in her section, cashing out clients and making change, when Zach strolled into the bar. He was wearing his usual jeans and T-shirt with that leather jacket, and when he claimed a seat at the bar, Murray reached for a beer glass. Zach waved him off and watched Jen with familiar intensity. She found herself nervous as she came to the bar to get change for a table.

"Hi," he said.

"You're early," she said. "Afraid I'd stand you up?"

"Just a regular Boy Scout," he said and held up two fingers in a salute. "Being prepared, that's me."

"So that must mean that you have a knitted avocado," she teased.

"Not yet. I'm working on it."

"Is that the favor you want?"

He grinned. "Don't sell yourself short, Jen. The knitted avocado is cool, but I've got a better idea than your knitting me one."

"One that involves more personal interaction, I'll guess."

Zach turned to Murray and heaved an ecstatic sigh that made Jen want to smack him. "Don't you love smart women?" When Zach turned, Jen could see that his skin was red on his cheeks where the fake sideburns had been.

Murray raised a meaty finger to expound, but Jen had to fight to not laugh out loud. He followed her glance and chuckled. "Battle scars," he said.

Zach raised a hand to his cheek and winced. "It's not nice to laugh at the wounded."

"What did you stick them on with?" Jen asked.

"Some stuff that ensured I won't have to shave for a week. Does it look bad?"

"Not really. For a person with a contagious rash."

"Or a venereal disease," Murray contributed. Jen laughed, knowing this would not be Zach's image.

"Thanks a lot," Zach said, sparing Murray a lethal glance. He winked at Jen. "I suppose that means you don't want to kiss it better?"

Jen felt herself blush. "Don't hold your breath."

Zach grinned. "I just might."

She went back to her tables with the change. She had a lot to do before leaving and was aware of Zach watching her the whole time. Kathy tried to chat him up, but he gave her only short answers, his gaze never straying from Jen. Lucy smiled at this and nodded at Jen with approval.

Funny how his presence made sense to everyone but Jen.

Just after one, she punched out. She got her coat and changed her shoes and hung up her apron. She phoned her mother and told her she'd be late because Zach had come to meet her, rolling her eyes when her mother insisted happily that she wouldn't wait up. Jen stuffed her tips into her wallet, liking that there was a good wad of them again, then tossed her backpack onto her shoulder and headed for the bar.

And Zach.

At Jen's suggestion, they walked to a new late-night coffee shop. Mulligan's was on Massachusetts Avenue, away from the tackiness of Central Square but not quite so trendy as those pubs closer to Harvard Yard. Jen liked how close the pub was to the T as it made her life simpler. She also liked how Murray had taken on an old pub, in a lovely building, and tried to give it new life with a new chef and a paint job. She was glad it was starting to work for him.

It was snowing, big, fat flakes that rolled lazily out of the darkness. The snowflakes waltzed in the glow of the streetlights and traffic was light. The hush—and the company—made Jen's sucker heart yearn for romance in a way that was entirely inappropriate under the circumstances.

At least, if she didn't want to get involved.

Once they turned down Lee Street, it was even quieter. The porch lights gleamed golden, the shadows were long but unthreatening. They could have been walking into a painting, one depicting a residential street in Europe decades before.

"It's like an old movie," Zach said, echoing Jen's thoughts. He made a frame with his hands. "Check out this shot. You wouldn't be able to guess where it had been taken."

Jen peeked into the frame he'd made with his hands. "Not with that old house on the right. It could be Paris."

"You wouldn't be able to guess when, either." Zach framed the virtual shot a couple of different ways. "Look. This way, I'd get that bit of wrought-iron fence in the corner."

Jen leaned against his shoulder and looked, proximity to him making her feel a tingle. "Too bad you don't have your camera. I'd buy a print of that shot."

"You would?"

Jen nodded. "It would be evocative. I can imagine looking at it and seeing different bits of it each time."

"Those are the best ones," Zach said, shrugging as he put his hands back into his pockets. "When they come out."

"It would come out," Jen said with assurance.

Zach glanced at her. "How do you know?"

"You know what you're doing with a camera. Like that shot in your apartment, the Venice one."

"You like that?"

Jen nodded, seeing no point in lying. "It's a great picture."

He smiled at her and his eyes were dancing again. "Then it's too bad this one is going to get away." He took her hand then and tucked it into his elbow.

She wasn't sure what to think of that, so she said nothing. It was intimate but not particularly sexy. It was a gentleman's gesture, the kind of thing he tended to do, and she tingled a bit from having her hand pressed against his side. Not a sexual gesture, then, but one that awakened sexual awareness in her. It was nice, though, walking along with him.

Nice and electric.

Zach stopped in the middle of the street and turned, looking up at the sky. "So, name the movie."

"White Christmas," Jen said immediately. "Where's Bing?"

"Right here." Zach started to sing "White Christmas," something that Jen realized she should have anticipated. She had a choice: she could be mortified, or she could join in for the chorus.

She went with option number two.

Zach had the gift of being able to keep pitch without accompaniment. Jen could keep pitch when she sang along with him, which worked. He moved straight to the chorus of "Blue Christmas," falling to one knee in his Elvis impression, which made Jen laugh. He leapt onto a light standard and swung around it, doing a passable Gene Kelly, "Singing in the Rain."

"It's not raining," Jen said through her laughter.

"Picky, picky. C'mon. Be happy with me."

"Why?"

"Why not? Being unhappy doesn't make the world a better place."

"Being happy doesn't keep bad things from happening."

"No, but nothing keeps bad things from happening. Why not enjoy life until they do?"

It made treacherous sense as a philosophy.

"Besides, I'm glad to see you."

"You are?"

"I am." Zach seized Jen's hand and spun her around on the empty street, then caught her close. Jen barely managed to breathe, she was so aware of him and the sparkle of his eyes. "Can you fox-trot?"

"No."

"Doesn't matter. Follow my lead, try to look like you know what you're doing, and no one will know the difference." He leaned close to whisper, his breath on her ear making her shiver. "Most people can't fox-trot, after all."

"A damn shame," Jen said solemnly, then gasped when he dipped her, spun her, and turned her. They danced back across the street in something that might have been a fox-trot and Jen realized she'd never done anything so silly in her life.

"You're making up the steps," she accused, when the variations showed no underlying pattern.

He gave her an arch glance. "I told you that most people can't fox-trot."

"Including you?"

"Where would I have learned to fox-trot? I was born eighty years too late."

Jen had thought that a few times herself, but didn't have a chance to say as much. Zach had changed to a waltz and had caught her close. She could waltz and so apparently could he. They swirled down the street, as light on their feet and graceful as snowflakes, and he hummed something vaguely familiar in her ear.

Because her heart was pounding far more than it should have been, because she liked being caught against his chest, and because she couldn't guess what he'd do next—or because she could guess and wasn't sure she'd be able to resist another killer kiss—Jen pushed him away in front of the coffee shop.

There was snow in his hair and on his eyelashes and he didn't push away very easily. He was smiling at her in a way that could make a woman believe the whole world spun around her and her alone.

"You're crazy," she said, trying to break the spell.

Zach tried to look rueful and failed. "It's been said before. You need fresh material, *honey*." He winked, then kissed her quickly, before putting his hands on her shoulders and bundling her toward the light of the shop. "What's your poison tonight? I'm thinking a decaf latte would be the way to go."

"Hot chocolate for adults," Jen agreed.

Zach smiled as he held the door for her. "Cinnamon, cocoa, or chocolate sprinkles?"

"They don't put chocolate sprinkles on lattes."

"They will if you grovel."

Jen paused beside him, knowing that was something she'd like to see. "Chocolate sprinkles then. Show me how it's done."

Zach laughed. "Anything for you," he said. His tone was light but his eyes weren't dancing the way they had been. He was watching her carefully and Jen found herself snared by the seriousness in his gaze. She swallowed, wanting very much for him to mean what he said. He smiled slowly and brushed his fingertips across her cheek, launching that army of goose pimples. "Honey," he said softly and Jen found herself blushing.

She hurried past him, not knowing what was going to happen and not really caring. She could feel herself falling head over heels in love, didn't really want to stop but knew it would be stupid not to stop.

It was one of Jen's favorite coffee shops even though it hadn't been open long. It was a little funky independent place with cozy corners and excellent coffee, run by a woman who could have been Natalie's long-lost sister. They never hassled anyone for lingering long over coffee and knitting (as Jen had, many a time) and always greeted regulars with a smile. She'd never been there at night and was amazed at how the low lighting made it seem mysterious and magical.

She sat, chin in her hand, and knew she'd remember this night for a long time. The snow and the mood in the coffee shop made her think of black-and-white pictures and old movies, of glamour and nostalgia and vintage dresses with hand-sewn satin trim. She knew, with curious conviction, that she could have said as much to Zach and he wouldn't have laughed at her.

He would understand and, quite probably, agree.

She liked that Zach was a gentleman without seeming to realize what he did. He opened doors, he kept a finger under her elbow, he insisted on getting her coffee and helping with her coat. Jen knew her mother would have gone wild over some implicit sexism in these gestures, but she liked it. She knew Zach didn't think she was too weak to take off her own coat. To have him do it made her feel feminine; it made her feel as if they were a couple. She didn't feel taken for granted.

She felt treasured.

She felt that he *was* glad to be with her.

That was kind of nice. She sat and watched him as he ordered and liked a lot more than his manner toward her. She liked his sense of humor and that he apparently had no shame. He wasn't afraid to take chances, but he wasn't as unreliable as he liked people to believe.

He teased the woman behind the counter and Jen heard herself gasp when the woman put chocolate sprinkles on the lattes.

She liked that Zach did whatever he said he would do, and also liked that if he didn't say what he was going to do, then anything was pretty much possible. She felt good in his company in a way that didn't bode well for the future well-being of her sucker heart.

This wasn't a good sign. She didn't even know what he wanted to negotiate yet. Maybe she'd been tricked. Maybe she was just opening herself to another heartache. Maybe she should bail now before she got in even deeper.

Then she realized that there was one surefire way to end this thing with Zach, one way to be rid of him for good. It wasn't the kind of thing she usually did, but it would work.

He'd be gone if she told him the truth.

Especially if she told him in a way that couldn't be misinterpreted.

Zach picked up the pair of double decaf lattes, their foam sinking under the corona of chocolate sprinkles, and turned to carry them back to the table. He could feel Jen watching him and was still trying to think of a good way to ask her about Christmas. She hadn't picked up the clue from the choice of songs, though it had seemed a brilliant opening at the time.

It didn't help that he wasn't particularly fired up about going to Gray Gables himself, much less facing the prospect of a Coxwell family dinner. It would be easier if Jen went with him, as he might then have one ally at the table.

Or he might not.

He glanced up as he crossed the floor and caught her eye. She looked a bit tired, which he could understand after the busy night at the pub. He was glad she'd agreed to come out with him when she could have gone home to bed. That was a good sign.

The next sign was less good. Instead of returning his smile, Jen reached into her shirt and pulled out what looked like a striped ball. She put it on the table in front of her, a challenge in her gaze.

Zach would have taken her challenge on principle, if he'd had a clue what it was.

He reached the table and put down the two big cups, glanced at the ball. It was knitted in pink-and-purple stripes that swirled around it. It was kind of flat on the bottom side and had a round pink pearl of a button where the swirls came together.

Like a cherry on top.

"No wonder Roxie loves you," he said, going with a joke. "You carry dog toys in your clothes."

Jen didn't smile. She shook her head minutely and was as serious as a heart attack. "It's not a dog toy."

Zach sat down, sensing that he was on thin ice but not really knowing why, much less what to do about it. "I'm not going to make any jokes about you playing fetch."

Jen just looked at him. Zach would have guessed that she was nervous, although he couldn't imagine a reason why this knitted ball would spook anyone.

For lack of a better option, Zach picked up the knitted ball. It was warm, presumably from being in Jen's clothes, which surprised him a little. He could smell that faint scent that she had herself, the clean smell of soap mingled with Jen's own skin. That scent shorted his circuits a little bit, just the way Jen did, but he forced himself to concentrate on the ball.

To keep his eye on the ball, as it were.

This was important. The ball was soft but heavier than he'd have expected. He turned it in his hand and was mystified. He propped his elbow on the table and held the ball between them. "Okay, I'll bite. It's not any kind of fruit I know."

"I'd guess not."

"What is it?"

Jen took a deep breath. Her gaze flicked away from his for only a second and she licked her lips before she spoke. She was really nervous, more nervous than he'd ever seen her. "It's a prosthesis," she said, her words softer than usual.

Zach was unable to immediately think of a body part of this particular shape, much less one that Jen was missing. "For what?"

Jen lifted her right hand and placed it flat on her left chest. To Zach's surprise, the shirt disappeared to nothing beneath her hand. The left side of her chest *was* flat, unlike the right side of her chest.

The breath left him completely.

"It's gone," she said, her words hoarse. "That fills the space instead." She lifted the knitted ball out of his hand, reached beneath her shirt, and presumably put it back into her bra.

Then she appeared to have two breasts again.

For once in his life, Zach didn't know what to say.

Jen took a sip of her coffee, blinking fast. Her words spilled in an increasing torrent once they started. "I know what you're thinking. You're thinking that I'm defective and you're right. I had cancer. I had a mastectomy. They cut it off." Her throat worked. "And I might get cancer again . . ."

"That's why you knit a cherry," Zach guessed, interrupting a speech that didn't promise to get more optimistic. He'd never had a date end in a complete emotional meltdown of the woman in his company and he saw no reason to start now.

Shit. A mastectomy. Didn't that only happen to older women? His mind stalled on the concept. He glanced at her chest, then looked away, knowing that she was watching his response avidly.

They cut it off . . .

Jen frowned into her mug. "I wasn't sure I'd live very long," she said, her tone flat. "I didn't want to leave stuff half done all over the place. It's terrible for people to have to go through everything and sort it out." Her throat worked again.

"You met other people during your treatment, people who didn't survive," he guessed again and she nodded emphatically.

"I wanted everything neat and tidy and organized. I didn't want to leave trouble for people. Loose ends in the knitting basket, that kind of thing." She heaved a sigh. "I finished things for dead people, out of respect for them. It's not easy . . ."

"It couldn't be."

She shook her head emphatically.

Zach watched her expression change, watched the shadows dance in her eyes. He couldn't imagine facing such fear in his own life. He couldn't imagine being given such a diagnosis, never mind how it would change his perspective and his life.

But Jen had gotten through it, she *had* survived, and it seemed very important to point out to her the merit of her achievement. "But the fruits keep getting bigger. You didn't finish that avocado in one go."

"No." She looked up, her expression wary. "I'm not dead yet, apparently."

The conversation could have ended there, and maybe Jen would have preferred it to do so, but Zach wasn't letting this go just yet. "So, what are you knitting now?"

She exhaled shakily. "I made socks. For my mom for Christmas."

"*Two* socks?"

A smile touched her lips. "She has two feet."

He pretended to shiver in delight. "There's nothing sexier than an observant woman."

"I'm not . . ." she started to argue, then gulped her latte.

And there was the crux of it. Zach heard the truth in what Jen didn't say.

She continued in a rush. "Anyway, I'm making a shawl for my grandmother now. I should get home and do some knitting before I go to sleep otherwise I won't get it done before Christmas."

She might have reached for her coat, her confession over. She was so certain that his interest in her would be eliminated by this truth that Zach understood Steve's crime.

He couldn't let her go.

He settled into his chair as if he'd be there for the duration, knowing that the position of his chair blocked her exit. "So, how long ago was it?" he asked lightly.

She looked at him. "You don't want to know."

"Actually, I do."

"Two years since I was diagnosed."

He watched her, seeing the barriers being erected, catching unexpected glimpses behind them and understood a great deal more about Jen Maitland. "Let me guess: that was when this Steve guy dumped you?"

She nodded without meeting his gaze. "It doesn't matter."

"Yes, it does. Just because he was an asshole doesn't mean all men are. It doesn't, in fact, mean that I am."

She shrugged, unpersuaded, sipped her latte, and didn't look as if she was enjoying it. Jen looked, in fact, as if she'd like to bolt.

But there was one thing Zach had to say to her first, even if it didn't change anything. "I'm sorry that I said what I said about you waiting tables and having no dreams," he said quietly and she stared at him. "I thought we had a lot in common, but the difference is that you had an excuse. I'm a loser, that was a fair shot, but you're a winner, Jen. You beat the worst bastard disease that there is. Don't forget that."

"I didn't call you a loser."

"Close enough." Zach decided a brief change of subject might let her find her equilibrium again. "I haven't lived with a lot of focus, shall we say, until lately. I didn't know what I wanted to do."

"Not until you weren't busy annoying your father anymore."

He smiled and turned his cup on the table. "Pretty much. That day I met you, when I had lunch with my old buddies, I realized that I didn't want to be like them. I didn't want to have the pursuit of money be my goal, because it's a crap goal."

"Money's a good thing . . ."

"But it's not the only thing."

"You can only say that because you have lots."

"No, I don't. I've been careful with what I had and I won't starve to death anytime soon, but money didn't keep my family from being the largest group of screwed-up individuals on the East Coast. It didn't make anyone happy. So I'm thinking that happiness is worth pursuing, not money, and am hoping that the money part takes care of itself." He met her gaze steadily. "You have to promise to not tell anyone this."

The barest smile touched her lips. "That you don't think money is so hot?"

"That I've been thinking profound thoughts about life, the universe, and everything. It'll destroy my reputation as a cavalier, selfish pleasure-seeker."

"You're not a cavalier, selfish pleasure-seeker."

"Damn! I thought I had you fooled!"

She smiled openly at that. "You blew it yourself, by making that deal for your mother's welfare."

"Mmm. There was that. It had to be done, though."

"Even at your own expense?"

"She's my mom, Jen. It's my job to take care of her."

She smiled beautifully then, smiled just for him, and his heart started to pound. "I registered to go back to college after Christmas," she said, her manner defiant. Zach wondered whether she was defying him, his expectations, or the cancer.

He felt a tenderness for her that shocked him to his core.

He wanted to protect her from everything, from the world and jerks like Steve and even from cells splitting in unauthorized ways. He wanted to stand beside her and hold her hand and watch her triumph over every obstacle.

He nodded and sipped his coffee, knowing that they'd entered a full truth zone. "Is going back to school what you want to do or what people expect you to do?"

"I wanted to finish my bachelor's degree."

"Why?"

She inhaled and fixed him with a look, daring him again to disbelieve her. She half laughed and shook her head. "Okay, I've never told anyone this."

"So, it'll be fair. One from me and one from you."

"Right."

"I'm ready."

She glanced around, as if someone might overhear. There was no one else in the cafe but the woman cleaning up behind the counter. "I always wanted to open a knitting wool store, with workshops and a place to knit and lots of wool," Jen confessed in a low voice. "I want to make a refuge for knitters, a place they can just be, where they can relax and knit and maybe heal a bit from the pressures of the world."

Zach smiled and sipped his own coffee.

"Don't laugh at me!"

"I'm not laughing at you. I'm thinking you'd be great at it. I can see you in an old house with pine floors that are polished smooth." He narrowed his eyes and refined his vision, sensing that she needed to know that he could see it, too. "There'd be big comfy chairs and rugs worn a bit, so you wouldn't have to worry about spilling anything on them. Warm and welcoming, like your mother's kitchen. Maybe you could have some old leather armchairs, you know how soft they get? And the color gets worn."

"Not leather," she said, her words carried on the barest breath.

"Right. Let's kill innocent polyesters instead. Or maybe you could have the chairs upholstered with kilims or Navajo rugs? That would be funky and cozy, and kind of tie into the whole wool thing."

"It would," she agreed with a smile.

"There'd be piles of wool, with little signs about the pros and cons of each kind. Handwritten signs." Zach gestured with one hand. "Tips from Jen for the uninitiated."

"Yes," Jen breathed.

"And there'd be knitters chatting and working at all hours of every day. You'd have to throw them out at night so you could go to bed. Maybe there'd be some plants in the window, because it would face south, right? All that sunshine."

"Good energy," she agreed.

"And hey, if there was some knitted fruit hanging from the tin ceiling, who's to quibble?"

Jen smiled and nodded and Zach didn't think he imagined that a tear fell. "Yes," she whispered, her throat working. "Yes, just like that. So, if I get my degree, then I can do a business plan and get a loan from the bank."

"That's a pretty long-term plan," he felt compelled to observe.

"I know." She gulped some coffee then reached for her back-pack. He saw that it frightened her to even speculate so far into her own future and he wanted, desperately, to give her a guarantee that no one ever got. "It's late. I have to go." She might have run, but Zach reached out and put his hand over hers. She halted, stared at him, fearful of what he would say.

It was, however, time for some truth.

"I don't know anything about what you went through, Jen," he said softly, never looking away from her eyes. "And I don't want to be presumptuous about how easy or how hard it might have been."

"You could never know . . ."

"No. I know." He swallowed and frowned, letting his thumb slide across the back of her hand before he met her gaze again. "But if losing your breast was the price of you being here tonight, drinking coffee with me, then I'm really glad you paid it."

"But I'm ugly now. I'm scarred—"

"Whoever told you that was blind and stupid, too," Zach said, interrupting her. "And just for the record, you could give me Steve's surname so I could go deck him one of these days."

"I wouldn't want you to get another shiner."

"He wouldn't have a chance to touch me."

She shook her head, tears falling into her lap as she looked down. "You haven't seen it. You don't know."

"I don't care. You're beautiful and that's that." He squeezed her hand beneath his own. "It doesn't even matter how I frame a shot of you, Jen. It's beautiful, every time."

She looked up at him, her eyes filled with doubts. He held her gaze, let her see that he wasn't lying to her, and slowly the skepticism faded away. "You're lying to make me feel better," she whispered.

Zach shook his head and let his fingers tighten over hers again. "Nope. I can't lie about beauty. It's part of the code."

"You never followed anyone else's code."

"This one's all mine."

To his astonishment, her smile broke free. There were still tears on her lashes, but she smiled at him. She turned her hand beneath his, so that their palms were together, so that their fingers entwined.

He waited, let her decide what she wanted to do, even though he had a favorite choice from the options available.

"Don't you live near here?" she asked hesitantly.

Zach grinned. "Close enough. Roxie's been asking after you, you know."

She looked across the coffee shop, then nodded once, such uncertainty in her expression that another onslaught of tenderness made Zach catch his breath. He stood and drew her to her feet. He pulled her close, sensing that she needed his touch, and kissed her again. When she looked up at him, he touched her cheek. "No lie, Jen."

"I know," she murmured with such conviction that his heart clenched. "Let's go. I could use a Roxie-fix."

"Everyone needs a little dog spit in their life, now and then."

"Or a lot of dog spit."

"Or a lot." Zach helped her with her coat and they left their lattes on the table, then walked hand-in-hand through the falling snow. There were no words for this moment and Zach didn't mind one bit.

Ⅰt had been so easy.

Too easy, a voice had murmured in Jen's thoughts, but she had ignored it. It was easy to go home with Zach, easy to imagine how they would tangle together, easy to think about what kind of a lover he'd be.

And if he only wanted sex, well, maybe Jen could live with that. (For the moment, at least.) Because the truth was that she wanted sex, too.

Sex with Zach.

Now.

They walked in silence to his apartment, the world around them painted in spinning white. She changed her analogy: it wasn't so much like an old movie as stepping into an Impressionist painting. Or being lost in a dream that she didn't want to end. This was a world she wanted to remain in, this was a moment in time that she wanted to last clear through eternity. There was nothing in it that mattered, nothing but the presence of the man beside her.

He'd been so sure.

Zach's fingers were tight around hers and their arms brushed as they walked together. It wasn't that cold and there wasn't much wind.

Just dancing snow.

He might think differently when he saw the scar, but Jen was bracing herself for that.

Maybe she wouldn't let him see it this time.

Maybe she'd take this moment and make it last as long as she could.

Jen couldn't help thinking that no matter what happened after this, the look in Zach's eyes in that coffee shop when he'd understood would make it all worthwhile. There had been compassion and surprise and admiration all mixed up together. He'd looked at her as if she'd conquered adversity, as if this night was as special to him as it was becoming to her.

That made her feel pretty damn good.

And she hadn't even had an orgasm.

Yet.

Chapter 12

When Zach opened the door to his condo, Jen was shocked, and it wasn't by the enthusiastic canine greeting she received.

There was furniture in the living room.

"Is this really your place?" she asked, pretending to check the number on the door.

He grinned, hung up her coat, then bent to clip Roxie's leash on to her collar. If Jen hadn't thought it impossible, she would have said he was embarrassed. He was certainly avoiding her gaze.

He wasn't just putting her on about trying to be an adult. He had listened to her and made some changes. She was impressed.

Jen wondered what other changes Zach had made.

"I just picked up a couple of things," he said, then reached for the door. "Do you mind? Roxie needs a pit stop."

"No problem. I'll just wait."

"Good." Their gazes locked and held for an electric minute, then Zach was gone. Jen took off her boots and left them in the foyer. She used the washroom, noting how clean it was. Since he really did live here, that was impressive, too. She peeked into the medicine cabinet and was reassured by its spartan interior. No prescriptions. That worked for her.

She went back into the living room, then, on impulse, turned out the lights that Zach had flicked on when they arrived. The falling snow brightened the room and the cascading flakes were all that she could see out the windows. It was quiet.

A haven in an unexpected place. The candles that had been burning the last time she was here were still on the window sill, as were the matches. She lit them, liking how their light mingled with that from the snow.

Once again, Jen had the sense that she had stepped out of time and space, into a place where there was nothing but tranquility.

She turned and looked, wondering if Zach had bought furniture just because of what she had said to him. He did have a tendency to listen when she least expected it.

Zach also had a tendency to do things that surprised her, but that she liked once she saw them. The same was true of the furniture. She never would have anticipated that he would have liked modern furniture, but he obviously did, and she liked that.

Now she could see that it suited him perfectly.

There were a pair of armchairs in the living room with an end table between them, plus a dining table with four chairs in the dining room. She moved the candles around, so that the room was filled with their golden light. The furniture looked as if he'd just dragged it back to his cave and not known what to do with it. There still wasn't a rug or any drapes, no art on the walls other than his single framed photo.

That one was so good, though, that Jen thought it deserved pride of place. She stopped to admire it again.

The furniture wasn't new, not by a long shot, although someone had taken care of it. There were a few scratches in the wood and the upholstery was hopelessly faded orange burlap, but he'd bought teak. Even in need of a polish, the grain of the wood gleamed. Jen could see that he'd gone after the arm of one chair in an attempt to clean it up, because that one shone more than the rest. The suite would look gorgeous when it was all polished.

Teak was Jen's favorite. She always thought the '60s Scandinavian stuff was underrated, given its sleek lines and solid quality. She ran one hand over the arm of one chair in admiration before it struck her.

Zach had bought used furniture. And not from fancy shop that refinished the past for the present. This looked as if he'd scored it at a garage sale or lucked out in a major way at the Salvation Army.

Jen felt a tingle. Did Zach intuitively know how to reduce, reuse, and recycle, or was he taking a page from her book? She remembered his car, which he'd had longer than he'd known her, and couldn't give herself credit. In fact, she had a growing suspicion that they had a lot more in common than she'd initially thought.

Which made her being here on this night even more perfect.

Jen sat in the chair with the polished arm and ran her fingers over the smooth wood. She sat in the flickering candlelight, watched the snow fall, watched the light play with the photograph he'd taken in Venice, and felt a weird mix of tranquility and excitement.

She was exactly where she needed to be. She couldn't make sense of that conviction, and she didn't really want to. She thought of her mother casting their astrological charts and declaring that their relationship was a fated one and knew it was true.

She knew it. She didn't know where it was going or how it would end, but she knew that being here with Zach was right.

And Natalie's youngest daughter had learned a long time ago that some things had to be taken on faith.

Zach was impatient with Roxie's quest for the perfect spot, because he was pretty sure Jen wouldn't be in his apartment when he got back upstairs. She'd be gone, having left a note on the fridge if he was lucky, and this would be the end of everything.

He couldn't do Elvis again.

Well, he could, but it wouldn't be as effective. Surprise wouldn't be on his side.

He hadn't even asked Jen about Christmas yet.

Neither of those were the real reason he was so anxious to get back upstairs.

Roxie seemed to sense his urgency—it could have been the way he tugged at her leash—because she headed back for the building in a power trot once she was done. She broke into a run once the elevator doors opened on his floor and Zach dropped the leash to keep from slipping on the wet tile. She went straight to the door of his condo, sniffled at the crack, and whimpered.

Zach was afraid that that was a bad sign. He spoke to the dog quietly, then opened the door, fully expecting to find his apartment empty.

Instead it was filled with candlelight. Zach froze on the threshold and felt for the first time as if he'd come home. Jen was sitting in one of his new chairs, as still as a statue.

She smiled at him and his heart stopped cold.

Roxie launched herself across the room for a second greeting, and Jen calmed her with enviable ease.

"She's crazy for you," Zach said as he shook the snow out of his hair and hung up his coat. "She dragged me back up here."

Jen patted the dog, who wagged mightily, catching her head in her hands. "You're so neglected, aren't you?" Roxie licked her hands happily. "You still look shiny and happy to me, so I'm not convinced," she said to the dog and Zach smiled.

Then Jen glanced up at him. "So, what's this all about? Why the sudden influx of furniture?"

Zach shoved a hand through his hair, not really wanting to talk about decor. "Well, it kind of turned up . . ."

Jen seemed to be fighting a smile. "Turned up? Does furniture often leap into your path?"

"It's been known to spontaneously manifest in my vicinity," he joked and she laughed.

"Then maybe you should take up a career as a picker."

"No, I've got a vocation. I think you can only have one."

"At a time, anyway." She regarded him warily. "You're not hanging out with people who deck you again, are you?"

Zach shook his head. "No. That was only a passing hobby."

"An infatuation."

"A flirtation at best."

She looked to the photograph. "But that's the real thing?"

Zach smiled, liking that she understood his ambition—such as it was—so well. "Yes. How'd you know?"

"You're good at it. Vocations are like that."

Zach sat in the other chair and watched Jen, liking her easy manner. The candlelight made dancing highlights in her hair, and made her eyes seem darker and more mysterious. Her skin looked golden, and the shadows beneath her eyes seemed to have faded. She looked serene, yet curious. He wasn't quite sure how to proceed, not knowing how spooked she would be about him seeing her missing breast.

And he really didn't want to mess up.

"Well, the truth about the furniture is that I was in Rosemount—"

"You went home? To your family place?"

"No. Not Gray Gables." Zach pretended to shudder.

"It can't be that bad."

"I don't really want to go and find out." Too late, Zach realized this bit of honesty would make the Christmas invite awkward. Rather than figuring that out, he continued his story. "I went to my sister Philippa's place. She lives in Rosemount, in her husband's aunt's house."

"Sounds complicated."

"It can be. I went to talk to her, but ended up bouncing a baby and painting the kitchen." He spread his hands. "See what I mean?"

Jen smiled, as if this confession pleased her. "I thought you

didn't get along with your family. You said you were all really good
at avoiding each other."

"We are. Usually." Zach thought about this. "Maybe we're getting over it. Anyway, someone on her street was having a garage
sale and I stopped to look. The price was really good and I like it,
so we made a deal."

"Don't say that you're cheap, but you're not easy," Jen teased.

Zach smiled. "I won't, because I'm feeling pretty easy right now."

"Are you?"

"Go ahead; have your way with me."

Jen laughed a little and blushed, then stroked the arm of the
chair he'd cleaned. "Are you going to reupholster them?"

"What's wrong with the orange?" he asked, pretending to be
oblivious to its splendid ugliness.

"It looks like you stole it from a dorm . . ." Jen started before
she glanced up and saw his smile.

"Gotcha." He leaned closer, flicked his fingertip across her
nose. She sobered and caught her breath, but didn't pull away. He
knew he had to go slowly. He smiled to reassure her, then caught
her hand in his, interlacing their fingers and pulling her to her feet.
"Let's dance."

"There's no music," she protested but she moved into his arms
all the same.

"Didn't stop us before. Do you want me to sing?"

"I kind of like the snow and the candlelight," she breathed into
his shoulder and he had to agree. They moved around the room
slowly, waltzing to no music. Zach closed his eyes and leaned his
cheek against the side of her head, pulling her a little closer.

She caught her breath but she moved closer, one hand on his
shoulder, one trapped within his. Her face was against his neck, her
nose was cold. He ran his hand down her back to her waist, letting
his thumb slide down the vertebrae. She shivered.

"What kind of upholstery?" she asked.

Zach's eyes opened in surprise. He forced himself to think of something other than how Jen felt and struggled to remember their conversation.

Upholstery.

Chairs.

Right. "I'll guess leather is out," he said, frowning. "Although it would look good."

"Nothing should die for the sake of appearances," Jen said sternly.

He caught her chin in his fingertips and forced her to meet his gaze. "My point exactly." Sensing that he'd wandered close to dangerous ground, he switched gears to make her smile. "On the other hand, the nauga lobby is pretty scary. I don't want to be answerable for dead naugas, do you?"

"Naugahyde isn't made of dead naugas," Jen chided, a smile in her voice.

"How many innocent polyesters should I see slaughtered for my upholstery? As a responsible human, concerned with my environmental footprint, I was thinking cotton."

"You're just trying to have your way with me, by talking about renewable resources."

Zach grinned. "You don't seem to have an issue with it."

"True." Jen stretched up and kissed him, surprising him to silence. "Go ahead, consider undyed hemp and you can have your way with me."

"Deal," Zach said. He kissed her before she could argue with that.

He'd been prepared to cajole her, but Jen surprised him again. She arched against him immediately and twined her hands into his hair, participating in the embrace as she never had before. She felt long and lithe and strong. Her kiss was demanding and his circuit board was melting faster than he'd ever anticipated it could.

Or would.

He swung her up into his arms and caught her against his chest. The twinkle in her eyes told him that their tempo was exactly right. He took his time, not wanting to spook her. "And you haven't even seen the bedroom suite yet."

Jen blinked. "You bought a bed?"

"Roxie was complaining about the futon's effects on her back."

"More garage sale stuff?" Jen was swinging her feet, her expression playful and seductive. Zach wished yet again that he had his camera.

On the other hand, he had his arms full and, given the choice, Jen was better to hold than a camera. "The same sale. I'm not a real power hunter. Yet."

She granted him a playful look through her bangs. "You're not going to promise to show me your etchings?"

"I have photos, and you've seen the only one I'm showing."

Jen glanced toward the Venice shot and smiled. "If you're only going to have one, it might as well be a beauty."

Zach was flattered and pleased that she liked the shot that well. "Applies to women as well as art."

"Should I take that to mean that you've been a collector in the past?"

"No, not me. A serial monogamist, maybe."

"You and my sister, Cin. I knew you were twins separated tragically at birth." She smiled up at him, then arched a brow. "So, is this bedroom suite teak?"

Zach nodded. "With a bookcase in the headboard." He carried her across the room and blew out the flame on a candle. Jen blew out another and between the two of them, the candles were quickly extinguished. The light changed from gold to cooler blues, but Jen's smile and the welcome in her eyes didn't waver.

Zach strolled into the bedroom, watching Jen check out his acquisition. He kicked the door shut behind them, saying good night to Roxie, who settled on the floor outside the door with a thump of bones on the hardwood.

"Nice," she said, and reached out a hand to stroke the headboard.

"A person could put her knitting on that bookshelf, come to think of it."

"Any particular person?"

"I only know one who knits."

Jen was pleased by that, Zach could see it in her smile. "I thought you'd say that a person would have better things to do in bed than knit."

"Good point. I should have said that."

"I'll forgive you this time."

"Provided I show you what better things people can do in bed," he teased.

"Be still, my heart," Jen said. "There's nothing sexier than a man who knows what a woman wants." Before Zach could comment on that, she pulled his head down for another searing kiss.

When they stopped for breath, he heaved a sigh. "If I walk into the wall and give us both a concussion, it'll be your fault," he teased.

Jen laughed. "You won't."

"You're trusting me a lot already."

"I wouldn't be getting naked in your bedroom otherwise."

Zach looked pointedly at her clothing. "I don't see you getting naked. Yet."

"You could help." She smiled and looked at him through her lashes, as provocative as he'd ever seen her. Her cheeks were flushed, her lips swollen, her hair tousled. Her expression was even more seductive because he knew she didn't realize how she looked.

"I'm taking that as an invitation," he said, then rolled backward onto the bed, carrying her with him. Jen gasped, then laughed as they tumbled together across the mattress.

Zach rolled her beneath him, his hand on her shoulder, and her laughter stopped as she looked up at him.

There was a beat when they eyed each other, when he saw her trepidation and wanted nothing more than to make it go away.

Jen swallowed and Zach kissed her again. It was a gentle, lingering kiss, but he knew he didn't imagine the electricity thrumming beneath it. He unfastened the top button of her blouse, then kissed her temple, her ear, her throat.

She was gorgeous and her uncertainty of that tore at his heart. He worked each button loose, leaving the shirt closed until they were all unfastened. Jen stared up at him, her breath coming fast, his hand rested on the indent of her waist beneath her shirt. The light of the snow poured through the window, painting her vulnerable expression with silvery light.

He smiled at her, wanting only to reassure her. "You could, you know, just be giving me a cover story here." She snorted and would have argued, but he dropped a finger over her lips. He replaced his finger with his mouth, finding that a much better solution. Jen seemed to like it, too.

"No story," she said when he lifted his head.

"I don't know. You're always putting people on, with this deadpan expression." He eased the top of her shirt apart with one fingertip, revealing her collarbone to his view. The light played in its curves lovingly. He bent and kissed it, liking how she caught her breath and arched against him. "I mean, Amazon warriors are a mythic race and all that, but there's nothing saying that they didn't really exist. Or even that they don't continue to exist. You hear stories, you know, about an underground society of women . . ."

"Living in the dark?" Jen demanded. "With spiders? I don't think so."

Zach chuckled. "Work with me here. What if there were Amazon warrior princesses still? They'd be tall and athletic and gorgeous. They'd keep their hair short." He shoved a hand through her cropped curls, swept his hand down her throat and eased the shirt open a bit more. "And they'd kiss like goddesses, for sure." He ran a line of kisses along her bared shoulder, then kissed her mouth again. "I'll bet they could really sing, too."

She was smiling. "You're making this up."

"But it sounds good, doesn't it? They'd face any obstacle fearlessly, they'd spit in the eye of Death." He pushed back the shirt and exposed her left breast.

Or where her left breast should have been. The pink and purple striped knitted ball was in her bra cup. It was a simple bra, a plain white one with underwires, no lace or frills. The cup was solid fabric so he could only see the edge of the knitted ball.

Something clenched deep within Zach, because he didn't expect what was beneath the prosthesis to be pretty. He felt Jen watching him and knew he had to be really careful.

He met her gaze. "They'd be independent and noble and opinionated," he murmured, then reached beneath her to unfasten her bra clasp. "They'd keep their steely gazes focused on what was really important." She seemed to be holding her breath, even as she arched her back a bit to give him access.

She wanted him to see, or more accurately, she wanted him to see her and not be revolted. Zach hoped he could do it. He eased the strap from her shoulder, lifted away the knitted prosthesis and put it on the bookshelf above them.

He looked down at her, seeing her uncertainty and fear. "And they'd ruthlessly use men for pleasure, kind of like an inverse harem."

She tried to smile. "Is that what you think I'm doing?"

"It's a risk. I'll just have to do my best, so you don't throw me back. You could give me a hint or two, you know, maybe out of pity."

"You don't need any hints."

"Good."

Jen almost laughed, then Zach swept her bra aside. She caught her breath and froze. He looked down at her scar, knowing she was watching, schooling himself to not flinch at the sight of it.

It wasn't as bad as he'd expected, but then, he had a ferocious imagination. It was odd, though, to see this roughly horizontal line where her breast and nipple should have been. The scar curled toward her armpit, smoothly healed but an inescapable reminder all the same. It looked savage and wrong, and he wished on some level that he'd seen her whole first.

But then, it was part of her, part of where she'd been and who she was. The cancer had reshaped her, as surely as the scar reshaped her chest. And when he thought of it that way, as a symbol of her strength, he could see beauty in its harsh line.

"Still think it was worth it?" she asked, her voice catching on the words.

He nodded. "I wouldn't miss your being here for the world."
He met her gaze. "What about you?"

She swallowed again, then nodded quickly. "I'm glad, too. "

"Does it hurt?" he asked and she shook her head.

"Not anymore." Her brow puckered. "Not physically, anyway."

He ran his fingertip gently along its length and she shivered.
This was part of Jen. He wanted to know it, as he wanted to know
everything about her.

"Don't pretend it isn't gross."

"It isn't."

"Don't lie to me. You chase beauty."

"Beauty is in the eye of the beholder. Maybe you've heard that."

"Was that yours?"

He grinned, letting his fingers gently learn the shape of her wound.
"You know, most warriors consider scars to be honorable."

"How so?"

"Scars are a mark of triumph, just like this one is. Scars mean
survival and persistence and victory. Scars mean strength and
power." He nodded at her with confidence. "I'm sure the Amazon
queens saw it that way."

"I thought I was supposed to be an Amazon. Shouldn't I be
telling you how we think?"

"Don't give away all of your secrets. I only ask that you be gentle with your love slave," he teased and she smiled a little, despite
the tears in her eyes.

"Maybe I'll have to lock you up until you learn to do it right."

"Promises, promises." He bent then and kissed the scar gently.
He felt her breathe deeply, then exhale, then whisper his name. He
didn't let her distract him from giving her pleasure. He wanted her,
but he wanted her to really want him.

She felt precious to him. He felt lucky to be with her. He wanted
her to know all of that, yet he didn't know how to tell her in words.

He'd have to show her.

Zach inhaled her scent, let his hands slide down around her

waist. He ran a trail of kisses down the center of her chest, tucked his nose into her navel, then and undid her pants with his teeth. He smoothed the pants off her long legs, using his tongue to tease her through her underwear while his hands were busy. The smell of her desire sent a electric jolt through him, made him peel off his own clothes in a hurry.

But this was going to take some time.

This was a moment to savor. There would never be another first time between them, and Zach was determined to persuade Jen of her desirability and her beauty before the sun rose.

The man was going to kill her.

Zach touched Jen with his tongue, teasing her to climax with embarrassing ease. Each time she got close, he stopped, cheating her of release, then started again. Her skin was on fire, she was writhing on his bed, she was ready to beg him to finish her off, and she didn't care.

He did this three times.

"I'll going to have to kill you for insurgency," she threatened, breathless and agitated.

He grinned. "It's worth waiting for."

"I'll remember that when it's your turn."

He chuckled, then moved behind her. His muscled strength was against her back, his arm wrapped around her waist. His busy fingers coaxed her to a frenzy again. Jen had never felt such desire. She arched back against him and moaned. He kissed her ear, whispered to her of what he was going to do to her, demanding to know what she liked best.

His erection pressed against her butt, and Jen liked knowing that he was as aroused as she was. He was huge and hard, so huge and hard that he couldn't possibly be turned off by her scar.

In fact, Jen forgot about her defect. There was only pleasure and Zach's wicked whisper and his dancing fingers and the heat building inside of her. As the heat rose again, she twisted and squirmed, but he held her tightly. His fingers were relentless and she loved it.

"Don't you dare stop," she managed to say.

"Me?"

"Promise me," she demanded, breathless.

"Or what?"

"I'll have you flogged, love slave. Bread and water for a week. You'll be locked in the dungeons with the spiders."

He laughed, his fingers flicking so surely against her that she gasped. She reached behind herself and grasped his erection, caressing him so that he choked a bit. "Okay, warrior queen, I promise," he murmured into her ear.

"Don't let go," she said, not letting go of him.

"Promise." Zach's arm tightened around her waist, his fingertips moved against her again and Jen felt her every muscle go taut. She struggled as the orgasm rolled through her, arched back, and dug her fingers into his arm with the fullness of release.

She was dizzy.

She was disoriented.

And she had to give serious credit to her mother's conviction that an orgasm was good for a woman's worldview. Jen's worldview was improving by the moment.

"Okay?" Zach asked and she smiled over her shoulder at him, uncertain how he could have any doubt.

"I think I woke the neighbors."

"No chance. I paid for extra soundproofing."

"For moments like this?"

"What can I say? I'm an optimistic kind of guy."

"Yes, I can feel your optimism." Jen closed her hand around his erection again and he caught his breath.

"Don't go playing with the toys unless you plan to buy," he growled and Jen laughed.

Jen rolled toward her stomach and slipped him inside her from behind. He muttered her name with a surprise that made her smile, then he swore a little.

"Do I need a credit check before I shop here?" she teased.

"Well, if that's how it's going to be, then I demand a view," he said, then pulled out of her. Jen had a beat to be disappointed before he rolled over, and lifted her atop him. He winked at her. "C'mon, honey, take me. I'm all yours."

Jen hesitated. He'd have a full view of her damaged chest if she sat astride him. It seemed to her to be a perfect recipe for erection failure. "Not like this?"

"Exactly like this. Nothing like a lady in charge. Or a warrior queen triumphant, as it were."

Encouraged by his easy manner, Jen sat astride him, taking him inside her in increments. She liked being able to watch his expression, liked how his eyes closed and he caught his breath. He wasn't faking his arousal, that was for sure.

And that meant that she didn't have to worry.

There was a lot of Zach and it had been a while since Jen had slept with anyone. It took her some time to accommodate him, but other than gritting his teeth and begging once for mercy, Zach didn't complain. She teased him a bit, getting her own back, liking how obviously he was pleased.

By her.

Once he was fully inside her, she leaned against his chest. She would have been content to kiss him and finish in that pose, but Zach wasn't having any of it. When their kiss broke, he caught her around the waist and lifted her back to a sitting position. Before she could argue, his fingers slipped between her thighs again.

"You'd forfeit this, the other way," he said, his smile wicked. "And it's my job as a love slave to ensure your pleasure every time."

"I can't come like this. And not again. Not so soon."

"How do you know? Have you ever tried it?"

Jen shook her head, finding herself aroused already. She gasped as his fingertip eased across her.

"Then let's try. What's the worst thing that can happen?"

"You could suffer a tragic penis-related accident."

"Not a chance. I'm lying in bed on my back."

"I could fall off the bed and break something and be left in a compromising position, thereby providing entertainment for paramedic personnel."

He shook his head. "I won't let you fall. Promise."

Jen believed his promise, at least. "People don't come simultaneously. It's a myth."

He arched a fair brow. "They said the Amazon warrior princesses were a myth. I'm thinking they had that wrong."

"So all myths are up for reevaluation?"

"Why not?"

Why not. It was all too easy to be seduced by this man, by his confidence and his curiosity. Jen leaned forward, bracing her hands on his shoulders. He smiled up at her, undeterred. "Okay, love slave, I'll bet you an orgasm that you're wrong on this one."

"Chicken," he said, his eyes sparkling. "Make it three orgasms and you're on."

Jen laughed and he moved inside her, making her gasp. Maybe he was right. "Deal," she agreed, not really caring whether she won this bet or not.

And that, she suspected, was Zach's point.

The phone was ringing.

Jen was half asleep, but waking up too fast for her preferences. The ring of the phone was insistent, nudging her out of warm, cozy, and contented slumber.

Where was her mother?

The phone rang again, close at hand. Jen opened her eyes, didn't know where she was, but saw the phone on the floor beside the bed. Good enough. She pounced on it, if only to shut it up. "Hello?"

There was a pause, as if the person on the other end hadn't expected a woman to answer the phone.

That was when Jen recognized her surroundings. She realized she was in Zach's bed, in Zach's apartment. It was morning. The bedroom was filled with radiant sunlight. The sky that she could see was a brilliant blue, and Jack Frost had done his creative painting on the windows. The frost sparkled coldly against the azure of the sky.

She snuggled deeper beneath the blankets at the sight and realized at the same time that she felt remarkably good for someone who had spent most of the night having enthusiastic sex.

Maybe because of that.

"Hello?" A woman said. "Did I call Zach Coxwell's place?" She said the number quickly.

"I think Zach's gone to walk the dog," Jen said, her cheeks burning at the obvious implication of her answering the phone. Her gaze fell on the alarm clock on the windowsill. It was 8:15. "Could I take a message?"

It was pretty obvious what she was doing in Zach's apartment this early on a Thursday morning, and no one was going to assume that it was to play secretary. Jen was embarrassed to have even this stranger be aware of it.

The caller wouldn't be a stranger to Zach, though, and Jen wondered who she might be.

The woman laughed. The sound was friendly and Jen relaxed a bit. "Would this be the elusive Jen?"

Zach had talked about her?

"I'm Jen, although I'm not sure I'm that elusive."

The woman laughed again. "And here I was doubting your existence. I'm sorry. Oh, I'm Maralys Coxwell, by the way, married to Zach's oldest brother."

Jen sat up straighter. "The one who shops vintage?"

Pleasure filled Maralys's tone. "Yes! Why, do you shop vintage, too?"

"Uh-hmm. So, what's your favorite shop?" This was Jen's trick for understanding other women, because if you knew where they liked to shop, you knew a lot about their income, their taste, and even their assumptions.

"Easy. My friend Meg's place in the North End: Twice Loved. It's between a bakery . . ."

"And an Italian take-out place. I love that store."

"Me, too," Maralys admitted. "I try to stop by at regular intervals to remind Meg to breathe."

"She does talk fast."

"But really has a heart of gold. You know, if you're ever looking for something special, you should tell her. She's good at hunting."

"Thanks. I'll remember that." Jen heard the door to the corridor, then the sound of dog toenails on the floor. "Sounds like Zach is back. It was nice meeting you, Maralys."

"Wait a minute. You're not done meeting me yet. Didn't Zach ask you?"

"Didn't Zach ask me what?" Jen met Zach's eyes as he came into the bedroom. He was still wearing his leather jacket and carried two steaming take-out cups of coffee. Roxie followed him, sniffing with pleasure at the bottom of the brown paper bag he also carried.

Zach shrugged in response to Jen's glance, obviously uncertain what she was talking about.

"He was supposed to invite you to Christmas dinner," Maralys said. "In fact, he's supposed to *bring* you to our Christmas dinner, since you're engaged and all. Didn't he tell you yet?"

Jen held Zach's gaze as she arched a brow. "No, Maralys, Zach didn't tell me about Christmas dinner."

At the mention of his sister-in-law's name, Zach winced.

Meanwhile, Maralys kept talking. "Well, I don't mean to surprise you, Jen. As you can imagine, we'd all love to meet you. I assume you are engaged again, seeing as I've, um, caught you at Zach's."

Jen fumbled for a plausible thing to say and couldn't come up with one. So she agreed, and tried to sound confident about it. "Of course, we're engaged again. We just had a little misunderstanding."

Zach looked at her and she shrugged, trying to communicate "What else could I say?"

"Every good relationship has to suffer an interval," Maralys said. "Lucky for you, yours didn't last eighteen years like ours did."

Jen had nothing to say to that.

Meanwhile Zach crossed the room and put the two coffees down on the headboard. He reached into the pockets of his jacket, removed a handful of creamers from one side and half a dozen packages of sugar from the other. He looked enquiringly at Jen, offering her choice of additions with a gesture. She nodded for both, and held up two fingers.

"Double, double," he said quietly. "Good choice. This place's coffee could be used to clean carburetor parts."

Jen put her hand over the receiver. "You make it sound so tempting."

"They're close so it's hot. That's a big plus. Maybe the only plus."

"We meet midafternoon," Maralys said into Jen's ear. "Although of course, everyone would understand if you had your own family arrangements that day. Do you have a family dinner?"

Jen felt put on the spot. Should she mention Christmas Eve at her Gran's? Or would that sound like she was agreeing to come to the Coxwells'? She watched Zach mix coffee, unable to read his thoughts. He didn't seem to be thrilled that she was talking to Maralys.

Had Zach been intending to ask her to Coxwell's himself?

Or not?

Or was he intending to ask somebody else?

Zach tugged two keys on a ring from the pocket of his jacket and dangled them from his fingertip. It was the jacket he'd worn the night before to impersonate Elvis, so she assumed the keys were for the motorcycle.

"Well?" Maralys prompted.

Jen was sufficiently distracted to admit more than she should
have. "Actually, we celebrate on Christmas Eve," she said, realiz-
ing too late what she'd implied.

"Great!" Maralys said with such enthusiasm that Jen had to
hold the phone away from her ear. "Then we'll see you on the
twenty-fifth."

"Um, I guess," Jen said, uncertain how to read Zach's grim attitude. She shrugged at him and he came to take the receiver.

"Thanks a lot, Maralys," he said and didn't seem very pleased
about the transaction. He sat on the bed beside Jen and offered her
the double-double coffee with his other hand.

Jen sat an increment away from him, not sure what to think.
She picked her shirt off the floor and put it on, feeling very naked
all of a sudden.

And a bit cold.

"I assume you called about the keys to the bike," Zach said with
some impatience. "And only accidentally got to meddle in my life."

Maralys said something and he grimaced. "I've no doubt that
you would have done it on purpose if you could have. Look, I
didn't leave the keys because it was too late to knock and leaving
them in the mailbox seemed like a good way to get the bike stolen."
He paused. "Yes, I know that James would have killed me if anything had happened to his baby. He made that pretty clear."

He listened for a moment and Jen stirred her coffee. It was disconcerting how he concentrated on the conversation and barely
looked at her.

But then, she had assumed that his pursuit had been only about
sex. She shouldn't be surprised that having sex should have dimin-
ished his interest. She got out of bed, patted Roxie, and went to the
washroom with her bra and her fake boob.

It would be easier to face the morning with her props in place.

Trust Maralys to screw up his timing.

Trust Maralys to shove him into a situation that he wasn't sure he wanted any part of. Zach had been hoping, actually, that Jen would invite him to her family's place at Christmas and the entire Coxwell festive ordeal at Gray Gables could have been missed.

Now that couldn't happen.

Zach sat on the bed and drank his coffee, not really tasting it, after he'd hung up the phone. Jen seemed to be taking a lifetime in the washroom, but then, how long had it been since he'd been waiting on a woman? He didn't like how quiet she had gotten, or how spooked she had looked when Maralys had popped the question, and he knew he could have eased her into the concept of meeting his family better than Maralys had done. Jen must have felt cornered, and he knew she didn't like that much.

Trust Maralys. She was about as subtle as a whack in the side of the head with a two-by-four. This was not the morning he'd planned. No doubt about it: any favor he owed James for lending him the bike was officially forfeit.

His coffee was almost gone and Jen's was stone cold when she came out of the washroom. She avoided his gaze and reached for her pants. "There was a new toothbrush in its package," she said, her tone cautious. "I hope you don't mind that I used it."

"No, that's fine. Did you find everything you needed?"

She shrugged. "More or less." She fastened her pants, then pulled on her socks as if she couldn't wait to get out of his apartment.

Zach felt about as smooth as a piece of steel wool. "I thought maybe we could go for breakfast this morning. There's a place around the corner . . ."

Jen forced a thin smile, a pale shadow of the one she usually flashed. "Sorry. I've got some things to do today."

"Right." Could this get any more awkward?

Jen paused before she left the bedroom. "Look. I'm sorry I answered the phone. I was half asleep and just grabbed it without thinking. If I'd been awake enough to realize where I was, I would have just let the machine get it."

"It's okay," Zach said.

"No, it's not." She looked straight at him for the first time. "You're annoyed that Maralys asked me to Christmas dinner. Message received: I'm out of here." She turned to leave and had grabbed her coat by the time Zach realized what she was saying and went after her.

"Wait a minute. That's not it." He caught her elbow and she regarded him warily. "Okay, I'm not happy that Maralys leapt right in, but not because she invited you. I just don't like the way she did it. I was going to ask you, but in my way."

Jen's skepticism faded a little. "Am I supposed to tell you that you're cute when you try to squirm out of a tight corner?"

"Am I?"

"Not nearly cute enough." She shoved her other arm into her jacket and reached for her boots. "It's okay, Zach. I get it. You're off the hook."

"But I don't want to be off the hook! I wanted to invite you for Christmas dinner." He shoved a hand through his hair and tried to find a rationale that she would understand. "If only to have someone relatively sane to talk to."

Jen's lips twitched. "Relatively? Thank you very much."

"You know what I mean."

"You've got a helluva way of flattering a woman into agreeing with you." She didn't look as ready to run, though, and Zach knew he was making progress.

Sort of.

He leaned against the door frame, blocking her exit in the process. "The thing is that I haven't given you a very good impression of my family, so I wanted to work up to inviting you to Christmas."

"It's December twentieth, Zach. Just how long were you going to take to work up to this?"

"It's December twentieth? Already?"

She laughed under her breath and pulled on her boots. "You don't fool me. You know what day it is. You just weren't going to ask me. Stop trying to pretend otherwise."

Zach went with the truth, as damning as it might be. "Okay, caught. I wasn't sure I would ask you." Jen glanced up with surprise. "But not for the reason you think." He leaned closer and dropped his voice, his gaze unswerving from hers. "I like you, Jen. I like you a lot. And the fact is that meeting my family, even forewarned, could scare the bejabbers out of any thinking woman."

A cautious smile curved her lips. "Presumably I'm in that camp."

"You're the warrior queen," he said, watching the tension ease from her gaze. "This dinner could easily nix our whole deal here, and even though you do owe me a family extravaganza, I'm not quite ready to nix this deal." He shook his head. "And to be totally honest—"

"You can do that?"

"When I have the right motivation." He looked at her hard, trying to tell her that she was exactly that motivation. "To be totally honest, I don't even want to go for Christmas dinner myself."

She stopped trying to run. "Don't they cook turkey with giblet gravy?"

"Who cares? Gray Gables is one place I'd be happy to never go again."

"Gray Gables?"

"Where I grew up." Zach glanced down. "Where my father killed himself."

"Ah." Jen watched him carefully. "Your not going there doesn't change the fact that he's dead."

"I know. I know." Zach shoved a hand through his hair. "I'd just rather not."

"What's the worst thing that can happen?" Jen asked. "They flick peas at you and throw you out of the house?"

He chuckled despite himself. "I know, it's stupid. And no one throws food: my mother would toss us all out for that."

"You want me to come along just to protect you?"

He met her gaze steadily. "I want to be with you, I'd just rather that we were together somewhere else."

The corner of Jen's lips tugged into a smile. "Too bad Maralys got to me first, then."

"If she could have planned it, she would have. You don't mind going then?"

"I can't let you go alone, not now."

"Thanks." Zach reached out and touched Jen's shoulder. She moved closer, watching him carefully and he smiled. "Let's start over," he murmured. "Good morning."

She smiled then, really smiled. "Good morning," she said, then reached to kiss him. She wrinkled her nose then and hesitated. "You smell like you've been licking carburetors."

Zach laughed. "Sorry. It's the coffee." He grabbed her by the hand and headed for the bathroom, then brushed his teeth again. "What do you say to a whole-grain bagel?"

"Is that a lawyer joke?"

"No, it's supposed to be an offer you can't refuse."

Jen leaned in the doorway, smiling as she watched him. "There you go, sweet-talking me with whole foods."

"Hey, whatever works." He rubbed a hand over his chin. "I'd better shave first. Maybe you should take off your coat again."

"Afraid I'll make a run for it when you're at a disadvantage?"

"Pretty much."

Jen looked at him, the warmth of her smile making Zach think of what they'd done the night before, never mind what they could do together in the future.

"Okay," she said. "I haven't had my coffee yet, anyway."

She hung up her jacket and retrieved the coffee. Roxie bounced along beside her when she went into the living room, and Zach heard Jen talking to the dog. He smiled when Roxie brought her a favorite toy and Jen exclaimed over it.

Disaster had been narrowly averted and lo, it was good.

Chapter 13

Jen was glowing when Zach and Roxie walked her to the T station later that morning. She was walking on air when Zach gave her a kiss good-bye and grinned when he muttered that it should be illegal for her to melt his Jockeys in public. Jen paid her fare, smiled at the conductor, and rode home blissfully happy.

She'd never had so much fun in bed, that was for sure.

And she'd never had a partner so determined to both give and receive. Her impulse to go with Zach the night before had definitely been a good thing.

Life was good.

Jen floated through her day, ignoring her mother's comments about the beneficial power of orgasm. She headed to Teresa's later that day, filled with significantly more optimism about the evening ahead than she had been earlier.

Orgasm was potent stuff.

Or was it love?

Either way, Jen was going with it.

• • •

Teresa's apartment was every bit as glamorous as Jen remembered, and the black cashmere prosthesis didn't help that much.

It was always a bit daunting to step into Teresa's home, always an occasion to feel underdressed and inelegant. It would have been more intimidating if Jen hadn't helped with the decorating, or if she hadn't known how much of the work Teresa had done herself.

It was still perfect. Always perfect. Jen didn't imagine for a minute that even if she lived alone, her home would be perfect. There'd always be a bra hanging from the bedroom doorknob, or a boot on its side beside its partner in the foyer. There'd be a dirty tea mug in the sink and a towel that wasn't hung exactly perfectly in the bathroom. Jen didn't worry about such things. They were how, in her opinion, you could tell the difference between real homes and those fake homes featured in magazines.

Teresa's apartment shouldn't have actually had a live occupant. It was elegantly decorated in pewter and white, and always made Jen feel as if she was standing inside a cloud. The tables were chrome-edged with mirrored tops; the cushy sofa was upholstered in silvery leather; the shaggy white rug on the floor looked like the hide of some alpine beast. The walls were pale gray, the vertical blinds matched that hue perfectly and the floor was a darker anthracite.

Even the art was pale and ethereal, prints pressed between layers of glass framed in silver, a framing technique that let the wall show where the mat would otherwise have been. The view out the windows, looking over the glitter of Boston and the ocean beyond from the forty-second floor, added to the sense of it being an eagle's aerie.

As did the quantity of Teresa's stash. The stash poured out of closets with the slightest encouragement, where it was trapped into color-coordinated boxes. The stash seemed to find these boxes too confining, because it spilled on to the floor and piled on the couch in a glorious riot of color and texture with amazing speed.

It could have been said that Teresa's nest was well feathered, but feathers were about the only natural fiber that she hadn't yet managed to collect. She had alpaca and llama and musk ox and angora and mohair. She had wool in a hundred varieties from merino to superwash and every color in the rainbow. She had sock wool and aran-weight wool and fingering weight and chunky. She had Lopi and baby wool and every damn weight in between.

It was a kind of nirvana to be let loose in Teresa's stash and to admire her new additions. The two friends sat on the floor, piling skeins and balls of wool across the couch, the floor, and the coffee table, drinking cranberry martinis and retrieving stray balls from the pouncing paws of Teresa's tiger-striped tabby. Gingerbear finally retreated under the couch, his eyes bright as he watched his prey being moved back and forth, his tail thrashing against the floor in anticipation.

Jen had brought her knitting, including the completed avocado. The sum of her work and her stash appeared meager in comparison to the marvels of Teresa's collection. Teresa, after all, had knit a glittering twin set for evening wear—with a daring halter—a bikini and four shawls since Jen had seen her last. Teresa gave the avocado a critical inspection, asking questions about its construction, then pronounced it "brilliant."

"What's next?" she asked, pouring their second crantinis even though Jen's was only half gone.

"I don't know. First I have to finish my Christmas knitting."

Teresa sat back in surprise. "Go on—you're making gifts?"

Jen nodded. "Well, yes, you see . . ."

"Wait a minute. This is Ms. I-Can't-Commit-Beyond-a-Cherry sitting before me, isn't it?"

Jen smiled. "It seemed time to get past that. The avocado was a bigger project, after all."

Teresa regarded her skeptically. "How many Christmas gifts?"

"I've made socks for my mom," Jen began, unpacking the gifts from her backpack.

Teresa exclaimed over the little cable on the heel of the socks for Natalie and fingered the wool with approval. She put on the mittens for M.B. and framed her face with them. "They're so soft and thick! Comforting and mysterious, just like M.B." Before Jen could comment on that, Teresa admired the lace scarf that was still on Jen's needles for Gran. "You'd better get moving or that will be a hanky by Christmas Eve."

"I know. Do you mind if I knit?"

"No, go ahead. I'll just drink to excess instead."

"You don't have a project in the works?" Jen asked with surprise.

Teresa shook her head firmly, threw back the rest of her crantini and changed the subject. Jen knew it would be better to wait, that the truth would come out in time. "So, why are you knitting like a fiend? Is there something you aren't telling me about your prognosis?"

Jen looked up in surprise. "You don't think these are death gifts?"

"I wouldn't put it past you to be that organized."

"I'm fine."

"Good." Teresa considered Jen. "You look good. You look, in fact, suspiciously happy."

"Maybe I am."

"Maybe you're getting some action."

Jen laughed. "You sound like my mother."

"And you sound like the Jen who was my roommate, all those many years ago. She had an infectious laugh like that." Teresa stuck out her hand. "Welcome back."

"I wasn't that bad."

"You've been pretty grim. And you know, not unreasonably so. I would have been downright morbid, but you're tougher than you look." She winked, softening her words with her expression. "So, what gives? Who's the guy? And what are you knitting for him?"

Jen gave her friend a quelling look. "I'm not going to invoke the sweater curse."

Teresa laughed. "Ah, the infamous sweater curse. Does every man run in terror when the woman he's dating makes him a sweater?"

"There must be a bunch of them who do, otherwise there wouldn't be a curse."

"True. All true. Did you knit Steve a sweater?"

"No."

"Maybe you should have."

Jen laughed.

Teresa drank, watching Jen's response with interest. "I never thought you'd laugh about that bastard."

"Well, I am."

"Good. So, tell me about the new guy. You must be serious if you don't want to scare him off." Teresa mixed another round of drinks. "Not to mention that glint of sexual satisfaction I see in your eye."

"Jealous?" Jen teased, fully expecting that Teresa would be seeing someone. Her friend never seemed to lack for male company.

To her surprise, Teresa nodded. "You bet."

"You're not seeing anyone?"

"Not since Mark." Teresa shrugged. "It just seems so pointless, kind of like my job. I'm tired of ambitious and driven people, and I sure as hell don't want to date any more of them."

"I thought you were one of those people," Jen said. "I mean, you don't make CFO without working pretty hard. It's what I've always admired about you."

"But what's the point, Jen? I just get to work harder. I'm surrounded by people like me, all chasing more money and more toys and finding themselves less satisfied all the time." She drank, then grimaced. "Some days, I'd like to drive over my cell phone and BlackBerry and smash them to bits, so no one could call me up out of the blue and demand that I answer for something. Some days, I'd just like to get into the car and drive away from it all." She looked around the gorgeous apartment with dissatisfaction, then forced a smile. "But then they'd come after me when the lease payment wasn't made, wouldn't they?"

"It wouldn't look good for a CFO to get nailed for nonpayment of personal debts," Jen said, trying to make Teresa laugh.

"True. All true. But then, wouldn't bailing on the CFO job be the point?"

"What would you do instead?"

Teresa sighed. "I just don't know. It's the only thing I know how to do, although sometimes it feels that I spend more energy playing office politics than doing my actual job." She shrugged and topped up their glasses, although Jen's was still full. "Sorry. I must just have PMS."

"It's too soon for you to have a midlife crisis."

"Maybe it's my biological clock."

"I didn't even know you wanted children."

"I don't know if I do, either. It would be nice, though, to have the choice before it gets made for me."

"Ambitious men make good providers," Jen noted, trying only to be helpful.

Teresa half laughed. "But they make crap fathers. I should know. You know, you're lucky in a way that your father just bailed."

Jen remembered the crushing disappointment of finally meeting her father when she was twelve, only to have him prove to be completely disinterested in her. He'd made an excuse, bolted—to the relief of both of them—and she hadn't seen him since. "No, but there were times when I wished there'd been more."

"Only because you're such a giving person. Think what kind of attitude you could have caught from a man like that." Teresa dismissed Jen's father with a wave, knowing as she did all the details of the one story Jen had about him. "You were better off with Natalie checking your chakras."

"I guess so."

"I know so. You don't have much baggage, or at least less than you would have if he'd hung around and messed with your expectations."

"Maybe you do have PMS," Jen said in a teasing tone. "Or did you catch grim from me? I didn't think it was contagious."

"You're right. I'm sorry. I've just gotten everything I thought I wanted, at least the parts that I can get myself, and it seems like so little." Teresa picked up Gingerbear and spoke solemnly to him. "I should be like you, and be happy with having one ball of wool to play with."

"You have enough stash that you could open a store," Jen noted.

Teresa shook her head. "No way. Then other people would want to touch my stash, even buy it and take it home. I could never let that happen."

"But I'm touching your stash."

"I know where you live." Teresa gave Jen a fierce look. "If anything's missing tomorrow, I'll come get it back."

"Are you sure you can take me? What if it was something I really wanted?"

"Then I'd have to be sneaky and get Cin on my side." They laughed together and Teresa drank some more. "Do you have any stash yet?" she asked abruptly.

"No. I'm buying on a project-by-project basis."

"No loose ends? Pun intended?"

Jen shook her head.

Teresa wagged a finger at her. "*You* could have a knitting store. You have the discipline to not fall in love with every skein that came in the door and not to take it personally if someone wanted to buy yarn from your store."

Jen smiled and decided to admit her secret dream, again. "I've been thinking something similar for a while," she acknowledged, feeling bolder about the idea after Zach's open approval. "I registered to go back and finish my degree this winter. I'll be done by the end of summer term and I was thinking about putting together a business plan and taking it to the bank."

Teresa sprawled on the floor, with Gingerbear on her chest. "You know what? Bring it to me. And you don't have to wait until your degree is finished."

"I really appreciate your taking a look at it for me," Jen said, thinking that Teresa's financial advice would be a great asset.

"I'm not just taking a look at it, Jen. I'm talking about investing."

Jen gaped at her friend in astonishment.

"Jen, the biggest variable in the success or failure of a small business like a shop is the character of the proprietor. I know you and I know you'll work harder than anyone else could or would to make this work. You care, and that's what makes the difference."

"But it could take a lot of money . . ."

"I make a lot of money, Jen, and I have all my retirement savings funds nicely topped up. I want to do something with my money that makes me feel like there's a point." She smiled and toasted Jen with her glass. "You being happy teaching people how to knit seems to me to be a way to make the world a better place. If I can help you do that, I'm in. I'm always up for living vicariously, if all it means is writing a check."

"But I still need to do the market research . . ."

"Of course you do. I'm no sucker!" They laughed together, then Teresa pursed her lips. "The location is going to be what makes or breaks it, Jen. There are so many yarn shops and so many online sources. You're going to have to find the perfect place, with ambience and no competition."

"Maybe a smaller town, with tourist trade."

"That would be good. You could sell online, as well." She picked up the avocado and admired it. "Teach workshops in knitting fruit or sell your patterns, too. You could start a trend."

"I don't think so," Jen retorted but she was thinking about Teresa's advice and getting excited about the prospect of opening her shop. Could the dream that she couldn't even voice several weeks before be so close as that? It seemed like it.

Teresa fingered the lacey hat for Cin. "She'll love this," she said. "It's just funky enough. What are you making for Pluto?"

Jen winced. "I don't know. The only thing I could think of was a sweater, but I'm running out of time."

"Ticktock," Teresa said. "Does he still use that shoulder bag?"

"The one that looks like it fell through the space-time continuum from 1972?" Jen asked.

"It's too dirty to have made that quick of a trip," Teresa said. "Honestly, the thing looks like he's dragged it around the planet eight or ten times."

"He pretty much has. He takes it everywhere."

"Then that boy needs a style upgrade."

"He'll never part with it . . ."

Teresa waved off this objection with one hand. "How do you know that he's not secretly desperate for a replacement but doesn't know where to find one? Besides, we can solve this easily."

"How?"

"We'll make him a bag and felt it. It will be very chic and useful, too."

Jen frowned down at the incomplete lace shawl. "But I don't think there's time. And I don't know how to felt . . ."

"I'll proxy knit for you," Teresa said breezily. She was already picking through her stash. "I can get it done tonight if I get to it and stop drinking. You'll see." She held up two balls of heavy wool. "Black or blue?"

"The indigo one. It looks more natural."

"Good plan. I'll do a Fair Isle thing with this lighter blue." Teresa pulled out some thick needles and cast on. She worked with daunting speed, giving her all to the project once she had committed to it.

As usual, Jen was impressed by her friend's drive.

"So," Teresa asked after she had established her pattern stitch. "Tell me about the mystery dude. Is he like Steve?"

Jen choked on a mouthful of crantini. "About as different as a guy could be, which is funny if you think about it."

"How so?"

Jen ended up having to tell Teresa the whole story of Zach from the beginning, which made Teresa laugh out loud more than once. "You should be the one taking pictures," she charged, when Jen told her about Zach impersonating Elvis. "This guy sounds like a hoot."

"He is." Jen smiled to herself. "He makes me laugh."

"And maybe that's good enough," Teresa said quietly. Jen glanced up at her friend's sober tone. Teresa shrugged. "You've got to know, Jen, that this is the kind of guy that is around for a good time but not a long time."

"Well, I wondered." Jen looked down at her work, finding herself disappointed by her friend's reality check. Then she wondered why she hadn't been skeptical sooner. She and Zach had made no plans to get together before Christmas Day, though, and nothing had been said about any connection after she repaid her debt to Zach and played fake fiancée at his family dinner. He hadn't even asked if she'd been working this weekend. Never mind New Year's Eve.

Doubt took root in her sucker heart and grew a little leaf.

Teresa leaned over to bump shoulders with her, apparently sensing her change of mood. "But you know, Jen, maybe what he's given you already is good enough. You've had fun, you're happier than you've been, and you've become confident enough to go back to school and pick up your life again. All that and great sex, too. There are people who've been married for decades and gotten less out of their relationship than that."

It was true. Logically, Jen knew as much. She decided to stick to her knitting and be glad of the gifts Zach brought her way. It would be greedy to expect anything more.

Even if she was feeling a bit greedy, she'd get over it.

Sooner or later.

Christmas Eve dinner at Natalie's was an event to look forward to. Jen always enjoyed it. Each year, Natalie picked a theme and they decorated and cooked accordingly. It was a collaborative effort and the guest list tended to be flexible.

Natalie's compromise with Gran was that Gran would attend the Christmas Eve dinner as a party instead of a religious holiday.

In recent years, they had begun singing Christmas carols on Christmas Eve again, in lieu of going to church, which suited pretty much everyone. The annual family gift exchange was sufficiently traditional to please both Gran and Natalie, although they had argued the pagan roots of Christian tradition to death years ago.

This year, they were cooking Chinese food. Jen had found some red paper lanterns in Chinatown and hung them throughout Natalie's big kitchen and out to the porch. Her contribution to the evening was hot-and-sour soup, which was five-alarm stuff, as well as vegetables in a spicy Szechwan sauce.

M.B. had brought chopsticks and dumplings for appetizers with various dips, and fireworks for afterward. He was busy showing Gran how to use the chopsticks, with mixed success.

Gerry was chopping vegetables in the kitchen with his usual vigor—could the man do anything by half measures? Jen didn't think so and simply tried to stay out of his way.

Gran had arrived with some take-out deep-fried chicken bo-bo balls with red sweet-and-sour sauce. Natalie had put them into the fridge, but would have to heat them up again before they ate.

Pluto had managed to bring his guitar. He parked himself in one corner of the kitchen and strummed while everyone else worked.

Cin was the last to arrive and she was in what Gran called a royal mood when she did arrive. "Ian's not coming," she said, flicking the door shut with more force than was necessary. She peeled off her coat and chucked it in the direction of the coat hooks, not troubling to pick it up when it landed on the floor.

"But why not?" Natalie asked, glancing up from her stirring and frying. "He always comes."

"He's working," Cin said, as if this was a sin beyond redemption. She thunked a big bottle of wine on the counter so hard that it might have shattered if the glass hadn't been so cheap. Jen guessed Cin intended to drink most of it herself. "Just like he's been working every day and every night since Thanksgiving." She heaved a sigh. "I've *tried* to be understanding—"

"You couldn't be understanding to save your life," Pluto teased and got a glare for his attempt to be funny.

Cin returned to her lament. "But I've run out of patience with it and with him." She peeled away the foil around the top of the bottle with impatience. "I think I'm going to move out. It'll probably be months before he notices, but whatever."

"Why would he be working so much?" M.B. asked, the voice of reason. As always, he focused on logic and tried to take the emotional charge out of Cin's attitude. "Do you two need extra money?"

Cin threw herself into a chair, not having any of it. "We always get by. No flights to New York for lunch to buy diamond rings, but that's never been an issue before."

"I thought you were thinking of buying a house," Natalie reminded her daughter.

Cin scoffed. "We could both work double time until we're dead, and still be unable to afford real estate in this town."

"Then move to another town," Pluto suggested. Cin threw a pillow at him. "Come on, answering the phone at Nature Sprouts isn't exactly an irreplaceable career opportunity."

"I like it here," Cin said, sulking the way she did when she didn't want to be talked out of sulking.

"Maybe Ian has new responsibilities at work," Gran suggested, ever the supporter of such thinking. "You can't fault a man for being ambitious, or taking advantage of opportunity. Why, he could be trying to get a promotion!"

"Except that Ian never has been ambitious before." Cin wrenched open the screw top on the wine and glowered at them all. "I can't ask him because I never see him. Not to mention the fact that I can't even tell you the last time we had sex."

Jen and her grandmother were the only ones apparently thinking that this was too much information.

"But you are mentioning it," Pluto teased.

"Obviously," Cin snarled.

"Nothing like a good orgasm to improve a woman's mood," Natalie said as she stirred.

"Works for both genders," Gerry said and the two smiled at each other. M.B. rolled his eyes and got a cup of tea for Gran, who looked ruffled.

"She never learned such talk in my house," Gran muttered and M.B. made a soothing noise that seemed to reassure her.

"I always thought she was an angel," Jen confided in her grandmother. "But a naughty one."

Gran laughed in surprise, almost spilling her tea in the process.

Meanwhile, Pluto perched on the chair beside Cin, his manner playful. "I don't suppose the timing of Ian's sudden work schedule is in any way linked to your turning him down."

Cin glared at him. "I've never turned Ian down for anything." She got a tumbler from the cupboard and poured herself a healthy serving. "Maybe that's the problem. The man has my number and he knows it."

"Nobody has your number," Jen contributed. "You change it all the time."

"Or have it unlisted," Pluto teased.

Cin ignored them both. She threw back a gulp of wine.

Jen cleared her throat. "Did he hear us on the phone?"

"When?" Cin demanded, her eyes narrowed.

"When you were talking about upgrading, and saying you'd have Zach's love child."

"You didn't!" Gran protested. Natalie choked back a laugh and Cin, for the first time in Jen's memory, blushed crimson. "That was a joke," she insisted. "And I was at work anyway."

She'd seemed pretty serious to Jen, but Jen thought it a bad idea to say as much.

"Oh, come on," Pluto urged. "You told me about him proposing with the Batman ring from the cereal box. You said you laughed at him."

"Cincinnati McKee!" Gran said in shock and put down her teacup. "You didn't do such a thing!"

"Pluto mentioned it at Thanksgiving," M.B. observed.

"I thought it was a joke," Gran said. "One in very bad taste."

"Of course I laughed at him," Cin said indignantly. "It was a joke. You're supposed to laugh at jokes: that's why people make them."

M.B. looked skeptical. "You're saying *Ian* made a joke?"

Pluto grinned. "Ian, the straight arrow you've been living with for ten years, the guy who couldn't hold on to a punch line if it was Velcro'd to his hands?"

Jen bit back a smile. It was an apt analogy. Ian was stoic and noble and good to Cin. He could be charming, but he was not funny.

Zach was funny.

Cin fidgeted. "It was a joke. I know it. He was just teasing."

M.B. sat down beside Cin in the silence that followed. "Was it?" he asked gently. She looked up at him, clearly uncertain. "Are you sure? Maybe you hurt his feelings."

"Of course, I'm sure it was a joke," Cin insisted. "He couldn't have been serious. It was a green plastic Batman ring that he got out of the cereal box, for goodness sake!" She turned to Jen. "And where's your rock from Tiffany? That would be an engagement ring. That would be a proposal that a woman could take seriously."

"Material waste and overconsumption," Gerry intoned as he carried plates to the table. "What difference does it make what kind of ring it is? It's a symbol of the connection between two people, no more than that. A circle of grass should suit you just as well."

"Or a green plastic Batman ring out of a cereal box," M.B. noted. Cin took another swig of wine and looked sour.

"Or the key ring off a pop can," Pluto said and rolled his eyes. "Women are big for that option."

"You've tried it?" Jen teased and he laughed.

"Not with any success. C'mon, let's see your rock."

Jen shrugged. "I don't have one."

"No time to charter a plane to fly to New York with your busy schedule?" Gerry asked, his tone acid. "I suppose planning a huge wedding does cut into your leisure time."

"I'm not planning a big wedding," Jen said.

"But the Coxwells are," Natalie said.

Jen left that one alone.

"I think the biggest diamond on the eastern seaboard was his ambition, wasn't it?" Gerry sneered.

Jen met the older man's gaze and decided she'd had enough of his bullying. "Hasn't it ever occurred to you, Gerry, that some people will sometimes say something untrue just to pull your chain?"

Pluto laughed. M.B. coughed into his hand, but when Jen looked, his eyes were twinkling.

Gerry inhaled and straightened. "I don't see anything funny about my expressing a concern for the future of the planet . . ."

"Except that you're so serious about it," Natalie interjected. "Whatever happened to mutual tolerance? Remember 'peace, love, and understanding'? We don't have to all have the same answer to every question."

Natalie and Gerry eyed each other from across the kitchen, and Jen sensed an unfamiliar vibration between them. It looked to her as if Gerry was waiting for Natalie to blink, while Natalie simply smiled back at him, her chin held high. The expression in her eyes was a bit harder than it tended to be when she looked at Gerry. They stared at each other for a long moment, then his lips tightened and he strode back across the kitchen to the stove.

He slammed a pot lid and Natalie ignored him.

"I don't have a ring because Zach and I aren't getting married," Jen said quietly, feeling it was best to make the truth clear to her family.

"Yet," Natalie supplied with vigor. "It's in your charts that you'll be together and really, there's nothing wrong with taking your time."

"You mean we won't be going to a wedding at the big Episcopalian church in Rosemount after all?" Gran demanded. "I've told all my friends and I've already bought a hat."

"It'll happen, Mom," Natalie reassured her mother before Jen could say anything. "All Jen and Zach need is a little space."

Jen felt everyone look at her, then look away.

Cin, of course, hadn't really been interested in the conversation around her. "I'm sure Ian has a girlfriend," she complained, taking the conversation back to her own woes once again.

"Well, if you turned him down, it's hard to blame him, isn't it?" Pluto asked.

"He wasn't serious!" Cin wailed.

"Sounds like he was," Jen couldn't help but note.

"Maybe you should ask him," M.B. suggested.

"While you can," Pluto added quietly, but Cin ignored them all. She was too busy draining her glass of wine and getting herself another one.

"We're almost ready," Gerry said, sounding long-suffering.

"Don't forget my bo-bo balls," Gran said with anticipation and Natalie got to her feet. "They're so good."

"Of course, Mom." Natalie returned to the kitchen, opened the fridge, and removed the little brown paper bag. Jen could see her mother over the island that separated the eating area from the work area of the kitchen. Natalie hummed a little as put a pan on the stove with a bit of oil in the bottom, waited until it was hot, then popped the deep-fried balls of chicken into the fat again.

What Jen could also see but Natalie could not was Gerry's face. He stood beside the sink, watching Natalie work, his expression one of horror.

"What are those?" he asked in a tone that indicated he already knew the answer.

"Bo-bo balls," Natalie said. "Mom's favorite. They have chicken in them and are deep fried. I'm sure you've had them before."

"But this is a vegetarian kitchen!"

"Live and let live, Gerry," Natalie said impatiently.

"Is that what they said to the chickens before they were slaughtered?"

Natalie turned to face Gerry, the take-out dish of bright red sauce in her hand. "Would you please put this in the microwave for a minute?"

Gerry recoiled. "What is that stuff?"

Natalie shrugged. "The sauce."

"Sweet-and-sour sauce," Gran contributed cheerfully. "It has pineapple chunks in it."

"Oh," Gerry said in an arch tone. "From one of those New England organic pineapple farms?"

Natalie glared at him and held the dish closer to him. "Just heat it up."

"How many kinds of food coloring are in this crap, Natalie?" Gerry demanded. "What kind of toxins are you putting into your body?"

"The same kind I've put into it for eighty years," Gran said as she pulled up a chair to the table. "Seems to be working out just fine so far."

Gerry looked at Natalie. "You can't mean to let anyone ingest this kind of garbage in your house?"

Natalie took a step back, her expression hardening in a way that Jen had rarely witnessed. Natalie's children were completely silent, knowing the portent of that look well despite its rarity, and Natalie spoke very softly. "There are things, Gerry, that are more important than abstract principles."

"Name one."

"Love. Respect. Tolerance. There's three." Natalie pushed past him and put the plastic bowl into the microwave, then punched in the time and hit start. "I am blessed to have my mother in my home this holiday season. We don't agree on everything, but a bo-bo ball here and there isn't going to condemn the planet to oblivion."

"How can you talk like this?" Gerry demanded. "You know about pineapple plantations. You know about the ill effects of food additives like color and preservatives. This stuff probably wouldn't degenerate in a hundred years."

"Then if I eat enough of it, they won't have to embalm me," Gran said cheerfully. "That'll save chemicals."

The microwave beeped and the chicken balls sizzled in the pan.

"Peace, love, and understanding to you this holiday season," Natalie said sweetly as she reached around Gerry and took the sauce out of the microwave.

"I can't believe it!" Gerry said. "First you let Jen eat turkey . . ."

"She needs animal protein," Natalie said mildly. "The doctor said she was anemic and it was the only solution. And Mom bought an organically raised bird."

"Shockingly expensive," Gran said with a shake of her head. "But it was good, wasn't it, dear?"

"It was delicious, Gran," Jen agreed. "The best turkey dinner ever."

Gran beamed and gave Jen a hug. "Worth every dime to see your blood built back up again," she said huskily. "I'm glad you'll have Zach to take care of you in the future."

"What's the matter with all of you?" Gerry asked, coming to the table. "Can't you see that eating this kind of garbage is what made Jen sick in the first place? Can't you see that you're poisoning yourselves? Cancer . . ."

Natalie slammed the pot on the stove and silence claimed the kitchen completely. Jen looked down. Gran laid a hand over Jen's. M.B. came to stand behind her, putting his hands on her shoulders. Cin put down her glass and looked daggers at Gerry.

"Hey," Pluto protested. "You're out of line, man."

"We don't say the C word here," M.B. said softly.

"Denial doesn't change anything," Gerry said and Jen caught her breath. "We're poisoning the planet and poisoning ourselves and every single goddamn bo-bo ball just makes it worse. We are what we eat and by careless consumption, we sicken ourselves and weaken our own population with disease."

Natalie poured the chicken balls into a bowl and brought them to the table, putting the bowl down with a thump. She put her hands on her hips and glared up at Gerry. "Are you suggesting that my daughter deserved to be sick?"

"I'm saying it's inescapable, if we don't respect . . ."

"Respect seems to be a problem here tonight," Natalie said, interrupting him so sharply that Gerry fell silent. "As does common courtesy."

"But—" he protested.

"But *nothing*," Natalie said fiercely. "My daughter never did anything to deserve her illness: no one could be sufficiently evil to have to endure what Jen went through. I have fed my children with the best food I could find and I have nurtured them with all the love in my heart and I have kept them safe and I have taught them everything I know, and shit still can happen. And no one who believes otherwise has any right to be in my house."

"Are you asking me to leave?" Gerry asked, clearly confident that this could not be the case.

"No," Natalie said and waited a beat. "I'm telling you to."

He stared at her, shocked.

"And don't bother coming back," she said, tossing him his coat and opening the door to the porch.

Gerry sputtered. He turned to the closely packed group at the table as if seeking support. It was a long shot, no matter how you looked at it.

Pluto stood up and started to clap. "Right on, Mom," he said, his eyes a colder blue than they usually were.

"Don't let the door hit you in the ass," Cin said, joining his applause.

"Well said, Mom," M.B. contributed.

Gran held fast to Jen's hand.

Gerry looked at them all, shook his head, swore, then strode into the night. Natalie slammed the door behind him and turned the lock, leaning her back against it to regard her family. There were tears shimmering in her eyes, Jen saw.

"Don't you dare believe any of that," she told Jen.

Jen shook her head. "The oncologist told me it was a random mutation that couldn't be traced to any single event or cause."

"And after a decade in medical school, he probably knew more about it than Gerry," M.B. said flatly. He gave Jen's shoulders a squeeze, then went to take his place. There was a bustle of food getting to the table and people seating themselves and Cin sharing her wine.

Then Cin surprised Jen once again. She whistled for silence and lifted her glass high, smiling at Jen across the steaming food. "To our Jen and her first anniversary of testing 'clear.' Let's drink to many, many more."

They cheered and drank and then Jen lifted her own glass. "One more," she said. "To all of you, for helping me get through it."

"To family," Natalie said. "Because no matter how we argue, we're here for each other when it counts."

"Which is a good thing," Pluto said. "'Cause you can pick your nose, man, but you can't pick your relatives."

Cin threw a napkin at him as everyone groaned. They drank the toast, then Gran looked over the table. "Doesn't this look nice?" she asked no one in particular, then insisted that Jen begin to ladle out her soup.

Chapter 14

Jen's knitted gifts were well received that night. Natalie exclaimed over the socks and put them on right away. M.B. pledged he'd wear the mittens home that night. Cin tried on the hat, then returned to her excessive wine consumption with the hat still on her head. Pluto declared the shoulder sling bag to be the perfect thing and immediately moved stuff from his canvas sling bag into the "much more funky" knitted one.

Gran wrapped herself in her lacy shawl and beamed with pride. "I never imagined that when you learned to knit, you'd one day make something like this," she said, her voice warm with affection. "Now, you go and get that envelope in the side of my purse."

Jen got the envelope, thinking her grandmother had brought a Christmas card for the household. To her surprise, it was addressed to her.

Gran smiled. "Go on. Open it."

Jen was embarrassed, feeling that she had been singled out from her siblings. They didn't seem to have any issues with it, though, and she wondered what they knew that she didn't.

"Go on," M.B. urged, bumping his shoulder against hers. "Open it. Cin's dying of curiosity."

Cin snorted, but she put her wine aside. "Do it, Jen."

"A little music to set the tone," Pluto said, and strummed on his guitar. He chose "White Christmas," which made Jen think about doing a fake fox-trot down Lee Street in the snow with Zach.

Would that happen again?

Was once enough?

Her throat tightened and she tore open the envelope without further ado.

There was a bank statement inside the envelope. It was hard to read the tally of numbers in the candlelight, so Jen looked to her grandmother for an explanation.

"Once upon a time, a baby girl was born," Gran said, her fingers entwined in the ends of the shawl Jen had knit for her. "And the grandparents of that little girl were very excited, even though they were already grandparents three times over."

"She's talking about you," Pluto said to Jen.

"Thanks for the clarification," Jen said and they all laughed.

Gran continued. "Now, because the grandfather of that little girl was the kind of man who worried a great deal about the future, and because the father of that little girl was not the kind of man who worried much about anything at all, the baby's grandfather opened a savings account for that baby. He put fifty dollars in that account and he left it there. And every time that little girl had a birthday or lost a tooth or got a good grade in class or won a blue ribbon at a track meet, he put a little bit more money into that account. Sometimes it was twenty-five dollars and sometimes it was only ten. He put fifty dollars in when she was baptized, and a little bit every Christmas. And he never took any money out."

Gran took a sip of her tea. "That little girl grew up and her grandparents came to love her more and more with every passing year. And the money in that account, through the miracle of compound interest and that grandfather's contributions, grew as surely as the little girl did. When she was eighteen, he changed the name on the account to make it hers and only left himself with the ability to deposit."

Gran sighed and looked around the room at the rapt faces of her family. Jen looked, too, and her heart clenched at the affection in their expressions. Her mother's kitchen was a good place to be.

She hoped with sudden ferocity that she would have her own kitchen one day, adjacent to her knitting store, and that people would feel as welcome there as they did here.

"Because he was the kind of man who took care of things quietly," Gran said, "he never said anything, either to the little girl who had become a woman or to his own daughter. When he was ill at the end, he made me promise to tell you, Jen, about your money when the time was right." Gran looked into her teacup and blinked back a tear. "But I never knew when that time was, because for a long time after he was gone, I couldn't even think about finishing things he had started. I couldn't really think of being without him, even though I was. Finding a time was the last thing on my mind."

Jen got up and went to sit beside her grandmother. The older woman held fast to Jen's fingers, her own hand shaped by time and experience, her grip strong. "He would have been so proud of you. He was proud of you always, but if he could see you now, well . . ."

"He can see her now, Mom," Natalie said softly. "Can't you feel that Dad's here with us?"

"Don't you go talking your strange nonsense with me now," Gran said with affection and the two women smiled at each other in the glow of the red paper lanterns.

Gran squeezed Jen's hand. "He told me, Patrick did, that I would know the right moment to tell you about this. I thought that a lot of nonsense, if you must know, the kind of nonsense your mother tends to talk . . ."

"So, you see? I came by it honestly," Natalie joked.

Gran harumphed. "Last week, Natalie told me about your go-ing back to finish your degree in January and it occurred to me that you might need a little bit of money. I knew that this must be the very moment that Patrick had told me about."

Gran swallowed. "And when I told Natalie, she told me about the medical bills, and your student loan." She looked up at Jen, her eyes bright. "I had no idea, my dear. I suppose I am a silly old woman, but I didn't realize that it was so expensive to go to col-lege. I never even finished high school myself. And I had no idea how much medical care costs when you have no insurance." She tightened her grip on Jen's fingers. "I'm very sorry that I didn't give this to you sooner, dear. I feel as if I failed you."

"Of course, you didn't," Jen protested, bending to kiss her grandmother's cheek.

"I could have set your mind at ease sooner."

"You did. You were there with me. I couldn't have gotten through it without you."

And it was true. The power of her family's love had been the one constant in Jen's battle with cancer, the one force that she had been able to rely upon. They had all been there. They had taken turns driving her to treatments, they had sat up with her when she was ill, they had held her hand and given her the strength to keep fighting on those days when it didn't seem there was a lot of point. Without them, she knew that she might have given up the battle. She looked around the room and wished that she had knit more for them, had knit gifts for them sooner, had somehow shown the magnitude of her love for them with wool and needles and time.

Gran held fast to her hand. "I know what it is, dear, to have nothing but love to offer a man who has a great deal more than that to his credit. I want you to be able to start fresh with Zach, to not have the past trailing along behind you. Go and look properly at that statement."

In the light over the stove, Jen looked at the balance on the statement and nearly choked. It was a lot of money, enough to pay all of her bills and change left to pay for her remaining tuition and books. She would be able to finish her degree and start fresh.

She looked at her family with astonishment. "We should share it," she began but they interrupted her as one.

"You need the break, Jen," M.B. said firmly.

"It was always for you," Gran insisted.

"Your father left you nothing but his name," Natalie said softly. "Cin's father paid her tuition. M.B.'s father took him on vacations in the summers. Pluto's father has always encouraged his music."

"And he still puts me up when I'm in New York," Pluto added.

"We need to take care of you ourselves," Natalie said. "Although that wasn't my expectation in the first place, that's how it worked out."

Gran reached up and kissed Jen's cheek. "On the other hand, it means you're all ours."

Jen, all choked up with tears, couldn't think of anything better than being part of her weird and wonderful family. She hugged them all and knew a relief that went beyond financial concerns.

Her knitting shop dream seemed suddenly a lot less insane than it had just a week before.

Christmas Day was sunny and cold. Zach, to his surprise, felt a bit of anticipation mingled with the dread he'd been fighting since agreeing to go to Gray Gables.

Maybe that was because he was going to see Jen again.

Maybe that was the only good thing about the day ahead.

He had good news himself—on the adult front—but that wasn't why he wanted to see her so much. He picked Jen up, right on time, and she was waiting for him, almost as if she was anxious to see him, too.

She was wearing a vintage suit, black and camel, with a silk scarf at her neck and only the barest dash of lipstick. She looked both retro and modern, feminine and austere. Her smile of welcome made everything in him turn hot, then cold.

"You look great," he said as he took the white poinsettia from her. It was wrapped with a plaid ribbon, and was clearly a hostess gift. He thought it was a good choice for Leslie. "Very Coco Chanel."

Jen's smile broadened, lighting her face. "When in doubt, go classic. You didn't give me a dress code so I guessed." She fussed a bit with the cellophane over the plant and the plaid red bow around the package. "Is this all right?"

"Perfect. Leslie likes poinsettias." Zach arched a brow. "Independent of them being the result of virtual slave labor and excessive pesticide use in the third world."

"And unnecessary air transport," Jen reminded him with a smile. She sobered as she straightened his tie. "You look nice," she said, and he knew that wasn't really what she wanted to say. "I'm sorry that my family was so awful to you."

Zach shrugged. "They're protective of you and there's nothing wrong with that." He winked at her. "Besides, I'm getting my own back today."

"From what you've said, your family sound like a pack of ogres."

"Maybe they'll be on good behavior for the holiday," he said and opened the door.

"Then why don't you look as if you believe that?"

Roxie barked with enthusiasm, jamming her head through the gap between the front seat and the door frame so that she could greet Jen, and spared him from answering. "No slobbering," Zach said, to no discernible effect in Roxie's behavior.

Jen laughed and patted the dog, admired the big red bow around her neck, then coaxed the dog back into the backseat with an ease Zach could only envy.

Although her feat had something to do with the dog toy she produced from her purse for Roxie. Roxie settled onto the back seat to chew her Christmas present with gusto.

"Cheap trick," Zach said.

"It worked, didn't it?"

Zach had to give her points for that.

"You'd better give me the plant here," Jen said. "I think it might be too cold for it in the trunk."

"Roxie really wants to be your dog," Zach said after he passed Jen the plant. "Just snap your fingers and she'll run home with you."

"I'd never tempt her to leave you alone," Jen teased. She glanced over her shoulder. "Are your presents in the trunk?"

"No. They decided on a lottery to keep things simple." Zach produced a small wrapped box from his suit pocket. "I only have the one."

Jen seemed perplexed. "No food contribution?"

Zach shrugged. "Unauthorized additions to the menu are frowned upon." He regretted his words immediately, because Jen looked more uncertain about her attendance today. "They aren't so bad," he said as he pulled out from the curb. "At least, they have better PR recently."

"That's not very reassuring."

"It's the best I can do."

She turned and he felt her watching him. "You don't really want to go, do you?"

"I'd rather be drawn and quartered. Come to think of it, Leslie's a medieval scholar. Maybe that's the entertainment she has planned for the day and they're all being nice just to sucker me in."

Jen chewed on her lip and studied him for a while, and he wondered how much of his reluctance over this trip she could see.

"Just tell me: are we still engaged or not?" she finally asked. "And when is the wedding? Or is there to be one?"

Zach nodded. "Good plan. Let's get our story straight. The problem is that we never did that trip to Tiffany . . ."

"And we aren't going to," Jen said firmly. Zach refused to think about what her attitude meant.

Maybe it was just about the flight to New York.

Maybe she still thought he wasn't the kind of guy a woman should marry. That was a more annoying prospect than Zach thought it should have been. He focused instead on the problem at hand.

"So, let's say that given our dispute about the kind of ring you'll be wearing for the rest of your life," Zach said, making up the story as he went, "we've decided to delay the wedding arrangements."

"You could say that the church was already booked."

Zach shook his head. "My mother would know, or she would find out. Let's keep it simple and blame our own indecision."

Jen, to his surprise, didn't seem to be happy with this scheme.

"What's wrong with that?" he asked.

"It sounds like something you would do, but not like something I would do. I like to have a plan."

"But they don't know you."

"Aren't they supposed to think that I'm good for you?"

"Well, I don't know. According to the original scheme, we should be trying to make them hate you, the way you wanted your family to hate me."

"But they didn't hate you."

"And I don't think my family will hate you either."

"So, why are we doing this at all?"

Zach knew his line was that Jen owed him, but that wasn't the reason that he wanted her to come to Christmas dinner. It wasn't because Maralys had managed to corner them on this, either.

He frowned as he negotiated the exchange to the highway, then decided to go with the truth. "Because I don't want to go at all, but I know that I should. I'm still new at this being-an-adult thing, and am enough of a chicken that I want you to be with me for this."

She regarded him with a twinkle in her eye. "And the fact that you could talk me into it by talking about me owing you was just a bonus."

"Maybe the ends justify the means." He cleared his throat and tried again. "I suppose it's not much incentive that you'll get a good turkey dinner for your efforts."

"I love turkey dinner," Jen admitted. "You might be surprised what I'd do for a good homemade turkey dinner."

"There's a tempting opening. Does the appeal diminish if I tell you that it will probably be catered?"

Jen turned to look at him in her surprise. "A catered Christmas dinner? Your family doesn't cook it themselves?"

Zach decided not to tell her about his mother's history of excessive alcoholic consumption on holidays and his father's criticism of everything in his house that fell less of perfection. She'd likely get out of the car and run if he did.

Hell, he might get out of the car and run if he thought too much about the fact that he was driving straight toward the place he most wanted to avoid. "They used to, but decided it would be easier to just order it in."

"That's not all of the truth."

"It's as much as I'm going to give you right now."

Jen watched him carefully. "You're serious about the catering."

"I am."

"Isn't part of a holiday working together to create a meal and then sharing it?"

"Maybe in some places. Coxwell holiday celebrations are endurance tests."

"No wonder you dread it," Jen said softly.

"Sorry." Zach put his hand over hers for a moment, feeling like a total jerk. "I shouldn't have asked you to come."

"Do you want me to be there?"

"Yes," he answered without hesitation.

"Because you're a big chicken?"

"Pretty much."

Jen turned her hand so that their fingers entwined. "Then I'm glad to be going with you. Maybe it won't be as bad as you expect."

"Maybe not," Zach acknowledged, but he didn't believe it for a minute.

He took the back road toward Rosemount and changed the subject, telling Jen about his various adventures growing up here. He wondered just who he was trying to cajole into approaching the festivities with an open mind.

They passed Mary Lake and he told her about teaching his younger sister to drive. He told the story of how he had taken Phil out on the frozen lake to show her how to turn doughnuts on the ice, and mimicked how Phil had shrieked when he had first driven the car on to the ice. Jen laughed. He told her about his recent deal with Phil's husband, Nick, to not teach their young son to drive when it came time, and she laughed harder.

He found that he was enjoying himself. His childhood did sound idyllic, now that he recalled it. They passed the forest where he and his friends had come to indulge in forbidden pleasures on Friday nights, once upon a time, and he told her about the chief of police hunting them down one summer night.

"Did he catch you?"

"No. There were too many mosquitos for him to go the distance."

"But he knew who you were?"

Zach nodded. "We had to hide deeper in the bush to get away from him. He came looking for us the next morning at our homes and had a serious talk with each of us, based on the evidence of our having zillions of mosquito bites ourselves."

Jen laughed. "And did it make any difference?"

"We changed our locations, but were otherwise pretty indifferent. I suspect that he thought we were mostly harmless. He's a big-picture kind of guy."

"You must have loved being in such a small town," she said with a sigh. "I would have loved it."

Zach looked at her in astonishment. "Go on! It was a place I couldn't wait to leave."

"Why?"

"It was boring. There was one movie theater and it played the same movie for weeks at a time. Do you know how many times I saw *Star Wars*?"

"No."

"Neither do I. I stopped counting in the low sixties."

"But it must have felt safe. Secure."

"It was that. Confining and restrictive. Prisons are like that, too, you know. We were all jockeying for position to run into the big wide world and never come back. Did you grow up in the city?"

Jen nodded. "My mother was always worried about something happening to Cin and I. We spent a lot of time together as kids, watching out for each other, and M.B. got stuck on guard duty even more."

"It made you all pretty close."

"There is that, but independence is important to kids, too. You must have known your neighbors, and been recognized in the shops because of whose son you were."

Zach gave her a dark look. "And you think that was an advantage?"

"Yes." Jen nodded firmly. "I think that's exactly the kind of security that kids need. You could have freedom in that town, because everybody knew everybody. You could be warned of who to avoid and your family wouldn't have to worry about you out riding around on your bike alone."

It was true. "But that cuts both ways, Jen. There are people who could never shake their apparent reputation, even if they didn't actually fit it. Kids of men who were said to be trouble, for example, were assumed to be trouble themselves, even if they weren't."

"But you didn't have that problem, did you?"

"No, just the opposite." He grinned. "I was supposed to be upstanding, like everyone else in my family."

"I'll bet there were people who refused to believe that you could be anything else."

Zach chuckled, knowing it was true and that he had used it to advantage once or twice. "Probably."

"I think it must have been wonderful to grow up in a small town, even if you saw the same movies over and over again." Jen spoke with such resolve that Zach took her implicit dare.

"Oh, come on, you don't even know what it's like. I'll show you what a little hick town it is." He turned onto the road that ultimately became Main Street, knowing that Jen's illusions would be lost when she saw just how little there was of greater metropolitan Rosemount. They passed the two old churches, the Episcopalian one on the left and the little Catholic one on the right, drove around the ancient maple that had been left in the middle of Main Street in front of the Town Hall, and emerged on what passed for downtown.

Zach was sure Jen would laugh. It looked so pathetic and dated to him.

But she was charmed. "Oh! It's like an old-fashioned Christmas! I didn't think anyone did this anymore. Zach, it's like a postcard from the past."

He looked again, and saw that she was right. Beyond the old light standards and parking meters that gave you an hour of parking for a quarter, there was a certain charm.

There were cedar ropes hanging from the store fronts, fairy lights twinkling within the dark bows. The old two-story buildings that comprised Main Street, with the apartment for the shopkeeper over the shop itself, looked pretty well tended when he looked at them instead of assuming he knew how they looked. The windows were joyously decorated for Christmas with ribbons and sleigh bells and angels and shepherds.

He slowed down, purportedly to let Jen have a better look and really looked himself. An automated Santa waved with a jerky gesture from the window of Chisholm's hardware store, where Zach knew for a fact that Mr. Chisholm could find any part that anyone needed somewhere in the vast store. It was good to know a hardware store like that one.

Mrs. Purdue was still selling twin sets at Style for Ladies, although the offerings in her shop window were in more punchy colors than he remembered them being before. Chartreuse and fuchsia had never been among the options, Zach was pretty sure.

The pole on Mack's Barber Shop was still turning, looking like the stick of a candy cane amidst the holiday decorations. Zach had had his first haircut in Mack's big old leather chair, which was still there in pride of place.

There had been changes, too. The diner had been repainted, and looked even more retro than it had before. The coffee shop with the all-day breakfast had become a bistro with a French awning; the five-and-dime store was gone and a home decor shop with a lot of wicker had taken its place. There was now a bulk food store and a chic little coffee shop that belonged to no chain Zach knew.

And there were vacancies. The movie theater was closed for the season, according to its sign. MacCauley's Bookstore that Matt had frequented was gone, its dark windows empty except for the FOR SALE sign.

"It's wonderful," Jen said and Zach saw Rosemount through her eyes. He remembered a thousand lazy summer days, scoring a popsicle at the corner store, then riding his bike down to the wharf with his buddies. He turned down the street that went to the docks and rolled down his window, remembering the salty bite of the winter wind off the Atlantic. There was a nature trail and a dog park now, in precisely the location where people had always hiked and walked their dogs.

"Can we go back downtown?" Jen asked. "Is there time?"

"I've never been obsessed with being on time before," Zach admitted, wanting only to make her happy. He drove back to Main Street, seeing its appeal for the first time in years. "It might frighten the locals if I showed up promptly for a family function."

Jen laughed, then urged him to stop beside the empty shop that had been MacCauley's.

"Dinah Dishman," he said, reading the realtor's sign. "I wonder whether that's the Dinah Dishman that Phil used to babysit."

"There can't be two people with that name."

"True enough."

"So, I guess someone stayed in Rosemount, after all," Jen teased and Zach had to smile.

"I guess so." He saw how hungrily she looked at the space and remembered something she had told him before. "There's no knitting shop in town," he said, hazarding a guess.

Jen flashed him a smile. "I noticed that."

He leaned across her, considering the building. "It's on the north side of the street," he noted. "It would have that sunshine."

Jen tightened her grip on the poinsettia as she looked. "I like the door. Does it have beveled glass?"

"Yes, I remember it. And the lock is heavy, brass I think. There used to be a little bell inside that rang when the door shut, and Mr. MacCauley would come out of the back. He was always carrying a cup of coffee, though I never saw him drink any of it."

"Mr. MacCauley?"

"It was his bookstore. Matt will know why it closed: he spent entire weeks here when we were kids. We had a joke that if Matt was missing, we'd call Mr. MacCauley to check on him."

Jen smiled. "See? That's what I mean. I like the sound of that. It's the kind of environment my mom tried to create for us, but she could only do it within our house."

"Or when M.B. went with you."

Jen nodded, her gaze clinging to the empty shop front. "We'll be late," she said, showing a reluctance to go to Gray Gables that Zach could understand.

"It will only fulfil expectations," he said, trying to be cheerful. He turned onto the road that climbed to the house, dreading their arrival more with every moment. Instead he focused on the glimmer of an idea he'd just had, a gift that Jen might like a whole lot more than a trip to New York and a Tiffany rock on her finger.

"Come on," Jen teased. "What's the worst thing that can happen?"

"I don't think I want to envision that."

"Don't worry: I'll protect you, no matter how mean they are."

"You should know what you're getting into before you make promises like that," Zach said. He reached over and squeezed her hand, not wanting her to feel as much trepidation as he did.

No doubt about it, he was very glad to have Jen with him.

And he didn't want his family to scare her off.

Gray Gables was like something out of a magazine. Jen felt her mouth drop open as Zach turned into the long curved driveway. The house sat at the end of the drive, imposing and elegant, exuding history and privilege from its every brick.

It was a mock-Tudor house, probably from the turn of the last century, and had been built with no care for expense. She didn't doubt that there was a huge rose garden in front of it in summer, or that the garage—which was a separate building—could comfortably accommodate half a dozen cars in lieu of the horses and carriages it had once held.

"It's huge," she whispered in awe.

"Only seven bedrooms," Zach said and she turned to look at him in shock. He grimaced. "They don't all have ensuites, although my mother will probably see that fixed one of these days."

It could have been a hotel, but Jen guessed that Zach wouldn't appreciate that suggestion.

"How many people live here?" she asked instead. The place would be full of antiques, like a set in a movie, she was sure of it.

"Four. My brother Matt bought out the rest of us after my father died, so he lives here with his wife and daughter, Annette. My mother also moved back here with them, as this was her family house." Zach shrugged. "They originally built it as a summer cottage."

Jen gaped despite herself. Cottages in her experience were little shacks, built by the hands of their owners, with no heating systems beyond a wood stove and no interior plumbing at all. You could see through the walls of cottages if you squinted at the corners.

A cottage. Her mind stalled on the notion of anyone considering this to be a minor vacation residence.

Zach parked at the end of a line of cars which were more modest than Jen might have expected and heaved a sigh. "Well, I guess this is it," he said, with no Christmas cheer at all.

Jen couldn't find her voice to assure him that it wouldn't be as bad as he feared.

He helped her out of the car, releasing Roxie with complete confidence that the dog was safe. It was so far to the road that his certainty was deserved. Roxie made a pit stop in the snow, then ran for the door, her tail wagging mightily in anticipation.

"See?" Jen said. "Roxie thinks it will be okay."

"Roxie has never been here," Zach said. "She has an innocent trust in the goodness of strangers."

"Don't say that's undeserved."

"It could be." Zach smiled, looking a lot less Tigger-like than Jen expected of him. "We might as well get this over with," he said and Jen knew one way to encourage him.

"Not yet," she said, snagging his sleeve. He glanced down at her in confusion. "We're supposed to be crazy in love with each other, remember?"

Before he could make a joke, Jen reached up and kissed him. He slipped his hand around her waist and pulled her closer, deepening their kiss just as she'd hoped he would. Jen wrapped one hand around his neck, not caring that the poinsettia was getting a bit crushed between them.

"Merry Christmas," she whispered when he eventually lifted his head.

A smile tugged at the corner of his lips. "It's feeling a lot merrier all of a sudden," he murmured then ducked his head to kiss her again.

"Hey, keep it legal out there!" someone shouted from the doorway. Roxie barked and dove into the house, almost sending the man flying into the snow. "Whoa!" he shouted cheerfully, but Roxie was gone.

It sounded like two other dogs began barking inside the house.

Zach turned to the taller man at the front door, who also wore a tie. He looked as if he'd left a suit jacket somewhere and had his shirtsleeves rolled up.

"Jealous, James?" Zach demanded in a teasing tone. "I see that you and Maralys haven't managed to melt all of the snow yet. Are you losing your touch?"

"Hey, give us a chance. We've been peeling potatoes since dawn, under orders of Leslie." James wiped his brow with mock exhaustion. "She's quite the task maker, and you're here just in time to mash them. Tell you what: I'll find you an apron to match that suit."

"I thought they didn't make dinner themselves," Jen whispered, wondering whether Zach's brother was joking.

"So did I," Zach replied, looking astonished. "Come on, let's see whether it's really true." He took her hand in his and led her to the steps and his smiling brother.

Who didn't look that scary, after all.

"You must be Jen," James said when Jen reached the front door. His smile was warm and welcoming. He offered his hand. "It's wonderful to meet you. I'm Zach's eldest brother, James. My wife, Maralys, talked to you on the phone."

"Cornered you on the phone," Zach corrected. "And conned you into agreeing to come today."

"Don't be spreading rumors about me unless I can hear them," a slender redhead said, stepping past James to offer Jen her hand. "Hi. I'm Maralys. Fab suit."

"Same to you," Jen said, knowing that she was in the company of a fellow vintage enthusiast. "Is that Balenciaga?"

"No, it's a repro. Meg makes them out of vintage fabric, using vintage patterns." Maralys spun and modeled the green shantung suit. It looked like something out of a fifties fashion magazine.

"It's gorgeous," Jen said, admiring the fabric and cut. "I'd never have guessed."

Maralys gave her a mischievous look. "Oh, we have so much to talk about."

"I think we all have reason to chat with Jen," said a beautiful older woman. She was dressed to perfection in modern couture, but her warm smile meant that Jen didn't feel as intimidated as she might have done.

Zach took Jen's elbow. "Jen, this is my mother, Beverly Coxwell. Mom, Jen Maitland." Beverly's fingers were a little bit cold but her handshake was firm, and her gaze direct. Jen felt an immediate accord with her because she sensed that the older woman was tougher than a casual observer might guess. Beverly's smile widened ever so slightly, as if she too found more than met the eye in Jen, and Jen knew that they would get along just fine.

If, in fact, they ever saw each other again. James urged them into the foyer, which was as lavish as Jen had expected. No one else seemed to take much notice of their surroundings though and she tried not to gape.

People poured into the foyer of the house, calling greetings, exchanging hugs, and kissing Zach on the cheek. It was noisy and familiar in a way. A whirlwind of introductions followed, including those to Roxie and the two large poodles that evidently belonged to Beverly. (Jen thought it apt that they were named for luxury products: the white one was called Champagne and the black one was named Caviar.) There were three teenagers, two toddlers, and a baby, Beverly had a date, Maralys's father held court in the living room by rapping his cane repeatedly on the floor. There weren't nearly enough aprons to go around once Leslie began muster the troops for dinner.

To Jen's surprise, they weren't that different from her own family. The setting was more posh and they were more fancily dressed, but the bickering between siblings, the jokes at each other's expense, and the memories they dredged up and tossed across the kitchen were pretty much the same.

They sat in the dining room, under the glittering chandelier, upon antique chairs. The gleaming cherry table could be glimpsed through the cutwork linen cloth, and the silver flatware was heavy enough to be sterling. The fine English china was passed around the table, each dish loaded with familiar favorites. Jen complimented Leslie on how wonderful the meal looked, Matt said grace, then Jen knew the interrogation would begin.

But the Coxwells asked Jen a lot fewer questions than her own family had asked Zach. She did sense an undertone of approval when she said she was going back to school, but no one said as much. They were polite and interested, and a whole lot nicer to her than her own family had been to Zach. Maybe they didn't think he needed protection. Jen might have accused Zach of misleading her about his family, but he looked more surprised by the easy camaraderie than she was.

"May we see your ring?" Beverly asked Jen during the interval between dinner and dessert. It sounded like a loaded question, and that impression was amplified when everyone around the table took an avid interest in Jen's answer.

"I don't have one," she admitted with a smile.

Zach closed his hand over hers. "We're having a hard time deciding what kind of stone would be best," he said smoothly. "I mean, Jen will be wearing it for the rest of her life . . ."

"Which is precisely why it should be an important piece of jewelry," Beverly said crisply.

"We were thinking of going to Tiffany . . ." Zach began but Beverly interrupted him.

"To buy a new stone?" Her tone was incredulous.

James started to chuckle. "Maybe that's not the real issue," he suggested, flicking a glance at Maralys. "Maybe Zach wants a favor, Mom."

They all chuckled and Zach, to Jen's astonishment, blushed. "No, I, no . . ." he stammered for the first time since she'd known him.

Maralys, who was sitting near Jen, put her left hand on the table. "Meet the Byzantine Queen ring, a Coxwell family piece."

Jen had noticed the stunning gold ring with its cabochon red stone earlier but took the opportunity to look at it more closely.

"It's beautiful."

"It's good luck for a bride to wear a family piece," Beverly said with resolve.

Philippa put her right hand on the table. "Grandma Coxwell's emerald," she said, letting the square-cut stone in the dinner ring catch the light. Her own wedding band was plain gold, which only made the family ring look more spectacular in contrast.

Jen was awed.

"An aquamarine set with amethysts," Leslie said, touching the gorgeous brooch that she wore at her throat. Her wedding band was also plain, but it was clear that she treasured the brooch.

"From Aunt Beatrice," Beverly said with satisfaction. "My sister didn't have children of her own and made me promise before she died that I'd give her favorite brooch to the bride of one of my sons." She smiled at Leslie. "I knew Leslie wouldn't likely wear a large piece daily, so the brooch was a good choice for her."

"Plus it looks medieval," Matt said, smiling at his wife.

"I love it," Leslie admitted.

"It's beautiful," Jen agreed.

Beverly smiled at her youngest son. "Is it really that you can't decide on a ring? Or is it that you're afraid to ask for what you really want your bride to wear?"

Zach shook his head and smiled, sparing a glance to Jen. "I would never have asked you for any of your jewelry, Mom. You have to know that."

"But what if I offered?"

Zach squeezed Jen's fingers before he answered his mom. "You have to know the one I think would be perfect."

Beverly's smile broadened as she surveyed Jen, then she rose to her feet. "Will you all excuse me for a moment?"

It didn't take a rocket scientist to figure out where she was going. They were going to give Jen something from the vaults, but their engagement wasn't real. "What are you doing, *honey?*" Jen whispered under her breath to Zach.

He spared her a confident smile. "Just go with it, *honey*. Trust me."

Jen tried not to look skeptical. She didn't have to manage for long, because Beverly swept back into the dining room, an old ring box in her hand. "Give your bride a ring that counts," she told Zach and pushed the box into his hand.

He seemed to be overwhelmed by her choice, even without opening the box. "I was thinking of the other one . . ." he began but Beverly interrupted him sharply.

"This is the right one."

Jen wondered what was in the box, or what memories it conjured for both of them. Beverly was blinking back a tear when she resumed her place and Zach took a moment to finger the silver box before he turned to Jen. He seemed to be composing himself and she saw a glitter of tears in his own eyes when he met her gaze.

"Will you wear my great-grandmother's ring?" he asked, his words husky.

There was only one right answer. "I'd be honored," Jen said.

Zach opened the ring box, which had a lining of garnet velvet. Nestled there was an old cameo set in a filigree gold frame. It had to be an inch and a half long, the background golden brown, the profiles a creamy ivory. A man and a woman were depicted in silhouette facing the left, the woman's hair coiled elaborately on her head. The man was behind the woman, and both of them smiled ever so slightly, as if laughing at a private joke.

As if they were happy. When Jen looked closely, she saw the man's left hand upon the woman's left shoulder, the fingers of the woman's left hand entwined with his, and a ring upon her hand that looked about the same size and shape of this one.

Zach took the ring and Jen's left hand and slid the ring onto her finger. It was a bit loose on her ring finger, so he put it on the middle one where it fit perfectly.

"It belonged to my grandmother," Beverly said, her words thick. "My grandfather had it made for her when they went to Italy and she wore it ever after in place of her wedding band. My mother wore it as a dinner ring." She smiled and took a sip of her water. "It has many happy memories for me, and I hope that it will be good luck for both of you."

"Thank you, Mom," Zach said, still holding fast to Jen's hand.

"Thank you," Jen said. "I'm honored to wear it." It was true, all true, and when the family toasted them and Zach gave Jen a kiss, there was a dangerous moment when she hoped with all of her sucker heart that this fake date might be the real thing after all.

The way that Zach kept hold of her hand did nothing to discourage that hope, however foolish it might prove to be.

Chapter 15

This couldn't be Zach's family.

They looked like his family. They sounded like his family. But they didn't act at all like the family he knew so well.

They were getting along.

They were talking about real things, encouraging each other, chatting about everything and nothing, teasing each other. There was no sense of strain and there were no brooding silences.

For the second time in a pretty short period of time, Zach felt that the people he had thought he knew best had gone and changed without serving him appropriate notice.

But this time, it was a good change. Unlike the lunch with his buddies, Zach found himself wanting to linger with his family, wanting to spend more time with them. They were generous with their humor, their intelligence, and their smiles. His mother had floored him with the surrender of this ring for Jen because he knew that it was a precious one to her. He was awed and honored that she had parted with it, for his bride's hand.

Contrary to expectation, he was enjoying himself. He sat at the dinner table and marveled at the change one person's absence could make.

His mother was drinking sparkling water, instead of the sherry that was her nemesis, laughing and apparently not missing the alcohol. Her companion, Ross, was charming and seemed to easily prompt Beverly's laughter. In fact, he'd never seen his mother sparkle as she did on this day.

Zach's brother James was more at ease than he used to be, protective and teasing the way he'd always thought older brothers were supposed to be. Matt seemed more happy than ever, more comfortable in his own skin. Phil practically glowed and it wasn't just postpartum hormones. His siblings were happy, happy in their marriages, happy in their lives, happy now that they weren't letting their lives be shaped by one man's determination.

Zach held Jen's hand and felt a commonality with his siblings that he'd never felt before. He understood now the force for change that one person could be in his life. Jen smiled at him, glancing up through her bangs in that mischievous way that drove him crazy and he knew that impulse had once again steered him straight.

His mother's gift was as sure a sign as there could be that she approved of his choice. Beverly's approval, in fact, made Zach fully understand why Jen had protested the idea of a fake engagement: Beverly would have been livid to have learned that she was being tricked.

It was a good thing, then, that this wasn't a trick. Zach had known for a while that this wouldn't be a fake engagement if he had anything to say about it.

He suspected that Jen would have a good bit to say about it, and he was still getting his proverbial ducks in a row, but having his family be less confrontational and challenging than he'd anticipated was a welcome surprise. At least they wouldn't be nixing the deal for him.

In fact, he had a feeling that everything was falling into place.

Zach had followed his instincts and impulse had once again delivered him precisely where he needed to be. Jen was good for him. Jen was perfect for him. Jen made him happy and prompted him to plan for the future. His mother's family ring looked perfect on her finger and Zach was determined to keep it there.

He just had to convince Jen that he was right.

The Coxwells exchanged presents in the living room after dinner, in front of a roaring fire that Matt had built in the old fireplace. Zach couldn't remember the fireplace being used, and was as impressed as Jen by how inviting the room was with the blaze on the hearth. People pulled chairs into a rough circle, moving the furniture that had never been permitted to move in Zach's childhood. They even perched on the arms of the sofa. The kids sat on the floor, which had been forbidden in Zach's memory.

Annette put some Christmas CDs on the stereo and Leslie lit the tree. It was a large spruce, set before the bay window that faced the street, lit with white fairy lights and adorned with the full array of ornaments collected over the years as well as some additions. Phil poured eggnog for everyone and Johnny, James's younger boy, passed chocolates.

"It's like a movie," Jen whispered to him, her eyes bright with wonder.

"Maybe we're on the wrong set," he whispered back. "But maybe we should stick with this one." She rolled her eyes and laughed at him.

James's elder son, Jimmy, proved to have drawn Zach's name in the lottery. The parcel was flat and heavy, so obviously a book that Zach had to say something. "It must be that pet canary I've been wanting," he said solemnly and Jimmy threw a wad of used Christmas paper at him.

To Zach's delight, it was a coffee table book from *National Geographic*, highlighting the photography from that magazine for over a century. Zach couldn't resist opening it and flipping through the pages.

"I like this one," Jimmy said, pointing out an arctic landscape.

"What about this one?" Zach asked, turning instead to a photograph of tribesmen, their faces each telling a thousand stories. "How'd you guess I'd love this book?" he asked.

"I had a couple of hints," Jimmy said, then looked toward Maralys. She tried to look angelic and failed, then the two chuckled conspiratorially together.

"Hey, I was going to ask if you ditched those old magazines of mine," Zach asked Matt.

"No, they're yours. They're still in the attic."

"Maybe I'll pick them up one of these days."

"Jeez, the floors will probably rise a couple of inches once all the weight is removed," Matt teased.

"The house will be lopsided," Jimmy said and everyone chuckled and they moved to the next gift in the lottery.

There were lots of laughs as the gifts were opened. None of them were enormous but each seemed a perfect choice: the gifts showed a thoughtfulness that Zach hadn't known his family members possessed, as well as a familiarity with each other's tastes that was surprising. Leslie had even wrapped a box of European chocolates for Jen to ensure that she felt included. It was easy and comfortable as holidays had never been at Gray Gables in Zach's memory.

Finally Matt unwrapped the Montblanc pen that Zach had chosen for him. He smiled as he held it aloft and everyone made approving noises.

"I thought every writer needed one," Zach said and Matt grinned.

"I suppose you'll want me to be waving a publishing contract around soon," he said.

"No excuses left," James teased. "Not with the pen."

"All the words you need are packed right in there," Maralys said. "All you have to do is coax them out."

"That's all?" Matt said with a laugh. He turned to Zach. "It's great. I've always wanted one of these and I like the burgundy." He turned the fountain pen in his hand, testing the weight and Zach could see his admiration. "Thanks."

A hum of conversation began easily again, and the teenagers disappeared to check something on television. The party spread out again, some people cleaning up the dining room, others helping Leslie with dessert in the kitchen. The three dogs went outside and came back in again, shaking snow all over the kitchen and tracking a bunch of it into the living room as well. They romped around a bit, got told, then laid down with heavy sighs.

"You should come and see what we've done," Matt said to Zach.

"To what?"

Matt smiled. "You'll see. Come on." He turned and left the living room, waiting for Zach in the foyer.

Zach offered his hand to Jen. "Want to come along?"

"Where are we going?"

Zach shrugged. "Maybe it's the nickel tour. They might have made some changes to the house that Matt wants to show off."

"How long is it since you've been here?" Jen asked in an undertone as she walked beside him.

"Not long enough," Zach said with a smile, then followed his brother.

"What do you mean? It's an incredible house."

"But it wasn't always a happy one."

She gave him a serious glance. "It seems happy today."

"It does. That's why I'm a bit disoriented." He smiled before she could say anything. "Maybe you've cast some kind of spell on them all."

Jen laughed, but there was no time to say anything more before they caught up to Matt. To Zach's dismay, his brother headed for the back of the main floor. There weren't many rooms beyond the stairs except the kitchen and there was one room that Zach really didn't want to visit.

His father's study had been at the back corner of the house. It had been a cozy room, all dark wood bookcases and chairs upholstered in oxblood leather. There had been a fireplace and a large Persian carpet and French doors that opened to the back of the property. It had always seemed to Zach to be a room from another time, lifted from a Victorian gentlemen's club, whisked across the Atlantic and reassembled for the pleasure of some forebear.

There might as well have been lions at the door, because entering his father's retreat had been forbidden except by invitation. Those invitations had tended to be issued to Zach when he was in trouble and summoned by his father to hear his punishment. The trial always occurred in his absence and he was, as far as he'd ever been able to tell, always guilty.

That wasn't why he didn't want to see the room, though.

His father had killed himself in his study. Robert had stood at his desk, in his military dress uniform, and put his service revolver into his mouth before firing it. Zach knew all of this but hadn't seen the result.

His imagination had done pretty well conjuring images all by itself. If he'd been the one to take possession of the house, he would have barricaded off the study, or maybe the whole corridor, or maybe even had this chunk of the house physically removed. It had to be better than cleaning that up.

But Matt walked straight toward the study, each step making it less and less likely that he could be going anywhere else. When there was no other possible destination and the closed study door loomed at the end of the corridor, Zach halted in the hall. "I appreciate the thought, Matt, but I'm not sure I want to go to Father's study."

"It's my study now," Matt said firmly, so firmly that Zach looked at him in surprise.

"You can work in there? After what happened?"

Matt paused, his hand on the doorknob. His smile was rueful. "Are you kidding? I couldn't even come down this corridor for about three months and I never thought I'd willingly cross the threshold again. I was going to therapy—" He nodded to Jen, who was very quiet and still. "I'm sorry, Jen. You've been tossed into the middle of this. Our father killed himself in this room. I discovered his body, which was his intention, and met with a therapist for the better part of this year to deal with the shock."

"I see," Jen said softly. "That was probably a good choice."

"It was less of a choice than a necessity once the nightmares started," Matt acknowledged. "Anyway, the therapist said it wasn't healthy to have this room here, effectively sealed off. She said it would create its own ghosts if we gave it that kind of power, and that we had to reclaim it from tragedy if we were ever going to live normal lives in this place." He gave Zach a hard look. "It helped me a lot, and both James and Phil have seen it as well. I thought it might be good for you to see it, too." With that, he threw open the door.

Zach wasn't hot to cross the threshold, but Jen tugged his hand. "Chicken," she said under her breath, softening the word with a smile.

"Damn straight," Zach breathed and she chuckled.

"I promised to protect you." When she smiled so encouragingly, Zach couldn't resist her. He folded his hand more tightly around hers, took strength from her surety and followed Matt.

"Oh!" Jen said. "It's lovely."

It was. To Zach's surprise, the room had been completely changed. It might have been in a different house altogether.

The Persian rug was gone, as was his father's desk and the heavy old oak chairs. The dark green walls had been repainted in a caramel color and the bookshelves had been stripped and stained in a honey tone. The floor was polished hardwood and the new rug was black and gold.

The desk looked like something from the 1930s and the swivel desk chair was stainless steel with black leather upholstery. The draperies were lighter and simpler than the old festooned velvet ones had been, just pleated honey-hued cotton.

He walked around, admiring what Matt had done. The room

looked bigger and brighter, and had positive feel to it. The fireplace surround had been changed to a bronze Art Deco one, maybe salvaged from somewhere, and a modern painting hung over the mantel. It was elegant and chic, updated but not too much of a contrast with the rest of the house. Zach liked it a lot.

"Was it that bad?" he asked, surprised that they would have had to get rid of all the furniture.

Matt shook his head. "No. There are services that clean up crime scenes after the police are done, and they did a pretty good job. It was just that the room was so evocative of Father and of what he had done." Matt smiled and shoved his hands into his trouser pockets. "I had to kick out his ghost, and you can believe that half measures weren't going to evict him from here."

Zach smiled. "No, I'd bet not. This is amazing."

"It's very bright, but warm, too," Jen said, running her fingertips across the top of Matt's wood desk. "I can imagine that it's a good place to write."

"It is," Matt said. "I can pull back the drapes and the room is filled with sunshine. You can see all the trees behind the house and hear the birds when the windows are open. Or at night, with a fire, it's good, too. It's quiet back here and I can put some jazz on the stereo and be in another world."

"I like when it snows," Leslie said, having appeared silently in the doorway. "We light the fire and turn off all the lights, and watch the snow fall." The couple shared a smile that heated the room a bit and Zach imagined that other activities also happened in this room. There was, after all, a couch upholstered in a nubby caramel cotton that faced the French doors.

"You've claimed the space for your own," Jen said with a smile and Matt nodded.

"Exactly." He sighed and looked around, then met Zach's gaze. "I hope it doesn't offend you that we're making changes at Gray Gables. It's important to Leslie to make the house her own in some ways, and it was critical to me to reclaim this space from Father."

"It's not up to me," Zach said. "It's your house now."

Matt smiled. "No, until I pay all of you off, it's still in joint possession. Given the schedule we worked out, it's going to take a long time."

"You'll get there." Zach shrugged. "You needed to be able to carry the debt."

"You're right: we'll get there."

"I think it's good that you're making changes," Zach said, liking the room more with every passing minute. "Houses shouldn't be museums, Matt. They have to change, to reflect the people who live in them. I like this a lot. I can imagine you here."

"Thanks." Matt frowned. "That's not the only reason I wanted you to see this, Zach. I believed that it was my fault that Father killed himself and that's why the therapist said I had to address that."

Zach stared at his brother in shock. "But how could you think that?" he demanded. "It was my fault that Father killed himself."

"Be serious. I lost the Laforini case that very day—"

"No." Zach interrupted Matt firmly. "No, it wasn't your fault. It was my fault. I called from New Orleans that night. I called from jail to grovel. I called to ask for help after getting myself into a situation that would demand his attention." He shoved his hands into his trouser pockets, echoing his brother's pose. "And oh, did I get it."

"You can't think it was your fault," Matt argued. "You were thousands of miles away. You'd been gone for a couple of years."

"No." Zach shook his head. "You did me the favor of handing out some truth in New Orleans, so let me return the favor."

"Okay."

"I finally pushed Father too far: that was what he told me on the phone. I had pot in my possession when I was busted; I was trying to sell some to an undercover cop, if you recall, which was the reason why I did get busted. There was no avoiding the truth about my being the black sheep of the family any longer, and he really let me have it on that phone that night." Zach frowned in recollection. "I thought he was going to have a heart attack while we were on the phone. He told me that whatever shook out of my stupid prank would be all my fault."

Jen came to his side and looked up at him with concern. "So when he killed himself, you blamed yourself."

Zach took her hand. "It was only logical."

"But wrong," Jen said. "Suicide is a personal choice."

"Maybe he was fed up with all of us," Matt said. "He gave me an ultimatum when he summoned me here to meet him. He said we'd never talk about the Laforini case again if I came, which sounded like a pretty good deal. I had no idea that he meant to kill himself while I was driving out here to make that be true."

Jen looked between the two of them, her eyes wide and her expression horrified. Zach thought a bit late that she might conclude that insanity ran in his family.

"Our father was battling depression," James interjected, stepping through the doorway. Zach could tell from his expression that he'd been listening, that maybe he'd followed along to check on things like the big brother he was proving to be. "Robert didn't ask anyone for help. He simply solved the issue as he saw fit and left all of us blaming ourselves for what he had done."

"Well, that's not unreasonable," Beverly said, appearing behind James. "I did leave him and insist upon a divorce, which he found very embarrassing. It certainly put an end to his political ambitions and it wasn't foolish for me to think myself at least partly responsible for Robert's choice."

"You don't anymore," James asked and Beverly shook her head.

"No. But Robert had a talent for ensuring that everyone felt guilty for his own choices."

"And he didn't like me marrying Nick," Phil said, easing her way into the room, as well. She bounced her baby on her hip and nodded at Jen. "My father had firm ideas of which kind of people counted and Nick's family, the Sullivans, weren't on his list."

"But you married him anyway," Jen said with approval.

Phil's lips curved. "I was too much in love to do otherwise."

"Good for you." Jen and Phil smiled at each other in complete understanding. Zach watched and hoped that meant that Jen might be feeling at least a fraction of what he felt for her.

Meanwhile Beverly tapped James on the shoulder. "Discovering that you weren't his biological son was very difficult for Robert, seeing as you were the only one who had followed in his footsteps."

"He didn't accommodate anyone but himself, Mom," James said quietly. "You can't blame yourself for what he chose to do."

"I know," she admitted with a sigh and a smile.

"None of us can blame ourselves," Matt said with resolve. "He made his own choices."

Beverly smiled across the room at Zach. "Just as we have to make our own choices." They all smiled at him then, seemingly approving of the changes he was trying to make in his life. Jen stood close beside him and he felt as if he really had finally come home.

Because he was in love.

He realized as much standing in his father's study, watching Jen smile, seeing his mother's cameo on Jen's finger. He probably should have realized as much sooner, because his feelings for Jen had been driving his actions pretty much since the day he'd met her, but introspection wasn't one of Zach's hobbies.

And in a way, it was more fun to be struck by lightning like this, to be standing on Christmas Day, surrounded by family, and abruptly realize that his heart was gone. It was in the keeping of one Jen Maitland, and she'd have it forevermore, whether she wanted it or not. Even more incredible, Zach knew that what he had done so far was only a tiny increment of what he would do to make Jen happy, or to coax her to love him. He stood there and looked at her, and yearned for her, and knew that everything in his life had led him to this moment.

Jen glanced up, maybe feeling his gaze on her, and met his gaze. Zach smiled a little and a twinkle lit in her dark eyes. She smiled a small smile that could have been a laser weapon, given its ability to dissolve his few inhibitions from any distance, and he hoped again that the electricity he felt was mutual.

One thing was for sure: he was going to find out.

"I love this room," Beverly said with resolve. "It was always a depressing little hovel, even before Robert did what he did. I could just walk in here and get the blues, probably because it was so oppressively dark."

"The French Deco look was your idea, Mom," Matt acknowledged. "And it was a great one."

"Thank you, dear. I'd toast you with a little digestif, but coffee will have to do, at least for me."

"You're doing great, Mom," James said, squeezing her shoulder.

"I've been forced to do well with all of you watching me like hawks," Beverly said, but there was laughter in her voice. "It does get easier, although I would love that coffee."

"I'm sure it's ready by now," Leslie said, then led them all back to the dining room for dessert. When Jen would have followed, Zach snagged her hand. The others continued down the corridor to the kitchen, leaving the pair in the study that had been reclaimed by Matt.

"Do you need a moment alone here?" Jen asked, unable to read Zach's mood. He seemed quiet and thoughtful, which made her wonder what was in his thoughts. Was he troubled by his father's study, or by his brother's renovations?

"No. I need a moment with you," he said, pulling her into his arms.

She went willingly, liking his embrace. He didn't seem as concerned as he had earlier. He smiled down at her and she wasn't sure what to think. "Are you okay?"

"Never better." Zach took a deep breath and nestled her more tightly against him. "So, I've been wanting to know, are you the kind of warrior queen who has arcane magical powers?"

Jen smiled, unable to guess his point but knowing from his playful tone that he was teasing her. "Arcane magical powers like what?"

He shrugged. "Like spell casting or super voodoo."

"Super voodoo?" Jen echoed skeptically. "That sounds like something you could pick up at the brain store. Who could be into super voodoo?"

"I think you're pretending ignorance to put me off the trail," Zach said. "I think you want me to underestimate your awesome powers."

"I don't have any awesome powers."

"No? Then explain my family today."

"I think they're nice . . ."

"My point exactly. Someone cast a spell on them, compelling them to act like nice, normal people when in reality, they're bonkers."

Jen laughed. "I think you were putting me on about them. I think that they really are nice, normal people. Otherwise, it would be a really complicated trick."

"See? They've got you fooled."

When Jen laughed again, Zach bent and quickly kissed her. She caught her breath in surprise, then kissed him back.

When Zach lifted his head, he gave a low whistle. "Weapons-grade Jockey annihilator," he teased.

"Speak for yourself."

He grinned wickedly. "I'll take that as a compliment." He winked, then continued in a more serious tone before Jen could say anything. "I think they're changing, actually. Say what you will, warrior queen, but I think you're the catalyst responsible."

"Be serious! I've only met your family today . . ."

"Then that's some potent magic you've got in your pocket."

"I didn't . . ."

"I meant for me." He was so serious that she looked up at him. He was watching her, marvel in his gaze, so intent the Jen's sucker heart skipped a whole bunch of beats. "I love you," he said and she was shocked into silence.

Zach bent and slowly kissed her, stealing every thought out of her head with his own persuasive magic.

When he lifted his head, the intent in his gaze made her knees go weak. His words were husky, convincing Jen that she wasn't the only one left dizzy by their kiss. "You've got some other magic brewing, too, warrior queen," he said, tucking her hair behind her ear and kissing her temple.

"What do you mean?"

"I've never had an out-of-body experience before the other night, but I'm pretty sure I saw Pluto."

"I think you were in your body when you were sharing it with me."

Zach grinned. "Then maybe you were out of body with me."

Jen frowned as if in thought, just to give him a hard time. "I did wonder if that was Pluto on the right, just before the second orgasm."

"I wonder whether that's where it always is," Zach mused.

Jen swallowed, feeling audacious and not really caring. "I suppose there's one way to find out," she said slowly, watching Zach's smile broaden. "So, want to see about riding moonbeams?"

"Are you propositioning me, warrior queen? Or is this a command performance?"

"Does it matter?"

"No. I'm yours to command." Zach laced his fingers through hers and led Jen back toward the kitchen. "How fast do you think we can eat dessert and get out of here?"

Jen felt again that sparkle of anticipation, the lightheartedness that she was coming to associate with Zach's presence, and she abandoned herself to the moment. "Not fast enough," she said, laughing at Zach's rueful smile.

"You've got it in one, warrior queen. I'll give it forty-five minutes."

"An extra orgasm if you manage it in thirty," Jen dared him.

Zach slanted her a look. "You're on. You know, maybe you should look into motivational speaking as a career option," he teased, and they strolled back to the kitchen together. "Because you're motivating me in a major way, and I don't even think you're really trying."

"Yet," Jen said and he laughed.

Jen felt radiant with happiness when they joined his family. She wasn't going to question anything or think too much about anything or allow doubt to ruin a wonderful day.

She was going to go with this and savor everything that resulted from it.

Zero. An abstract concept, a mathematical trick stolen from the Arabs—did they tell the authorities that nothing was taken?—the digit zero is worthless in itself but adds an order of magnitude to any other digit it joins. One becomes ten, ten becomes one hundred, quantities gain in magnitude all because naught cozied up next door.

So, on the one hand, zero makes something from nothing.

On the other, zero is the bottom line. To be reduced to zero is to be annihilated. To have one's efforts come to naught is to fail, and to fail so spectacularly that there's no room to quibble. Zero visibility means none at all, zero zero means no visibility in either distance or height, which might ensure that your vehicle is reduced to, well, naught. Nothing left, nothing at all, nothing to lose are all expressions of absence. A null set includes no elements: it is said to be void. To be null is to be without value or consequence, to be devoid or empty of any quality that counts.

So to speak.

Yet, mathematically speaking—can we have a third hand?— zero is a whole number. (Or is that a hole number?) It's the cipher between positive and negative integers, between the positive end of the scale and the negative. Zero anchors the scale, it holds the balance, it makes the extremes possible if not palatable.

Is zero everything? Or is it nothing? Or it something in between? Is it exclusive or inclusive? The total or the null? Does the void encompass everything, or is it something beyond the sum?

If nothing else—ha ha—zero remains a cipher in another sense. After all, in the game of tennis, a score of zero is called "love."

Is there a bigger mystery than love?

Is there a better reason to risk the whole shebang, the whole shooting match, the whole kit and caboodle? Is there anything other than love that leaves you empty with its loss, or fills you to bursting when it's reciprocal? Is there any better reason to bet all that you have, on the chance that you could win so much more, however slim that chance might be?

It must be, because we all do it, all the time. Maybe there's nothing else worth making that gamble. Maybe the best things, or the things most worth winning, demand the biggest potential sacrifice. Maybe the score only counts when you offer your all.

After all, nothing ventured means nothing gained.

All for one and one for all.

All or nothing.

The phone rang in Zach's apartment. Jen opened one eye, then snuggled deeper under the covers when she saw that Zach was still in bed with her.

"You should get it," she said, cuddling up closer to him. She wasn't wearing anything other than the cameo ring and the air was chilly.

"No rest for the wicked," he complained and she laughed.

"I've heard that. Is it yours?"

"Nothing like an audacious warrior queen in the morning," Zach growled, then kissed her. He propped himself up on his elbow and smiled down at her, appreciation in his gaze. "In fact, nothing else can compare." They kissed again and the room got much warmer.

The phone continued to ring. "Isn't it early for this?" Zach leaned over Jen to snag the receiver, not waiting for an answer. She closed her eyes, not intending to hurry out of bed anytime soon. She'd linger here and maybe they'd make love again.

"It's for you," Zach said, rolling his eyes.

"For me?"

The dog barked in the living room and Zach rolled out of bed. "Coming, Roxie!" He picked his underwear off the floor, then pulled a T-shirt out of a drawer, dressing hastily.

To Jen's surprise, Cin was on the phone.

"Oh my God, Jen, I just had to tell you. I'm sorry to call and interrupt but if you've been at it all night, then you need a break anyway . . ."

"Or maybe some sleep," Jen interjected.

"I'll be back," Zach mouthed from the doorway and Jen nodded.

Cin's laughter bubbled down the phone line. "Well, I had to tell you and if I hadn't called, you'd want to kill me for not calling—"

"That's hard to believe."

"But I phoned Mom and she said you were there and so I had to call and tell you . . ."

"You haven't told me anything yet."

Cin squealed. "Ian, Ian, oh my God, Ian, you won't believe what he did."

Given Cin's predictions of doom on Christmas Eve, Jen decided not to guess. "I probably won't, but tell me anyway."

"Oh, is this a bad time?" Cin asked, in a sudden and uncharacteristic attack of consideration.

"It might have been, but that's okay."

"Well, I think this is worth an interruption." Jen made no comments about getting even by returning the favor one day. "Remember how Ian was working so much?"

"I recall you mentioning something about it." Jen found her blouse and pulled it on, wrapping it around herself.

"Well, he was trying to make extra money and he did, and he bought plane tickets and you'll never guess where we're going."

"We? As in both of you?"

"He's taking me to New York!" Cin screamed into the phone, almost delirious in her joy. Jen held the receiver away from her ear. "We're going to Tiffany to get an engagement ring, because he said that was obviously what I wanted. It'll probably be a small ring, but I don't care. We're going to New York and we're going today and we're going to take a carriage ride in Central Park and Jen, isn't it the most romantic thing you ever heard? Can you believe it?"

Jen believed it. She'd known for a long time that Ian was crazy about her sister. He didn't say much, but he put up with Cin with such good humor, and teased her out of her moods, and spoiled her shamelessly.

"I think that's wonderful," Jen said and meant it.

Cin gushed on. "He got down on one knee last night and proposed, and he had roses and he had the plane tickets and he said he loved me and I just couldn't believe it. I mean, I felt so awful for doubting him, and you know, I'm just going to have to love him more than anything and love him forever to make up for that."

Jen smiled. "I guess you will. But, um, didn't you already love him more than anything?"

Cin let out a long sigh of contentment. "Yes. I think he knew it before I did."

Jen chuckled to herself at that. "I bet he did," she said, feeling warm and happy for her sister.

"I think—" Cin's voice caught. "I think we're going to try to have a baby, Jen. Ian has always wanted kids but I just couldn't . . ."

"You wanted a commitment from him first," Jen suggested quietly.

"I guess I did."

"And now you've got it."

"Well, there are no guarantees, Mom will tell us that, but I know he really cares. He worked hard to give me what he thought I really wanted and that really touched my heart."

"You'd better not tell him you'd have gone with the Batman ring, if you'd known he meant it."

Cin giggled. "No, not for a while anyway. But you know, I will tell him one of these days, so don't laugh if I end up wearing both rings, maybe together."

"I promise."

"I gotta go, sis. We've got a plane to catch but I wanted you to know. Maybe you can tell Mom." Her tone turned wicked. "Or maybe you have news for her yourself. Should we plan a double wedding, on Valentine's Day?"

"I wouldn't want to steal your thunder."

"I don't care, Jen. I'm just so happy. All the rest is just detail." Cin blew a kiss into the phone. "Be happy, sis. I'll see you at the end of the week."

"I won't wait up."

Cin chortled. "It looks like no one should bother waiting up for either of us anytime soon."

And then she was gone. The apartment sounded empty without Cin's exuberance. Jen looked down at the cameo ring and knew that, Cin's expectations to the contrary, there would be no double wedding.

The fake date was over.

Because the fact was that if she and Zach had been serious—or if he really did love her—they'd have plans beyond dinner with his family on Christmas Day. There were no future plans between them, because they had no future. They'd had sex, which was great in itself, but it wasn't a long-term plan.

Jen got out of bed, dressed quickly, then put the cameo ring carefully on the teak headboard. It wasn't hers to wear, as lovely as it was, and the sooner she ended the charade, the easier it would be.

Although it wasn't very easy to leave even now. She reminded herself that fated relationships weren't always about happily ever after. Sometimes they were about lessons, or wisdom that needed sharing, or about recharting one's course. She and Zach had done all that, and Jen didn't want to wait around to find out that that was all he wanted. She wasn't going to stand and wait for the inevitable.

This would end on her terms.

It would end right now.

Jen told herself to appreciate what she'd been given, to concentrate on the good. She let herself out of the apartment and went down the stairs so she wouldn't meet Zach on the elevator. She went out a back door and walked briskly down a side street, hailing a cab as soon as she could.

Although Jen told herself that it was for the best, her sucker heart didn't believe her.

Zach came home with two take-out coffees, two whole-grain bagels, and an excited dog. He found the ring immediately and knew what it meant. He stood in the doorway of the bedroom with those two coffees, noted the open bathroom door, and took Jen's departure as the indictment it was.

His euphoria was gone, as surely as Jen was gone.

He hadn't measured up yet.

But he wasn't done. Not by a long shot.

There was one thing Jen didn't know yet, one thing he wasn't going to tell her until everything was in place.

In fact, he had a lot of work to finish today in order to make everything come together.

He was going to need both of those coffees himself.

Chapter 16

It was the thirtieth before Teresa and Jen made the drive to Rosemount to check out the old bookstore. As they drove, Teresa told Jen about her visit home to Kansas City, a whirlwind holiday tour that seemed to involve lots of food, lots of drinking, and lots of babies.

Jen knew she didn't imagine the wistfulness in Teresa's tone when she described her sister's newborn daughter.

"They're noisy and messy, you know," she teased. "And exhausting to have around all the time."

"Oh, I know," Teresa admitted. "It's just about choice."

Jen didn't say that there were lots of ways to lose that particular choice and that having a partner didn't necessarily mean having babies, but Teresa gave her no chance.

"Who knew that being empowered to have a career meant losing the power to make all the choices that were so easy for women before?" Teresa peered at the sign. "Is this the exit? Are we here yet?"

Jen gave directions, having scored a map from the Internet to supplement her memory. After all, Zach had taken a back route and she'd been completely charmed by his stories and the appearance of the town in the snow.

It was real, though, more real than she remembered. There were cars parked downtown and a few people walking along the street. More than one took a good look at Teresa's navy Honda Accord, as if they thought they should know her.

As if there couldn't be any other reason to be here other than living here.

Teresa parked in front of the bookstore and exhaled. "Wow. It looks perfect." She glanced up and down the street. "Nice old downtown, too."

"I know. It's so pretty decorated for Christmas."

"But beyond that, Jen, there's still traffic. Look how few empty stores there are. In most old towns, the downtown core is gutted. These people still shop here, which is a good thing."

"I didn't think of that."

"And this shop is right in the middle of the main block, on the north side of the street."

"It'll get sunshine."

"That's always the best retail space. People walk on the sunny side of the street."

"I didn't know that."

"That's why rents are higher on the sunny side of the street." Teresa gave Jen a sharp look. "But what about Fake Date Boy? Isn't he from here?"

"He said he couldn't wait to get away. I don't think he'd been back in a long time, and even then, I don't think he ever comes downtown."

Teresa watched her closely. "You never told me about Christmas Day."

"It was lovely." Jen forced a smile, knowing she wouldn't fool her friend. "For a reciprocal fake date."

Teresa winced. "So the inevitable happened?"

Jen nodded and Teresa gave her an impulsive hug. "Better for you, Jen. I could see you were already falling. It's better for you to get out while you still could."

"That's why I ended it."

"You ended it? Even better." Teresa sat back and eyed the storefront. "So, onward with the plan."

"What do you mean?"

"Well, we came all this way. Let's have a look."

"But it's too soon. I won't be done school until the fall . . ."

"Be serious, Jen. Opportunity doesn't knock very often, and I've got to think that there was a greater purpose in your hooking up with the man."

"Other than great sex and mutual satisfaction?"

Teresa laughed. "I know. It should be enough in itself, without the security of real estate. You really could be lucking out here."

"We don't even know how much it is. It's probably expensive . . ."

"Oh, you're too skeptical! It's still for sale and who knows how long it's been for sale. They might be ready to make a deal."

"You don't know that . . ."

"Look around, Jen. Its advantages might suit us, but Rosemount doesn't look like a hot and happening real estate market." Before Jen could answer, Teresa had rummaged in her purse and quickly punched in the phone number from the sign. "Calling Dinah Dishman," she said, smiling for Jen.

"But it's too soon . . ." Jen protested.

Teresa waved her off, then frowned as someone answered the phone. "Hi, yes, I'm looking for Dinah Dishman." She paused, then smiled. "Yes, I wanted to know about the property you have listed for sale. Um, let's see, it's a shop. The address is 272, um—"

"Main Street," Jen supplied.

"Main Street, in Rosemount." Teresa paused to listen. "Oh, it's not a shop? It's the whole building? With an apartment over top and a small yard in the back, which includes parking?" She made a face and gave Jen a thumbs-up.

Jen was convinced that she couldn't afford it.

Teresa listened for a minute, then her eyes widened. "Yes, I am driving a navy Honda Accord." She met Jen's gaze with confusion. "Why do you ask?" Teresa listened, then looked at the phone. She covered the mouthpiece. "She said to look back."

Jen and Teresa turned as one to look through the back window of the Honda. A woman was waving from the window of the diner across the street.

"That would be Dinah," Teresa said.

"Meet Dinah in the diner," Jen said with a grin.. "There's a joke in there somewhere."

"Something about dishes," Teresa agreed. "Let's meet her now and worry about the joke later."

Dinah Dishman could well have been the girl that Zach's sister Phil had babysat. She looked to be in her midtwenties. She had brown hair, tugged up into a ponytail, and still had freckles on her nose and across her cheeks. She wore glasses, had a quick smile and an easy manner that put Jen immediately at ease.

She looked to be working in the window booth of the diner. There was a empty coffee cup pushed to one side, an iPod and earphones cast to the other, paperwork all over the tabletop and her cell phone presiding in the center. She had the announcement page from the newspaper folded and highlighted, too.

The diner was otherwise empty, although there was a clatter coming from the kitchen, as well as what sounded like muted music from a radio. Jen thought it might be an oldies station. The diner was very clean, and could have been transported through time from the fifties.

"Forgot my yellow Realtor blazer," Dinah said with an apologetic smile. She was wearing jeans and a red blouse with the sleeves rolled up. That wasn't much different from Jen's jeans and blazer, but Teresa's designer casual wear stood out. "It's usually pretty slow for real estate in Rosemount between Christmas and New Year's, but I can still answer your questions." Dinah swept up her paperwork and piled it onto the bench seat on one side.

At her gesture of invitation, Teresa slid into the bench on the opposite side of the booth and took the lead. Jen hadn't intended to take this any further than showing Rosemount to Teresa, so felt as if she was along for the ride in more ways than one.

"Actually, all of our questions have to do with that shop or building that's for sale," Teresa said, gesturing across the street.

"Would you like a coffee? Or tea?"

Teresa looked impatient at this offer, but Jen smiled. "Thanks but we don't want to be too much trouble."

Dinah laughed. "It's my brother's place. I've washed enough dishes that he can spot me the occasional cup of coffee or tea."

"I'd love a cup of coffee," Jen said.

"I guess I'll have one too, then," Teresa agreed.

Dinah got up to pour it herself and brought the two cups back to the table. She refilled her own, as well, then brought cream in a pitcher and some spoons. "I wait tables here, too," she said, her smile turning rueful.

"As well as selling real estate?" Jen asked.

"A person needs a broad economic base to survive in a little place like Rosemount," Dinah admitted. "I like it here enough, and I like multitasking enough, to make it work."

"Does your brother do other things as well as run the diner?" Jen asked. "Because that seems like a lot of work."

"He does a lot of catering, in partnership with my other brother who owns the bistro across the way. Between the two of them, they joke that they feed a third of Rosemount every day and all of it when there's a wedding or a funeral."

The women smiled at that. Jen thought it sounded great to be in a smaller place, although she could tell that Teresa was less enamored of the idea of a small pond. Her fingers were already tapping in impatience. "So, what can you tell us about the place across the street?" Teresa asked.

Dinah winced. "It's sold."

Jen was unable to fully hide her disappointment.

Dinah smiled. "There's a conditional offer, which is why the sign hasn't been changed, but I'm pretty sure it will go through . . ."

"Conditional upon what?" Teresa asked.

Dinah straightened. "I don't think I'd be breaking any confidences to tell you that it's a financing condition. Obviously, the issue is that a lot of bank personnel are away for the holidays . . ."

"If the buyer was certain the financing would go through, there's be no financing clause in the offer," Teresa noted.

Dinah studied her warily. "No, I suppose not. But I do think that it will go through."

"But you don't know."

"No, I don't," Dinah said carefully. Jen could see her back rising.

"And financing clauses do fall through," Teresa insisted.

Dinah flicked a glance at Jen. "That's true. If you're interested in the building, I can call you if that happens."

Jen wouldn't have bet a nickel that that would happen.

Teresa leaned forward. "We've just driven from Boston to see it. Don't you think it would save all of us a lot of time if we saw the building now? That way we'd all know if we were interested, if the financing clause fell through."

Dinah sat back. Jen could tell that she wasn't used to people playing as assertively as Teresa did. But she reached into her folder and pulled out a listing, sliding on to the table between them. "Here's the listing price," she said, tapping a number on the page. Jen's eyes widened but Teresa made no outward sign of surprise. "I'll tell you that it's higher than is typical for Rosemount, because the building is on the historic register and it's structurally in excellent repair." She glanced up. "It's a premium property, and although it's an estate sale, the family wants their price."

Teresa was working her way down the listing, her fingertip pausing on the square footage and the description of the apartment. "One kitchen, one and a half baths?"

"There's a washroom with toilet and sink on the main floor, that Mr. MacCauley used to let customers use."

"The insurance will kill you on that," Teresa noted. "How high are the ceilings?"

"Twelve feet throughout. There's a tin ceiling on the main floor, in the shop," Dinah said, and Jen caught a glimpse of her enthusiasm for the space. "Hardwood floors throughout. The kitchen upstairs could use an update, but the plumbing and wiring were done in the seventies and should be okay."

Teresa was still reading. "And a full basement? How high is the ceiling down there?"

"Nine feet. The foundation is stone, about three feet thick."

"And the basement is dry?"

Dinah nodded. "It's a premium property," she reiterated. "Because it's listed on the register, it won't be possible for the new owner to make substantive changes to the building."

"We wouldn't want to." Teresa glanced up, drained her coffee cup and smiled. "Can we see it? Maybe now?"

When Dinah hesitated, Teresa leaned forward. "Wouldn't you like a backup plan in case the offer does fall through? Seems to me you've got nothing to lose."

"Sure," Dinah said, although there was little enthusiasm in her voice. "Let me get the keys."

"I think you could have been a little less pushy," Jen said to Teresa when Dinah had left the table.

"Why?" Teresa cast her a confident smile. "Time is precious, Jen. We came here to see it and we're going to see it. No wasted trip for us."

"Unless it really is sold."

"Even so, you'll know a Realtor here."

Jen watched the Realtor's body language and wasn't sure that Dinah would be calling anyone who knew Teresa Tremaine anytime soon.

The three women went across Rosemount's Main Street in silence, stamping their booted feet on the sidewalk as Dinah unlocked the old door.

Jen crossed the threshold and lost her heart.

The tin ceiling was gorgeous, intact, and original. The transom over the oak door she'd already admired had the address etched into the glass, surrounded by etched curlicues. The main window had been replaced, simply because it was large and had been broken at some point in time, and now was double glass. Above it, the original stained glass window that was the same width remained.

The store interior was surprisingly bright, even without the electric lights on. The store occupied the whole first floor of the building, one corner at the back blocked off for that small washroom. The high windows across the back wall had been replaced with glass blocks, which let in more light. In the middle of the space, a stair went up to a locked door at the summit, and beneath it, a door that could be locked led to the basement.

The old counter was there, also made of oak, its surface polished smooth from countless transactions. The counter was J-shaped and wrapped around the space claimed by the staircases. Telephone jacks and wiring seemed to have been passed through the building in the stairs.

There was crown molding around the ceiling, wood molding that was carved into the furling shapes of acanthus leaves. The floor looked original, too, and was made of wide planks of oak. Jen could smell the beeswax used to polish it and she could see the square heads of the old nails used to hammer it down.

"It was the general store a hundred years ago," Dinah said. "Mr. MacCauley, who ran the bookstore here for ages, tried to keep it as original as possible."

"He did a good job," Jen said, unable to resist touching the smooth surface of the counter. "It's beautiful."

Dinah studied her. "Are you from here?"

"No."

"Then how did you find out about the listing? I didn't put it on the Internet."

"I was here, visiting with friends, and saw it. I'm looking to open a shop and it just seemed perfect." Jen turned away before

Dinah could ask any questions about who Jen's friends might be. "Can we see the apartment?"

The apartment desperately needed an update. Teresa grimaced at the kitchen and bath and muttered something about needing to gut it that obviously offended Dinah.

"The layout is good," Jen said of the kitchen. "I could paint the cabinets, lay a new linoleum floor, maybe put in new counters, and it would look great."

"The bathroom, though," Teresa said, gesturing with one finger as if she was afraid to touch anything.

"I like the tub," Jen said, admiring the claw foot iron tub in one corner. "Again, I think paint and new tiles would make a world of difference. I don't think it needs that much work."

Dinah smiled at her.

The apartment had wonderful big windows as well, three facing the street from what would be the living room and three facing the modest back lot. Two were in the bedroom and one was in the tiny kitchen. There was an alley that serviced the parking spaces behind each of the buildings. She sighed and glanced around, admiring the hardwood floor and the bannister that coiled at the summit of the stairs.

"It's great," she said, listening to the comparative quiet outside. "I love it."

"You're one tough negotiator," Teresa teased.

Dinah almost smiled, but then her cell phone rang. Jen and Teresa strolled to the back of the apartment to give Dinah some privacy, although her voice echoed in the empty space. "I think there's room for a garden," Jen said.

"A couple of chairs and a cooler," Teresa said. "You might be able to make a patio without checking with the historic preservation people."

"I'd think you could lay some stones for it. It wouldn't be permanent and would look nice. I'll bet if you open the windows, you can hear the sea."

"I'll bet you couldn't get a date in this place, if you walked down Main Street naked," Teresa said with a sigh. "Are you sure this is what you want?"

It wasn't exactly what Jen wanted, but it was the closest approximation she could make on her own. Maybe, just maybe, she'd meet some small-town guy with similar values to her own.

Maybe she'd already done that.

"Yes, it is. It's perfect," she said to Teresa just as Dinah came back.

"Sorry to give you bad news," she said, not looking overly sorry at all when she glanced at Teresa. "The condition has been cleared: the building is sold."

Jen wasn't in a good mood when she got home. She was feeling as if everything she wanted was just coming close enough to tempt her, then was being snatched away by unseen forces. She was annoyed and tired and looking forward to going back to work at Mulligan's that night, even if it meant singing to an empty pub.

She'd be singing, anyway. Motown music always cheered her up. Having a shift meant that there was no time to have dinner with Teresa, but they were going to hang out at Teresa's on New Year's Eve.

"Call us a couple of wild spinsters," Teresa said when she dropped Jen off. "Bring your knitting and I'll pick up the bubbles. No guarantees that you'll keep gauge once we start on the champagne, though."

Jen smiled and waved and tried not to think of Zach trying to divert her from killing him by offering a glass of champagne.

Natalie's house was empty, no one answering when she yelled. There was a note propped up beside her mug. *Gone to water Cin's plants,* her mother had written. *Drink this.*

The green leafy stuff in Jen's mug smelled more like anise this time. She smiled and filled the kettle, uncertain she'd drink this stuff either. The phone rang and she answered it without thinking. "Hello?"

"Is Guinevere Maitland there please?"

Jen sat down heavily. She knew this woman's voice and was not particularly glad to hear it. "This is Jen."

"Hi, Jen." The woman's voice warmed. "This is Dr. Levittson."

Jen's voice didn't warm as much. Maybe that was because she felt as if she was suddenly in freefall. "Hello, Dr. Levittson."

"I'm glad to have caught you at home," the oncologist said. "I came into the office this week to catch up on paperwork and your mammogram results are here."

"Yes," Jen said, closing her eyes in fear. She thought it unlikely that Dr. Levittson would call to chat about a clear mammogram result. The kettle began to boil but she ignored it.

The doctor cleared her throat. "Jen, there's something I don't like the look of in your right breast. It's small, it might just be a calcification or a cyst, and really, if I was talking to another woman of your age with no personal or family history, I would just keep an eye on it. The fact is though, Jen, that I want to be proactive here, given your history."

"I understand."

"Listen to me, Jen. I don't think it's anything, but I want to be sure. You must remember that we talked about the fact that recurrence is most likely in the first two years after the initial diagnosis."

"I do," Jen said, her eyes filling with tears. Not again. It couldn't come back again. It couldn't steal everything from her again, not when she was finally finding her stride again.

But cancer could and Jen knew it and that was why she was so very afraid. She clutched the phone cord in her fingers, barely noticing how cold they had become.

"I've called the lab," Dr. Levittson said and her matter-of-fact tone was reassuring. What Jen had liked about Dr. Levittson was that the woman always gave the impression of having everything under control. Whether it was true or not—and it couldn't be true, really—her assurance and confidence had always been reassuring to Jen. "Unfortunately, they're backed up in January, what with the holidays and all, but there's a cancellation on the tenth. I want to do a fine-needle biopsy and I'll be there myself to make sure we get a sample from the area in question. Can you possibly make that date? It would be at two-thirty, otherwise we're into February."

Jen couldn't even imagine declining this appointment. She'd do whatever was necessary to know the truth as soon as possible.

"I'll be there." Her voice was small and tight and she sat curled on the stool by the phone. Her guts were writhing into knots.

Dr. Levittson cleared her throat. "Jen, I don't want to frighten you. You know that mammogram equipment is very sensitive and we have many more false positives than was once the case."

"That's what they said last time," Jen acknowledged and Dr. Levittson sighed.

"I was afraid you'd say that."

"I'll see you on the tenth," Jen said, wanting only to get off the phone.

"Yes. Try not to worry." Dr. Levittson's voice lightened as she used an old joke they had shared. "And eat your veggies, Jen. Those leafy greens are good for you."

Jen tried to laugh lightly but failed. The kettle was boiling, but she had no time to pull it off the stove. She ran in the other direction and barely made the bathroom before she vomited.

She knelt on the tile floor and cried as her body emptied itself. It was back. Or maybe it wasn't. Never mind the financial burden: she was sure the uncertainty would kill her as surely as the cancer could.

Jen wiped her tears, knowing they wouldn't help. She couldn't put her family through the ordeal again, not without knowing for sure. Jen decided she'd say nothing until—or unless—Dr. Levittson said the big C really was claiming real estate in her right breast, too.

Maybe not thinking about it, or not talking about it, would diminish the boogeyman's power.

Or maybe not.

Either way, this time she was going to drink the tea her mother had left for her. Jen didn't figure she had a lot left to lose.

The box was delivered on the tenth of January.

Jen was heading out the door, panicking about being late for her needle biopsy. She'd been dawdling, worrying about which prosthesis to wear, which was the least of her troubles. The truth was that she was terrified and avoiding what frightened her most seemed like good sense. She hadn't told anybody, which had left all of them ignorant and confident, and seemed to have only increased her own fear.

She opened the door to find a courier on the doorstep, wearing a baseball cap pulled down low. He had his hand on the bell but hadn't pushed it yet.

Before she could say anything, he offered a small box to her.

It was addressed to her, but it was from the Holland-Mercer Art Gallery. The address for the gallery was downtown, and Jen was sure she'd never been there.

"Are you sure this is right?" she asked.

"Package for Jennifer Maitland," he said.

His voice sounded familiar.

She looked up at him for the first time. Her heart stopped cold when she met that dancing green gaze, then galloped off to distant horizons. "Zach?"

He grinned and cocked a finger at her. "Gotcha."

"Not really." Jen felt herself blushing. The man shouldn't have been grinning at her, as if he was glad to see her. She certainly shouldn't be glad to see him. "What are you doing here?"

"Making a delivery."

"For this gallery? This is what you decided to do with your life?"

Zach laughed. "No. I have a better plan. Maybe I just wanted to see you again."

"Why?"

"The usual reasons." He bent and stole a kiss, his smile fading as he gave her a considering look. "What's wrong?"

"Nothing," Jen lied. "I'm late, that's all."

"Liar," he said. "You look like you haven't slept."

"Oh, well, working too hard, I guess."

He considered her for a moment, then gestured to the box. "Go on, open the package."

"I can't right now. I'm late."

"Then bring it with you and open it on the way." He was practically bouncing, doing his Tigger imitation again, and Jen knew he was itching for her to open the parcel.

"I don't think that will work . . ."

"I'll give you a ride."

"Oh, you don't have to do that."

"But I want to. Come on. Where are you going? Early shift at Mulligan's?"

"No. Look, you can't drive me. You can't."

"If you're late, you won't get there on time on public transit. Besides, I'm playing courier today. I'll happily courier you wherever you want to go."

"But . . ." The truth was that Jen didn't want to tell Zach where she was going.

"Jen, unless you're going to Timbuktu, it's not a problem. Come on, you're not putting me out. I'm offering." Zach strode toward the red Neon, which Jen now saw was parked at the curb. Roxie was in the backseat. She saw Jen and barked. "That's the bark of joy," Zach said. "You can't let Roxie down now."

Jen locked the door behind herself, knowing she'd lost. She'd get him to drop her off close to the clinic, but not right at the door.

It would save her time and wouldn't give her secret away. It was a rationalization and Jen knew it. She could use a dose of Zach's irrepressible optimism.

She spoke to Roxie through the back window—which Zach had rolled down for her—and nearly got licked to death. Zach opened the door for Jen and she got in, laughing as Roxie nuzzled the back of her neck.

"She likes you," Zach said as he got in.

"I hope so. It would be a bit weird if this was how she greeted people she didn't like."

He laughed and Jen felt better. "Go on, tell me that you missed me. That you're not sleeping nights because you're pining away for me."

Jen scoffed, because she knew he expected it. "If I admitted that, it would only encourage you."

"And we've agreed already that I'm incorrigible," Zach said with false solemnity. "Should I sing?"

"No, please don't."

He clucked his tongue, making a chicken sound, and Jen found herself glad to be in his company again. The car seemed full with the three of them, because it pretty much was. She gave him an intersection, lied about being late for a class, and he didn't question her. Once they were en route and he'd scolded Roxie for steaming up the windows—which had no discernible effect—he tapped the box with a fingertip. "Go on, open it."

"I should be the one who's curious, not you."

"But you aren't, and I know you should be. Go on, it's good. I know because I packed it."

"It's probably booby-trapped," Jen said, giving the box a shake. She was curious, although she wasn't sure she should be. It couldn't be a print of one of his photographs and she couldn't think of what else he would give her.

"Quit thinking and start tearing," Zach counseled.

Jen opened the outer envelope and pulled out the box inside, her heart stopping cold at its distinctive turquoise color. It was a Tiffany box, but not one for a ring. It might have held a necklace or a bracelet because it was large and flat.

Jen couldn't think of a thing to say. There was suddenly not quite enough air in the car. They stopped at a red light and she turned to meet his gaze. She stared at him for a long potent moment, thinking of the things they'd done together, thinking about how much she'd like to do some of them again.

Zach seemed to be thinking similar things. The air was electric between them.

She licked her lips without meaning to do so. Zach caught his breath and put the car into gear, sending it skipping into the intersection as the light turned green.

"You might not have missed me, but I've missed you," he muttered.

"I'm sorry," she said. "I shouldn't have just left after Christmas night."

"Run, I think is the correct verb," Zach said, showing some irritation. "You didn't leave, you ran."

"You're just mad because I beat you to it."

"I wasn't going to run," he said so firmly that she half believed it.

"You would have tossed me out, then."

"Not a chance." He winked at her. "You ran, Jen, maybe because you didn't have all of the information."

"You're going to tell me that there's more info inside."

"Pretty much. Open the box."

"I can't imagine what you're up to," she said, turning the box in her hands. It was light and didn't rattle.

Maybe it was empty. A fake present to commemorate fake dates.

"There would be one good way to find out."

Fair enough. Jen untied the silver ribbon and opened the box. To her surprise, there was an invitation nestled in the tissue paper inside. It was gilt-edged but not stuffy, the edge of the card cut in a funky pattern.

THE HOLLAND-MERCER GALLERY
cordially invites you to attend

Before and After: A Retrospective
A new exhibit of photographs
by Zachary

January 23 to February 14, 2007
Artist's Reception—January 22—8:00 p.m.

There was a telephone number at the bottom of the card to RSVP.

Jen looked at Zach in surprise. "Is this Zachary you?"

Zach nodded grimly. "The very same."

"It doesn't have your surname."

"That would be the point."

"I don't understand."

Zach frowned, more serious as Jen had ever seen him. "A lot of things have happened for me—and not happened for me—because of my family name. My father and mother both have lots of connections. I wanted to do something myself, to see what I could accomplish myself, without anyone easing the way or cutting me slack because of who my father was."

"You wanted to be assessed on your own merit."

"And it's scaring the crap out of me, by the way." He flashed her a confident grin, making her doubt that anything could scare the crap out of him.

Jen turned the invitation over thoughtfully. "And the gallery agreed to that, when they decided to show your work?"

"They don't know my surname. I never told them."

"So you got the show—"

"—the old-fashioned way. I took my photographs to an old teacher, who had once challenged me to make something of myself." He smiled ruefully and spared her a glance. "Unlike anyone else I know."

Jen felt herself blush. "I'm sorry that I said what I said . . ."

"Don't be. You were right. Anyway, Mr. Nicholson knows Tom Holland, who agreed to look at my portfolio. I got lucky: Tom not only liked my work but he had a late cancellation that would have left him with empty walls. One of his artists changed to another gallery and he was scrambling to put something together."

"You had enough work for the show?"

"Hardly!" Zach laughed. "Where do you think I've been these past two weeks? I've been killing myself to get enough done to be framed. And now, it's in Tom's hands. I just have to show up and sparkle at the preview." He took a deep breath, as if he was nervous, which Jen knew had to be an impossibility. She'd never met anyone more confident in her life. His voice dropped low enough to make her shiver. "I'd like it if you could be there, too, Jen."

Jen swallowed and looked down. "I might have to work," she lied, knowing that she might have an even more pressing engagement.

With an oncologist.

"And I'm making a personal appeal," Zach said impatiently. "I'll talk to Murray if you want. I'll drive you to work when you need to leave."

"You'd leave your own launch party?"

He nodded tersely. He stopped at another red and gave her a hot glance. "I'd really like you to be there."

It was hard to think that he was putting her on, his manner was so sincere, but Jen had to ask. "Why?"

Zach shrugged and she guessed that his answer would only be part of the truth. "It's kind of your fault, isn't it?" he said lightly. "You challenged me and this is the result. Don't you think you should check it out?"

Jen watched him for a moment, thought about what he'd said and guessed. "You're really worried about this."

"Does it show?"

"Not really."

"Good! Never let them see you sweat, right, Roxie?"

Jen put the invitation carefully back into the box, smiling a bit that he'd gone to some trouble to get a Tiffany box. "What does your family think of it?"

"I don't know."

"Will they be there?"

He spared her a wry look. "*Everyone* will be there to see me fall on my face. Trust me. They've been waiting for this moment for a while."

"I doubt that you'll fall on your face." She spoke softly, wishing that she could be there. Maybe she'd go see the show on her own. "I'm sure it will be great."

"You make it sound as if you're turning me down."

Jen reached for the door handle as they reached the corner near the intersection she'd named. "You can let me out here."

"I'm not stopping until you RSVP."

"You have to stop."

"I can go three hundred times around the block. Just watch."

"I'm late!"

"And I'm stubborn. Jen, I love you. If you want to ditch me, that's fine, but I want to show you the change you've made in my life first. If nothing else, it could give you a sense of accomplishment."

She didn't say anything, just looked out the window, wondering whether she dared to believe him.

"Hey, I don't plan fake weddings with just anybody." Zach glanced her way. "Did you think I just said that at Christmas to get you to come back to my place?"

"It did occur to me."

Zach swore.

"It's not that crazy," she argued. "It's been a couple of weeks, Zach, and I haven't heard from you . . ."

"And have I heard from you?"

"I didn't confess to being in love."

"True enough." He gave her a hard look. "Does that mean you're not?" He looked very unhappy with her, more frustrated and irritated than Jen would have believed possible. She wanted to tell him that she loved him, but then, she didn't want to admit to anything that could be used against her.

She was, after all, running late.

"Okay, I'll ask you an easier question," Zach said, his annoyance clear. "Will you come to the show?"

Jen pushed a hand through her hair in indecision. She was acutely aware of what Zach wanted to say, but couldn't fight her own sense that it was foolish to promise what she might not be able to deliver.

Maybe it would be better to hurt his feelings now than to risk him hurting hers. Maybe the simplest answer was the best one. "Maybe I need to check my Day-timer," she said, unable to just decline.

"Maybe you should do it now," Zach growled.

"Maybe I'll get out the car anyway."

"You'll have to jump." He was angry. There was no doubt about it, and Jen was sure he wasn't putting it on. His eyes were flashing and he was changing gears more roughly than he usually did.

"You really want me to be there?"

"Why else would I invite you?" he demanded, his voice rising. "Why else would I go to the trouble of trying to get your attention . . ." He turned to face her, his eyes flashing. "Yes. I would like you to be there. This show wouldn't have happened without you kicking my butt. It only seems right that you get to see what you've done."

"That sounds ominous."

"It isn't meant to be." He slipped the car into a parallel parking spot, then caught her hand before she could bolt. "What the hell

are we doing at this intersection? Tell me the truth this time, Jen."
He spoke with such conviction that Jen was frightened by his per-
ceptiveness. "There's nothing in this area that could have anything
to do with one of your classes."

"You don't know that. You don't even know what I'm taking."

"You're upset and I'd like to think it's not because I finally
turned up on your doorstep. Okay, I should have called. I'm sorry.
I wanted to surprise you with something that was done. I wanted
to show you that I'd changed. I wanted to impress you with a big
gesture." He arched a brow. "It's working brilliantly, I can tell,
so I'm hoping there's another problem here. Is something going
on, Jen?"

It was tempting to admit the truth to him, but Jen chose not to
do so. "I . . . I'm just late," she said, knowing that her excuse was
lame. "I hate being late."

"And you stink at lying," Zach said quietly. He sat back and
watched her, his expression inscrutable. "Okay, so there's someone
else. Okay, you're throwing me back." Jen stared at him, shocked
by the conclusion he'd made and by how hurt he appeared to be.
"But please come to the show, Jen, even so. For old times' sake, if
nothing else."

Jen opened her mouth to correct him, then closed it again. Maybe
it was easier this way. "I'll see what I can do." When he looked
lethal, she offered a bit more. "I'll try my best. Really."

Zach was simmering. He watched her for a long electric moment and Jen felt herself respond to him. As previously, she wanted
to make him smile, but it was much worse this time. She wanted to
make him smile by making love to him. She wanted to confess her
own love for him. She wanted to tell him what was happening and
to have him pledge to stand beside her the whole way.

But it was too much to ask and Jen knew it.

She wouldn't ask so he couldn't refuse. She turned to open the
car door, heard him swear, and walked away, her vision blinded
with tears. His car didn't move for a long time. Jen knew it because

she heard Roxie whimper and felt Zach's gaze boring into her
back. She brushed away her tears.

Why did doing the right thing seem so wrong?

Jen stopped and looked back. Zach was still sitting in his
parked car, watching her. When she paused, Roxie barked but
Zach didn't move.

Then she knew that it felt wrong because it *was* wrong. Once
upon a time, she had taken chances. Once upon a time, she had
been impulsive. Once upon a time, she had dared to ask for what
she wanted.

And to expect to get it.

Once upon a time, she had been, in fact, a lot more like Zach
Coxwell that she had been lately. The cancer might have taken that
boldness away from Jen, but she could have it back. She could have
her life back, her hope back, her sense of optimism back.

She just had to ask for what she wanted, instead of surrendering and accepting its absence. She loved this man, loved his crazy
sense of humor, loved his surety that anything was possible. Just
holding his gaze from a hundred feet away, when she couldn't see
the green of his eyes but could feel the heat of his anger, made her
guts clench. She loved his determination to live life to the fullest, to
learn from his mistakes and to start again, as many times as was
necessary.

He hadn't been avoiding her. He hadn't dumped her and moved
on. He'd been working hard, preparing for the very first exhibit of
his photographs. She was desperately proud of him for seeking out
that opportunity, then seizing it once it appeared. He wanted her to
be there and she had seen in his eyes how important her presence
was to him.

He'd asked for what he wanted. He'd confessed his love for her.
Why didn't she have the nerve to trust him?

Jen marched back toward the red Neon, terrified of what might
result from taking this chance. Zach might run. He might disappear as quickly as Steve had done.

But losing Zach would hurt more than losing Steve.

Jen's heart was pounding and she knew she was shaking, but her stride didn't falter. It had been a long time since she had dared to even say what she wanted.

On the other hand, it was even more frightening to consider that she might be walking away from happiness without giving it a real chance.

Chapter 17

Zach couldn't believe it when Jen turned and walked back toward the car. Roxie barked with enthusiasm, her joy at Jen's return rocking the car on its shocks.

Something was wrong, though. Zach could see it in the way Jen moved. He'd had that sense before, but now it was redoubled. She was shaking and her steps were filled with defiance, not her usual confidence. He got out of the car and waited for her, a cloud of doom gathering around his heart.

She was coming to give him bad news.

She was going to tell him that she was in love with some other guy.

She was preparing to hurt him, something that wouldn't be easy for Jen to do, but she would do the right thing and be honest with him. He admired her, even as he feared what she would say.

Jen surprised him, yet again.

She stopped in front of him and took a shaking breath. She had

a card in her hand, although she didn't give it to him right away.
"Look," she said, her voice wavering. "I don't know if I can be at
your show, but it's not because I don't want to be. I'm proud of
you, proud that you've decided what you wanted and have gone after it. Don't think otherwise."

Zach shoved his hands in his pockets to keep from touching her,
sensing that she had drawn away from him. She looked down at
the ground, then met his gaze. He was shocked to see the tears in
her eyes.

She took a deep breath. "You're right, something *is* wrong. I
haven't told anyone because it's too early to know for sure." A tear
escaped, trailing down her cheek and she wiped it away impatiently.
"The thing is that I'm late for a needle biopsy. The mammogram I
had for a routine check last week showed some abnormalities in
my right breast and my oncologist wants to take a sample to be
sure."

Zach stared at her in shock. "It's back?"

Jen shook her head, loosing a number of tears. "I don't know.
That's why the test is being done. It's too soon to know for sure,
but the point is that everything is kind of up in the air right now."
She fumbled with the card, not showing her usual grace, then
shoved it at him. He took it from her shaking fingers.

"This is the clinic." Jen half laughed. "I don't need the card
anymore because I could walk there in my sleep." She looked up at
him and he understood that she was giving him a chance to run. He
saw her vulnerability and wanted to gather her up, take her home,
keep her safe. She swallowed, her throat working. "So, um, maybe
I'll see you around."

Before he could answer, she walked away again, moving quickly
down the street toward the clinic. Zach looked down at the card,
swore, then leapt into his car. He squealed the tires as he pulled
away from the curb, and used every trick he knew to get home
quickly.

"You're going to hang out solo for a while, Roxie," he told the dog as he double-parked in front of his condo building. "But I promise that it will be worth it in the end." He left the car running, took the dog upstairs, locked the door, and ran.

He broke seventeen traffic regulations getting to that clinic, but he made it in five minutes.

Jen heard Zach's tires squeal as he drove away. She winced but didn't look back. The sound told her everything she needed to know. The man couldn't wait to put distance between himself and a defective member of the female gender.

Maybe all men were like that.

Maybe if she got through this test and everything came out clear, she'd go to his show and tell Zach what she thought of him. She didn't know whether to be livid or to sit down and cry.

They were backed up at the clinic, and it was a few minutes before the receptionist could take Jen's information. She was standing at the counter, trying to appear composed, and wondering whether her credit card would melt in the receptionist's hands, when someone came to stand behind her. She caught a whiff of soap and cold air and the smell of Zach Coxwell's skin right before his hand landed on the back of her waist.

Her heart stopped cold.

"Need a different card, honey?" he asked and the bottom fell out of her universe.

She glanced back, saw his proffered credit card, the familiar strength of his hand, then dared to look up. She trembled inside. He was still angry with her and she didn't trust his presence fully yet. "No, thanks. I think this one's fine." She met his gaze and swallowed. "Honey," she added.

He flashed a grin at the receptionist, all cocky confidence, and Jen's knees went weak. "Roxie isn't happy about being dumped home alone," he said, his tone conversational. "I think she knows that you're worried. You know how sensitive she is to your moods."

So that's where he'd gone. And why he'd driven off so quickly. Jen made a mental note not to assume that she could guess what Zach Coxwell was doing in any given situation. The man had a talent for challenging her assumptions. Her heart warmed and she smiled at him, seeing his own annoyance fade a little.

He captured her hand in his and she dared to hope.

The receptionist smiled politely and gave Jen back her card, telling her to take a seat and wait. One of the ladies waiting moved so that they could sit together and Zach thanked her graciously. He sat right beside Jen, his shoulder bumping hers. He was the only man in the waiting room, and the other women watched him openly.

"I didn't think you'd come," Jen said quietly and earned herself a stern look.

"I had to stop by to kill you," Zach said lightly. He claimed her hand again and gave her fingers a squeeze. She saw a flicker of anger in his eyes. "What the hell do you think you were doing, not telling anyone that you were having this test done?"

"I didn't want to worry anyone . . ."

Zach interrupted her before she got any further. "I don't know whether to be more pissed off that you thought I was lying about loving you, or that you thought I was like Steve."

"But, I . . ."

"I mean, come on, Jen. There's not much worse you could say to me than that you think I'm like that jerk."

"Well, I didn't. Not really."

"But you were afraid I was."

Jen looked down at her hands. Zach knotted his fingers with hers and leaned closer to make his point. "The point of loving someone is that you worry about them, Jen." Zach's words were emphatic and his tone was low. She met his gaze and there wasn't a flicker of laughter in his eyes.

He was not putting her on.

"The point of loving someone is that you are there when that person needs you, and vice versa." He shoved his other hand through his hair, which made him looked rumpled and disreputable and unpredictable. He gave her a simmering look. "Although I can't believe I have to explain to Natalie Sommerset's daughter what it means to love somebody."

"I wanted to wait until I knew the test results for sure . . ."

"But the uncertainty is what's eating you alive," Zach insisted. "That's why you can't sleep." He brushed a fingertip across her cheek and Jen nearly melted at the tender gesture. "The uncertainty is the part you most need to share, Jen, because not being sure of what's in front of you lets your imagination go wild."

"I'll say," interjected an older woman on the other side of the waiting room.

"Nobody asked you to carry this burden by yourself and nobody who loves you expects you to do it," Zach continued. His grip on her hand was crushing but Jen was glad of it. He was here, and there was no mistaking that. "I love you, Jen." He smiled crookedly. "And that means that you're stuck with me."

"For better or for worse?" she ventured and he laughed. It was probably the first time anyone had ever laughed in this waiting room. The other women watched with interest.

"Something like that." He pursed his lips. "In fact, exactly like that." He turned a sparkling glance on her. "You see, I've been thinking that this fake engagement has its limitations."

"Does it?"

"One big one, really. A fake date and a fake engagement means a fake wedding." He held her gaze steadily. "And I don't want a fake wedding. Not with you."

Jen's mouth went more dry than it already was.

Zach looked down at their linked hands. "The thing is, Jen, that I had to prove myself to you. I still eat frozen burritos and I still don't have a lot of furniture, but I know what I want to do. You helped me find that and this show, I'm hoping, is the first step on that path." He shrugged. "Who knows whether it will work, but it's an opportunity and one that is a step in the right direction. It's one of the first things I've ever wanted."

"Not the first thing?"

He smiled at her, his grin so warm and wicked that Jen got goose pimples. "No. That was you."

Jen didn't know what to say.

Zach spun out of the chair. He dropped to one knee in front of her, and kept a firm grip on her hand. The other women tittered but Jen had eyes only for Zach. "I love you, Jen Maitland," he said with such conviction that her heart squeezed tight. "I want to be with you every step of the way, I want to take pictures of you and travel with you, and just hang out with you. I want to argue with you and plan with you and build a life together. I want to be there every time you smile and I want to hold you every time you cry." He kissed her palm, then met her gaze, his own earnest. "So, will you marry me, for real?"

"No breakup at the altar?"

"Ideally, no. It would hurt my mom's feelings, and then I'd have to learn to brood." His voice deepened and he was serious again. "I mean the real thing, Jen. What do you say?"

Jen smiled at him, feeling happy and excited and fearful all at the same time. "Yes," she said. "Yes, I will."

Before she could kiss him, he snapped his fingers. "By the way, I found something you forgot." Zach reached into his pocket. He pulled out a wadded paper towel.

"A present from Roxie?"

"No, this is better." Jen didn't know what to expect until he unrolled it and revealed his mother's cameo ring, nestled safely there. "It suits you," he said, offering the ring.

Jen went to push her middle finger through it, but Zach shook his head. "It's been resized," he said.

She pushed her ring finger through it, awed that he had such optimism—or confidence—in her reply. The ladies in the waiting room applauded. Jen didn't care, just leaned forward and kissed

Zach. He brushed off his jeans and took his seat beside her again, his arm tight around her shoulders.

"What if I'd said no?" Jen teased.

Zach grinned and held her close. "I would have rephrased the question."

"You're confident."

"It's a gift."

"Jen Maitland," the receptionist called and reality intervened all too soon.

The oncologist let Zach accompany Jen, when she claimed him as her fiancé, provided that he stayed out of the way. Zach stood back as he was bidden and watched the technician position Jen on the table. Jen breathed more quickly out of her fear, but she didn't show any other emotion. He couldn't see her right breast, where it protruded from the table, because of the technician and the doctor, but he could see Jen's face.

She looked small and pale and frail and vulnerable. He wanted her out of here. He wanted her healed. He wanted cancer to go away.

But it wasn't likely to listen to him.

Jen closed her eyes when they slid the needle into her breast. The oncologist spoke softly to her. Long moments later, the doctor stepped away and Jen opened her eyes. Her gaze flew directly to him: he winked at her and gave her a thumbs-up, which made her smile thinly.

Never mind decking Steve, he'd like to deck whoever was in charge of distributing cancer among the human population.

Dr. Levittson put a hand on Jen's bare shoulder. "It will take a couple of days to hear back from the lab. Don't panic if I don't call you before Monday. Remember: I'm being cautious and proactive here."

"Maybe you should have my cell number," Zach said. Jen

looked surprised but he just smiled at her. "Jen doesn't know yet, but I'm kidnapping her for the weekend."

"But I have a class tomorrow," Jen argued.

"Then skip it. This is worth it."

"You're leading me astray again," Jen complained.

"No, I only lead you into temptation. What you do when you get there is up to you." Zach winked at Jen and she laughed.

Dr. Levittson smiled in her turn. "Sounds like exactly what the doctor would order. Have fun."

"We will," Zach said.

Jen sat up slowly, but Zach knew she was still worried. He gave her a hand to get down from the table as she seemed a bit unsteady. "Sore?"

"Not so bad," she said, although she was pale.

"Come on," he urged. "Let's get Roxie and go home."

"But . . ."

He stopped her protest with a kiss. "No arguments. Just trust me."

She glanced through her bangs and gave him that little pixie smile, the one that turned his world upside down. "Okay. I will."

"I'm going to hold you to that," he teased, relieved when her smile broadened.

The traffic was miserable.

By the time they went to Zach's place and picked up an exuberant Roxie, ensured that Roxie had a chance to relieve herself, and stopped at Natalie's for Jen to pack a bag, it was six o'clock. The roads heading out of Cambridge were choked with commuter traffic.

There was nowhere to stop for dinner and eat anything remotely good for them, so they decided to keep going. Natalie had hastily packed them a few sandwiches on her fresh bread—made with wheatberries this time—but there weren't any parks to stop for a picnic. Jen unwrapped vegetarian sandwiches and poured green tea from the thermos Natalie had also filled, Roxie watched the food move between passenger and driver with avid interest, and Zach drove.

It seemed to take forever to leave the congestion of the city behind. Zach refused to name their destination, but they were headed northeast. When they turned out toward the coast, Jen unrolled the window a bit and just enjoyed the drive. Roxie stuck her head over Jen's shoulder to sniff the breeze and Zach told a few bad jokes. Jen was happy, or as happy as she could have been given the uncertainty of waiting for lab results.

Jen must have dozed off because she woke up when the car was bumping slowly along a dark road. It was unfamiliar to her, although she could see the silhouettes of buildings to one side. Trees adorned with snow rose high on the other side of the car, houses beyond them. There was no traffic and no streetlights, just Zach peering up at the buildings in the darkness as if he wasn't sure where he was going.

He finally turned into the parking spot behind one that had no lights.

"No one's expecting us," Jen said.

"I think this is it," Zach said. He pulled a key ring out of his pocket and turned on the light in the car to sort through them.

The key ring had a hang tag that said *272 Main Street.*

Jen read that and knew where she was. She raised her hands to her mouth in surprise and stared at Zach. "You bought it," she whispered. "You were the one who bought MacCauley's bookstore."

He flashed her a grin. "No. We bought it." He extricated the second set of keys and handed them to Jen. "It's jointly owned. Welcome home."

Jen was incredulous. "But you didn't know . . ."

"Yes, I did, Jen." Zach tapped his chest and looked fierce. "I knew, right here, that we should be together. Even without your mother's astrological charts." He grimaced. "I was, however, a little less certain that you knew the same thing." He grinned at her. "I am shameless enough to use all possible arguments in my favor, including real estate."

"You bought this place and made it joint, not knowing what I'd say?"

"I followed my instincts."

"You're crazy."

"New material, Jen, you need new material. And don't say that before you see the mortgage. Your name's on that piece of paper, too, although James may cut us some slack on payments." He smiled at her. "I knew you'd like this better than a trip to New York and a ring from Tiffany."

Jen didn't know whether to laugh or cry. "You're right. I do." She threw her arms around him and made her feelings clear with a resounding kiss. Roxie barked with impatience, making them end their kiss all too soon.

"She's right," Zach said. "Getting caught steaming up the windows is a bad way to meet the neighbors for the first time."

"With melted Jockeys, too," Jen teased and he laughed.

"Come on. Let's go in. I hope the furnace is still on."

They spilled out of the car, gathered their things, then made their way to the back door. They laughed together in the darkness as they tried to get the key in the lock, and Zach talked about a first improvement being a new light.

Then they stood, hand in hand, in the space that would be Jen's wool shop. Jen had a lump in her throat the size of Rosemount. The furnace was on, churning away in the basement, although they didn't flick on the lights right away. Roxie trotted through the whole building, her nails echoing on the hardwood floor, the sound of her sniffing resonating in the empty space.

"It's perfect," Jen breathed.

"I thought we'd keep the condo at least until you finish your degree," Zach said. "Then we can decide what to do with it."

"It might be handy, but maybe too expensive to keep."

"We'll work it out. I think this will be home, though."

Jen smiled. "So do I."

"You'll need shelves and inventory." Zach strolled the length of the space, looking at it. "Quite a lot of it, really."

"But Teresa wants to be my partner and investor. I already know that she loves this space."

"Then all you need is a name."

"Oh, but I have that already," Jen said, hearing the laughter in her own voice. He turned to look at her and she loved him so much that she couldn't believe her luck.

But then, she'd known what she wanted and asked for it.

She'd wanted Zach. She smiled at him, knowing that she exuded confidence the way he so often did. "I'm going to call it the Black Sheep, since that's who brought me to Rosemount in the first place."

Zach was clearly flattered. "I like it."

Jen crossed the floor to him and put her arms around his neck. "And I love you, Zach Coxwell. Thank you for following me today."

He snorted as he caught her close. "As if I could have gone anywhere else." They smiled at each other, then Zach sobered. "It's going to be okay, warrior queen."

"I know," Jen said and she believed it. "Because we'll face everything together." She smiled at him, feeling mischievous. "So, are you planning to kill me the way I tried to kill you?"

"You bet," Zach said with a laugh. "Pucker up, sister Jen," he said, his tone teasing, then bent to kiss her thoroughly.

Jen was cleaning the kitchen in the apartment when Dr. Levittson called Zach's cell on Friday afternoon. The oncologist immediately apologized for being wrong. Jen practically danced across the hardwood floor as the doctor explained that the biopsy was benign, then insisted that Jen book another mammogram in six months.

"Let's be proactive," Dr. Levittson said and Jen agreed.

She hung up, dialed and made that appointment, then leapt on Zach when he returned from the hardware store five minutes later.

They fox-trotted across the empty apartment after she told him the news, making up the steps as they went and laughing at each other in their happiness. Roxie bounced around them and barked, sensing their joy.

"What if we don't get married in February?" Jen asked and Zach froze.

"What do you mean?"

She grabbed his collar and gave it a shake. "I mean, what if we get married sooner?"

He smiled slowly, a smile that warmed her to her toes. "You're blowing off the asiatic lilies and roses?"

"All I want is you."

"Ditto." He gave her a look that was filled with mischief. "Think we can find the justice of the peace tomorrow?"

Jen smiled, not having thought of that soon, but liking the suggestion when she heard it. "Rosemount isn't that big."

"No, it's not. I think we can do it."

Jen laughed, thinking a quick and small wedding would be the perfect solution. She was going to follow Zach's impulse and surrender to the moment.

She knew she was going to be getting better at that with every passing day.

It's Dinah Dishman, the Dishing Diva, here on Radio Rosemount on Monday, January 25, with all the latest gossip about what's going on in and around Rosemount.

Your eyes didn't deceive you, ladies: Zach Coxwell is back but that boy is taken. The lucky lady is Jen Maitland, formerly of Cam-

bridge. *Fear not, ladies, you'll be able to catch glimpses of the happy couple around town: they've bought the building that used to be MacCauley's Bookstore and are already living in the apartment upstairs. Rumor has it that the happy couple tied the knot right here in Rosemount, sometime earlier this month, and just dropped into the JP's office one Friday afternoon.*

That Zach Coxwell is something else, isn't he? I can believe that Jen was swept off her feet. There are lots of us in town who would have gone for that deal, but the Diva isn't dishing those names. Your secrets, ladies, are safe with me.

For now.

Jen tells the Dishing Diva that her knitting store will be opening in the former MacCauley's and the Diva is advising you to watch for a grand opening in September. The store's to be called the Black Sheep, which I'm sure has nothing to do with our boy Zach's reputation. Nuh-uh-uh. Has he mended his ways? Or will life get more interesting in Rosemount? Stay tuned.

Our boy Zach has been busy. After all his travels, he's the star of a one-man photography show down at the Holland-Mercer Gallery in Boston. The grand opening was on Friday night and rumor has it that not only does our local-boy-made-good have another show booked for later in the year but that this one is already sold out. Shake your booty on down to Boston to check it out through the end of February and see where Zach has been.

Not to mention—although of course I am mentioning it—there was a private reception for the newlyweds last Saturday, at the Coxwell digs we all know and love, for five hundred of their nearest and dearest, including yours truly. Gray Gables was hopping, courtesy of an ancient karaoke machine, the like of which I would never have expected to see at a Coxwell party. It was some kind of fête—those Coxwells know how to turn it on. In case you were wondering, both bride and groom can really sing.

Darlings, I fox-trotted the night away and practically wore holes in my fave shoes, just to be able to bring you the real dish.

The fashionistas among you will want to know that the bride wore Balenciaga for the reception, a perfect little retro number conjured up by Meg Erickson, owner of the vintage store, Twice Loved, in Boston's North End. In fact, the Dishing Diva can divulge that the talented Meg is considering a move to digs in our own delectable town, the better to concentrate on her custom dressmaking. Shhhhh—the tentative name of her new biz is Vintage Interventions and I'm thinking that real estate on Main Street has suddenly gotten more valuable. You heard it here first, boys and girls.

Got news? Got gossip? Call the Diva and let's dish down at the Dishman Diner. Call me, too, to sell your house or help you buy real estate in town. I'm your single source for everything you really want to know, darlings. Listen for me daily on Radio Rosemount, simulcast on the web for you, me, and everyone else who's dying to know the dish on what's going down in Rosemount.

AUTHOR'S NOTE

Yes, you really can buy a knitted prosthesis like the one Jen wears in this story. Check out www.titbits.ca.

If you'd prefer to knit your own, visit the archives of www.knitty .com. The founder of Titbits, Beryl Tsang, supplied her pattern in the Fall 2005 issue of *Knitty*—but be warned that her introductory comments are very funny.

ABOUT THE AUTHOR

Since selling her first medieval romance in 1992, **Claire Cross** has seen more than thirty of her books published. *The Beauty,* part of her Bride Quest series, was her first book to land on the *New York Times* Expanded List of Bestselling Books. Two-time winner of the Colorado Romance Writers' Award of Excellence and two-time nominee for the *Romantic Times* Career Achievement award, she has written historical romances as Claire Delacroix for Warner Books, Bantam Dell, and Harlequin Historicals, as well as contemporary and paranormal romances as Claire Cross for Berkley Books. Visit her websites at www.clairecross .com and www.delacroix.net.